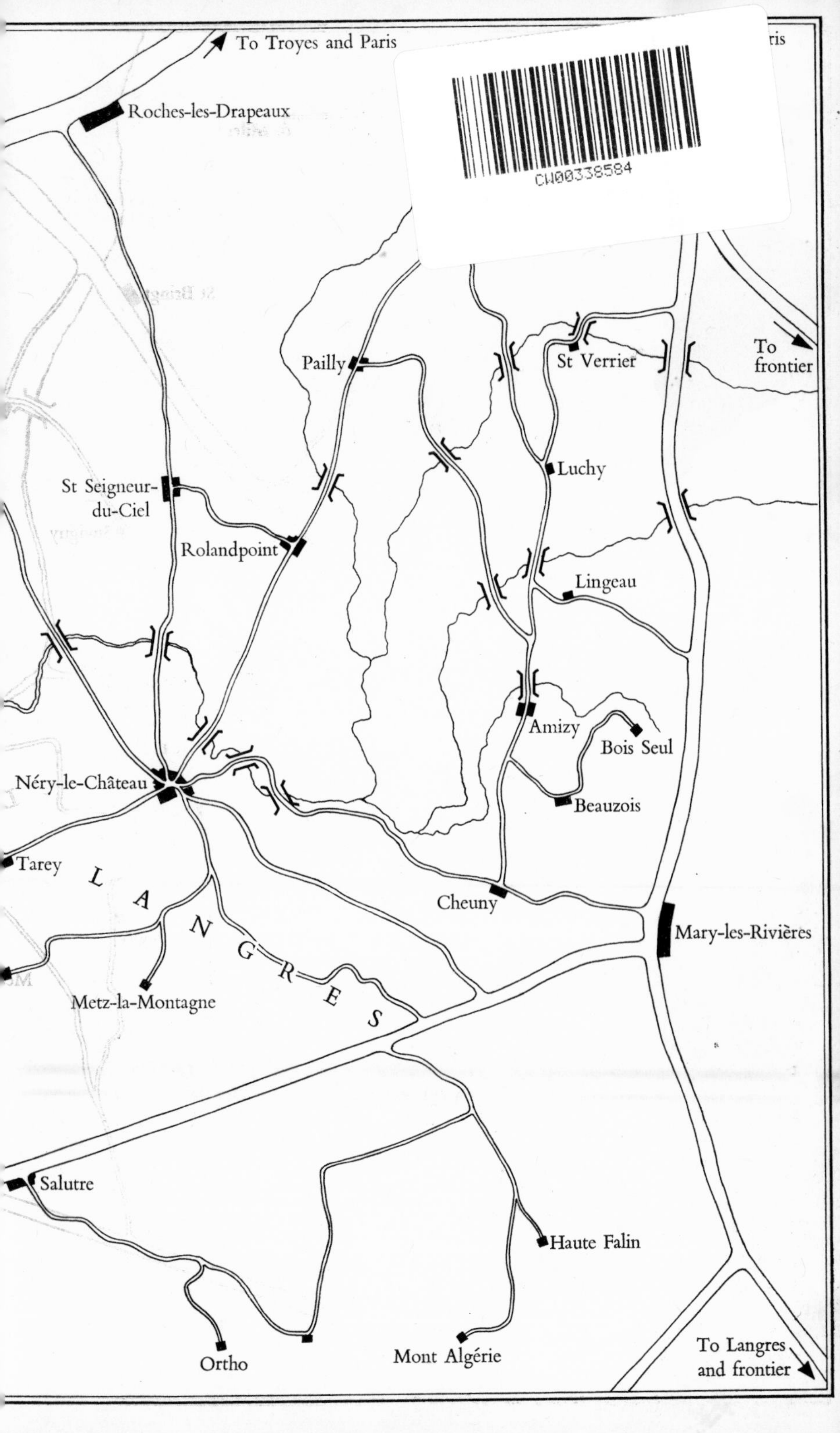

To Troyes and Paris
Roches-les-Drapeaux
Pailly
St Verrier
To frontier
Luchy
St Seigneur-du-Ciel
Rolandpoint
Lingeau
Amizy
Bois Seul
Néry-le-Château
Beauzois
Tarey
L A N G R E S
Cheuny
Mary-les-Rivières
Metz-la-Montagne
Salutre
Haute Falin
Ortho
Mont Algérie
To Langres and frontier

CW00338584

ARMY OF SHADOWS

Also by John Harris

Novels

The Lonely Voyage
Hallelujah Corner
The Sea Shall Not Have Them
The Claws of Mercy
Getaway
The Sleeping Mountain
The Road to the Coast
Sunset at Sheba
Covenant with Death
The Spring of Malice
The Unforgiving Wind
Vardy
The Cross of Lazzaro
The Old Trade of Killing
Light Cavalry Action
Right of Reply
The Mercenaries
The Courtney Entry
The Mustering of the Hawks
A Kind of Courage
Smiling Willie and the Tiger
Ride Out the Storm
Take or Destroy!

History

The Somme: Death of a Generation
The Big Slump
Farewell to the Don (as editor)
The Gallant Six Hundred
The Indian Mutiny
Much Sounding of Bugles

For Younger Readers

The Wonderful Ice Cream
The Sword of General Frapp
Sir Sam and the Dragon
Sam and the Kite
A Matter of Luck
A Tale of a Tail
The Fledglings
The Professionals
The Victors
The Interceptors

John Harris

ARMY OF SHADOWS

A novel of the Resistance

Hutchinson of London

To
our good friends of many years,
Christian and Maryelle Risoud, and
their friends in Paris and Burgundy,
who have become our friends

Hutchinson & Co (Publishers) Ltd
3 Fitzroy Square, London W1

London Melbourne Sydney Auckland
Wellington Johannesburg and agencies
throughout the world

First published 1977
© John Harris 1977

Set in Intertype Times

Printed in Great Britain by
The Anchor Press Ltd and bound by
Wm Brendon & Son Ltd
both of Tiptree, Essex

ISBN 0 09 128450 3

Author's Note

Though many of the events described in this book actually took place, it is nevertheless a work of fiction. The Resistance in the Côte d'Or region of Burgundy managed to show its defiance of the Germans in its own way and without the personal assistance of members of the British forces. The Plateau de Langres is an actual place, but most of the names in the maps will not be found in the Guide Michelin.

I am indebted to Frenchmen who described to me what it was like to live under the Occupation, and to the writings of those British agents who operated in France – in particular to *S.O.E. in France,* by M. R. D. Foot (HMSO, 1966), for its coverage of the whole Resistance scene, to *Maquis,* by George Millar (Heinemann, 1945), for its view of the last days of the Occupation in Burgundy, and to *Accidental Agent,* by John Goldsmith (Leo Cooper, 1971), for its description of Resistance tactics.

Part 1
DARKNESS

Les temps heroïques sont passés.

Léon Gambetta

1

'Fighter!' Urquhart shouted. 'Right astern, skipper! Below and closing fast!'

The German plane was still no more than a swiftly moving shadow and it had obviously been stalking them for some time hidden against the black patches of forest below, but now as it began to climb, Urquhart, with his sharp, experienced eyes, had picked it up at once from the rear turret of the Lancaster.

They had all been in that pleasant euphoric state with the job well done and, even if not relaxed, had begun to feel they were reasonably safe. It had been a long flight down to the butt end of Europe, wearying and different but not too arduous and certainly nothing like as dangerous as Berlin or the Ruhr, the best defended targets in Europe.

Urquhart was still peering downwards to his left, watching intensely, as Crombie's voice came back in answer to his warning. Quite steady. Crombie was always unflappable. He was a Regular like Urquhart, a thin, ascetic, reserved type none of them had ever got to know well. 'Keep an eye on him, rear gunner,' he said. 'He's bound to sniff around a bit to see if we're awake.'

'Right.' Urquhart answered equally steadily, then his voice rose in a sudden yell of alarm. 'Not this one,' he screamed.

'This one's a nut! He's not even stopping to look! He's – coming – *straight in!*

The fighter came snarling up to the slower bomber in a long curve, seeking a position underneath and astern of the starboard wing – a black, deadly, evil thing – and Urquhart yelled again into the intercom.

'Now, skipper! Corkscrew *now!*'

Even as the fighter's weapons system spat long curving lines of tracer at them like coloured slots on rails, Urquhart's guns also began to hammer and the Lancaster twisted to the right, its speed cut dramatically as Crombie snatched at the throttles. The fighter, a Messerschmitt 110, Urquhart saw now, flew straight into the stream of bullets and the four Brownings jumped and clattered again as he fired in short deadly bursts between which he could actually hear the empty cartridge cases rattling in the chutes. Most of the German's shots had gone wide, he knew, and for a moment as the Lancaster picked up its course and speed again he thought they had missed it altogether.

His mouth twisted in a grin that was more a grimace at the thought that anyone should be bold enough to try consequences with Crombie who was a squadron-leader with the D.S.O. and two D.F.C.s and, picking the best tradesmen in the squadron to fly with him, had the best shot in the group looking after his rear end. It was because Crombie was so good that they also had on board the journalist doing a war correspondent stint for his newspaper and the wing-commander from Air Ministry who wished to see the flak in the south for himself.

'Got the bastard,' Urquhart said into his microphone as he leaned forward to watch the Messerschmitt swing away on one wing-tip and begin to curve downwards, trailing a streaming tail of fire. 'He'll not bother us any more.' But then he realized the Lancaster must have been hit, too. Through the excitement and the roar of his own guns, he remembered hearing the thump and crack of explosions behind him and someone's yell of fear or pain in the intercom, and he now waited quietly for instructions to come from forward about what to do, confident that what Crombie ordered would be right, as it had been right in every other emergency they'd been through together.

The silence from the front of the aircraft continued and Urquhart grew uneasy, wondering what had happened. They had expected the trip to be to the Ruhr and the tension in the briefing room had been thick enough to cut with a knife as they'd waited for the gen, with everyone in his own little oasis of loneliness, doubt and fear. The news that it was to be Genoa, not the Happy Valley, had put them all in a good humour, with Crombie's crew of experts listening idly while the newcomers took their copious notes, hoping they were spinning the charm that would bring them safely home. Crombie's crew had been to Genoa several times before and they knew that, though reinforcements had moved south to protect the Italian cities, compared with Hamburg or Berlin or Essen, there was still nothing much to worry about.

Until now.

Two minutes before, Urquhart had been enjoying himself. The weather was gin-clear and they'd seen the Alps in full moonlight, with every snow-covered peak gleaming white. They'd used the lights of Switzerland as an aid to navigation and Urquhart had even identified Mont Blanc and the Matterhorn. It had been a piece of cake. Even the flight north, well behind the rest of the squadron because of the extra circles Crombie had made round the target so his passengers could see what was going on below, had been a piece of cake. Then, shortly after turning for home, they had run into an electrical storm over the mountains which, if an interesting experience, had also been slightly eerie. The heaped cumulonimbus had glowed and flared with internal lights and for the first time Urquhart had seen that phenomenon remembered from school books, St Elmo's fire, brilliant electric-blue sparks between his gun muzzles, the propellers four iridescent rings, the aerial wires running with glowing globules like fluorescent raindrops.

There were still no orders from forward and suddenly the silence worried him.

'Hello, skipper! Rear gunner here. Everything all right?'

There was another long silence. Down below he could see France in full moonlight with a curiously reassuring clarity, especially where snow sprinkled the high ground, and he could pick out towns, cottages, châteaux in wooded parks, and small lakes like jewels. The moon made every tree, every hedgerow, every house stand out sharply in the crystal clearness of the night. Then a window opened and he saw a silhouetted figure looking up, and someone quicker-witted than the rest swung his door to and fro so that the light behind it gave him the V-sign.

There was still no sign of life from forward. His thoughts had occupied a mere matter of seconds since the attack and now an unexpected thin flick of fear came, icy against his flesh.

'Hello, skipper. Rear gunner here – '

Tucked away down at the stern of the huge aircraft, it was hard to tell without leaving the turret what had occurred but he guessed now that they had been badly hurt. In fact, because the German pilot had not been an *Experter*, most of his shots had gone wide, but four of them had done tremendous damage. One of them had exploded behind the Lancaster's cockpit, slightly wounding Crombie and killing Arnold, the flight engineer. The second had mortally wounded the newspaperman, the wing-commander from Air Ministry and Stone, the bomb aimer, who just happened to have moved aft to the navigator's position. The third had exploded against the frame of the mid-upper turret, removing an arm from Udell, the gunner, and sending a splinter of steel through his throat. The fourth had hit the inside of the starboard inner engine, blowing off the cowling, peeling back steel, severing pipes and causing a colossal hole just aft of the navigator's table. Like the Messerschmitt, the Lancaster was also dying.

Urquhart was growing anxious now. For the first time he discerned a different note in the beat of the engines and saw that the ground was nearer than it had been before he'd seen the Messerschmitt. Since they hadn't been going to Happy Valley, they'd been trying an experiment and had flown low right across France, climbed to bombing height near Genoa, then dropped down again for the return trip. 'With the invasion expected any time now,' the group-captain had told them at the briefing, 'we're trying to show the French people that they're not forgotten, and a few Lancs thundering low over their homes will let them know what we've got when the time comes.' It had sounded fine, but no one had warned them to expect a German night fighter in an area where they didn't normally operate.

Suddenly Urquhart began to wonder if he were the only man alive in a flying *Mary Celeste* peopled by ghosts and he flicked the switch of his intercom again.

'Skipper – ' he began, but then Crombie's voice came at last. It seemed quite steady and Urquhart's thumping heart quietened at once.

'Bit of a shambles up here,' the voice said. 'We'd better count noses, I think. Answer, everybody, so we can see who's still around.'

'Rear gunner here, sir,' Urquhart said thankfully. 'I'm okay.'

There was a long pause, because the order was usually that the mid-upper gunner answered next, then Neville answered, his voice a little shaky. 'Navigator here, sir. I'm okay.'

There was another long pause and Urquhart was shocked to hear no more answering voices. Crombie's voice came. Still steady. He was a stiff, unsmiling man, unapproachable to all of them save Urquhart who was the oldest member of the crew and, like Crombie, had been in the war long before the others had even thought of joining up.

'Rear gunner,' Crombie said, formal as ever, the procedure as correct as if the A.O.C. were listening. 'Make sure there aren't any more fighters about, then come forward and see what's happened. Navigator, come up to the cockpit. I think I need a little help.'

Urquhart peered round him then centred his turret and opened the door to climb back into the body of the machine. Immediately he was aware of a roaring gale funnelling down the dark shaft of the fuselage, scattering papers and setting something that had been blown loose flapping with a wild clanking noise.

'Christ,' he said. Stumbling forward, he stopped by the mid-upper turret. 'Uddy,' he called. 'You all right?'

Then by the light of the torch in his hand, he saw the whole interior of the aircraft was covered with blood mixed with oil from the hydraulics.

'Uddy!'

Udell was huddled over his guns and, seeing the shreds of his right arm and the blood on his face, Urquhart came to the not unnatural conclusion that he was dead. In fact, at that moment, he was still alive but he had no more than seconds to live. Collins, the radio operator, was huddled over the ruins of his sets. His helmet was torn and there was blood on his face but he seemed to be still alive, and Urquhart got him out of his seat and lying down. The blood on his face appeared to be from a minor scalp wound; but there was more on his chest and it was impossible to tell where it came from, so that Urquhart could only make him as comfortable as possible and move further forward to see what other damage had been done.

The aircraft suddenly began to shudder and he became aware of torn metal clappering in the slipstream. There were flames inside the fuselage but he found an extinguisher and managed to put them out, working with difficulty in the heavy clothing he had to wear for the icy rear turret. Just in front of him there was a gaping hole, and between the flapping struts and stringers that set up a high-pitched whirring noise among the clattering he could see the ground passing backwards beneath them and the moon on a winding river.

Neville, a tall, good-looking, dark youngster with the thin intelligent face of a student, was bending over Stone, the bomb aimer, trying to drag him out of the way. 'He's had it,' he said, his voice uncertain with the knowledge that it might be his own turn next. 'I'd better get forward.'

The newspaperman was still breathing but the wingco from Air Ministry, an armchair boffin without wings who'd been generous with his cigarettes, seemed to have had it, too. Arnold, the flight engineer, was lying behind Crombie's seat, obviously dead, and there was blood on Crombie's face, though he didn't seem too badly hurt and was struggling with the controls. When Urquhart arrived, Neville had already joined him.

As Urquhart reported, Crombie raised his eyes and it was Urquhart he spoke to, not Neville.

'What about the others?' he asked.

'They seem to have had it, sir. Except Collins and the newspaperman. They've both been hit, though; I think, badly. How about you?'

Crombie turned his head. 'I'm all right. I don't think it was much. Most of the blood came from Arnold. He fell on top of me.'

Crombie seemed to consider the situation. He was still wrestling with the control column and Urquhart saw the air-speed was already down and still falling in irregular jerks on the dial. The altimeter showed three thousand feet with the needle still sinking.

'I can't get her up,' Crombie said. '*Or* down. I don't think we're going to make it.'

Although they knew that what he said was correct, the announcement came as a shock. Because the attack had been unexpected, there had been no thought in their minds but that they'd get back to England, land safely and eventually finish their tour and go off on a long leave with the prospect of safety when it was over. Now, within seconds, six of the men who'd been in the plane had been killed or mortally wounded and the chances of life for the other three were slender.

Crombie spoke over his shoulder. 'You'd better bale out.' he said.

Neville glanced at Urquhart. He was a newcomer to the crew, having just taken the place of a navigator who'd broken his wrist in a mess-night binge and, with Crombie as his captain, he was still a little nervous. The thought of leaving the bomber, crippled as it was, obviously shook him. Despite the shuddering and the whirr of metal, the shattered bomber still somehow represented safety.

'How about you, sir?' he managed.

'Never mind about me,' Crombie said. 'I can see some

pretty wide-open spaces down there and, if I can, I'm going to drop her down in one.'

'Why can't we all try it?' Neville asked, unwilling to think of jumping.

Crombie's head turned. 'Because I'm telling you to bale out,' he rapped. 'That's why. I know what I'm doing. It might not have occurred to you yet, but there are two extra people in this aircraft and if you bale out and the Germans don't see you, they'll assume the aircraft had its normal complement. You'll have a chance to bolt for Switzerland. We're not so far away from it here. Head for Pontarlier.'

'Pontarlier,' Neville repeated, like a hiker asking the way.

'The border's not far from there. I'll follow you if I make it.'

Urquhart glanced at the air speed indicator again. The speed was still dropping. Very soon, since they couldn't put the nose down, the Lancaster would stall and that would be that. The machine was already wallowing and right wing low as though it was going to slide off to starboard at any minute. The loose metal was clappering more loudly now and the air coming in through the hole in the nose was icy. Crombie was hanging on to the control column like grim death, his feet jammed against the rudder bar. He was obviously in pain because his face was twisted and covered with sweat.

The shuddering became worse, as though something had fallen off one of the engines and set up a vibration which was throwing everything out of synchronization. It was violent enough to shake the entire aircraft, setting loose things jangling and making their teeth rattle in their heads. Crombie's whole frame was shaking with the motion but Neville clearly still couldn't manage to think of diving into the empty air when, despite the shuddering and the roaring gale howling down the fuselage from the enormous hole near the navigator's table, he still had his feet on something reassuringly solid.

'We might be able to help, sir,' he urged.

'Don't be a fool!' Crombie snapped. 'Can you get the injured out, Urquhart?'

'We can try, sir.'

'Right, do that. And make sure everybody else is beyond help. Let me know when you're going and then I'll go myself through the hole behind me. It's big enough.'

They didn't argue. Urquhart knew that Crombie was preparing if necessary to sacrifice his life to give them a chance. It was the sort of thing he'd do without thinking. An officer's first job was to see his men comfortable. He didn't eat until they'd eaten and he didn't bed down until he knew they'd bedded down. In the same way, he didn't run for safety until he was sure all his men were safe, and he didn't jump out of a crippled aircraft until his men had gone. Regular officers were sometimes snotty bastards but as often as not they came from a line of Regulars, and honour was bred in the bone. Crombie was far from being a lovable man but he knew exactly where his duty lay.

Leaving him to his battle with the controls, they struggled aft but had only just bent over the wireless operator when the machine seemed to hesitate. It was as if a heart-beat had been missed. The clappering of torn metal was violent now and to it was added a new and ominous clanking noise. It was obvious they were never going to make it and they had just clipped on their parachutes when they felt the aircraft lurch. Then the nose dropped violently, flinging the two of them with Collins and the newspaperman and the bodies of Stone and the wingco into a heap. In a second, the Lancaster was going down in a twisting dive which pinned them to the floor. Fighting with clenched teeth to separate themselves, they dragged themselves free.

There was no longer any question of waiting to bail out or get Collins and the newspaperman out. Now it was a question of 'Could *they* make it?' It was obvious that something had broken and Crombie had lost all control.

'Get out!' Urquhart yelled and, now that the time had come, Neville didn't hesitate. Urquhart followed him. After four years of war he'd acquired a sixth sense that told him when the time had come to quit.

But it was harder now because the aircraft was on its side and he was being pressed to the floor. With an effort, he dragged himself to the hatch and flung himself through. The angle was awkward and his foot caught the opening a resounding whack, but he barely noticed it as the blast of clear cold air seized him and whipped him away.

For a second or two he allowed himself to fall through space, turning head over heels. Then, with a bang, the parachute opened and he was swinging in mid-air, conscious that he'd been given a chance to live. Almost immediately, caught by the moon, he saw another parachute a hundred yards away on his left and slightly below, and he guessed it was Neville.

In the distance he saw the flash of moonlight on the perspex of the mid-upper turret and a few seconds later a glow of red as the aeroplane, the whole thirty tons of it, smashed into a disused barn. It tore off the trees that surrounded the building, then demolished the wall and the roof in a crash that sent bricks and tiles and timbers flying, before hurtling out of the opposite side, taking with it a shattered cart, two mangled goats, a few chickens and a rusty harrow, finally coming to a stop in a crater ten feet deep. Inside it were the bodies of everybody who had been on board except for Urquhart and Neville.

2

Urquhart's thoughts as he floated down were mixed.

Having slipped through the German panzers in France in 1940 to escape unhurt from Dunkirk, and then survived the disasters of Greece and North Africa, he had come to expect that he might emerge from the war untouched. Now, if nothing else, it seemed he was going to sacrifice his freedom.

Below him he could see mile upon mile of forest round a wide patch of open land, the snow silvery in the moonlight, and he wondered what was waiting for him on the ground, because he'd heard of crews being murdered by the Germans for the bombing of their cities.

He saw the trees rushing up to meet him, and the next moment his feet touched earth. Immediately he was conscious of a searing pain and remembered banging his left boot on the escape hatch as he'd dived through. Picking himself up, he thumped the buckle of his parachute harness so that it fell away from him, and turned awkwardly on his heel, wondering what to do.

Then he remembered the compass sewn into the seam of his battledress blouse, the German money and the handkerchief in his back pocket with a map on it, and decided it was up to him. Rolling up his parachute and harness, he held them to his chest and hobbled to the edge of the clearing. There was a barbed wire fence and he scrambled underneath it and sat down, panting, until he could gather his thoughts.

The moon through the trees made them look like the bars of a prison. For a moment, as he remembered Crombie, he felt deflated and depressed, finding it hard to believe that everybody in the crew but himself and Neville was dead, together with the anonymous-looking wingco from Air Ministry and the newspaperman, both of whom had seemed far too old to go tearing round the night sky.

It seemed important that he should find Neville. With his experience, he felt responsible for him. Neville's family were wealthy and he had a degree from Cambridge and had always quoted history at the rest of them in a smug way that had seemed to suggest they were a lot of uneducated morons. It had annoyed Urquhart and infuriated Udell, the mid-upper gunner.

Perhaps because Neville had been new to the crew or because he'd taken the place of a man they'd trusted, perhaps simply because he still had that enthusiastic innocence about him that had gone for ever from the older men, Urquhart had never quite been able to hit it off with him. Even the fact that he was practising Church of England while Urquhart was a non-practising Catholic had seemed to add to the irritation.

Urquhart frowned. They were an ill-assorted bloody couple, he decided, and they hadn't known each other long. There was an undoubted mutual dislike between them and they had surely never been intended to fight a personal war together.

He stuffed the parachute into the undergrowth and as he straightened up he heard twigs crackling. Immediately he heard Neville's voice calling his name and he climbed to his feet, furious.

'Over here!' he snapped. 'And, for Christ's sake, shut up! You'll have the whole bloody German army on to us!'

Neville appeared between the trees carrying his parachute. 'You all right?' he asked.

'No,' Urquhart said bluntly. 'I've done something to my foot.'

'I think the rest bought it.'

'I don't think they knew much about it – except for Crombie.'

Neville was silent for a moment. 'You know,' he said at last, 'that was a bloody brave thing Crombie did. He stayed in so we could escape.'

'He might have got out.'

'I didn't see another parachute.'

For a moment, Urquhart was silent, thinking; then he lifted his head. 'You know, Crombie was right,' he said. 'They'll not bother to search for us if we hide the 'chutes.'

'We might even be able to pinch some civvy clothes somewhere,' Neville said. 'Off a scarecrow or a clothes line or something.'

Urquhart stared at him coldly. Neville's enthusiasm was that of a schoolboy. Why the hell did it have to be Neville, he thought with a bitter sense of injustice. Why couldn't it have been Udell or Collins or one of the others – even Crombie, come to that? With Neville, he sensed that he'd be making all the decisions.

Neville shuddered. His thoughts seemed to be following the same line. 'Poor buggers,' he said. 'You know, somebody ought to recommend Crombie for a gong.'

'Why?'

'For what he did.'

Urquhart shrugged. 'He wouldn't have thanked you

for it. I don't suppose he even considered he was doing anything very unusual.'

They were silent again. It was a cold night and they were both suffering from delayed shock. Neville spoke again, slowly, almost painfully.

'Piece of chocolate?' he said. 'I always keep my ration for eating on the return journey.'

It was then that Urquhart realized how hungry he was. 'Thanks. How about a cigarette?'

'Got some?'

'About three. They're a bit bent.'

They finished the chocolate and lit the cigarettes, carefully shielding the flame of the match. There wasn't a sound about them and they were silent for a while before Urquhart spoke again. 'Fine bloody ending to a tour,' he said. 'I'd only four more trips to do, and then there was a nice office job at an O.T.U. lined up for me. Training new boys.'

'Not any longer.' Neville always knew the snags. 'There are so many intrepid birdmen about from the Empire Training Scheme these days, they don't need any more.' He stared round and shuddered.

'Crombie – ' he began and Urquhart whirled savagely on him.

'Shut up about Crombie, for God's sake,' he snarled. 'That's what we joined for, isn't it? To get killed. Now, for God's sake, stop binding.'

'Doesn't it mean anything to you?'

'Look, I was at Dunkirk and a few other places. I've seen it too often to get hot under the collar about it.'

'You've got no bloody feelings!'

'Because I don't smear them all over the bloody walls, it doesn't mean I don't feel things just as much as well-bred, nicely-brought-up little men like you. I've discovered in the end it makes no bloody difference. It doesn't lick Hitler any quicker and it just makes you and everybody else miserable. Nobody believes that being in a war's one long round of happiness and jollity, but we can at least make it bearable by not dwelling on the bloodiest bits. For what it's worth, I liked Crombie; though, because he was an officer, I don't suppose he ever thought much about me. But he'd got me home safely more times than I like to remember so he meant something to me. Now shut up.'

Neville was silent for a moment. 'Sorry,' he said, and even that irritated because he sounded like a kicked dog.

Urquhart looked about him. 'Where are we?' he asked. 'Any idea?'

Neville shrugged. 'North of Dijon. But not much north. Côte d'Or area. Somewhere on the Plateau de Langres.'

'What's it like?'

'Pretty empty. It's roughly a triangle standing on its tip. Bounded by Châtillon and Langres to the north, with Dijon in the south. It's wooded and high – though nothing like the Vosges. I passed through it by car once or twice on the way to Nice before the war.'

'Did you now?'

'We used to have a house down there for the summer.'

'Filey was where we went – if we went anywhere at all.'

'It's nothing but woods and fields and deep valleys. No big cities. Just a lot of small places that call themselves towns but really aren't much bigger than villages: St Seine-l'Abbaye, Aignay-le-Duc, Sémur-en-Auxois, Baigneux-les-Juifs.'

'Good place to hide?'

Neville managed a smile. 'Well, the Germans couldn't possibly patrol it all. It's mostly farming. It's an isolated area and they're an uncommunicative lot. Even their guide books say they're as wooden as their own trees. Burgundy used to be an independent monarchy in the Middle Ages. Philip the Bold came from here.'

'Who the hell's Philip the bloody Bold when he's at home?' Urquhart growled, knowing that another of Neville's historical diatribes was on its way.

'One of the dukes of Burgundy. Fought against the English at Poitiers –'

'One thing,' Urquhart said, interrupting before he could get going. 'Plenty of wine.'

Neville even had the answer to that one. 'Not here,' he said. 'That's further south. Here it's straightforward farming.'

Urquhart was on the point of a retort but he changed his

mind, deciding that quarrelling wouldn't help much. 'How far can we go by the woods?' he asked. 'To that place the skipper mentioned.'

'Pontarlier? A lot of the way. But what do we eat if we stick to the woods? I think we'll have to shelter in one of the villages.'

Urquhart was staring about him. 'Well,' he said, 'it'll soon be daylight, anyway, and we'd be bloody silly marching about Occupied France in British uniform, wouldn't we? I think we'd better wait until tomorrow night.'

Urquhart was the first to wake. A jagged blade of sunlight was driving through the trees into his face like a nail driven into wood, penetrating, rigid and hostile.

For a moment he lay still, aware that, despite his flying clothing and the parachute that was wrapped round him, he was stiff with cold and for the last ten minutes had been trying to force himself to stay asleep. Expecting to see above him the roof of the hut where he normally slept, he wondered where he was; then, with a shock, the memory of the night came back and he recalled twisting uneasily in the darkness in a nightmare of being trapped inside the Lancaster.

For a long time he lay in the damp grass staring at the sky, which seemed incredibly blue through the bare trees. Then he drew a deep breath and sat up. The snow was beginning to melt in the sunshine, the water dripping from the undergrowth and catching the light like jewels. His foot was throbbing and tight inside his boot and he stared down at it disgustedly, wondering why the hell he'd had to complicate things by damaging it. Climbing to his feet, he hobbled with difficulty to the edge of the trees and stared over the clearing where he'd come down. The land looked purplish in the early light, and there was no sign of life beyond a single spiral of grey smoke rising from the valley beyond the curve of the hill where he could see the spire of a church. As he turned, he saw Neville had also wakened and was climbing to his feet.

For a moment, he stamped his feet and slapped his arms about him; then Urquhart pointed.

'There's a village over there,' he said.

Neville fished in his pocket and produced a Mars bar. 'Breakfast,' he said.

'Your clothes must be stuffed with them.'

'This is the last.'

They ate the chocolate; then Urquhart produced the last cigarette, lit it and passed it to Neville. They finished it smoking alternately.

'We'll get cracking as soon as it's dusk,' Urquhart suggested.

'What about your foot?'

'I'll manage. I walked all the way from Brussels to Dunkirk in 1940. What have we got that we can use?'

'Bloody little. Compasses, maps and some German money – which, come to think of it, won't be much good in France.'

Urquhart stared down the slopes at the white Burgundy countryside. It was wide, foreign-looking and empty. All through the winter the offensive had gone on against Germany and he had never realized what was beneath him. Northern France had become familiar to him in 1940 but down here there was a strange unbelievable distantness, so that he felt he didn't belong; bare and empty, but different from the bareness of the flying field with the Lancs lined up black and menacing on the perimeter track, and emptier than the emptiness of the flat Yorkshire meadows that surrounded it.

He felt slightly worried, but not afraid because he'd already been involved in three campaigns as an infantryman and was confident in his own skills.

'I wasn't thinking of escape equipment,' he said. 'I was thinking of special qualifications. I mean, you're a navigator. That's a help.'

'How about French?' Neville asked. 'Can you speak French?'

'A bit. More than a bit, in fact. I learned it at school and I was in France from September, 1939, till they chucked us out. I can get by.'

'Enough to sound like a Frenchman?'

'I think so. You?'

'I told you. My family used to spend every summer in Nice.

I also took a degree in European History and I had to learn it for that. I did a lot of research.'

Urquhart nodded. 'I've noticed.'

They dozed and chatted through the day, conscious of the emptiness of their stomachs. Then as the sun disappeared and the shadows began to creep across the countryside, Urquhart climbed to his feet. His foot felt as if it were about to burst. 'I think we ought to get moving,' he said.

He broke off a stick and, limping heavily, led the way to the road and along it in the shadow of the trees, following the curve of the hill.

'Where are you going?' Neville asked, running to catch up.

'Anywhere. Anywhere away from here.'

'It won't be much good if we don't know where we're going, surely to God.'

'It won't be much good if we do,' Urquhart said, hobbling energetically along. 'But, for Christ's sake, let's do *something*, even if it's wrong!'

'With that foot you ought to be resting.'

'I've told you – ' Urquhart's voice sounded savage ' – I'll manage.'

The sprinkling of snow seemed to have laid a blanket of silence over the countryside and there was no sign of life.

'Think the bloody place's deserted?' Urquhart asked uneasily.

'This is France, old boy,' Neville pointed out, cheerful now that the knowledge and experience was his. 'Not England. The villages are a bit further apart.'

They set their course towards the church spire in the next valley and Neville began to hesitate. 'It's a long way,' he said eventually. 'What are you expecting to find when we get there?'

'Christ knows.' Once again it was Urquhart, not Neville, who was making the decisions. 'Somewhere to hide. Somewhere we can steal some food.'

They walked without speaking for a while, awkward in their heavy flying boots.

'If we get as far as Switzerland – ' Neville began.

'If.'

'If,' Neville said doggedly. 'I shall sit out the next twenty years of the war there. Plenty of food in Switzerland.'

'Don't kid yourself,' Urquhart growled. 'It won't be that long. The second front'll come soon.'

There was silence again until Neville announced bitterly that he had a blister. 'Two, I think,' he added.

The sweat standing out on his face, his teeth gritted against the pain in his foot, Urquhart gave him a sour look. Then Neville indicated the houses in the valley below them. 'I reckon this is where we start to be careful,' he said. 'There might be the odd German about.'

As he spoke they heard the low growl of a lorry engine and Urquhart slapped him on the arm and dived for the trees. As they huddled among the wet undergrowth in the last of the light, they realized that what they heard was not one lorry but a whole column of them. Lights were coming up the hill and they managed to make out the shape of heavy canvas-topped vehicles, led by motor cycles, scout cars and a large Mercedes staff car.

'The odd German,' Urquhart breathed. 'It's the whole bloody German army!'

The lorries were grinding up the hill in low gear, packed with soldiers sitting face to face, with their rifles between their knees, their helmets strapped behind their shoulders. They were obviously not expecting trouble and were singing a German marching song of the sort that normally took the beat from the step so that they kept perfect time.

'Die Wirtsleut und die Mädel,
Die rufen beid: O weh!
Die Wirtsleut, wenn ich komme,
Die Mädel, wenn ich geh . . .'

Urquhart's face was bleak. He'd heard the songs in France in 1940 and in Greece and the North African desert in 1941, and he hated them as he hated everything that symbolized Nazism. 'Where are they going?' he asked.

Neville shrugged and Urquhart turned on him angrily. 'You're the bloody navigator,' he snapped. 'You're the man with the maps. You know France, you say. Okay, then, pull your finger out and think.'

Neither of them seemed to consider it odd that he should talk in this way. Though Neville was a pilot officer, Urquhart was the older and the more experienced and it seemed normal enough for him to jockey Neville along, chivvying him into using his wits.

'Paris and the north, perhaps,' Neville said. 'Perhaps heading for the N74 to Nancy and the German frontier.'

They set off again. The village was further away than it had seemed and there appeared to be some activity going on in the valley. They could see lights moving, but not fast enough to belong to vehicles, and they decided to wait. After an hour or two the lights disappeared and they entered the village warily by the glow of the young moon. Whatever had been happening seemed to have stopped, and there were no lights at all now and no sign of life.

It was a small place set below the plateau, the sort of place which, cut off from the mainstream of events, hadn't changed much in three hundred years. The names in the registers would be the names on the gravestones, their owners from families that had been born there for centuries, receiving their Confirmation and their first Communion there before marrying and finally dying and being buried there.

In the light of the moon the honey-coloured walls were touched with silver. The main street wound down out of the woods to where a stream crossed the road, then out again at the other side of the village. The houses were of worn stone and shabby almost to the point of neglect, with weather-beaten corners and timbers. Grass grew in tufts from clefts between the stones, and the roadway, crudely asphalted but like the rest of the village neglected after years of war, was silent under their feet from a thick trodden carpet of the droppings of farm animals. It had a country smell about it, of grass, decaying leaves and old wood, and Urquhart sniffed the air appreciatively.

'Smells like home,' he observed.

The roofs were higgledy-piggledy and overhung here and there with trees. Occasionally there were big double gateposts without gates that marked a larger house or a farm. Surrounded by crooked stones and gaunt family vaults, the church stood with the presbytery in a triangle of neglected grass and it was from round the presbytery door that there came the only light they could see.

There was a bar, dark now but with the usual fading advertisements for Dubonnet, St Raphaël and Byrrh; and two shops, both of which appeared to be practically empty, their windows filled with showcards rather than goods.

'We're not going to find anything here,' Urquhart said.

Opposite the presbytery a disused water mill, its wheel stationary, loomed over the road and they crouched down by the stream under the hump-backed bridge beyond it to wash their faces. As they knelt they became aware of the sound of a car engine and in desperation looked round for shelter. 'In here!' Urquhart said.

Followed by Neville, he waded under the great wooden box containing the mill wheel. Behind it and above there was a compartment just big enough for them to crouch out of sight, and they had just huddled down in the darkness when lights appeared, making vivid slashes between the crooked planks of the wheel box as a lorry swung into the village and stopped.

Urquhart had picked up a little German in Africa and he scowled as he listened to the soldiers talking. 'They're going to take the bloody place over,' he whispered. 'It'll be crawling with 'em by tomorrow.'

A scout car appeared and slid to a stop by the lorry with a squeal of brakes. There were four men inside and with the lifting moon they could see three of them were officers. While the driver waited, they crossed to the presbytery and banged on the door.

As it opened they began to speak in French and the men in the mill box could just make out what was said.

'The Abbé Jean-Baptiste Pol?'

The voice that answered was low and subservient. 'I am the curé.'

'I command the 117th Pionierbataillon, 7th Sicherungs-regiment. We're looking for the Château de Frager.'

3

The Château de Frager was situated in what had once been parkland at the southern edge of the village. It was badly neglected, with broken fences and fallen trees destroying the symmetry of the wind-breaks. The house itself was a square ugly building of grey stone, with high windows, cornices and ledges under a mansard roof. Like the estate, it was also neglected, and the gardens, hedges and yew walks were ragged with lack of attention.

When the Germans appeared, the Baronne de Frager was still at dinner and they were shown into the room by a frightened old manservant. The German colonel, a thickset, blond man with a paunch, bowed from the hips.

'Colonel Klemens, madame,' he said, stiffly polite. '117th Pionierbataillon, 7th Sicherungsregiment. These gentlemen are Major Klein-Wuttig and Captain Tarnera, of my staff. I'm taking over from Colonel Marx of the 9th. My guns are at Rolandpoint and my tanks, under Captain von Hoelcke, are at St Seigneur, where there's more room. As Néry is central, headquarters will be here.'

With her companion, the Baronne had risen, an old, old woman like a dry stick, with hands that were knobbly with arthritis. She was small but her slimness made her seem taller, and her face, crossed with wrinkles like a spider's web, was rigidly expressionless. Despite her great age, her hair was a bright red and was quite clearly dyed. For lack of anything better, she had been toying with an andouillette, one of the tripe sausages of the region, and, long since bored with it, was only too willing to push it aside and wait for the German to enlarge on what he'd said.

He had moved away, his eyes roving restlessly across the walls, the furniture, the painting over the fireplace. He seemed to have forgotten her, and one of the other officers, the handsome pale-faced youngster with cold blue eyes and reddish hair whom he had introduced as Major Klein-Wuttig, pointed at the floor between his feet. 'We shall require the best rooms, old woman!' he said. 'You'll be given two hours to move into the servants' quarters.'

The German colonel brushed him aside. His manner had none of the other's hectoring arrogance. 'Who lives here, madame?' he asked.

The old woman's eyes flashed and she glanced at her companion, a withered old man as ancient as she was herself, dark-skinned, faintly Spanish-looking, with a beak of a nose that was as thin as a scimitar.

'*I* live here,' she said. 'With this gentleman; a manservant, Joseph; a girl, Euphrasie Doumic, who comes every day from the village to act as maid and do the laundry; a cook, Henriette Scholl; and a gardener, Gaston Psichari, who lives in one of the outbuildings. He is considered to be simple.'

Colonel Klemens nodded. 'There's another one, I'm told. A young man. Your grandson, perhaps.'

The old woman's face tautened. 'My grandson lies near Sedan,' she said. 'You killed him in 1940, as you killed my husband and son in 1914.'

Klemens inclined his head. 'I regret as much as you do the tragedies of war, madame. Then your great-grandson, perhaps. Where is he?'

The old woman sniffed. 'I'm sure he won't be breaking the curfew,' she said. 'He's probably in bed with a girl somewhere.'

Klemens turned away, staring at the walls again. The Baronne stared after him. She was dressed in what appeared to be a shabby kaftan, beneath which was what had once been a fashionable evening dress, though it now looked faded and as if it badly needed replacing.

'This is my home,' she pointed out acidly. 'It's been declared a museum. Under Occupation law, museums cannot be occupied.'

Klein-Wuttig turned stiffly. 'We know that old chestnut,' he said. 'The minute you hear us coming, you grab every bit of rubbish you've got and stuff it into the place and say it's a restricted building. You won't get away with it here.'

The colonel turned from examining the pictures. 'Madame, I know perfectly well that my predecessor,

Colonel Marx, occupied this place. I intend to also. We shall use the mairie for offices. I shall need to see the maire.'

The old woman's head jerked up. '*I* am the maire,' she said. 'The de Fragers have been maires of Néry-le-Château since before the Revolution. My great-grandson will take over from me when he is old enough and – ah– has acquired some sense of responsibility.'

The German turned to the old man alongside her. He was as odd a figure as she was, with his hollow cheeks and sagging clothes. He had a monocle on a broad black ribbon jammed in his eye and wore a toupee that looked as artificial as the Baronne's hair.

'Name?' he barked.

The old man jumped. 'Balmaceda, monsieur. Edgar Balmaceda.'

'Relation?'

The Baronne's head lifted again. 'Monsieur Balmaceda is an old friend. He's an artist.'

'Not a very good one, I'm afraid,' Balmaceda said gently. 'I know about art but I have little skill.'

The German was staring round him. There were a few small artifacts about the room and he picked up a pottery figure and studied it. 'I'm interested in art myself,' he pointed out. 'I shall enjoy being surrounded by such things as I know you possess.'

'Then I hope,' the Baronne snapped, 'that you'll manage to keep warmer while you're doing it than I have. The central heating's always been inefficient and now there's no coke and no coal because you Germans have taken it all. My fireplace has not seen a fire since January, 1942, and I'm driven to wearing my late husband's sheepskin coat which he wore as a cavalryman in the High Atlas years ago in a better war than this one.'

Klemens' expression remained unaltered. 'The valley's surrounded by trees,' he pointed out. 'There's plenty of wood.'

'There's less than there was because you're taking that, too, to pay off the costs of the Occupation – as you've taken the church bells, the gates and the railings of every house in the village that possessed them – and work has been forbidden in the forest since your last brush with the Maquis.'

Klemens was obviously not interested in the village's woes. His eye was held by the picture over the empty fireplace. It was surrounded by fading wallpaper, as though what had originally hung there had been much bigger. It showed a pond with weeping willows and two or three girls in classical poses staring at the water. 'Would that be a Corot?' he asked.

The Baronne's mouth, wrinkled as if it were stitched, stretched in a sarcastic smile. 'It would not,' she said. 'Some insignificant artist. I don't even know the name.'

'You have other paintings?'

'I've told you. This place is a museum.'

'What does it contain?'

'Nothing worthy of your attention. This is an out-of-the-way place.'

Klemens frowned. He seemed to be growing angry. 'We shall see,' he said. 'We shall see.'

By the following morning there were three lorries in the street and German soldiers were everywhere – several of them sitting on the wall of the hump-backed bridge, smoking, so that the two men in the box of the mill wheel could smell the fragrance of their cigars and cigarettes. Alongside the bridge the ground sloped down from the road to the stream where they had knelt to wash their faces the night before, and the Germans had torn down a fence and built a fire there to make coffee.

The first villager to appear was an old man in a beret, blue smock and trousers, his feet in the banana-yellow rubber boots all French farm-workers seemed to wear. He was carrying a fork and a sickle and he edged along the wall past the Germans as though afraid they might stop him. Doors began to open and a few children appeared, wearing black school pinafores over their clothes, to stand staring at the Germans as they gnawed at pieces of dark-coloured bread. One of the Germans offered chocolate but the children shook their heads and edged away.

By this time, Urquhart was hanging on to his sanity only with difficulty. His foot seemed to be breaking out of his boot with the pain of his injury. His whole leg felt numbed by it, and it seemed to be threading its way insiduously up into his body so that he couldn't think and hardly dared to move.

The previous day's sun had gone and the morning was chilly, with a cold wind blowing through the ancient wood of the mill box so that, in their wet clothes, the men inside were wretched and cramped with not moving. During the late afternoon, a German scout car appeared and they could see a German sergeant giving orders. Eventually the lorries disappeared, grinding slowly up the street, and as it began to grow dusk, Urquhart glanced up and down the empty village. Seeing no one, he cautiously lowered his injured leg and began to climb down. It was difficult and painful and he had to take a long time. A door clicked as he was halfway out and he struggled hurriedly back to shelter. The priest had emerged from the presbytery and in the last of the light they saw he was a burly man with a vast paunch, grey hair and thick spectacles. He was smoking a curved pipe and holding a glass of red wine. Walking across the road towards the mill pond, he stared down into the water as though looking for fish. He appeared to be singing to himself.

'Au bois, mesdames,
Au joli petit bois.
Qu'est-ce qui s'y promènera?'

He paused; then, moving along the stream nearer the mill box, still staring into the water, he began to sing again.

'Attention, messieurs.
Attention, s'il vous plaît.
Il y a une sentinell-e
Au-delà du petit pont.'

'The bugger's warning us,' Urquhart breathed.

'He can't be.'

'He says there's a sentry at the other side of the bloody bridge!'

Neville was inclined to disagree, even to disbelieve Urquhart's claim to be able to understand French. With the youthful arrogance of the university graduate, nothing, he felt, that had been picked up in a village school and added to during nine months' campaigning in the north could measure up to his own capabilities. 'It's part of the song,' he said. 'It's obviously part of the song.'

Urquhart turned on him furiously, his anger increased by the nagging pain in his foot. 'For Christ's sake,' he snapped, 'I know what it means! He was telling us to be careful!'

The priest had turned back to the presbytery now and they heard him sing again:

> *'Attention, messieurs!*
> *Il arriv-e tout de suit-e.*
> *Attention! Attention!*
> *Attention un moment d' plus!'*

Finishing his wine, he spat into the stream and turned in the doorway, smiling, as a German, his rifle slung, appeared within the field of vision of the men in the mill box.

'By Christ, he *was* warning us!' Neville said.

Immediately the cold feeling of being alone was replaced by a warm one of being among friends. Somewhere, in this outlandish little village, not very pretty, obviously not prosperous, there was someone who was prepared to help them. It had seemed that in the whole wide land of France there had been no one, but now, suddenly, Urquhart felt sure they were surrounded by allies.

It was just growing dark when the priest reappeared. This time he was carrying a string bag containing a bottle and half a loaf of bread. On his head he wore a dusty black shovel hat, and his old grey boots – like those of a farm-labourer – splashed in the puddles as he trudged out of sight, conducting a conversation as he went with the invisible sentry.

Hungry, cold and cramped, they had lapsed into a shivering half-sleep when a sharp click above their heads made them jump. In his surprise, Neville almost fell off his perch. A faint, fading torch shone on their faces, and above them they saw a trap-door. Because it hadn't been opened for years, they hadn't noticed it in the shadowy interior of the mill box, but it had obviously been placed there by the mill owner in the days when the mill had worked, to repair and oil his wheel.

'*Messieurs!*' A low hoarse voice whispered to them. '*Suivez-moi! Par ici!*'

Neville glanced at Urquhart and the voice came again. Urgently.

'*Vite! Vite!*'

Coming to life, Neville scrambled to his knees and, reaching up, grasped the edge of the trap-door. Stiff with twenty-four hours of crouching, he almost fell, but a strong hand came down and, grabbing his clothing, dragged him through so that he sprawled on a worn wooden floor thick with dust and old flour. Urquhart followed him and, as the trap-door thudded softly to, in the light of the torch they could see the great stones of the mill and a pile of empty grey sacks.

'*Ça va, mon vieux?*' The shadowy figure in front of them spoke in a hoarse corncrake voice. '*Vous parlez français un peu?*'

'*Oui.*'

'*Pas les deux?*'

'*Si. Tous les deux.*'

'*Oh, mon dieu!*' The Frenchman sounded amazed. 'Not just one Englishman who speaks French, but *two*! *Quel sang-froid!*' He grinned. 'Father Pol told us you were here. He saw you from the presbytery.' He tapped his chest. 'Me, I am Hyacinthe Reinach. Sometimes they call me the Alsatian or Boche d'Est because I came here originally from near Strasbourg. My trade is wood, and this is Néry-le-Château. During the Revolution they called it Néry-le-Fond, but we don't like change much round here and after it was over they changed it back again. You are from the aeroplane that crashed near St Seigneur-du-Ciel?'

'It sounds like it.'

The Frenchman looked puzzled. 'But, messieurs, there were seven bodies in it. The Germans found them all. It was a Lancaster, and they carry only seven.'

'This one carried nine.'

The Frenchman grinned and spread his hands in a gesture of pleasure. 'Then you are safe, my friend. They assumed there were no more.'

They followed the Frenchman down a set of wooden steps to the yard and, entering a building smelling of horse-dung, climbed through a sliding wooden window which had lost its slats. Beyond, they found themselves in another yard which appeared to belong to a forge. The Frenchman said nothing and opened a gate which led into a narrow lane fringed with grass. Still without speaking, Urquhart grinding his teeth at the pain in his foot, they moved along a wall to a point where the stones had collapsed, leaving a narrow gap. At the other side was a high ugly building surrounded by stables.

'Château de Frager,' Reinach said.

'The Germans are here,' Neville whispered in a panic.

Reinach nodded. 'But not on this side, monsieur. Leave it to me. I've worked here on and off for years. Repairing furniture. Replacing panelling. At the moment I'm repairing the Baronne's bed. The de Fragers have fornicated in it, slept in it and died in it for three hundred years. No one will question me.'

They followed him between tall old outhouses until they were standing beneath the great building which reared up above them with steep roofs, turrets and chimneys, on a small mound that rose gently to the front and fell away steeply at the back, so that there was an extra floor behind and below the rest of the house. In front of them stone arches were stuffed with winter hay, at which Reinach dragged so that a whole wedge of it, tied with string, came out. Behind, there was a narrow gap against the wall like a passage.

'We're not a wine region,' he whispered. 'But if we're wealthy we still have cellars to store it.'

He slipped behind the hay and motioned to them to follow. A yard or so along, there was a great square door of thick worn planks that hung awkwardly from a crumbling pillar. Beyond it was an arch and another broken door, and beyond this a vaulted cellar containing empty wine vats on gantries. Stonemason's tools lay about, together with square blocks of stone.

'It goes right back under the château,' Reinach explained. 'With half a dozen smaller ones leading off. They stuffed the harvest in here when the Germans came in 1870 and 1914. In 1940 they were too damned fast. You'll be safe here.'

He disappeared, closing the door behind him, and they sat down in the darkness to wait. Neither of them spoke, both of them conscious of the emptiness of their stomachs and the dry dusty atmosphere of the cellar. After a while, they saw a glimmering of light between the cracks in the door and stood up as it opened. Reinach was the first to appear, followed by an old manservant in a green baize apron and black alpaca jacket carrying an acetylene lamp. They saw, now that the light fell on Reinach's face, that he was a large squarely-built man in blue smock and trousers, with a flat cap sideways on the back of his head. He gave them a wide grin that showed a mouth only half-filled with teeth. Behind him was a tiny woman withered as an old apple but with outrageously red hair. She was dressed in what appeared to be a long sheepskin coat. With her was an old man wearing a toupee, his thin frame hidden in a shabby overcoat.

'Madame la Baronne,' Reinach introduced and the old woman held out her hand.

'You must kiss it,' Reinach whispered, and Neville bent over the withered claw.

'You're welcome here,' the old woman said in a cracked ancient voice. 'The de Fragers have lived here for three hundred years.'

She gestured with her thin fingers, quite unperturbed, as though she received escaping aircrew every day of her life. 'My great-grandson, the Baron, should be here to welcome you, too,' she went on, 'but he's away on business at the moment. He's a good de Frager, however, in spite of his youth – not like some who carry titles these days. The Vicomtesse de la Chattel at Bourg was once a chorus girl and has a lover who works the black market. She's even a collaborator and what can one say about someone who collaborates?'

She sniffed as though she'd caught the whiff of a bad smell. 'The old aristocracy's been infiltrated by the middle class, of course, and lack of money has kept most of us from shutting out the vulgar, but this family at least has escaped the need to "manure the land" with moneyed marriages. Our title dates from the Monarchy; not the Empire, which doesn't even impress the servants. The people one sees in the salons nowadays are either nobodies or Germans. Three times I've seen those filth in my country. They're upstairs in my salon now.'

The old manservant produced cheese and a bottle of wine and, turning her back abruptly, the old woman headed for the door. Reinach paused and winked. 'She's not such a cold fish as she looks,' he whispered as she disappeared. 'Look, I'll show you something.'

Deep in the cellar, he indicated an arch almost blocked in by a half-built wall. Beyond the old stones that were being used, in the light of his torch they could see paintings stacked one against another in the dusty shadows. Alongside them were vases, glassware, chairs and roped trunks.

'The Baronne's,' he said. 'Her husband collected them for her. But she cuckolded him with the old boy with the wig. He's an artist and she was his mistress. He used to come to copy the old masters and he had dozens in his attic in the end because they were at it for years; every time the Baron went out, he dropped his brushes and they popped into bed.' Reinach gave a little cackling laugh. 'When the Baron finally died and they were free to do as they pleased, they were too old to enjoy it any more.'

Neville indicated the paintings. 'What are they doing down here?'

'When the Germans arrived in 1940, they made it an Occupation law that museums weren't to be abused or occupied, so everybody grabbed everything they valued, declared it a treasure, and stuck it in the château so the Germans wouldn't steal it. But they occupied the place anyway, in the end, and when that fat idiot, Goering, started grabbing everything we couldn't get the stuff back.'

The empty mouth widened. 'When this lot didn't arrive on

time, we grabbed our chance and stuffed everything that was worth anything down here and filled the château with rubbish. Théyras the mason's building the wall. One more day and it'll be bricked up, and then they'll never know there's anything behind it. They won't even know the paintings existed.'

The following day seemed interminable. Urquhart knew his temperature had risen and the pain in his foot now was agony. Neville suggested taking the boot off but, guessing that they hadn't finished their wanderings, Urquhart refused in case he couldn't get it back on and spent the day in a blur of pain.

As the faint cracks of light they could see through the door disappeared with evening, Reinach returned and they slipped out of the cellar into the darkness of the courtyard. There was no sign of life as they edged between the outbuildings into the park.

It was difficult following Reinach among the trees and Urquhart kept blundering blindly into bushes. They seemed to have walked right round the village, with his mind only a red blur, when they breasted the brow of a hill and saw a faint chink of light below them and made out a huddle of ancient buildings surrounded by a windbreak of horse chestnuts.

As they began to descend, it started to rain. At first it was only light but it soon grew heavier until it plastered their hair over their eyes and they were spitting it from their mouths.

'*Mon dieu*,' Reinach spluttered. '*C'est comme une vache qui pisse!*'

Vaguely aware of a dog barking, Urquhart saw a woman muffled against the weather, a man's heavy coat over her shoulders, a man's hat pulled down over her eyes, a man's boots on her feet. Then he was being pushed blindly up a ladder into a loft full of straw. Conscious of the drip of rain through the roof and the warmth generated by the cows below him, he felt the place whirling about him and, putting his head back in the straw, he quietly and entirely without fuss slid into unconsciousness.

4

For a while Neville stood staring down at the man lying in the dusty straw.

Urquhart was good-looking in a strong, rugged way. His nose was straight and his jaw-line firm but he was powerful-looking rather than handsome with his fair hair and ruddy complexion, like someone who enjoyed being out of doors. He was normally a man with a great deal of energy but he always used it sparingly in a stolid, deliberate manner so that he never seemed to be in a hurry, and at that moment he was still, his eyes closed, his muscular body curiously helpless-looking.

'What's the matter with him?' The voice that came from the shapeless bundle of men's clothes alongside Neville was light and he realized that the woman who'd met them wasn't as old as he'd thought.

Then, as she lifted the lantern she carried, the light fell on her face and he saw even that she was little more than a girl, with smooth cheeks and a clear skin under the ugly man's hat she wore. Her hair, damp and lank from the rain, hung over her face, but as she lifted her head he saw clear unafraid eyes staring at him from the shadows.

'Is he ill?'

'No,' Neville said. 'I think it's his foot. He damaged it.'

An older woman appeared at the top of the ladder, a woman with greying hair and red cheeks who looked as though she might be the girl's mother.

'He's hurt,' the girl said. 'He'll have to come inside the house.'

The older woman said something under her breath, gesturing fiercely, and the girl turned on her. 'He can't stay here,' Neville heard her whisper.

It took some doing to get Urquhart down the ladder again but, with help from the girl, Neville and Reinach managed it. He showed no sign of consciousness as they carried him into the house and up the stairs and laid him on one of the beds. The older woman bent over him to stare more closely.

'He'll be all right,' she said shortly. 'He looks tough to me, that one.'

Neville nodded. 'I suppose he is,' he agreed. 'He was pretty fit. He was a regular soldier who transferred to the air force.'

'Are you a regular soldier?'

Neville was faintly hurt at the thought that he even looked like a Regular. 'Not me,' he said firmly.

The girl had managed to unzip Urquhart's flying boot and pull it off. 'His foot's swollen,' she said. 'How did he manage to walk?'

Looking at the bruised and darkened foot, Neville couldn't imagine, but it seemed typical of Urquhart with his strong hard body that he had.

'I don't know,' he said. 'He did it as we parachuted from the aeroplane.'

'One thing,' Reinach said. 'When he's better, we can get you away quickly. You speak French. Most of them can't.'

'When can we set off?'

The girl turned. Still bundled in the old clothes, she was bent again over Urquhart, unfastening his shirt at the neck and loosening his battledress. 'Not yet,' she said shortly.

As she pulled the blanket up and arranged an eiderdown covered with pieces of patchwork material, Neville leaned forward.

'When then?'

'A week or two. Perhaps more.'

The first thing Urquhart became aware of as he came round was that it was daylight and Neville was bending over him, looking anxious. Then he realized a doctor was holding his foot, that he was in a bed, and that there were two women watching too; one an older woman with greying hair and red cheeks; the other a girl, whom he recognized at once as the woman he'd seen the night before. She had a splendid figure, a straight back and thick chestnut hair, and she was smiling reassuringly to show even white teeth.

'This is Doctor Mouillet,' she said in English. 'He say you have some broke bones in your foot.'

The doctor smiled apologetically. 'You must keep it very still for a day or two,' he said. 'There is no plaster in Occupied France for French fractures so I have had to bandage it. When the swelling goes down I'll tighten it so you can put it to the ground.'

Urquhart frowned. 'How long will it be before I can walk on it. I want to get over the frontier and back to England.'

The doctor straightened up and moved to the door with the women. 'There'll be no walking for you for a while,' he said. 'Perhaps in three weeks you'll be able to walk just a little, but certainly not as far as the frontier.'

When the doctor had gone, Urquhart stared furiously at Neville.

'I'm staying too,' Neville reassured him quickly. He had been wondering all night how Urquhart with his background, his simpler education, his regular service and North Country upbringing, would accept the enforced stay in France and the need to adapt himself to foreign patterns and culture, and he had decided it was up to him to see him through. 'After all,' he said, 'we're members of the same crew.'

Urquhart decided he sounded like a boy trying to play the game according to the rules he'd learned at public school. 'I think you're barmy,' he said. 'If I were you, I'd shove off.'

'And leave you here?'

'It's your job to escape.'

'Together. We'll do it together.'

Oh, Jesus, Urquhart thought. I really am stuck with this one. 'I'd be all right,' he growled. 'I'd cope.'

'We'd be better together. I know France, remember. I spent a month here every year of my life.'

'And I spent nine months here soldiering in 1939 and '40,' Urquhart snapped back. 'You learn a lot about a country that way; especially when you're running for your bloody life.'

Neville was a little disconcerted by his ingratitude but before he could say anything the girl reappeared. She now wore a bright flowered dress, a spotless apron and what looked like her best shoes with high heels. She carried a tray which she put down on Urquhart's knees. Behind her the older woman carried a large coffee pot.

'For the English the bacon,' she announced, her Rs like rolling drums. 'This is not usual in France, you understand – especially these days when the meat ration is eighty-eight grammes and it is a public holiday if you get it – but you will be hungry.'

The bacon turned out to be ham, but there was an egg – undercooked in the French fashion but an egg nevertheless – and toast cut from a baguette and shrivelled almost black in the oven.

'We do not have tea,' the older woman said. 'But we have butter and honey, which are very good for the digestion.'

The sleep had sent Urquhart's temperature down and he tucked into the food with enjoyment.

The two women studied him from the end of the bed. 'I am Marie-Claude Defourney,' the girl said. 'This is my mother, Madame Lamy du Roux. When you saw me last night, I was in my disguise. We cannot get new clothes under the Occupation, of course, and my cousin in Dijon, who grew out of his at eighteen, even had to join the police force to get some more. Today I am très swing and in my battle-dress.'

She was tall for a French girl with firm breasts and a brown skin and she was clearly independent, intelligent and sturdy-minded, with a vibrant personality and more education than her surroundings might suggest. 'There is also a dog outside,' she went on. 'Called Elsie. She was brought here as a puppy but she spends most of her time at the Dréos' forge down the lane. Sergeant Dréo is the smith. He has a grandson, Jean-Frédéric, who is fourteen, who takes her with him wherever he goes. He has taught her to sit up when we say "Winston Churchill" and "Charles de Gaulle" and to growl at "Hitler". She also barks at German cars but I think this is because she barks at *all* cars. You must write down your names because sometimes we can send messages to England. There is a radio operator in Rolandpoint nearby.'

She glanced round the room and for the first time Urquhart became aware of the vast feather bed and an enormous Norman wardrobe with a mirror where he could see himself, burly and square-faced, his chin dark with reddish bristles. 'You must forgive the dust,' she went on. 'We have had to neglect the house to keep the farm going. We have no man about the place, you see. The 135th Regiment drew its reserves from this district in 1939 and all our young men have disappeared. My husband went with them.'

He didn't dare to ask where he was and she shrugged. 'He was killed at Albert in 1940 and my father died last year. Now there are only two of us. Most of the young men who were left escaped to North Africa or to join General de Gaulle. Some have been taken to work in Germany. Some joined the Resistance. I was going to marry one of them. He was killed by the Germans near Suvigny. Twice they've destroyed the Resistance in this area.' She paused and drew a deep breath. 'You are lucky. One group of Germans has just gone. The others don't know you, so as soon as you have papers you'll be safe.'

She had brushed aside her gloom defiantly and, clearly dying for information, was gazing at them with shining eyes. 'Is it true there are still cinemas in England?' she went on quickly. 'And that the cows are milked by machines and the fields are fertilized not with dung but with scented products made in factories? And what about the Free French? When will they return to France?'

Urquhart and Neville glanced at each other and she pushed on eagerly. 'General de Gaulle has promised to drive the Germans from our soil,' she said. 'We've heard it on the radio. I remember clearly what was said: "In this historic year of 1944 we shall bring you tremendous news." Doesn't *that* mean they're coming?'

'I suppose it does.'

'When do *you* think they'll come?'

'God knows,' Urquhart said.

'But you must have seen signs! The troops marching to the ships! The preparations!'

'There are unbelievable precautions,' Neville pointed out.

She seemed satisfied. 'Of course. I understand. You have been sworn to silence. But it *will* be France, won't it? It can only be France. And all France knows it will be soon. We get many messages.'

'Who do?'

'We do. On the radio. From the British Broadcasting. For this area they are always prefaced by the words "D'Auguste à César" and then we know we have to listen. After that there are two lines from La Fontaine that tell us the message is for us.' Her eyes became sad. 'That was a long time ago, of course. There have been no messages lately.'

As Urquhart finished eating, they heard a bicycle bell outside and a voice calling. A few moments later the priest appeared in the doorway. Fat, ugly, his eyes hidden by thick pebble glasses, he looked warm with pedalling and there was a rank smell of sweat about him.

'God shower his blessings on you, my sons,' he said. 'I am the Abbé Pol.' He picked up the paper on which they'd written their names. 'Neville,' he said, reading it in the French fashion. 'Ewer-cue-'art.'

'Urquhart.'

'Urk't?' The old man's eyebrows shot up. 'It is not possible!'

They assured him it was; especially in Scotland where such names originated.

'You are not English, then?'

'Yes. I'm English."

'But you have the Scottish name.'

'I'm still English.'

Father Pol looked at Madame Lamy and it was quite clear they were mentally touching their temples to each other.

Neville tried to express thanks for their rescue. 'We thought when we heard you talking to the Germans,' he said, 'that you were a collaborator.'

'Not me.' Father Pol's heavy shoulders rose in a shrug. 'But it's also pointless sticking out one's neck to get a martyr's crown; especially with the church calendar already crowded.'

He accepted the coffee Marie-Claude brought and lit his pipe to fill the room with clouds of acrid smoke. 'We suffer badly with the Germans stealing all the fats and greases we need,' he said, 'but history's full of nations defying God and prospering, so we must bow before His will and endure.'

He took a sip of coffee, extending his lips and sucking it up as if he were a vacuum cleaner. 'It's a matter of attitudes,' he went on. 'Father Xavier at Rolandpoint abuses them at mass every Sunday, yet he survives.' He shook his head. 'I think the Holy Ghost is working overtime for him, and I prefer myself not to demand too much of the Lord. I'll wait until the odds change a little.'

He took another noisy sip of coffee. 'I was at Verdun as a young man, you see,' he said. 'And there was so much dying there for nothing, I decided that when one *has* to die, it must be for something worth while.'

As they talked five other men arrived, one of them Reinach. They all wore stiff black suits as though they were being interviewed for a new job and they appeared one after the other, with discreet intervals between them, riding down the muddy farm road on ancient bicycles with threadbare tyres; one without tyres at all and clattering like a set of old tin cans. As they gathered in embarrassed silence round the bed like mourners at a wake, Marie-Claude produced glasses and they began to introduce themselves, carefully avoiding looking at the drinks as though there were a secret agreement not to.

'Thomas Dréo, smith.' The first one was a straight, solid elderly man like a rock, with a creaking artificial leg. He had black eyes that flashed brimstone and spiked moustaches so aggressive they seemed to throw off sparks. 'Late sergeant of the 17th Alpine Regiment. I fought against the Germans in the last war and would have fought against them in this if they'd let me, in spite of my age and my leg.'

'He has the Médaille Militaire for extraordinary valour,' Reinach pointed out. 'As well as the Croix de Guerre and several citations.'

Dréo shrugged. 'It was nothing. It was expected of me My father also lost a leg – at Belfort in 1870, when it was the only city in France to withstand the Prussians.'

'Under Denfert-Rochereau,' Neville said and Dréo's eyes lit up.

'Oh, mon dieu,' he crowed. 'We have a historian of France among us.'

Reinach shrugged. 'The English aren't bad,' he observed. 'Some are even quite likeable.'

Dréo warmed to his theme. 'My grandfather fought in Algeria and my great-grandfather at Waterloo, and my son fought in this war and lost a leg at Sedan in 1940. Although we have only two legs between us, we run the forge and make a business of sorts collecting scrap.'

The diatribe looked like going on all day but Reinach pulled one of the other men forward.

'Théyras, Maurice.' he said. 'Mason.'

The mason was a prematurely old man with a wry smile and a hump back. 'I have no military service because of my back, but it doesn't stop me having feelings. I've finished the wall. They'll never find our pictures now.'

Reinach pushed him away before he could get too involved and pulled another man forward. Casimir Ernouf had the shoulders of an ox, pale blue eyes and fair hair so that he looked almost German. 'I am the quarryman,' he said. 'When the German filth allow me to work.'

'And I am Reinach,' the carpenter said, pushing him aside. 'Because Alsace was occupied in 1870, my service did not start until it was liberated in 1918. I speak German because I am Alsatian, French because I am French, and Polish because when France went to the aid of Poland in 1919, I went there to finish my army service. In addition to working with wood, I am also a mechanic – and I own a charcoal business which I bought when it was bankrupt because it allows me the legal use of a lorry for which I have a police pass. I live by Système D – by my wits – and believe firmly in le sang-froid. I have no teeth because the Germans knocked them out with a rifle when they first arrived in 1940, and I don't wear false ones so that I shall remember what they did every time I eat.'

Despite his cheerfulness and empty clown's grin, there

was a whole well of hatred beneath Reinach's words. He gestured at the fifth man, a miniature human being with a sly darting glance, who had arrived carrying a brief-case and wearing a black homburg that looked far too large for him. 'This ordure,' he said, 'is Emile-Auguste Moch.'

'With no service,' Moch said.

'He calls himself a commercial traveller but he's really in the black market and everything he does is either illegal or dangerous. He has a petrolette, which is a small motor bike, and we call him the Gardien du Fond, because his house is deep in the Fond St Amarin, which leads out of the village towards Belfort, and because "fond" also means "oddments". In addition to bringing information about the Germans, you see, he looks after our needs with odds and ends from the black market. So far he's not been caught.'

No one had yet looked at their glasses. Then, as Madame Lamy drank, everyone else drank, too, as though a signal had run round the room. Father Pol smiled.

'They do say,' he observed with satisfaction, 'that the spirit we distil here can be used in a blow torch.' He gestured and a great waft of body odour came across. 'We are Néry's council of war.'

'Here to do what?' Urquhart asked quietly.

'We are the Resistance,' Dréo said. 'We wish to decide whether you're shot-down fliers or Gestapo agents. The Gestapo is up to all the tricks.'

'They look like airmen to me,' Reinach commented.

Dréo gestured. 'We have to be sure.'

Reinach grinned. 'Well, they're certainly not French. No self-respecting Frenchman would say he was English. But they can't be German, because they're far too intelligent.'

'If they *are* English,' Moch said, 'they'll be able to tell us how to bowl a maiden over and what is the silly mid-on. The agent at Rolandpoint gave me this question because no German would know the answer.'

It seemed a strange way of deciding their nationality, and there was a surprising levity about the conversation, but Urquhart realized that running beneath it there was a shrewd thread of enquiry that was barely detectable. When they seemed satisfied they changed the subject to the invasion.

'When will it take place?' Théyras asked.

'We don't know.'

'They can't be English,' Ernouf said at once.

'It can't be long,' Father Pol pointed out. 'The General Montgomery has returned to lead the Eighth Army. He is Norman, of course, that one. French, like Winston Churchill.'

They seemed settled for a long discussion, standing around the bed, sombre and black, in a way that reminded Neville of Rembrandt's 'Night Watch', and Marie-Claude sighed and went none too willingly for the bottle to refill their glasses. Théyras leaned over to Neville.

'That's a good girl, that one,' he whispered. 'And did you ever see such buttocks?'

As Marie-Claude returned, Neville found himself eyeing her approvingly, deciding she'd probably been better educated, with more straightforwardness, more politics, more Shakespeare and more knowlege of sex than any English girl of comparable age.

'The British Broadcasting spoke again yesterday.' Théyras started the discussion once more. ' "The Germans believe in overwhelming force," they said. "Soon they will know what overwhelming force is." I liked that. It was clever.'

Reinach seemed more interested in events nearer home. 'The Germans have taken over the château,' he announced.

'What are they like?'

'Like Germans. The Baronne tells me the colonel's already looking for the paintings. He's fat and blond, and the back of his neck has short hairs on it like a pig's.'

'There was a little of God's grace in one of the last lot,' Father Pol observed quietly. 'There's another with these – a Catholic from the Rhine. He's been already to ask if he might receive Confession.'

'You said "no", of course,' Madame Lamy said.

'I said "yes",' Father Pol snapped. 'I was sent here by ecclesiastical authority, and until ecclesiastical authority sees fit to remove me, no one asking God's mercy will find *me* wanting. In the eyes of God, he's one of His subjects.' He stared defiantly at Madame Lamy who glared back at him, quite willing to give as good as she got. He turned to Urquhart. 'Are you of the faith, my son, or do you follow that chilly English dogma that's a cross between Catholicism and bastardized Lutheranism?'

'I'm a Catholic,' Urquhart said.

'And do you go to church?'

'Not very often.' Urquhart had never suffered from self-doubt and never permitted himself to be questioned about what he did. It was typical of him that he had no nickname and had always remained 'Urquhart' and nothing else to his friends.

Théyras interrupted. 'Perhaps your German friend, Father, has some suggestions as to how we might get rid of them.'

Reinach shrugged. 'There are so damned many we should turn the place into a spa and make money. Germans like spas, and we've only to bury some good German bodies in the stream where it comes down from the hills to give it the proper flavour.'

'It isn't a joke,' Dréo snapped.

'Who said it was?' Reinach snapped back.

Urquhart and Neville eyed each other, faintly embarrassed. The discussion had started so proudly but the pride was obviously only a screen for tension and edgy nerves; a striving for defiance that was betrayed by every word that was spoken as strain and the suffering of the Occupation.

There was a long silence then Dréo spoke. 'Every Frenchman feels the need to wipe out the shame of 1940, you understand,' he explained stiffly. 'We had bad leaders.'

'That's what everybody says,' Marie-Claude joined in. 'We're good at explaining. That's all we do – talk. We French talk too much.'

Dréo shifted uneasily. 'At Rolandpoint they're ready for anything,' he growled. 'They once cut the railway lines from the forest to St Seigneur.'

Reinach shrugged. 'And for that pleasure,' he said, 'fifteen men were shot. To me it didn't seem worth while, especially as they repaired it within a day.'

Dréo wasn't put off. 'They have an arbalette, a rocket-launcher for destroying tanks. They got it from London by parachute. They also have a transmitter and an allied agent called Arsène who visits them.'

'So I heard.' Father Pol frowned. 'And if *I* have heard, then probably the Germans have also heard.'

Dréo was still pursuing his theme. '*We* have guns too,' he said. 'And I have my old Laurelline.'

'A recuperated fusil-mitrailleuse from the last war, smuggled home and hidden under the floor of the forge.'

'She is spotlessly clean. She could still kill Germans.'

'It's not enough,' Reinach said. 'Apart from that, all we have are a Sten gun given us by the Rolandpoint réseau, three revolvers, two Belgian automatic pistols, two old Lébels from 1918 and a few hand grenades which someone left outside until they were rusty. We are humiliated.'

'Then spit,' Marie-Claude's mother snapped. 'I am a good spitter. It is good for the juices.'

Father Pol drew a deep breath. 'France does not stand alone,' he pointed out. 'De Gaulle said she didn't. "The flames of French resistance must not and shall not die," he said.'

'They nearly have,' Madame Lamy snapped. 'Of course Elsie wags her tail for Winston Churchill and growls when Hitler's mentioned. But that doesn't get us far. All we have left are young boys.'

'Who don't know how to fight.' Marie-Claude frowned. 'This isn't a big place. It's not a pretty place or well known. We have a window in the church dating back to Henri IV and a few fine carved statues in the frieze over the altar. But the church bells have been stolen to make guns and we have nothing that's beautiful so that even the tourists never come here. We have two bars – one since the Germans closed one down – two grocers with no groceries, a butcher with no meat, a post office and a mairie. We're not famous or clever or brave. Sergeant Dréo's got a wooden leg and so has his son, and probably his grandson will eventually have one, too, because they seem to run in the family. Mère Ledoux's barman, Vic, slips into the wood with Chrystalline Gaudin, Dr Mouillet supports a mistress in Bourg-la-Chattel and the Baron is just a posturing boy. We have four farms, two good, mine very bad. Hyacinthe Reinach's a scoundrel, Father Pol's sometimes a bore and I am badly in need of a man about the place. Who are *we* to take on the Germans?'

There was a long affronted silence, then Father Pol shrugged. 'We *can't* take on a German army that isn't defeated,' he said. 'We all saw them arrive. They were dusty and dirty but they were singing. They sang magnificently. They came as conquerors and that was what they were. That's what they still are – despite North Africa and Russia. When they came here, I saw Commandant Verdy de Clary weeping, despite the rosette of the Legion of Honour he wore. He was weeping for things he wasn't strong enough to stop. We're *still* not strong enough. We just have to be patient.'

Colonel Klemens at the Château de Frager was also trying to be patient. Outside, rain drummed against the windows and his small eyes glittered and his hand strayed to the back of his head to scratch at the short gingery hairs there that so annoyed Reinach. Behind him stood Tarnera, while Klein-Wuttig sat at the table. In front of them the Baronne and Balmaceda waited.

'You're an artist, monsieur,' Klemens was saying slowly, gesturing at the painting over the fireplace. 'Would you say that was valuable?'

Balmaceda shrugged. 'Well, yes and no,' he began.

'Yes *or* no!' Klein-Wuttig snapped and the barked word seemed to make him jump in his seat. 'Answer properly!'

Balmaceda's frightened eyes lifted. 'It's hard to say, monsieur.'

'I don't expect exactitude,' Klemens said gently. 'What is its value? Great or small?'

'Not great. Not small. It's by an unknown artist, but the painting is skilful, the style has merit. The colours are good.'

'How old is it?'

'Last century, monsieur.'

'Who was the artist?'

'A Dijonnais by the name of Wemille.'

Klemens' head turned. 'Ever heard of this Wemille, Tarnera?' he demanded.

Captain Tarnera shrugged and Klemens strode across the room and gestured with his crop at another painting. 'How about that one? Valuable?'

Balmaceda gestured. 'I'm an old man now, monsieur. I don't know much about – '

'I know who you are!' Klemens said more sharply. 'I've looked you up. You were a dealer in Paris and a copyist of skill. You've spent a great deal of time in galleries and you know the masters. Give me a proper answer.'

Balmaceda's thin body tautened. 'Little value, monsieur. Late-nineteenth-century artist – Jeannot Monjaret.'

Signing to them to follow, Klemens strode through the house, through the dining room and the hall, up the stairs and to the bedrooms, jerking his crop again and again at the pictures on the walls. 'How about that one?' he demanded. 'And that?'

Balmaceda's distress was growing. 'Last century, monsieur. George-Marie Planel. No great value.'

'That?'

'Pierre-Jean-Hubert Loupias. No value. An unknown, monsieur.'

When they'd seen every painting in the house, Klemens began to go round the furnishings. Balmaceda's replies remained depressingly the same and after a while Klemens dismissed the old people and turned to the two officers.

'There's something damned funny going on here,' he said. 'When I was in Torcé-en-Vallée, my commanding officer was Colonel Dannhüber. He knows about paintings and he had a major on his staff called Kaspar, who used to be curator of the Stadtmuseum in Hamburg. They came through here in 1940 and Dannhüber once told me to keep an eye open for the paintings. He mentioned a Corot, I remember, a Prud'hon, and a Fragonard, as well as Troyons,

Daubignys and a few others.' His voice rose. 'Well, I *am* keeping my eyes open. And I'm seeing nothing!'

Tarnera's dark intelligent eyes contained a hint of amusement. 'Perhaps they've been stolen, Herr Oberst,' he suggested. 'Perhaps Colonel Dannhüber – '

'Colonel Dannhüber's just arrived in Dijon,' Klemens snapped. 'He's now *General* Dannhüber, and Major Kaspar is *Colonel* Kaspar. If *they*'d taken the paintings I'd have heard of it.'

'Then perhaps Reichsmarschall Goering's been helping himself. National Socialism's been a good excuse to grab most of the world's treasures.'

Klein-Wuttig's eyes snapped up. 'One day, Tarnera,' he barked, 'your tongue'll lose you your head. Some people mind about that sort of talk.'

Tarnera refused to be put off. 'It's more than likely, all the same. I hear that his ante-chamber's knee-deep with fraudulent dealers all trying to tread each other underfoot to sell him something. Pictures would go well with his jewels and Roman togas.'

Klemens slapped at his boots with his crop. 'Find out, Tarnera,' he said.

Tarnera's jaw dropped. 'Find out, Herr Oberst?'

'Exactly. Find out. It's public knowledge what Goering has at Karinhall. He's boasted about it often enough. Very well, try a few of his friends. You're an ex-newspaperman with contacts at the ministry. Find out.'

5

To everyone's surprise Urquhart was up within four days, his foot inside a rubber boot, and moving doggedly about the bedroom with the aid of a stick.

'You must be potty,' Neville said. 'Getting up so soon.'

Urquhart was quite unmoved. 'Never could lie in bed,' he said.

'You'll probably do it permanent damage.'

Urquhart shrugged. 'Either it or me. If I stay in bed I'll do *me* permanent damage. I like to be on my feet and able to move – especially with the bloody Germans all round me.'

Neville gestured. 'We're all right here.'

Urquhart turned. 'How do you know?'

'Well, for God's sake – !'

'Because Marie-Claude's pretty, and Father Pol's a bit like Friar Tuck, and Reinach's a sort of Scarlet Pimpernel? You want to grow up, son. Trust nobody. It's safer.'

'For Christ's sake, they've already risked their lives more than once for us – '

'You read too many romantic novels,' Urquhart said cynically. 'The reason France went for a burton in 1940 was because everybody thought everybody else was a jolly decent type. Most of 'em were, but there were a few who weren't. I prefer to rely on me.'

The following day Neville found him hobbling round the farm.

'How the hell did you get down the stairs?' he asked.

'Elbows and backside.' Urquhart's reply was laconic. 'Not difficult.' He stared round him, sniffing the air. 'Not a bad place,' he said approvingly. 'Must have been a good farm once.'

It was an old farm, built like a fortress, with tiled roofs marked with lichen, the kitchen table as solid-looking as if it had been made two centuries before. There was a hot water tank with a fat pipe going through the wall, a battery of ladles and cooking utensils under a picture cut from a calendar showing kittens and roses, and opposite, a yellowing photograph of three men in uniform bearing the words 'Morts pour la Patrie' and the dates '1914–1918.' Outside was a stack of hutches containing stolidly-munching Belgian rabbits, and beyond, down a short winding road terminated by gateless stone pillars, the blunt spire of the church.

On Urquhart's insistence, within days Marie-Claude produced papers for them.

'Work permits,' she said, handing them over. 'Also identity cards and certificates from your employer, without which you can be taken to Germany for the Service de Travail Obligatoire. You've become Robert-Charles Neville and Jacques Urquaert. Robert-Charles Neville is my cousin from Nice – because you've spent much time there, of course, and acquired a southern accent and could answer questions about it. Since my husband is dead you have come to help with the farm. Because *you* have a northern accent, Jacques Urquaert's a Belgian worker. We're allowed to have one because there's no one else, but unfortunately, at the moment, he has an injured foot because he was kicked by one of the cows.'

She paused. 'Because he is one of the family, the cousin must live in one of the bedrooms. Because you are a Belgian hired labourer, you must sleep in the attic. I have made it nice. You will understand, I hope.'

Urquhart grinned. 'Of course,' he said. 'Naturally. Mustn't let the hired help get too big for his boots.'

She gave him a quick, hurt look and turned away. Neville's gaze followed her, frankly admiring. She seemed to sense it and stopped in the doorway.

'There have been others,' she said, 'and we have sent them on their way. At the moment, though, it's difficult because it costs three thousand francs for fares and bribes and, with the Germans expecting the invasion, they suspect everybody. I shall be sorry to see you go because it's pleasant to have men about the place again.' She indicated the old clothes she wore. 'Normally, I would not work on the farm, you see. My husband had studied at agricultural college and we expected to be prosperous. But instead he is dead and I am alone. You will not understand the problems.'

'I might,' Urquhart said quietly. 'My father was a farmer too.'

She gave him a quick, calculating look. 'You know about farming?'

'English farming.'

'Cattle are cattle and grain is grain. Broken fences are the same anywhere and cow dung doesn't change its smell. If you understand farming in England, you will understand it here.'

Rather to Neville's surprise, the Resistance he'd heard so much about in England seemed to be almost non-existent and certainly didn't keep up the running battle British propaganda suggested. Most of those engaged in it were mere boys who'd fled to the woods to avoid being sent to Germany to work. They lived for months in camps hidden in the trees, depressed, lacking arms, food, equipment, sanitation, even clothing, their morale at rock bottom, their weapons rusty fire-arms from farmhouse walls, dynamite stolen from quarries, and a few old Mills bombs too dangerous to handle, sometimes even none at all.

'South of Dijon it's different,' Marie-Claude explained. 'The Germans erected frontier barriers down there in 1940 and to cross from Occupied France into Vichy France you had to show a passport. But until France was totally occupied, you could also see British films and read Swiss newspapers down there and it was always easier to organize a resistance against the future. In the north we decided it would be wiser for the time being to do as we were told and, before we knew where we were, many found themselves trapped into collaboration.'

She frowned. 'It was a little like roulette. You were allowed to win at first to encourage you to lose your fortune later. We discovered that we didn't know what God's grace was until evil took its place.'

Neville frowned. He'd had no idea what the French had been enduring. The only thing they'd had to hold on to, it seemed, was the knowledge that de Gaulle was in London planning their liberation.

'But what about your ex-soldiers?' he asked. 'The survivors of 1940?'

Marie-Claude's shoulders moved. 'There's one here – Commandant Verdy de Clary. Like all the others, his goals were "correct". He always lived and died by "honneur et patrie", "le devoir" and "la tradition", and to fall on the field of honour was the most important thing of all. Unfortunately he can't understand that the field of honour can be the woods and the hills, because those who've fled there aren't always very presentable and are often Communists.'

Within three weeks Urquhart was limping easily about the fields behind the house and, because he was bored, he started to do small jobs, mending fences and walls, and insisted on Neville helping. Neville was none too keen. Unlike Urquhart, he'd never done the work before and he was clumsy and soon bored.

'You're supposed to be helping run the place,' Urquhart growled when he protested. 'So you'd better. In case the Germans ask.'

For another two weeks, watched by the delighted Marie-Claude, they worked about the boundaries of her land and in the stackyard until Urquhart's limp had almost gone. So far, they'd kept well away from the village, moving about only behind the farm and in the fields where there were no Germans, and the most they saw of them were occasional figures in grey and lorries moving past the end of the muddy road to the street. Whatever had to be done in the village was done by Marie-Claude, dressed lumpishly in the heavy men's clothes and hat to hide her figure so that the Germans wouldn't molest her as she tramped alongside the old horse which pulled the rubber-tyred platform cart they used.

'It's as bad as being in jail,' Neville complained.

'And listening to you moaning all the time's like sharing a cell,' Urquhart said. 'We're not at Eton now.'

'I didn't go to Eton.'

'Well, wherever you did go. We're not at university either, punting on the Cam or taking tea with the dean. We're not even in the bloody officers' mess. We're here. In France. Pretending to be Frenchmen.'

'You don't like me much, Urquhart, do you?' Neville said.

Urquhart stared at him, a half-smile on his face, and Neville had the impression that he didn't give a damn either way.

'I've met worse,' he said. 'Chiefly, I wish to Christ you'd stop thinking about what you were, and remember what you are now.' He slammed a mawl into Neville's hands and picked up a heavy axe.

'We're farm labourers,' he said. He grinned. 'At least, ***I*** am. I'm Jacques Urquaert who sleeps in the attic. You, of course, are the cousin from Nice who has the spare bedroom, so perhaps you have the right to grumble.' The smile disappeared and an icy look came into his eyes. 'But not to me. Come on. We have stakes to cut and a fence to repair.'

They moved up through the woods behind the farm, Urquhart's face expressionless again, as though he'd already forgotten the quarrel. He seemed quite content to work, as if he felt it was a way of paying for his keep, a sort of pride in not being dependent.

Neville was frowning. He knew he was being churlish but Urquhart's very stoicism made everything seem worse. Even the trousers he wore, a gift from Reinach, were too loose so that he felt oafish in them, and he much preferred to remain where he could talk to Marie-Claude, making her laugh with mock gallantry and witticisms in French.

He was trudging behind Urquhart, indulging a little in self-pity and deep in thought, when he realized there was a German standing by the edge of the trees. He had a machine pistol slung from his shoulder and was studying them suspiciously, so that Neville found himself tensing and growing pale under the scrutiny. Urquhart seemed unmoved.

The German pushed his gun round the back of his shoulder and gestured. 'Who're you?' he asked in French.

Neville couldn't have answered to save his life. His throat seemed to have closed up and his tongue clove to the roof of his mouth in fear. Urquhart looked puzzled.

'*Hein?*'

'*Vos papiers!*' It sounded like 'vos babiers.'

'Ach!' Urquhart's expression changed to one of understanding and he fished into the old blue smock Marie-Claude had found for him. He turned to Neville. '*Papiers,*' he said. 'He wants our papers.'

The German seemed as unsure as Neville felt, and it

dawned on him that he'd been looking for game to augment his rations, and was putting on a show of authority to explain his presence to them. As he bent his head, making a performance of studying the documents, Neville saw that Urquhart's hand had tightened on the haft of the axe and knew that if necessary he was prepared to chop the German down with it.

Glancing round, he saw they were entirely alone, away from the village with no other Germans in sight, and hidden from view by a line of bushes. His throat worked because he knew that if the German started being difficult he hadn't the nerve himself to do anything about it. But then the German's head lifted and he handed back the papers with a smile.

'Belgian?' he asked. His voice was not unpleasant and Neville realized that he was approaching middle age and even had a friendly face.

'Yes,' Urquhart said.

'You're a long way from home.'

'Doesn't worry me. It's warmer here than Belgium, and there's more food and no wife, and the work's easy.'

The German's smile widened to a grin and he looked at Neville. 'You're a long way from home, too,' he said. 'And for you it's colder, I think. Colder than Nice, anyway.'

Neville found he couldn't answer and Urquhart's elbow jabbed at him so that he woke up.

'Oh, yes,' he managed. 'But *I* don't like the work. I'm not used to it.'

'Who is?'

The German waved them on and they stuffed away the papers, shouldered the tools and began to move up the hill again. For a while they didn't speak then Neville looked at Urquhart.

'Would you have hit him with the axe?' he asked. 'If he'd found something wrong with the papers?'

Urquart didn't turn his head. 'Yes,' he said.

'Think we got away with it?'

'Yes.'

The knowledge that they *had* got away with it, that the papers they'd been provided with could pass muster and carry them through all but the closest check, cheered them and gave them confidence. Within another week, they were moving freely about the village and even knew which houses would offer a slice of cherry tart or a glass of wine, that Father Pol was obsessed by the absence of fats, and which woman would take advantage of her husband's absence to make eyes at them; who slept with whom, and who was to be trusted, and all the gossip of the village and the villages around. Neither of them ever mentioned the men who'd been in Crombie's crew with them. It was almost as if they'd decided by mutual agreement that they'd never lived. Nobody questioned them. No one was curious and no one blamed them for the bombs that had been dropped on France.

Occasionally, one of the German orderlies from the château, a Westphalian called Hössenfelder, came to the farm. He was a grave little man in his early forties and, after at first simply watching, he shyly picked up a fork and started to help Urquhart with the straw and dung from the cow byre. 'At home I am a farmer also,' he said in his bad French.

Marie-Claude was delighted by the sudden influx of help. 'Next year,' she announced, 'we shall set down the south meadow to corn.'

'Next year,' Urquhart reminded her, 'we shan't be here.'

She gave him a shrewd smile. 'Perhaps the war will go on for a long time,' she said. 'Perhaps you'll have to stay longer than you think.'

She was earthy and full of good humour – the sort who could never be defeated – and it was quite obvious that the young men of the village had noticed her, too, because they were always calling on the flimsiest of excuses. Usually, she sent them packing. 'It's not an unwritten law that the backsides of women are free pasturage for the wandering hands of young men,' she said. 'They have no education and not much sense. They'd keep me pregnant, and all I'd do would be keep them in food and drink and warm in bed. They're after the farm.'

Only Lionel Dring, the son of Théodore Dring, the garde-chasse, seemed to be welcome. He was a tall, blond young man who'd studied forestry. Because he was not allowed to practise it – except for the Germans who were denuding the countryside of its trees – he worked for a farmer called Gaudin who lived with his wife, two sons and a daughter on the west side of the village. He was a shy, tongue-tied young giant and his excuses to see Marie-Claude were patently false.

'He's a good man, of course,' she told Urquhart soberly. 'He'd make a good husband. But he knows nothing about farming.'

'What are you looking for?' Urquhart asked. 'A husband to love or just a man to work the farm?'

She stared straight at him. 'Both,' she said.

That afternoon, as Urquhart hacked away with a billhook at an overgrown hedge on the other side of the hill where the stream ran down to the river, the sun came out – the first real warmth they'd had since their arrival. In the valley was a small dam Marie-Claude's father had built years before. It was hot down there and loud with insects and, since he was sweating, he stripped off his clothes and waded in. As he splashed about he became aware of Marie-Claude sitting on the bank watching him.

'I'm coming out now,' he said.

'Then come. I know what you look like. I've been married. I've seen a man before.'

Urquhart shrugged and climbed out to dry himself with his shirt. As he dressed, she handed him a slab of bread and a bottle of coarse wine she'd brought, and waited while he ate, her feet in the heavy boots she wore about the farm, her strong body relaxed but taut and pliant.

The first busy bees of the spring had begun to appear, droning among the bottoms where the first flowers were showing. A thrush in the top of an elm lifted its voice in song and the young grass, new and bright green, thrust upwards among the tufty brown stalks of the previous year's growth. But Marie-Claude seemed indifferent to the waking world around her and was studying Urquhart carefully – almost as if he were a prize steer, he thought – her eyes on his big frame, thick forearms and strong neck, and the planes and angles of his face.

She caught his gaze on her and turned her eyes away quickly. Then she looked back at him and smiled, boldly, defiantly, as though she had nothing to hide. 'You're a big man, Urk't,' she said. 'Strong. Well-made. Neville is slow and he isn't good with his hands like you.'

'I grew up on a farm,' Urquhart pointed out.

'Then why did you become a soldier?'

Urquhart shrugged. 'It was a small farm and I had four brothers. There wasn't room for all of us.'

'And after the war? You'll go back?'

He shook his head. 'When it's over there'll be trouble between them. I'm keeping out of it.'

She looked worried. 'If you're once a farmer. you're always a farmer. You can't push it aside like that.'

'I can leave it for the time being.'

'You're different from Neville.'

'Yes,' Urquhart grinned. 'He's young, virginal and idealistic, and he's read too many books. None of those things applies to me.'

She frowned. 'I didn't mean that. I meant that he's not of the soil.'

'He never had to be. His family have money.'

'A great deal?'

'More than was good for Neville, I suspect.'

'You are envious of him?'

'God, no! I'm envious of no man. I'm one of God's chosen few.'

She stared. 'Why?'

'Because I'm alive when I ought to have been dead a dozen times. Because I'm not worried about whether things are right and whether things are wrong. And because, unlike Neville, I can live anywhere I'm dropped. I don't need the trimmings he needs.'

'You cannot have many friends.'

Urquhart smiled. 'I don't need friends. I get along all right with me. Neville wants the things he's been used to. Friends. Background. Money. People with money.'

She sniffed. 'We have money, too.' She looked at him under a lock of dark hair that had fallen over her eyes. 'Before the war, this was a good farm. Even now there is no shortage of money. Just a shortage of men.'

That night, as they listened to the BBC, the older men came again. Urquhart suspected that, like Lionel Dring, they came as much as anything to look at Marie-Claude. Because of the curfew, they sneaked across the fields, leaving their homes by the back doors and slipping over walls.

The radio was an old one, and under the Occupation it was impossible to replace. From time to time the sound disappeared entirely and Madame Lamy had to rise, her Rs rolling thunderously as she complained about the Germans, to give it a thump with her fist to bring it back to life.

It had been behaving particularly badly this night and she was attacking it with vigour when the door clicked. As Marie-Claude went to answer it, Reinach poked his head round the corner into the hall and withdrew it, grinning his toothless grin.

'It's Patricia,' he whispered to Urquhart. 'Patrice de Frager, the Baron. He likes to think he's the symbol of the Resistance round here and prowls round at night, sometimes to Rolandpoint to see a girl, sometimes to St Seigneur, sometimes just to prove to himself that he can.'

The boy who entered was no more than nineteen, smooth-faced with fine dark eyes and a high thin nose. He was beautifully dressed in a shooting jacket and velour hat, and everyone stood up respectfully as he appeared. He didn't waste time.

'The German colonel's looking for the pictures,' he announced. 'My great-grandmother's worried.'

'So she should be,' Marie-Claude said. 'So should we all be.'

Father Pol shifted uncomfortably. 'Me,' he said, 'I'm fat, myopic, unfit and lazy.'

'It makes no difference.'

'My child, I know that and I'm ashamed. I'm even indifferent to comfort and cleanliness and I'm probably not even a good servant of God. But I'm an ex-soldier and a good hater of the Germans, and sometimes I wish the organ pipes in the church were the barrels of a multiple pom-pom.'

'It's a pity we can't infiltrate them,' Marie-Claude said, her voice suddenly thin and bitter. 'As they infiltrate the Resistance. My fiancé was killed because they had a tip-off and, because I was engaged to him and they thought I might be carrying messages for them, they took me to Gestapo headquarters in Dijon and I was forced to strip while they examined my clothes. They didn't even give me a blanket to put round me and I had to stand there naked in front of all those grinning men.' Her face was pink with shame and hatred, and she spoke with an angry desperation, her mind stiff with memories of twisted motor bikes and burned cars and fragments of bone among scorched helmets and broken weapons, and a sickly-sweet smell that was like nothing else on earth.

Reinach's eyes glinted. 'We got the man who betrayed them,' he growled. 'The St Seigneur and Rolandpoint réseaux caught his car. It stank of women and perfume and he had a tart with him and plenty of money. They were both informers and when he tried to run for it he was shot down. It was Brisson from Rolandpoint who did it. When the woman grabbed Brisson's clothes, he put his hands behind him so he wouldn't have to touch her, and she was pleading for her life when someone blew away the back of her head.'

No one said anything for a moment and Neville realized just how savage life had become in France. The Luftwaffe over London, the telegrams that came to the homes of the dead, the nightly losses of bomber command, all seemed strangely impersonal compared with this.

'There's one of the Germans who has his eye on Euphrasie Doumic, my mother's maid,' de Frager suggested and Reinach smiled his empty smile.

'That girl's eyes have turned a few heads in their time,' he said.

'Not half as many as her behind,' Madame Lamy rapped. 'Tell her to encourage him.'

Father Pol gestured. 'There's one other,' he said. 'The Catholic officer, Tarnera.'

'Will he talk?' Reinach asked. 'If he will, then you have a duty to France.'

'After my duty to God. I shall not be bound by what he says outside the Confessional, but what is said inside is between him and me.'

They seemed lost and bewildered, yearning to do something to prove they were men and Frenchmen, but unable to bring themselves to a point of action.

'They're born victims,' Urquhart growled when they'd gone.

Marie-Claude turned on him at once. 'With good reason!' she flared. 'There's hardly a family here that hasn't lost one of its men. They tried but they had no experience and the Germans ambushed their group and shot twenty-five of them. We put red, white and blue ribbons on the grave, and later, when they were brought down for burial in the village, there were hundreds of mourners and a tricolour on the tomb. A German officer tore it down and said that they were gangsters and pigs, and that we'd abused their generosity.' Her eyes flashed. 'Generosity! Mother of God!' She drew a deep shuddering breath, caught by her own inflamed pride. 'Last year they tried again. A few young men who'd managed to escape from Germany; a few who'd come from North Africa. Another agent came with another radio and again they got weapons. But the Gestapo caught one of their messengers – a boy of seventeen. They castrated him like a young boar to get information. They were all taken up to Mont St Amarin and shot. Every one of them.'

There was a long aching silence that Neville tried to break. 'And now?' he asked.

She turned on him sharply. 'After that do you expect any "now"?' she snapped. 'There can't be. There's nothing left.'

6

Colonel Klemens was irritated. He was well established now in Néry. The château was well run by Unteroffizier Schäffer and a staff of four, one of whom, Corporal Goehr, the cook, was making eyes at Euphrasie, the Baronne's maid; while the young Baron was stiff and polite without being friendly – except when he wanted a little extra petrol. Klemens knew he used it to visit girls and he gave it grudgingly because it was beginning to occur to him that somehow someone had put something across him, and he was beginning to grow annoyed. Sitting at the Baronne's dining table, flicking at his shining boot toes with his crop, he stared at the Baronne in a chair opposite, with Balmaceda's ancient frame drooping alongside her, as thin and dried up under his sagging clothes as she was herself, and just as ridiculous with the dark toupee that made a match with her hennaed hair.

'I've been round this house,' Klemens was saying angrily. 'I've studied every painting and artifact in it. And I've decided that for a family as great and old as this one, there's remarkably little here of any value.'

The Baronne shrugged. 'We were never wealthy.'

Klemens frowned. 'My information's different,' he said. 'My information is that your husband put his wealth into the soil. He bought land in the Jura and property in Dijon and other places.'

'Which – ' the Baronne sniffed – 'at the moment brings in nothing. The land in the Jura has been taken over by your army, much of our property has been sequestrated, while our vineyards south of Dijon have had to be sold to raise money.'

Klemens frowned. No one spoke. Standing with Klein-Wuttig, Tarnera hated the baiting of the old woman. He had a feeling that Klemens hated it too. He was a good-natured man under the surface, likeable and harmless and with a weakness for young women; but, like so many other Wehrmacht officers in France, a grabber with one eye on the future.

Klemens flicked at a speck of dust on his trousers and tried again. 'I also understand that your husband put a lot of money into paintings which, as you know, madame, are always a good investment.'

The Baronne said nothing, staring at Klemens without really seeing him. It was something she'd trained herself to do. The Germans were like the dung on the road through the village. It was there but one didn't comment on it. Klemens stared back at her with a look of baffled anger. 'You're not being very helpful, madame,' he said bitterly.

She gave a bark of laughter. It sounded like the squawk of an ancient parrot. 'You're an optimist if you think *any* good Frenchwoman would ever help *you*,' she said. '*I* wouldn't. *I'm* not the Vicomtesse de la Chattel at Bourg.'

Klemens glared. 'There's nothing in this place,' he snorted. 'Nothing! These "treasures" we see around us are village treasures. Vases from cottages. Paintings from farmhouses and the homes of retired bank managers and ex-officers. Of no value whatsoever, madame, because such people don't have the sort of money that's needed to buy *real* treasures.' He flicked at his boots again, trying to hang on to his temper. 'I know this because General Dannhüber, who is now in Dijon, was once billeted here. In 1940. For several nights. He was a colonel then. Perhaps you'll remember him.'

The Baronne's eyes flashed. Despite her age, there were deep glowing fires behind them. 'Since he stayed without an invitation,' she snapped, 'I'm not likely to forget him.'

Klemens lost his temper. 'General Dannhüber's a gentleman!'

'He's a German!'

Klemens managed to control himself. 'General Dannhüber is a connoisseur and *he* didn't see only rustic treasures! He saw things of value! He saw a Corot, a Fragonard, a Troyon and a Vigée Lebrun, to say nothing of several Nattiers and Daubignys and other things!'

The Baronne's shoulders moved expressively and Klemens slapped the table.

'Where are these Troyons and Fragonards and Daubignys?' he snapped.

The Baronne drew a deep breath. 'There were never Troyons and Fragonards and Daubignys.'

'There was a Corot!' Klemens indicated the painting over the fireplace. Round the frame there was an area of faded wall-paper.

'There was a bigger painting hanging there until recently,' he said. 'It's been taken away and that one put in its place. I've looked round this house. There are several places like that. Some are bigger. Some are smaller. You haven't been clever enough, madame. Those are the places where the Corots and the Daubignys hung, aren't they?' He sat bolt upright. 'Very well, where are they?'

'We sent a lot to the house in Nice.'

'We've radioed Nice,' Klein-Wuttig snapped. 'We've had the house there checked. The paintings are all small. Where are the ones that hung here? The big ones.'

'They were taken by the Germans.'

'When?'

'I can't remember.'

'By my predecessor?' Klemens asked. 'By Colonel Marx?'

'I can't recall.'

'I'll try to refresh your memory.' Klemens turned to Tarnera. 'Send a signal to Colonel Marx, Tarnera. Ask him. He's only at Nevers.'

May came and Neville began to grow impatient with waiting. Living in the country to Neville had always previously meant shooting, riding, fishing, walking and enjoying the views, while other people did the work. It didn't include smelling like a stable or using his hands and his muscles to do backbreaking jobs, especially when Urquhart could shame him by doing them with much greater ease. He grew short-tempered, and what little help he gave about the farm was slap-dash and careless. Urquhart worked slowly and stolidly, finding he enjoyed using his hands again, and his efforts made an enormous difference. Things that had been flung down and left, because there'd never been time to pick them up and put them away, suddenly began to disappear; fences that had been broken for years became taut and strong again. To Urquhart, a quiet man, calm in his own self-dependence, the work he did mattered little. He'd always had to work hard.

Hössenfelder, the German orderly, continued to turn up, even occasionally sitting in the kitchen drinking wine with them and being sentimental about his home in Westphalia. They tried to hate him but even Marie-Claude found his simplicity hard to resent.

'He loves the land,' she said, puzzled. 'And in this he's not so different from my husband – nor from you, Urk't.'

Urquhart's foot finally healed and two nights after Dr Mouillet had pronounced him fit, when they returned from the fields to the house, there was a smell of cooking and the tang of garlic, and Marie-Claude was standing at the fireplace, dressed in her starched apron, stirring a shining brass cauldron. There were two bottles of wine on the table, and there seemed to be a new smell of wax and polish about the place. Madame Lamy was chopping large chunks of bread with a guillotine.

'There is also an omelette,' Marie-Claude announced with a beaming smile.

Madame Lamy spooned soup into a large dish and slammed it to the table. 'Onion,' she announced. 'Very good for the digestion.'

Marie-Claude sat down as they ate, watching them with excited eyes. 'Tomorrow we go into Rolandpoint,' she said.

'Who do?'

'I do. And you do. We will take Hercule, the horse. He is a veteran of the Spanish Civil War and came here in 1939, having walked all the way from the frontier. He will pull the trap and you will accompany me.'

Urquhart and Neville stared at each other then back at Marie-Claude. 'Why?'

She sat back, her smile full of pleasure. 'Because we've had a message,' she said. 'Arsène's back and he's offered to take you on the first leg of your journey.'

Neville beamed. 'Where to?'

'The Spanish frontier.'

Neville's face fell. 'Why not Switzerland?' he demanded. 'It's nearer.'

'And twice as dangerous,' Marie-Claude said. 'Everyone heads for Switzerland from here. It's too well watched.'

Neville looked at Urquhart, wondering what he'd have to say, expecting anger. But Urquhart was smiling and he leaned across the table to kiss first Marie-Claude then Madame Lamy on the cheek. They seemed a little startled at this expression of pleasure from someone so undemonstrative and Madame Lamy slapped at him embarrassedly with her apron.

Marie-Claude sat still, watching him, a sudden lost look on her face. Outside, the twilight was descending like a grey veil, and Urquhart seemed to sense the sacrifice she was making for them.

'There'll be others,' he encouraged. 'Wait until the invasion. There'll be millions of them. With bulldozers and tractors. They'll make your farm like new.'

Next morning, accompanied by Elsie, they set off early for Rolandpoint. The trees were in leaf now and the muddy puddles had gone from the drive. Marie-Claude was in a gay mood, light-hearted and enthusiastic. 'Soon it'll be summer,' she said. 'And then the Free French will come.'

Urquhart was wearing a pair of black trousers with a pin stripe in them which had belonged to Marie-Claude's father, while Neville wore a black and white striped shirt and a black jacket over a pair of blue denim overalls. Both wore flat caps which they had pulled down over their eyes, only to have them pushed to the back of their heads again by Marie-Claude.

'You look like gangsters,' she had said sharply. 'Remember you're farm workers with nothing to be ashamed of.'

As they drove out of the village, the land, slow-curving and surprisingly warm in the sun, showed patches of young corn on the slopes, and along the road there were oats and young beet. Marie-Claude seemed completely in charge and they were both quite happy to let her run the show.

Rolandpoint was larger than Néry, a grey stone village

with its main street winding down to the inevitable Grande Place. The Chemin des Chats, a narrow lane slightly higher, ran parallel to it behind the backs of the houses, and there were several intersecting lanes, all winding between the crooked buildings to link courtyards and alleys. The woods were always close, while the little narrow-gauge railway that brought timber from the forests above Néry ran through the street on its way to join the main line at St Seigneur.

It had a softer, mellower look about it than Néry. Down in the valley away from the higher ground, the stones were less worn, the tiles less faded, the timbers less warped by the weather. Summer was in the air, too, to add an extra benison of colour, with blossom out near the Grande Place and a hint of perfume in the air. Occasionally they passed groups of Germans on bicycles or on foot, and once an infantry platoon on the march. They were marching at ease and several of them smiled and waved. To Neville they didn't look like murderers or men without pity, but Marie-Claude showed no sign of even having seen them. Though her expression didn't change, to her they were the enemy and there was no equivocation, no doubt, no half-measures in her hatred as she stared about her at the starved streets, the empty shops and the gazogène cars which ran on charcoal gas and had to be stoked up every few kilometres.

'Everybody uses bicycles these days,' she said. 'They say Paris is like Hong Kong and in the Champs Elysées there are so few cars you can actually smell the fresh air.'

Women clattered past on wooden-soled shoes and, as they approached the Grande Place, they heard the high hooting of a lorry, aggressive and imperious. Two trucks passed them, moving at full speed so that the people in the roadway had to run for safety. They were Wehrmacht vehicles and Elsie immediately placed her paws on the side of the cart and barked furiously at them.

'One of these days,' Urquhart said, 'one of them will shoot her.'

There were pictures everywhere of Pétain, the old man who was in control of France under the Germans, with notices giving instructions on how to send parcels to the

Frenchmen who were still prisoners of war. Marie-Claude frowned but continued to chatter cheerfully.

'You must always remember,' she advised, 'that in places like Rolandpoint there is one day with, and one day without.'

'Without what?'

'But alcohol, of course! You cannot buy it, and it's possible for escaping fliers to give themselves away if they're not aware of this. The people who live here, of course, know *exactly* whether it's 'with' or 'without'. They say it's to conserve the country's wine stocks but it's obviously only going into German bellies. Even the collaborators hate it.'

She indicated a notice printed in red and black. 'An S.S. announcement of the execution of Communists and men of the Maquis,' she said in a flat voice. 'They're everywhere. Both the notices and the S.S. The Miliciens are the worst. They're French and the scum of the jails, and they know how Frenchmen think and which questions to ask. You're lucky to be leaving. For you, the hardest thing will be the walking. Just keep away from the cities, that's all. The Germans are always worse in the cities. Under the surface, I think they're really afraid of us and this is why they go in for terror and torture. It's our strongest ally.'

There seemed to be a great number of soldiers about the streets and Neville looked round uneasily at them. 'Do they check papers?' he asked.

Marie-Claude shrugged. 'Sometimes.'

'What's the drill?'

'The drill?'

'In case they stop us.'

'I shall think of something.'

'Don't you have a plan?'

'What's the use of a plan when the drill's different every time.'

As they reached the village centre, Neville realized he was tensing himself against the back of the cart, his foot jammed hard against the side, his jaw set and his teeth clenched. He forced himself to relax and glanced at Marie-Claude. If she were afraid she showed no sign of it, and sat straight-backed and undaunted in a way that pleased him somehow, her head up, the white column of her neck straight, her eyes wide, a slight frown on her brows. Only the tightening of her lips hinted at what she was feeling.

The German soldiers eyed them incuriously. The cafés were open and at one German officers were eating breakfast.

'When they first came,' Marie-Claude said, smiling reflectively, 'they put wire round them to keep the French out. But during the night schoolboys put up notices, "Wild beasts. Keep away", so they took it down again and we use them, too, now. We take our bicycle pumps in with us and hang them on the hatstands next to their belts and holsters. They hate it.'

As they turned the corner, they saw a line of men standing at the next crossroads. some of them soldiers, some in the uniform of the Gestapo, others still in civilian clothes.

'The *rafle*!' Marie-Claude spoke quietly, her expression unchanged. 'The round-up. They might be looking for British airmen, French resistance workers, young men for forced labour in Germany, or merely their own deserters.'

'What do we do?' Urquhart demanded.

'Nothing. They're too busy to worry about us at the moment. Whenever they hold one, every woman in the place wraps up anything she can find to make a parcel and lets herself be stopped. It delays the searching and helps anyone who has to, to get away.'

Neville had licked his lips nervously. As he gathered his feet under him, ready to run, Urquhart laid a hand on his arm.

'For Christ's sake.' Neville breathed, 'we're just putting our heads in a noose.'

'Shut up,' Urquhart growled. 'Or are you afraid?'

Neville's head jerked round. 'No,' he said. 'I'm not.'

'Well, you're putting on a bloody good imitation of somebody who is.'

The insult steadied Neville, as it was intended to, and he frowned as Marie-Claude's voice came. 'They'll shoot anyone who tries to bolt,' she said. 'And Arsène will already have gone to ground.'

The old horse continued to plod towards the line of men.

Then, abruptly, without any sign of panic, Marie-Claude pulled on the reins and the horse swung between two large gate-posts into a muddy yard surrounded by buildings. An old man with a thin sly face came towards her.

'Pigs, Bona,' she said quietly. 'I want pigs.'

The old man looked nervous, well aware of what was happening further along the street. 'I haven't got pigs,' he said.

A woman appeared. She was older than Marie-Claude, pretty and plump, but sharp-eyed as though she knew everything that went on. She wore thick powder and heavy eye make-up, and as she stood near the cart Neville caught a whiff of a suffocatingly strong perfume. Her legs were good but she wore shoes with heels so high she was pigeon-toed when she walked. Her dress, new and obviously acquired on the black market, was so tight it showed the bulges of flesh round her hips.

She stared up at Marie-Claude, her expression hostile.

'We have no pigs, Marie-Claude,' she said. 'Not for sale.'

'Today you have,' Marie-Claude said sharply. 'I want one. Two would be better. One for me. One for the Germans.'

'You heard what my father-in-law said.'

'Give me the pigs, Ernestine,' Marie-Claude snapped. jerking her head at her passengers. 'I need them.'

The woman stared at her for a moment, then at Urquhart and Neville. Finally she turned and hurried away across the muddy yard. 'Give her the pigs,' she said to the old man.

A flicker of a smile crossed Marie-Claude's face and she jumped to the ground. 'Get the back off the cart,' she commanded.

'Do we hide here?' Neville asked as they lifted the catches.

'Of course not. If I drive in here with you, and out without you, they'll search the place at once. We came in to buy pigs and when we've bought them, we go out again, back to where we came from.'

Half an hour later, there were two half-grown pigs in the back of the cart, and Neville and Urquhart were splashed with mud and pig dung, and panting with the exertion of hoisting them in. The old man produced a net which they draped over the two sullen animals and tied into place, then the old horse began to splash out of the muddy yard.

The round-up seemed to have finished. A soldier in a doorway glanced at them but he saw only what had entered, plus two disgruntled pigs, and he made no move to stop them. Without speaking, they jolted out of Rolandpoint back towards Néry, not speaking until the houses were behind them and they were already climbing the hill. Then Urquhart noticed that Marie-Claude was smiling.

'What's so funny?' he asked.

She gave a little laugh. 'It's always good to put something across Ernestine Bona,' she said. 'I now have two pigs and Ernestine has two less.'

'You don't like her?'

'Anyone kissing her would come away looking like a baker's assistant. She once tried to steal my husband.'

'Does she work with the Nazis?'

Marie-Claude's eyes flashed. 'She helped with the pigs, didn't she?' She chuckled. 'She'll never condescend to ask for them back and *we* need pigs. We haven't had pigs for a year.' She gave them a broad unashamed grin. 'You ate what was left of the last lot.'

Neville glanced at Urquhart. 'What about us?' he asked.

'What about you?'

'It seems to have put paid to us leaving.'

She shrugged. 'Father Pol always did think you were unwise trying to leave so soon.' She laughed again. 'Tomorrow we must clean out the old sties. You'll be able to do it for me.'

She began to sing softly to herself and Neville looked at Urquhart. He was surprised to find him grinning.

'Do you get the impression,' Urquhart asked, 'that we're being put upon?'

7

There was only one thing in everyone's mind: the invasion waiting just across the Channel, holding back only for the days of fair weather when it could be launched against the shores of France.

There was no fear anywhere that it wouldn't succeed. With the Germans already out of Africa and in trouble in Russia and Italy, and with the vast industrial might of America behind it, failure just couldn't be conceived.

'After all,' Marie-Claude pointed out, 'there are a quarter of a million men waiting in England, and the British Empire, the United States and Russia are a formidable combination to take on, even for Hitler's Germany.'

They could hear the RAF going over at night, and learned that Auxerre and Tonnerre and Châtillon-sur-Seine had been bombed because they were junctions leading to the invasion coast. They also heard of the Resistance blowing things up in Besançon and the Doubs next door, where the Resistance was stronger because the high ground was higher and they were harder to get at. Occasionally they even heard of sabotage in Dijon, which was an important German military administration centre for north-eastern France, and of damage done to railway points and turntables. The townspeople seemed better at that sort of thing than the country-dwellers.

Their lack of success was something that bore heavily on the men of Néry. Twice they had failed and suddenly the good hard life of the fields and the pleasure of cheating the Germans with high prices for their food was no longer enough. They were beginning to itch for action again. Every man in France was beginning to itch for action, and the men of Néry had old scores to settle.

As the Germans well knew.

'According to our predecessors,' Colonel Klemens was saying, 'Resistance cells sprang up here in 1942 and 1943 but were totally destroyed. Since then there's been nothing.'

Tarnera and Klein-Wuttig waited. There was obviously something on the colonel's mind.

'However,' he went on, 'Dijon's had a report that a parachute drop took place here recently and I want supervision of the villages in the command to find out where it went to. Dijon suspects Rolandpoint and I want a man there to keep an eye on the place.'

'I'll go,' Klein-Wuttig said at once.

'Disguised as what?'

'I'll find something.'

'See that you do. Go and see Major Doench at Rolandpoint. Anything suspicious to be reported at once. We'll follow it up with a house-to-house search.'

The failure to contact the Resistance in Rolandpoint had drawn Urquhart and Neville closer together, Neville edgy and frustrated, Urquhart more philosophical and with an old soldier's calm.

'When *do* we go then?' he demanded of Marie-Claude.

She seemed unexpectedly cheerful. 'You don't,' she said. 'Without Arsène, you have to stay here for a while longer.'

Then her smile faded and he had the feeling that some secret tribunal within her was summing them up. He shrugged. Since she was obviously used to running things, they had to leave it all to her.

'How long will it take to organize the route again?' Neville asked.

'A month.' Her cheerfulness had given place now to briskness. 'Two months. Perhaps longer. Sometimes airmen have stayed hidden in attics for as long as three.'

As she disappeared, Urquhart stared after her, his expression puzzled. 'That girl's a bloody sight cleverer than I thought,' he said.

'What do you mean?'

Urquhart grinned. 'I have the sad dry taste of shattered illusions,' he said. 'I thought she was keeping us here for the glory of France. Instead, now, I think she's keeping us here because we're a bit of extra bloody labour about the farm.'

'I don't believe it.'

Urquhart looked at Neville's eager youthful face. 'People have a habit of belying their looks, old son,' he warned.

'Well, what if they do. I suppose we owe her a bit.'

'Okay.' Urquhart laughed. 'Then next time there's some muck-spreading to be done, let's see you at it, boy, with a bit of this same enthusiastic willingness to repay, instead of creeping up to it like an undertaker approaching a corpse.'

Quite clearly, Marie-Claude had them exactly where she wanted them and there was nothing they could do but accept it, able to do no more than fight the war at a distance through the BBC.

That night, Dréo, Reinach and Ernouf turned up at the farm to listen to the broadcast from London, all claiming that their own batteries had given up the ghost. Smiling his sideways withdrawn smile. Urquhart decided that they'd really come only to daydream about the mayhem they hoped to commit on the Germans when the second front became a fact.

'And since they haven't anything more lethal than those guillotine things they chop the bread with,' he thought, 'it's a pretty pointless bloody exercise.'

The radio behaved as if half its inside was missing, so that Madame Lamy was continually on her feet, pounding the case. Her efforts made little difference and reception remained poor.

Above the crackling, however, it was still possible to feel some of the excitement in the air. The announcer gave no dates but he seemed to be suggesting that the invasion was just round the corner. 'When the allies come,' he said, 'they will rely on your help. In no more valuable way can this be given than with information about the enemy. Observe him more closely . . .'

'How close do they want?' Marie-Claude snorted. 'He's already standing with one foot on our necks.'

She was shushed to silence and they listened wistfully to the long list of personal messages – *'Marie sends her best regards to Ratouf'*, *'Napoléon passa par le tombeau comme il a passé partout'*, *'C'était Anne de Bretagne avec ses sabots'* – messages that were meaningless to the Germans, but contained hidden instructions for those they concerned. Occasionally a personal message to a family to say their son was safe in England was slipped in, occasionally something insulting for the Germans, but none was ever prefaced with 'D'Auguste à César' and they were all aware that somehow the war was passing over their heads.

There was a long silence as the announcements finished, and a distinct sense of anti-climax. Marie-Claude looked angrily at the hopeless expressions on the faces around her.

'We weren't *expecting* any messages,' she pointed out sharply.

'One might just have come,' Ernouf said wistfully.

'To tell us what?'

'Well – ' Ernouf shrugged ' – we can't just sit here doing nothing. In Paris, Maquisards disguised as Milice got into the Ministry of Information and killed a few traitors.'

'And in Marseille,' Marie-Claude said, 'when they blew up a brothel the Germans used, the Gestapo destroyed the old port and sent thousands to concentration camps.'

Ernouf shifted uncomfortably. 'The Francs-Tireurs Partisans are active,' he said.

Reinach snorted. 'The FTP are Communists and don't fight for France. Whenever they murder a German officer the Gestapo take twenty innocent hostages. I spit on the FTP. All they do is raid banks for money, mairies for ration cards, and tabacs for cigarettes. There are more Frenchmen killed getting cigarettes than anything else.'

There was another long silence. One view seemed to be that active resistance would erode German morale, another that it was best to lie low until the invasion.

'We should kill Germans,' Ernouf said doggedly. 'That's the understanding.'

'Where?'

'Does it matter where?'

'It matters a lot,' Urquhart said. 'Where you do it dictates the sort of weapons you'll need.'

The older men looked blank. 'Has war changed so much?' Sergeant Dréo asked. 'At Verdun it was just rifles and machine guns.'

'There are a few refinements these days.'

Ernouf gestured. 'Then we must just kill them with what we've got,' he said. 'Wherever we can.'

'The guerrilla's job's not to hold ground,' Neville pointed out earnestly. 'It's to hinder the enemy's progress across it.'

They stared at him indignantly. 'Doubtless you'll know exactly what to do then,' Ernouf muttered.

'Yes, I will.'

'Well, what?'

'You don't have to look further than Wellington.'

They looked at each other, puzzled.

'Who is this Wellington?' Dréo growled.

Dring's shoulders lifted. 'He's nobody from here.'

'He defeated Napoleon at Waterloo,' Neville explained.

'Oh, *him!*' Dréo shifted uncomfortably. 'Napoleon wasn't himself that day.'

Neville grinned. 'No. He had piles.'

Reinach interrupted. 'Never mind Napoleon's piles,' he growled. 'What did this Wellington do at Waterloo that was so clever?'

'Nothing more than he'd done before with Napoleon's marshals.' Neville was vital with eagerness. He was no good about the farm and ham-fisted when it came to making repairs, but on his own subject there was nobody to touch him – certainly not in Néry – and he plunged into his theme with enthusiasm.

'He waited until Napoleon had exhausted himself trying to break into his lines. He did it at Torres Verdas. He did it at Busaco and half a dozen other places. He let his enemies fight for him.'

'So?' Dréo's expression was suspicious, even dangerous.

Neville's face was bright and innocent with youth and knowledge. 'So when you start something, make sure that the Germans can't hurt you, and then go for them as they retreat.'

Dréo swallowed the contents of his glass at a gulp. 'And when do you predict the Germans will start this retreat?' he demanded.

Neville smiled. 'After the invasion,' he said.

The argument went on late into the night and was resumed early the following morning outside the gate, as Reinach stopped his lorry to pick up scrap for Sergeant Dréo. Dréo and his son were with him, sitting in the back of the vehicle, their artificial legs stuck stiffly out in front of them.

Reinach had obviously been brooding all night, and he started off again at once as he shoved and heaved at an old harrow.

'We've got a few weapons,' he said in a low voice.

'I've seen them,' Urquhart said. 'You'll not get far with those.'

'I have two shotguns and a rifle,' Marie-Claude put in. 'I hid them in the woods. They're still there.'

'Rifles and shotguns,' Neville observed, 'aren't much good against Spandaus and Schmeissers and tanks.'

For once the two Englishmen found themselves thinking the same way, if for different reasons. To Neville it was simply an exercise in historical logic: A plus B equals C. To Urquhart it was nothing but the voice of experience. He'd been through it. Their unanimity obviously irritated Reinach.

'You two talk too much,' he snarled.

Urquhart indicated Neville. 'He knows what he's talking about,' he said. 'He's read the books and, what's more, they've stayed read.'

Neville grinned at him. 'And he,' he said, 'knows because he spent two years fighting the Germans. Hand to hand. Tooth and nail. Ask him.'

'Is this true?' Dréo asked.

'Yes,' Urquhart growled.

Three pairs of eyes switched to Neville and he gestured. 'For Christ's sake,' he said, 'before you start doing anything, why not get in touch with London and see what they can do to help?'

The struggle with the harrow stopped for a moment as they stared at each other. They all knew what London meant. Though Russia and America had come into the war, because London had been the first to defy Hitler in 1940 it was still London that mattered.

'There's the radio at Rolandpoint,' Reinach said thoughtfully.

The argument ground on, the harrow forgotten. Then Father Pol rattled into the yard on his bicycle. He wore his shovel hat over his eyes and had tucked his dusty soutane up out of the way of the pedals. Now that the weather had grown warm, his sockless feet were thrust into wooden sabots. He was in a hurry, pedalling as fast as his fat legs would go. As he reached the low wall that surrounded the kitchen entrance he flung the bicycle down, fell over it in his haste, and stumbled towards the group by the lorry. He stank of rank sweat.

'We're proposing a festival for Ste Amalie-de-Lachume,' he said loudly.

'Who's Ste Amalie-de-Lachume?' Reinach demanded. 'I've never heard of her.'

'My son, the Church has plenty of all-purpose saints no one has ever heard of that she can call on when they're needed. Even St Blaise for tonsillitis.' Father Pol was using his stomach to propel them towards the house. 'I need a committee. I'm proposing to ask the German commandant for special dispensation to allow us a little celebration with candles in front of the Henri IV window.'

As they crowded into the kitchen, he shut the door and leaned on it to recover. 'It's the absence of fats,' he said. 'It leaves one exhausted.' He drew a deep breath and went on in a rush. 'Trouble,' he said. 'Father Xavier sent one of his choirboys from Rolandpoint on a racing bike.'

The door jerked behind him and the two Dréos, who had somehow struggled down from the lorry despite their artificial legs, pushed him aside. When they were all inside, he started again. 'The Germans got a tip-off,' he said, 'and picked up a man near Rolandpoint with the cords from a parachute. He'd used them to tie up staves on his farm. They tortured him and found out where Arsène was. *He's* now in La Butte Prison at Besançon but he managed to get a message to his radio operator who bolted to St Seigneur. He's sitting there now with the radio and no one to give him instructions. The Rolandpoint réseau's scared stiff.'

Elsie began to bark, and Neville dragged out the milk yield book they had to keep for the Germans and started filling it in blindly. Urquhart grabbed a scythe that had stood by the kitchen door and began to remove the blade. Marie-Claude banged down a history of Néry she'd started to write as a young girl, long since abandoned and recently rediscovered as an excuse for when people visited the farm.

They were all talking loudly of Ste Amalie-de-Lachume when Madame Lamy turned from the window. 'It's the Baron,' she said. 'And Guardian Moch.'

De Frager was dressed dramatically in black, and Neville leaned over to Urquhart to whisper. 'He thinks he's Rupert of Hentzau.'

De Frager removed his hat with the sweeping gesture of a Cyrano and faced them with eyes that flashed so much he seemed to have been practising.

'We need every man we have,' he announced loudly. 'The Germans are going to lay on a raid at Rolandpoint.'

They all sat up at once and the sly smiles at de Frager's histrionics vanished.

'How do you know?' Reinach asked.

'Ernestine Bona,' Moch pointed out. 'She says that she helped Marie-Claude a little while back and it's up to us now to help them in return. They've got to get rid of their weapons.' He placed a piece of paper on the table. 'That's what they've got. I picked it up from Brisson who has the garage.'

Reinach was reading the list out loud. 'Two bazooka anti-tank guns; six Brens, with spares and extra magazines; thirty-six rifles; twenty-seven Stens, each with three hundred rounds; five pistols, each with fifty rounds; forty Mills grenades; twelve other grenades; a hundred and twenty kilos of plastic explosive; twelve thousand rounds of .303 ammunition; six thousand rounds of German Parabellum ammunition – ' he looked up. 'Mon Dieu, you can't hide that amount! There must be over a thousand kilos!'

De Frager gestured again. Like everything else he did, it seemed as if it belonged on a stage and had been rehearsed in front of a mirror. 'Do you propose to let the Germans find them?' he snapped.

'Surely they've got a look-out watching the place?'

'There's a man in black leather on a motor cycle,' Moch said. 'Brisson thinks he's an officer from Néry. He doesn't know where the weapons are but he's making sure nothing moves.'

'For God's sake,' Sergeant Dréo said, 'if we're caught trying to get that pile away they'll shoot the lot of us!'

Marie-Claude drew herself up, her eyes flashing. 'You've been saying for months that we must do something,' she said furiously. 'Well, here it is, that something! You've been on your knees for four years! Stand up for once! I'll supply the horse and the platform.'

De Frager gestured. 'I have a car,' he said wildly. 'Full of German petrol. Let's drive in at full speed and grab the stuff.'

They didn't even bother to answer him.

'Where's it hidden?' Urquhart demanded.

Moch's sly eyes flickered. 'In Brisson's loft.'

'What's behind the loft?'

'The yard.'

'And behind that?'

'Brisson's brother's place,' Dréo said. 'He used it for scrap. He worked with Brisson until they quarrelled. He's dead now.'

Urquhart leaned forward. 'Where does the yard lead to?'

'The other end of it's in the Chemin des Chats. They say it got its name because it's where all the cats do their courting and it always smells of cat-pee.'

Urquhart was silent for a moment and they all waited. There was something about Urquhart. His eyes were often sombre, even when he smiled, as though his life was an ocean of experience, and without conscious effort he could always dominate the room when he wanted attention. Not because he was handsome – he was far less handsome than Neville or de Frager – or because he had the gift of words. But in a smiling, sardonic way that managed to project personality, confidence and knowledge.

When he spoke again, it was clear his mind was busy with an idea.

'Can you get through to the Chemin des Chats from Brisson's place?' he asked.

'Not likely,' Moch said. 'There's a high wall. His brother built it when they quarrelled.'

'How high? Too high to get over with a pair of steps?'

'No, I suppose not.'

'Can it be seen from the main street?'

'No.'

'Where does the Chemin des Chats lead to?'

'Out of the village in the direction of Néry. The other way it goes down to the Grande Place. But it winds.' Moch's narrow face was bright and eager now and he seemed to have caught at the idea forming in Urquhart's mind. 'The Germans wouldn't see a thing – not even if they were standing in the Grande Place. We could get our men down there and carry it away in small lots.'

Neville gestured. 'For God's sake, if the village filled up with men from Néry, your German on his motor bike would see them immediately, wouldn't he? Where is he?'

'On the terrasse of Hytier's place – the Bar de la Frontière. Down the street from the Bona farm. He can see the whole street from there – even the garage.'

'Not the *back* of the garage,' Reinach pointed out. 'Not the lane.'

'Are there houses in the lane?' Urquhart asked. 'Enough for people to be moving up and down?'

'Plenty.'

Marie-Claude was leaning eagerly over Urquhart now. 'Go on, Urk't,' she said. 'You're making sense.'

Father Pol was not so impressed. 'How do we move the weapons up the lane?' he asked. 'And where to?'

Dréo's son slapped his thigh. 'The drain!' he said. 'Just above the village. It was put there when the place flooded in 1937.' He pulled a face. 'It's also a sewer of course – for the timber mill and the cottages on the hill. But we could hide them in there.'

'Better still,' Reinach said, 'why not put them in at the

top and take them out again at the bottom? It runs under the road and comes out in the wood, in a ditch that leads to the river. We could have a cart waiting down there.'

'How do you get them through?'

'Men in the tunnel,' Dréo's son said. 'I went through it myself once before I lost my leg – when my dog went in after a hare.'

'It's knee deep in mud and shit!'

'For the love of God,' Marie-Claude said. 'If you like, *I'll* go in.'

Reinach grinned. 'The old men use the bridge to sit on and talk. They could pass the stuff down as it arrives. But how do we get it up to them?'

'Over the wall and through the back of Brisson's brother's place.' Moch said. 'Then out into the lane. There's a window at the back of Brisson's loft. Brisson could handle everything. He's already wetting his pants with fear.'

'There are a thousand kilos of the stuff,' Neville pointed out soberly.

'And even with the Lord's help,' Father Pol said, 'that'll take some carrying. The Germans will soon notice if every man in the village disappears.'

'Then use women,' Urquhart said. 'Send them up to talk to the old men. Tell the old ones to fetch their husbands home to dig the garden. Tell them to go up to look for firewood. Old women carry bags. Young women push prams.'

'The stuff's heavy,' Moch warned.

'A Bren takes to pieces. And a woman can carry a stripped Sten in her shopping bag.'

Marie-Claude's eyes were shining. 'Ernestine Bona could organize them,' she said. 'She's not short of guts.'

'What about the rifles? And the rocket-launchers? You can't get those in a shopping bag.'

'Hand-carts,' Reinach said. 'Load them with sacks, wood, vegetables. Shove the weapons underneath.' He slapped his thigh and for the first time there was an eager light in his eyes. 'We can be there by midday and clear the place before curfew.'

'What about the big stuff?' Dréo's son asked. 'Brisson

can't even take a car to pieces, let alone a machine gun.'

'I can,' Urquhart said. 'I'll go over there.'

'I'll go, too,' Father Pol said. 'I'm too fat to climb into drains but I can go and help Father Xavier.'

'We ought to get a message to them,' Moch said. 'Before they do something stupid. My daughter's in the village with the petrolette. She can take it.'

While Father Pol began to write, Moch dragged his daughter out of Mère Ledoux's bar where she was drinking an ersatz coffee with Gaston Dring. She was fifteen, and brown as a young partridge, and Marie-Claude stuffed the message into her brassière between her plump young breasts.

'Ride fast,' she said. 'So that your skirt blows up. If they see your legs, they'll not think of looking anywhere else.'

As the little red petrolette roared off, Urquhart reached for Marie-Claude's ancient cycle. 'When are the Germans expected?' he asked.

'They make their searches at midnight,' Moch said. 'When they expect to catch everybody in bed.'

Urquhart grinned and drove at the pedals. 'Better make sure they *are* in bed then,' he said.

8

The rescue worked like a military operation.

When Urquhart cycled down the hill into Rolandpoint there were already four old men sitting on the bridge smoking, and he noted with satisfaction that they looked strong old men.

'The girl brought the message,' one of them said. 'What legs that one has!'

In the Grande Place German soldiers were standing about, evidently on the alert because there were two tanks and several lorries alongside the war memorial. Outside the Bar de la Frontière, the man Moch had described was drinking a coffee and Urquhart recognized him at once as a German officer from Néry. Women, children and old men seemed to be everywhere, all with their eyes on Brisson's garage.

He found Father Pol with Father Xavier, smoking in the sun on a bench outside the presbytery, watching everything that went on. Ernestine Bona, powdered, mascaraed and crammed into a tight red dress, was clutching a bunch of flowers as though about to place them in the churchyard. She was talking to the priests with Stephanie Moch whose face was still flushed with the wind of her ride and the joy of having done something illegal without being caught.

'For God's sake, Father,' Urquhart said, gesturing at the women up the street. 'Get those people moving about! Their eyes alone will give us away.'

Ernestine put down the flowers. 'I'll go,' she said at once. 'They don't like me much but they'll do what I tell them.'

As she disappeared, Urquhart headed for the Chemin des Chats. Entering the scrapyard that had belonged to Brisson's brother, he climbed the wall by the ladder that was already leaning there. There were two men working in the scrapyard and one of Brisson's apprentices standing on a pair of steps at the other side. The second apprentice was waiting under the window at the back of the garage, with Brisson in the loft above stuffing weapons into sacks as fast as he could. Stripping the machine guns, Urquhart slipped back out of the garage into the lane and laboured up again to the old men sitting on the bridge above the drain.

'Ready?'

The old men nodded and, climbing over the parapet into the bed of the stream, he peered into the drain. It was full of broken bottles and rusty tins. In the darkness he could hear splashing.

The men from Néry were taking up their positions, up to their knees in the mud and rubbish that washed down from the hillside. Despite the darkness and the foetid smell, there was a distinct atmosphere of excitement. Reinach, Ernouf and de Frager had gone round Néry demanding help from everyone. The women were told to gossip in doorways and the few men like Balmaceda, Théyras and the Dréos, who couldn't climb into the drain, the middle-aged and older women like Madame Lamy – even the Baronne – and the young boys and schoolchildren were ordered to make themselves obvious. The rest of them – with Marie-Claude and Gaudin's elder son driving rubber-tyred platforms – had set off for Rolandpoint by the roads through the woods.

'Ready?' Urquhart called, and Ernouf's voice came back. 'Send them as soon as you like.'

Cycling back down the lane, Urquhart turned towards the presbytery. Not far away Ernestine Bona was talking to a group of women.

'Cart first,' he ordered.

Ernestine smiled. 'There's one waiting round the corner with a load of turnips,' she said. 'The Germans look down their noses at turnips. It's as safe as houses.'

Waiting in a back kitchen, sipping a glass of wine, Urquhart watched the cart go past with a thumping heart. Five minutes later word came down that the two bazookas were safely away.

'Now the next cart?' Ernestine asked.

'For God's sake, no, woman! Use your damned imagination! Send girls up with prams and babies! They can shift a few Stens!'

Ernestine shrugged. Men normally didn't talk to her as Urquhart was talking to her. Because she had a ripe body and black market food and drink, they usually asked her permission instead of telling her what to do. 'I think the brats'll find it a bit uncomfortable,' she said.

Three girls with prams containing howling babies sauntered up the lane. Behind them a bony old man who had fought in the war of 1870 as a boy of fourteen hobbled past in an ankle-length overcoat, followed by a donkey-cart loaded with scrap wood, and a long crocodile of children.

Ernestine gave Urquhart a wide smile. 'I've fixed a school outing,' she said. 'They're going to draw wild flowers, and they all have satchels for their pencil boxes. There'll be room for a magazine or a Mills bomb.'

Urquhart grinned. 'For God's sake, make sure there's someone up there to pack them properly!'

Ernestine sniffed. 'All organized. Father Xavier's by the scrapyard and they'll stop to get his blessing. As they come back they can bring something else down to the classroom and we can pick it up there and take it round the back of the village. We've also started a line across the lane to Sosthène Doumouriez's cottage and over the wall to the window of Bertrand's shed. From there it goes down the garden, through the house and out of the front door, and up to the drain that way. There's another lot going through old Tessier's forge and across the allotment to the fields. They're wrapped in curtaining. The women put their washing on the grass up there, and there are leaves higher up that they collect for their rabbits. No one'll notice anything odd.'

During the morning, Klemens drove over to Rolandpoint himself to make sure everything was as it should be. As the car climbed the hill, a boy waiting with his bicycle in the trees at the top shot down the opposite slope past the old men.

'Germans!' he said as he passed and a bundle was hurriedly handed down with a warning from the bridge to Ernouf standing in the mouth of the culvert below. By the time Klemens's car rolled down the hill after the cyclist, the four old men were sitting on the parapet smoking and talking to three girls with prams.

All movement had stopped in the tunnel. The entrance contained only a trickle of water and thick mud. Further inside it was impenetrably black and filled with nauseous air, the only light coming from candles resting on bricks projecting from the wall. None of the warmth of the day penetrated the darkness, and everyone in the tunnel was icy cold.

Standing up to his knees in black slime, Neville could see other men waiting motionless – Reinach; the two Drings; Guardian Moch; Ernouf; Patrice de Frager; the Baronne's gardener, Psichari; Gaudin, the farmer, and his eldest son; and a few others, as well as a lot of teenage boys and even a few girls. Marie-Claude was near Lionel Dring, her unbuttoned blouse plastered to her breasts, her wet skirt clinging to her thighs, her hair escaping in damp ringlets from beneath the scarf she'd tied round it as the peasants did – though not for a minute did she look like a peasant. She saw Neville looking at her and managed a smile. Despite the unromantic circumstances, he was aware she'd been watching him and elation surged through him, so devastating he forgot what he was doing and almost dropped the package he was holding. As he smiled back, Lionel Dring frowned and abruptly lit a cigarette.

Every eye followed the smoke as it was sucked up by the draught through the manhole cover. Then Reinach snatched the cigarette from Dring's lips and threw it into the water. Dring stared at it, his eyes angry. 'You didn't have to throw it away,' he hissed. 'They're hard to get!'

'You deserve to lose it,' Reinach hissed back. 'You might have got us all killed! You still might have!'

As Klemens's car approached the bridge, the four old men perched on the parapet watched the blue tendrils of smoke ooze through the grids of the manhole cover, drift away, and stop. The girls with the prams drew a deep breath and let it out together as a sigh of relief. Half-way up the lane the crocodile of children with satchels on their backs was climbing towards the woods, and the old man with the donkey-cart was just passing them. There was nothing to arouse suspicion but on an impulse Klemens decided to make a spot check.

'Stop the car!'

As Tarnera halted the vehicle, it effectively blocked the road so that the old man with the donkey-cart couldn't continue. Klemens rose in his seat and stared at him.

The schoolmistress, walking at the back of the crocodile, saw what was happening. She was an inoffensive spinster of thirty-three whose fiancé had gone into the army in 1939 and had vanished as a prisoner to Germany. She had no idea when – or even whether – he would return but she prayed for his homecoming before her crucifix every night. It was a cruel joke round Rolandpoint that when he reappeared she'd be so old he wouldn't be interested, but she longed to do something to hasten his return and she wasn't lacking in spirit. As Klemens stared at the old man with the cart, she drew back her arm and, using all her strength, sent one of the older girls flying with a clout at the side of the head.

As the girl spun away, her head cannoned off her next door neighbour's who staggered back to knock one of the smaller children flat on its back. As it started to yell, its fingers were trampled on by one of the boys as they milled about, and in a moment the whole lot of them seemed to be screeching like a lot of factory sirens.

Klemens' head turned. The veteran of 1870 had disappeared into a cottage further down the lane. Almost immediately, a woman came out and started to run towards where the schoolmistress, shrieking vituperation at the girl she'd slapped, was clutching one of the younger children. She stopped by Klemens' car, fat, aggressive and angry.

'At it again?' she said. 'Bullying people! We have to live with you but we don't have to be knocked about unnecessarily.'

Klemens sighed and signed to Tarnera to continue. As the car jerked and disappeared down the hill, the schoolmistress put down the child she was holding and swept the girl she'd hit into her arms. 'Please forgive me, Françoise,' she pleaded. 'I'm so sorry! You know why I had to do it!'

Through her tears, the girl hugged her back. 'It's all right, mademoiselle,' she wailed. 'It's all right! It's all right!'

As the car vanished, everybody drew a deep breath. The veteran of 1870 reappeared and the stream of bags and brown paper parcels which had been passing over garden walls from near the school, down alleys, through back windows into next-door gardens, and across allotments, began to move again. The old man with the donkey gulped and jabbed at it with his stick. As it trotted off, he tottered after it, almost too scared to walk.

As the sound of the car died away, the glimmer of light from the manhole in the centre of the bridge was obscured. Someone began to whistle 'Madelon' and thump on the cover with his walking stick. 'They've gone,' a hoarse voice came. 'They've gone!'

The donkey clattered on to the bridge, the sound of its hooves echoing in the culvert below, and the flow of weapons began again. Where Neville stood, the sewer had been constructed to descend as a series of shallow steps, and they had to splash backwards and forwards in the foul-smelling black water which was never less than thigh-deep and in places up to their waists. The surface was alive with strange, little creatures and grey spidery insects which darted about, and the slime was noisome with leeches and worms. Occasionally one of the girls gave a stifled shriek of horror as she felt them on her legs, while the mud was so full of broken glass and tins with jagged edges they all had cuts on their hands and ankles.

The bazooka barrels needed two men to carry them and Neville stumbled and fell as he and Dring struggled with one, so that he swallowed some of the water. Spitting and spluttering, he almost vomited, but they managed to pass the steel tube on and saw it disappear down the chain. The cart that had carried turnips up brought hay down and took it to the other side of the village and round to the bridge by a different route. A woman carried a basket of laundry to the fields and brought down another full of sun-dried linen. Three old men who had decided to go for a stroll in the woods moved off with bulging pockets. A girl with a baby followed them.

'She has a grenade in its napkin,' Father Pol said tensely.

Then Dr Mouillet arrived in his car, for which he was allowed petrol by the Germans to attend his patients. Ostensibly he'd come to confer with his colleague in Rolandpoint, but when he left there were the barrels and stocks of two Bren guns under the rear seat of his ancient Citroën. As the car chugged away, Sergeant Dréo's grandson, Jean-Frédéric, and his friends arrived. Young Dréo's prize possession was a racing bicycle with a three-speed gear, butterfly nuts on the wheel-hubs and thin red Michelin tyres. It was new and distinguishable as such by its wartime lack of chrome, but it was fast and light, with the word 'Viking', printed in large letters on the cross-bar. He was intensely proud of it and called it his 'Spitfire'. In little groups, he and his friends swooped around the village with the Rolandpoint boys, revelling in the joy of speed; but they all had leatherette bags on the handlebars and the bags contained small metal objects. In one horrific moment, as he bounced over a gutter near Hytier's bar, Jean-Frédéric heard his bag tear and was shocked to see the blunt end of a Bren magazine sticking through. Grabbing hurriedly over the handlebars, he stuffed it back and rode on, holding it in place until he could stop with safety and transfer it to a pocket.

The crocodile of children returned at tea-time, their satchels heavy once more, and shortly afterwards a donkey with panniers full of winter logs for the stove arrived at the school to collect what they'd brought down. Outwardly Rolandpoint presented its normal appearance. People moved about in ones and twos. The men were all at work where they could be seen. Klein-Wuttig, eating bread and sausage outside the Bar de la Frontière, watched all the time by the proprietor, noticed nothing unusual.

'Last ten rifles,' Ernestine reported to Urquhart. 'They're loading a cart full of scrap for Sergeant Dréo and, since it all eventually goes to Germany, the Germans are well aware of it and never query it.'

When the old men on the bridge had lowered the last load and headed one after the other down the hill for Rolandpoint, those under the road splashed their way after it through the dark water. Where the culvert opened into a deep ditch in the wood, they began to emerge, men and women, boys and girls together. As Marie-Claude stumbled, Dring and Neville went to her assistance. She thanked them both, but it was Neville she allowed to put his hand under her behind and push her up the bank into the trees.

Ernouf was the last to appear. He was grinning and carrying a dripping sack. 'Grenades,' he said. 'And a Sten. Twelve oranges and a clarinette.'

Marie-Claude stared at him, a smile spreading across her face. Then she flung her arms round Neville and kissed him joyously. Because he was sulking, she also kissed Lionel Dring and, to make sure no one would complain, Patrice de Frager, Ernouf, Reinach, and a few others.

As they washed off the slime, no one worried about standing naked while youngsters scrubbed at their backs and legs and arms and when they were reasonably clean they changed into the spare clothes they'd brought. Then Moch handed round stone bottles of wine and cigarettes he'd acquired from the black market in Dijon.

Back at the farm, as Neville led the old horse away, his face still streaked with mud, Marie-Claude appeared from the house. She had already bathed and put on clean clothes.

'It's all in the woods,' Neville said. 'Wrapped in tarpaulins and buried. It's safe until we can hide it properly.'

By the time he'd cleaned himself, Madame Lamy had produced an omelette and there was a bottle of wine on the table. 'I think we should celebrate,' she said. 'Where's Urk't?'

Neville grinned. 'Urquhart's the last man you need worry about,' he said. 'Perhaps he was caught by the curfew and had to stay the night in Rolandpoint.'

When Madame Lamy disappeared to bed, Marie-Claude produced a bottle of marc. She seemed pleased and relieved, and as they raised their glasses, she stared at Neville, her brown eyes steady on his face, aware that they were alone and a little frightened by her feelings.

'Do you think I am attractive, Neville?' she asked abruptly.

He gazed back at her for a moment, his eyes holding hers. She wasn't beautiful in the accepted way and he knew she didn't expect him to tell her so. But she had the sort of face a man could live with, the sort of face that grew on you, awkwardly angled but with pale perfect skin and a cloud of chestnut hair, and those desolate grey eyes behind the humour that made him feel sobered and drained of excitement without knowing why.

'Yes,' he said and, putting down his glass, he leaned forward to kiss her full on the lips.

She studied him silently, a curious exhilaration running up and down her body. 'Kiss me again, Neville,' she said.

This time he took a little longer and made more of a job of it, and she responded with a painful intensity that surprised him. As he released her, she drew her breath luxuriously and stared at him with shining eyes. Then she moved away and stood with her back to him. He took a step forward and put his arms round her. She lifted his hands to her breasts and stood with her fingers over his, and they remained like that for a long time until he felt her give a deep shuddering sigh. She turned in the circle of his arms to face him, her eyes moist, and as he pulled her closer her arms went round him and she was crying softly and he was kissing her tears away. Her words surprised him.

'I wonder what it's like in Rolandpoint,' she said.

When Urquhart arrived at the Bar de la Frontière with Father Pol and Father Xavier, Klein-Wuttig had long since decided it was safe to leave and was on his way back to Néry to change into uniform. Brisson arrived with his helpers soon afterwards, looking hot and dusty but relieved.

'All gone,' he announced as he sank a demi-blonde at a gulp. 'There's nothing they can find. Not a thing. Not a single round. Where are you putting it?'

'Never mind where we're putting it,' Urquhart said. 'The less you know, the less you can tell if they ask.'

Brisson shrugged. 'All right. When do we get it back?'

'When do you want it back?'

Brisson mopped his face and grinned. 'We're in no hurry,' he said.

They were celebrating quietly, with Ernestine Bona paying freely, when a German scout car appeared in the street. A sergeant stood up in the back and raised a loud hailer.

'Curfew has been advanced by one hour,' he announced. 'Get to your homes! It starts immediately!'

Brisson shot a worried glance at Urquhart but Ernestine gestured. 'Stop worrying. They can't possibly know what happened!'

Father Xavier pulled at Father Pol's arm. 'I can find you a bed,' he said. 'And my housekeeper's been given a rabbit. If Monsieur Urk't – '

'Monsieur Urk't can come to my place,' Ernestine said quickly. 'No one's got enough food for *two* extra.'

Urquhart followed her from the bar, wheeling Marie-Claude's bicycle. Inside the house, she dug out a bottle of brandy. 'Help yourself,' she said. 'You did us a good turn today.'

The ravages of the day repaired with a fresh application of pungent perfume and so much eye make-up her eyelashes kept sticking together, she produced a meal of pork, vegetables, potatoes in oil, and lettuce. She was free with her wine and produced more brandy with the coffee; for a change it wasn't made of acorns, wheat seed and chicory but from real beans which, like the tight purple dress she wore, had been bought on the black market.

When her father-in-law had gone to bed, exhausted, she beamed at Urquhart. 'The Germans don't get *me* down,' she said. 'And if it causes my death I shan't complain. In Paris hard-working men collect potato peelings from dustbins and the city's lost its personality. There are no tripes in Les Halles these days, no onion soup, and no terrifying porters breathing garlic – just women searching for cabbage and turnip tops. It's astonishing – and terrible – what women will do for chocolate.' She laughed. 'You speak French well, Urk't. Where did you learn it?'

'In the north in 1940.'

'When the British abandoned the French.'

To Urquhart it had seemed to be the other way round. 'I walked from Brussels,' he said. 'Bombed every bit of the way. They picked on us to support the artillery of the rear-guard and I was one of the last out. Nine of us pushed a boat into the water and rigged a sail. We were picked up by a destroyer next day.'

'Then you became a flier?'

'In 1941 they said people in the army could volunteer. I was nearly killed in the rush.'

They were still sitting at the table at midnight when they heard the faint squeal of a vehicle braking carefully to a stop outside and Ernestine gestured.

'Upstairs!' she said. 'My bedroom. It's opposite the

stairs. Get moving. Get into bed. Without clothes. My father-in-law will answer the door.'

Urquhart flew up the stairs. Ernestine was right behind him, her nose to the shutters as she tore at the buttons of her dress. There were Germans in the street below. One truck was already visible and, as they watched, another rolled silently to a stop, its motor off, the driver treading gently on his brakes. From the back, steel-helmeted soldiers jumped down. Among them there were a few Milice who were joined by a group of gendarmes. A machine-gun was set up along the street, a grey figure squatting tensely behind it. A car ghosted to a stop nearby and an officer climbed out and spoke quietly to the man behind the gun. It was impossible to hear his voice and there was something sinister about the silence.

'There's a squad near Brisson's garage.' Ernestine whispered. 'And more down the street. Let's hope we get a gendarme.'

The Germans began to split up into groups and were joined by Feldgendarmerie, the metal gorgets of their trade catching the faint glow of the lights. Two of them approached a door on the opposite side of the street and they saw them lift their rifles. The banging was loud in the stillness.

'They'll be here in a minute,' Ernestine said.

As the hammering started downstairs, she leaped for the bed and grabbed at Urquhart. 'Hold me,' she said. 'For the love of God, you know what we're supposed to be doing, don't you?'

Despite the situation, Urquhart was becoming very much aware of what they were supposed to be doing. Ernestine was well-rounded and naked, and she was clutching him tightly.

'Behave as though you're interested,' she said. 'Men usually are, with me.'

They heard her father-in-law clump down the stairs, and the door open, and harsh voices below. As Urquhart's head lifted, Ernestine's hand went up and pulled it down again to her bosom. Boots thumped on the stairs, and Ernestine shot bolt upright, pushing Urquhart's face into the pillows. As she headed for the door, grabbing her nightdress from the end of the bed as she went, a police brigadier appeared, accompanied by a Wehrmacht corporal.

'Hello, Ernestine,' he said, grinning. 'We want to see everyone in the house.'

'There's only me and my father-in-law.'

'Nobody else?'

'Well – ' she paused, ' – my boy friend.'

The sergeant grinned. 'Well, I'm sorry to disturb your nesting, Ernestine, but we've got orders to search.'

She tore him off a string of abuse. 'Well, go and search. You'll find nothing here.'

The sergeant glanced past her towards the shadowy outline of the bed then he turned and eyed her admiringly. 'How about me some time, Ernestine?' he suggested. 'My wife would never find out.'

Her eyes flared. 'Go and do your searching! You'll not find much! Perhaps a little black market pork and a bottle of brandy, that's all.' She leaned closer. 'If you don't bother to count things too carefully, you might even find a bottle for yourselves.'

The sergeant winked and strode to the bed to drag back the sheets. Urquhart sat up slowly, his heart pounding.

'You pick 'em big, Ernestine,' the policeman said. 'Is he well-built all over?'

'Better than you, you miserable worm. Where does your wife go for satisfaction?'

The policeman glanced at the papers Urquhart offered. 'Jacques Urquaert,' he said. 'Belgian. What are you doing in Rolandpoint?'

Ernestine lifted her arms in a gesture of disgust. The nightdress went with them. 'What do you think he's doing, you oaf?' she said.

The sergeant handed the papers back and jerked his head to the door. 'Come on, Ernestine. Let's search the house. You needn't put your clothes on, if you don't wish to. We don't mind.'

The two men went out, grinning. At the door, Ernestine turned and signed to Urquhart to stay where he was. On edge, he began to dress, listening to the sergeant's gruff voice downstairs, old Bona's whines, and Ernestine's shrill vituperation. After a while, he heard the front door slam and a vehicle drawing away. Then Ernestine appeared in the room once more.

'What it is to have a reputation!' she said. 'People don't know how valuable they can be.' She laughed and tore off the nightdress; then, pushing Urquhart back into the feather mattress, literally dived after him.

'You can't leave till daylight,' she chirruped. 'And it's a pity to waste a well-built man.'

9

'Who told them, Wuttig?' Klemens snarled.

Klein-Wuttig frowned. 'Someone must have, Herr Oberst,' he said. 'Someone in the know.'

Pacing up and down in front of the fireplace, his hands behind his back. Klemens turned. 'There were only us, Dijon. Rolandpoint and St Seigneur,' he said, and Klein-Wuttig stiffened.

'Perhaps it's nearer home than that, Herr Oberst.'

'What do you mean?'

'Perhaps Tarnera let it out.'

'Don't be a damn fool!'

Klein-Wuttig's eyes narrowed at the insult. 'I didn't mean that he went out and told them what we were going to do, Herr Oberst. But he's far too friendly with them. He goes to see the priest. He goes to mass.'

'He also goes to confession.'

'It contains a suggestion of weakness,' Klein-Wuttig said stiffly. 'The French think he's a fool.'

'More likely they think he's a Catholic.' Klemens glared. 'I think you're talking out of the top of your head, Wuttig. You've got to come up with something better than that.'

Klein-Wuttig bit his lip. 'Dijon's pretty sore,' he said. 'They passed the information on to us and they expected results.'

'Then tell them they were mistaken and that the man who tipped them off has been shot.'

'He hasn't. He's disappeared.'

'Because he was given a good beating. I'd disappear if that happened to me, wouldn't you? He'll join the Resistance. There's nothing like a German beating to make a good French Resistance worker.'

As they talked, Tarnera appeared. 'We're having the inquest,' Klemens said. 'Wuttig thinks someone split.'

Tarnera smiled and Klein-Wuttig scowled. 'We're all aware,' he said. 'that there are a great many people in the Wehrmacht looking over their shoulders these days.'

'With the Russians at Odessa and heading for Sevastopol,' Tarnera said, 'it's natural enough.'

Klemens slapped his leg with his crop. 'What about the police?' he asked. 'Would they have split?'

'I doubt it, Herr Oberst,' Tarnera said. 'They try to avoid taking sides.'

'They *should* take sides,' Klein-Wuttig said. '*Our* side.'

'They're Frenchmen, Fritzi,' Tarnera pointed out. 'You expect rather a lot.'

'Give me time,' Klein-Wuttig said, 'and they'll *all* be on our side.'

'And good National Socialists to boot, no doubt.'

Klein-Wuttig opened his mouth to argue but Klemens waved him away. Klein-Wuttig scowled and left the room, and Klemens turned to Tarnera, his manner immediately easier, as if he'd shrugged out of a tight jacket. 'What do *you* think happened, Tarnera?' he asked.

Tarnera smiled. 'I think they've simply developed an instinct for danger,' he said. 'It would be normal enough after four years of occupation.'

Klemens shrugged. 'I told Fritzi to tell Dijon they were mistaken,' he said.

'I bet they weren't.'

'Of course they weren't. But we don't want an official

reprimand for failing. Next time, Sturmbannführer Frobinius and his blasted SS can do their own searching.' Klemens gave a sudden grin. 'Fritzi thinks *you* told them,' he said. 'He doesn't approve of your being a Catholic.'

Tarnera smiled. 'I suppose he imagines that when I go into the confession box I pour out the Fatherland's secrets. The only secrets the Abbé Pol gets to know are those of my soul.'

'So long as they contain none of mine. What's he got against you?'

Tarnera laughed. 'I caught him fondling his orderly in the bathroom. You know he's a homosexual?'

'Of course I know. It's nothing to be surprised about. It's fashionable in the Reich these days and his sort often go that way. All the same, you'd better watch it. People like that can be spiteful and I'm concerned for you.' Klemens smiled. 'I'm also concerned for me. Remember that. Did you get a reply from Colonel Marx about the pictures?'

Tarnera had deliberately dawdled. 'He's moved further north, Herr Oberst,' he said. 'I understand he's now up near Paris somewhere and communication's not easy because of the bombing.'

'Well, at least we know the paintings aren't in Goering's possession.' Klemens smiled. 'You're a rotten soldier, Tarnera, but you have your uses. That report you got on what's at Karinhall was an excellent bit of work. Let's now try Colonel Kaspar in Dijon. The general might have made a list. In the meantime, concentrate on this place. I want an inventory made.'

Tarnera's eyebrows rose and Klemens gestured. 'It's another way of looking,' he explained.

'Very well, Herr Oberst. I take it you want everything putting down – even the chamberpots.'

Klemens frowned. 'If they're of value.'

'Very well, Herr Oberst. I'll also earmark the transport to take the stuff back to Germany.'

Klemens' head whipped round. 'Who said anything about sending it to Germany?'

Tarnera shrugged. 'It's the common practice, Herr Oberst.'

Klemens coughed, knowing he couldn't draw the wool over Tarnera's experienced eyes. 'It behoves us to collect as much of what is valuable inside Germany as we can,' he grunted.

'If only to build a roof over us against the Allied bombing.'

'Shut up, Tarnera!' Klemens' face had gone red. 'That's no way for a German officer to talk.'

Tarnera's smile vanished. 'I'm not blinded by Party mystique, Herr Oberst,' he said. 'And neither, I suspect, are you.'

'Sometimes it makes me want to throw up,' Klemens admitted. 'But my tongue won't be the death of me all the same. So just stick to your inventory. You and I aren't fools, Tarnera. We both have a shrewd idea that Germany isn't going to win this war and that one day we'll have to withdraw to our own frontiers. When we do, we'll need all we can get to barter with for our immortal souls.' Klemens tossed down a sheet of instructions. 'In the meantime, you'd better inform the Baronne that we have to get an extra five thousand cords of wood for winter relief, to be transported to St Seigneur for despatch to Mannheim. There's also been another restriction on the use of vehicles and we're ordered to requisition horses and mules, and I want to know of every wheeled vehicle in the district. The Reich might have need of them before long.' He paused. 'Come to that, Tarnera,' he ended, 'perhaps you and I might too.'

The Baronne listened carefully to the orders Tarnera passed on. When he'd finished, she nodded and rose without a word.

As Tarnera opened the door for her, she eyed him carefully, trying to weigh him up. 'Why do you want my pictures, Captain?' she asked unexpectedly. 'You've been through France like an army of locusts. Aren't you satisfied?'

Tarnera smiled. '*I* don't collect pictures, madame,' he said. 'I don't collect anything.'

The Baronne paused. 'Does the colonel know anything about painting?'

Tarnera shrugged. 'Madame, these days, *no one* in Germany knows about painting. The edict came down from the high altar as long ago as 1937: Artists must no longer use colours other than those perceived in nature by the normal eye.' His smile returned. 'It marked the immediate departure from Germany of every worthwhile artist and every worthwhile painting.'

The Baronne eyed him warily, her old eyes shrewd. '*You* know about art, I think.'

Tarnera shrugged again. 'We all have our own ideas, madame. Boudissin feels that the most perfect shape, the sublimest image, is a steel helmet, and we go in a lot these days for steam baths of national sentiment and soulful elevation in the shape of challenging heroism – stern-visaged stormtroopers with flexed muscles or enormous bare-breasted Amazons. Ziegler's confections of lifeless nudity have earned him the title of "Reich Master of Pubic Hair". National Socialism claims to have taken the pretentiousness out of art. *I* think it's merely taken out the art.' The smile returned. 'But we don't discuss it, madame. What is on the walls is art, and that's that.'

She was still watching him. 'You are not a Nazi, Captain?'

'No, madame.'

'But you're here in France.'

'I'm still a German, madame. I endured the defeat after the last war when German prices rose and German values fell by the hour. You needed a barrow to carry your money and, if you delayed too long in buying, two. I'm pleased to see Germany great again.'

'Not for much longer, I think, Captain.'

Tarnera smiled again and said nothing, and the Baronne's stitched mouth twisted.

'Will my paintings be stolen?' she asked.

'I suspect they will, madame.'

'Is there nothing I can do?'

'I regret, madame, nothing.'

'Perhaps the arrival of de Gaulle will save them?'

'Perhaps not even that. We're a very efficient nation and we move very fast when we have to.'

She eyed him for a moment, treading warily. 'Could *you* not do anything?'

Tarnera smiled. 'I regret, madame, no. I value my head too

much. If I objected, I could find myself on the Eastern front fighting the Ivans, and I prefer to remain here where I can be among the first to bolt for home when the British and the Americans arrive.'

10

Urquhart returned from Rolandpoint two days later. He had made no attempt to communicate or explain his absence, and Marie-Claude's expression, at first anxious for his safety, changed to one of sullen anger when she learned where he was staying. Hearing him arrive, Elsie barked furiously and rushed out to fawn on him as he leaned Marie-Claude's bicycle against the wall. As he entered the house, Reinach was there with Father Pol, and his mouth immediately widened into an empty grin. It was known all round Néry where Urquhart had stayed and Marie-Claude's face grew stiffer still.

'I'm surprised you had the strength to ride back,' she snapped.

Urquhart smiled. 'They've started to commandeer vehicles in Rolandpoint,' he announced.

'Do you think we don't know?' Marie-Claude said coldly. 'We're nearer the fount of knowledge here.' She gave Urquhart another cold look. 'You look like a cat that's been at the cream. I suppose you were so busy you didn't notice that the curfew didn't go on all yesterday. I heard you stayed with Ernestine Bona.'

'Yes.'

'She's a Norman. They're like that up there. I suppose she pressed you.'

Urquhart's smile died as he grew angry. 'She suggested it because she's a brave woman and it was the only safe thing to do,' he said. 'And I stayed an extra day because I'm no man's slave – or a woman's either.'

It was obvious the reply had hurt Marie-Claude and she turned quickly and hurried from the room. Neville swung round on Urquhart.

'Christ,' he said. 'You could have let her down lightly.'

'Why?' Urquhart demanded. 'She wanted to know.'

'She believed in us.'

Urquhart laughed. 'You sound like a prefect who's sent for me to give me a whacking for telling dirty stories.'

Neville frowned. 'You know damn well what I mean.'

'No, I don't!' Urquhart's temper rose. 'I'm not a farm boy. I'm a senior N.C.O. in His Majesty's Royal Air Force and I'm going to behave like one. There's only one person I take my orders from and that's my superior officer, and sometimes not even from him.' He grinned. 'And don't tell me *you're* my superior officer, because it won't carry any weight. As far as I'm concerned, you're still a kid who's wet behind the ears.'

Humiliation stung Neville like a lash across the face. 'Sometimes, Urquhart,' he said, 'I think you're a bastard.'

'I *know* I am.' Urquhart smiled. 'But there's one thing I'm not – and that's hypnotized by my own visions. I'm what one of your class used to call the brutal and licentious soldiery, the poor bastards who held the fort in 1939 and '40 until everybody else wound up their affairs, closed their homes and resigned from their clubs, because joining the army was something that was beneath you lot in peacetime. Most of those people who stayed behind at Dunkirk were Regulars and, because of them, the Saturday-night Territorials and the newly-joined who'd been sent out for a bit of experience got away. The blokes they've got in the stalags in Germany and the ones they shoved under the sod were people like me, dimwits who hadn't sufficient intelligence or sufficient money to stay out of the army. Some of 'em even joined to get a decent pair of boots because there wasn't any work for them, but they were still the only trained soldiers we had when the balloon went up. So don't start delivering lectures on what's right and what's wrong to me, and don't start telling me how to behave. Some of those brutal and licentious soldiery knew more about behaviour than a few public schoolboy officers

I've seen, and don't you make any mistake about it.'

It was a brutal attack but Neville could see Urquhart's difficult pride had been touched and he tried to make peace.

'For God's sake,' he said, 'she was worried as hell about you.'

Urquhart looked up at him. 'Sometimes I'd like to hit her over the head,' he said. 'But I'm aware of that.' He smiled unexpectedly and slapped Neville's shoulder. 'Don't let it get you down, lad. We all get dragged along a bit. Even Sancho Panza was talked into it by Don Quixote.'

It surprised Neville that Urquhart had even heard of Don Quixote and he decided there was more to him than he'd realized.

'Did you really go to bed with Ernestine?' he asked.

Urquhart laughed quietly, but without mocking this time. 'Didn't they ever tell you never to bandy a lady's name about?' he said. 'They were much stricter about things like that in the sergeants' mess.'

The following day they heard that the Germans had caught one of the Rolandpoint réseau's messengers. He'd been sent to St Seigneur to cancel another parachutage that was due and had bumped into a German patrol. When he ran they shot him. Nobody talked, however, and two days later Néry sent a deputation to Rolandpoint for the funeral.

It proved a big affair, with several hundred mourners. A squad of German soldiers watched the ceremony but no action was taken and Father Xavier spoke an impassioned eulogy: 'Soldat de France, mort pour la patrie . . .'

Jean-Frédéric Dréo, who'd been a friend of the dead boy, went with Elsie who wore a thin ribbon of red, white and blue in her collar. Reinach approved neither of the eulogy nor of the red, white and blue ribbon, but young Dréo was unconcerned. 'Everybody's talking about what we did,' he announced. 'Even in St Seigneur.'

Marie-Claude's eyes flashed. 'Then they shouldn't be!' she snapped. 'Last time someone talked too much they shot seventeen men and their relations! Tell them to keep their mouths shut! What about the radio operator?'

'He's in St Seigneur. He's expecting a new agent to replace, Arsène.'

Urquhart smiled. 'He could help us leave,' he said.

Marie-Claude's head turned. 'Leave?'

'For Spain.' The smile became wider. 'That was the idea originally, if you remember.'

Marie-Claude made an indeterminate gesture. 'Things are different now.'

'Why?'

'Nobody knows the next link in the chain. If it's broken it takes a lot of doing to join it together again.'

Urquhart said nothing but Neville had a feeling he didn't believe her, and Marie-Claude hurriedly steered the conversation away from the subject.

'This radio operator,' Reinach asked. 'Can he still send messages?'

'Yes.'

'Perhaps he could send one for us.'

Marie-Claude's head lifted and she smiled at Neville. 'I think in Néry we've got our courage back,' she announced.

Urquhart raised his eyes. 'In case you haven't noticed it,' he said, 'you've also got a load of weapons.'

It was something that hadn't occurred to anybody before but when it did dawn on them, there was a sudden new excitement in the village and that night Father Pol, Reinach, Sergeant Dréo and Théyras turned up to play cards with Urquhart so they could discuss what to do with what they'd acquired so unexpectedly. As they played, Guardian Moch arrived, followed soon afterwards by Patrice de Frager, dressed as usual in his dramatic black.

'Suppose, when the invasion comes,' he said, 'that Rolandpoint want their weapons back? We'd be left with nothing.'

'Then we must acquire our own weapons,' Reinach said.

'How?'

'We have a radio operator and a radio. Surely he'll send *one* message for us.'

'Who'll draft it?' Urquhart asked quietly.

'Father Pol?'

Father Pol looked alarmed. 'I don't know anything about weapons.'

'Sergeant Dréo.'

'I'm just a simple soldier.' Dréo waved his thick knotted hands. 'I don't know how to draft messages.'

'Moch?'

'I don't know one end of a gun from the other.'

'Reinach then.'

Reinach's empty grin was faintly embarrassed. 'I wouldn't know what to ask for.'

Urquhart smiled and Marie-Claude rounded on him angrily. 'You're sneering at us, aren't you?'

Urquhart nodded. 'Yes,' he said.

Marie-Claude's eyes blazed, but before she could spit her fury at him, he went on, speaking calmly.

'You can't fight Germans with nothing but hatred,' he said. 'And that's all you've got at the moment. You're making up your minds to set about the best-trained army in Europe as if all it required was guns.'

'We *have* guns.'

'You don't know how to use them.'

'We should acquit ourselves well.'

'The Germans would tear the place apart. It's pride that's behind all your talk, that's all. You haven't even got a leader and any outfit without a leader's just rabble.'

'We've got no one with experience.'

'You've got Verdy de Clary.'

'That old mothball!' Reinach's look was full of disgust. 'All he does is sit at home, nursing his honour and looking at maps to explain why we were defeated in 1940.'

'He knows what to do,' Urquhart insisted.

'We could never accept him.'

'All right, then. Not him. It doesn't *have* to be a soldier. Just someone who knows how to give orders and make everyone obey him.'

There was an awkward silence. Then Théyras gestured at Father Pol, who shook his head hurriedly.

'I'm good at *paters* and *aves,*' he said. 'But I've forgotten all I ever knew about fighting.'

'Dréo?'

'Holy Mother of Mary – ' the spiked moustaches seemed to give off sparks ' – I have a wooden leg. I can't even run across the road to avoid a horse and cart, let alone up a hillside or climb a tree. It must be someone young – '

Patrice de Frager sat up a little straighter, his expression hopeful. He could just see himself as a leader of men and a hero. There would probably be a ceremony outside Notre-Dame with General de Gaulle pinning on the medal.

' – but not too young,' Dréo went on, and de Frager's face fell.

Neville lifted his head. He had been silent for a long time, still a little puzzled by Marie-Claude who suddenly seemed to have no eyes for him. The morning after Urquhart had failed to return from Rolandpoint, he had been dazed and awed by what had happened. There had been no argument, no pleading or persuasion, just a desperate longing for warmth and affection in both of them. It had left him thinking, in the uncomplicated manner of a boy, that there was nothing unexpected about it, that it was as normal as breathing and the natural outcome of their being together. But now, half in love, his eyes following her like a devoted dog's, he was startled to find she had no time for him and seemed troubled, aloof and indifferent, as if she entirely rejected everything that had passed between them – even cold, not speaking and confining herself to bitter remarks addressed to Urquhart.

'How about Reinach?' he said. 'He's big enough to punch anyone in the mouth and knock out his teeth. They couldn't knock *his* out in return, because he hasn't got any. He cuts the timber the Germans want, he's free to move about as he pleases, he talks to them. He goes to the château. He even has a lorry with petrol.'

Reinach frowned. 'I'm forty-six!'

'A perfect age,' Dréo said. 'Napoleon was in his prime at forty-six.'

'When Napoleon was forty-six,' Neville said dryly, 'it was 1815 – the year of Waterloo.'

There was a long silence. 'He had piles,' Dréo growled.

'You said so yourself. The English caught him when he wasn't ready.' He brushed the thought aside hurriedly. 'It *must* be Reinach,' he said.

There was a new eagerness in the room. Urquhart seemed to have put his finger on what was wrong.

'Since we have the weapons,' Reinach said, almost as though his new authority had taken hold of him at once, 'we ought to learn how to use them. I know of people in Dijon and Besançon who're in touch with the réseaux in the Doubs. We could send two men down there to learn how to use the rocket-launchers. They could then return here to teach us. Then when we get an agent in the district again, we could persuade him to let us have a parachute drop of our own.'

The others were all watching him eagerly, even de Frager.

'I'll go to Besançon,' he said. 'The Germans ignore me. They think God was a German junker and they treat me differently because I have a title.'

'Those Resistance chaps round Besançon are a rough lot,' Reinach pointed out. 'Communists, some of them.'

'I can keep my mouth shut.' It seemed it wasn't only Reinach who was growing in stature. 'Who else?'

'Lionel Dring,' Marie-Claude said quickly and Urquhart laughed out loud. Dring had been growing too possessive lately, and jealous of Neville, and she was eager to be rid of him. The realization that Urquhart knew what was in her mind irritated her and she found herself blushing.

By the following day, Reinach was begining to take his leadership still more seriously, even swallowing his pride sufficiently to see Verdy de Clary. The old soldier's manner was stiff and acid.

'The war ended in 1940,' he said. 'I was told by my commander-in-chief to lay down my arms.'

'Pétain!' Reinach thumped his forehead with the flat of his hand in frustration. 'That old stuffed dummy!'

Verdy's eyes flickered to where his medals rested on velvet in a small glass case on his desk. 'He's not an adventurer,' he snapped. 'Not like de Gaulle who's only a jumped-up brigadier-general who promoted himself overnight to head of the French nation. It's stupid to fight when the odds are against you. No battle's worth dying in when there's no hope of final victory.'

'What spirit!' Reinach grated as he outlined to the others what had happened. 'What courage! What cowardice!'

Urquhart, the regular soldier, disagreed. Army discipline, still strong in him, coloured his thinking and made his reactions instinctive.

'Cowards don't have a string of medals like he's got,' he pointed out.

That night the German-controlled French radio sounded nervous and twice as loud as normal with its warnings against resistance; the commentator, Jean-Hérold Paquis, urging strongly that the French people should throw in their lot with the Germans.

Madame Lamy pulled a face. 'He's another William Joyce, that one,' she snorted. 'Like Degrelle in Belgium and Quisling in Norway. No one listens to him.'

The BBC had also stepped up its urgings. 'Watch the Germans,' it said. 'Find out when they come and go and where they go to. Pool your knowledge. Give information to none but known patriots.'

When Reinach returned from taking Dring and de Frager to Dijon, he was full of alarm. 'All they could talk about down there,' he said, 'was the new weapons the Germans have. V-weapons, they call them.' He grinned. 'But at Besançon several kilometres of railway track have gone, with pylons twisted and engines upside down. The invasion *must* be coming. And this time we shall win because we have a myth. We have de Gaulle and Churchill. Who could make a myth of Daladier?'

'Perhaps they'll give you the Legion of Honour when it's over,' Madame Lamy murmured. 'For talking.'

'I'm not looking for medals,' Reinach said hotly. 'What we do'll go into the history books as much as what the armies do, and if we don't do anything, they'll be nothing except under the heading, "Occupation".'

There was a long silence then Guardian Moch twisted in his chair. 'There's a new agent in St Seigneur,' he pointed out. 'He's come to take Arsène's place. He can be found at a café called Le Petit Poucet. I could make contact.'

'What would you ask for?' Urquhart stopped them dead in their tracks.

'What do we need?'

'Rifles. Telescopic sights. Sten guns. Bren guns. Magazines. Ammunition.'

'Perhaps also mortars, grenades and even land mines?'

Urquhart's expression didn't change. 'Even rocket launchers, anti-tank weapons, field guns and, if you can get them, howitzers.'

'We're not conducting the defence of Paris,' Reinach growled.

Urquhart was unmoved. 'You could also start on the Rolandpoint weapons,' he pointed out. 'I could show you how to use them. I can strip, clean and reassemble anything you put in my hand. In the dark, if necessary.'

Reinach stared at Marie-Claude, then at Neville, then at Madame Lamy. His sarcasm had gone. 'I think we should go to St Seigneur,' he said.

Reinach's lorry was ancient but he pushed it along as fast as its age would allow, rolling and lighting his cigarettes as he drove with the accelerator pedal pressed firmly down, while Urquhart and Guardian Moch bounced about like ping-pong balls in the back. To make the occasion seem more innocent, Marie-Claude, dressed in her best for shopping, had climbed into the cab with Reinach who wore a pair of wide green knickerbockers – what he called 'les golfs' – and pretended to make a heavy set at her.

As they dropped into the town, they saw few cars or lorries apart from those owned by Germans, collaborators or tradesmen employed by the Wehrmacht. Dilapidated horse carriages waited at the station, with two-wheeled basket trailers behind bicycles, and only a few gazogènes moved about the streets. The shops seemed to be full of rubbish passed off as luxuries, but decorated always with the tricolour of France as though it were patriotic to buy them. 'Patrie,

Honneur et Courage' and Pétain's watchwords, 'Travaille, Famille, Patrie', seemed to be heavily overworked.

The café to which Moch directed them had the usual zinc-topped bar beneath pictures of Pétain and Charles Trenet, the singer, with another of Hitler for good measure – pointedly hanging on the door of the lavatory. It was a depressing place, with walls thickly painted with mountain scenes and an iron stove by the bar where the proprietress was trying to boil a kettle on burning sawdust that filled the place with smoke.

There was a brief whispered conversation and the woman disappeared to return with a greasy-looking man wearing a blue smock and beret, a fag end hanging from the corner of his mouth.

'He thinks he's Jean Gabin,' Marie-Claude whispered to Urquhart.

They all ceremoniously shook hands and ordered sausage stew. As they ate, the conversation remained inconsequential.

'The Germans are losing the war,' the man in the beret said. 'It's obvious from the bookstalls. They've got no sparkle any more, no ideas. Just the big German loudspeaker and the small Vichy loudspeaker yapping alongside.'

To Marie-Claude, writhing with impatience, it seemed they'd never get to the question of a message, but eventually Moch arrived at the point after a lot of cautious sparring. The agent was none too easy to convince but he finally nodded.

'So long as you can vouch for all your people,' he said. 'What do you want?'

A slip of paper and a *Carte Michelin* changed hands, and Moch jabbed with his thumb. 'That's the field. Right there.'

The agent nodded. 'We'll arrange the co-ordinates and broadcast them. You'll need a code – a phrase or a line of poetry. When it's broadcast, that's the night you'll know you have to wait.'

'They used La Fontaine last time,' Marie-Claude said.

'Then use him again. Do you know any?'

'I know the one about the crow,' Marie-Claude smiled. '*Maître Corbeau, sur un arbre perché . . .*'

'I prefer the one about "*La fourmi n'est pas prêteuse,*"' Reinach decided.

'That's the only one you know.'

The agent scowled. 'Make up your minds,' he said sharply.

'The one about the crow,' Marie-Claude insisted. 'That's the one they used last year; they'll know it's us again.'

The agent scribbled the lines down. 'Don't miss them,' he warned.

'We'll listen every night.'

The agent's sour face twisted. 'You needn't bother,' he said. 'They'll only come at the time of a full moon.'

As he rose to leave, Marie-Claude put a hand on his arm, and Urquhart could see in her face all the desperate longing of France for liberation, for freedom, even just for hope. 'Do you know anything about the invasion?' she asked.

'Why?'

'If you do, for the love of God tell us!'

The agent took his cigarette end from his mouth. 'I know nothing,' he said. 'They wouldn't tell *me,* anyway.' He managed a twisted smile that was meant to be encouraging but looked as though it belonged to an undertaker sizing up a corpse. 'I can tell you this, though,' he ended. 'It's coming, all right.'

11

It was Tarnera who noticed the new spirit in the village. Something had happened to the place. It had been obvious for some time that one or two people had begun to have stirrings in their minds. Now it was as if they were *all* engaged in a vast conspiracy.

For safety the word had been passed round that the Germans were no longer to be talked to, in case some hint of what was in their minds was dropped. Even Hössenfelder, the orderly from the château, was discouraged from helping at the farm.

Like everyone else, Tarnera guessed that they were on the brink of something tremendous. It was deep into May now and he was well aware that for Germany events had reached the top of a steep slope down into the darkness and were already on the move again. It was clear the tide had turned and that eventually they were going to lose the war. The U-boats had been beaten and the Luftwaffe was broken. The Russians had smashed the Wehrmacht in the East, and even in the Pacific and Burma the allies were beginning to sweep everything before them.

Then they heard that Cassino, which had been holding up the allied armies in Italy, had fallen and it didn't escape Tarnera's notice that the place wasn't just another stronghold but part of the battle for the Italian capital.

'In case you haven't realized it, Fritzi,' he said to Klein-Wuttig, 'we've just entered on a new phase.'

Busy at the table, Klein-Wuttig looked up. 'What do you mean?'

'Rome will fall before long.'

'Rubbish.'

'I'm glad you think so. I even hope you're right.'

'There's nothing to fear.' Klein-Wuttig was armoured by his faith. '*Hitler ist der Sieg*. The Führer is Victory itself.'

Tarnera laughed. 'Fritzi, you're an incurable optimist. You know the current joke in Berlin: They stuck a notice outside an old folk's home – "Closed. Due to Call-up." Men of sixty-five are being called into the Volkssturm, Fritzi. Mind you, they say you're exempt if you can prove you have a father serving at the front.'

Klein-Wuttig's expression was frozen on his face. 'You think the war's a joke, Tarnera, don't you?'

'If I didn't I'd have cut my throat long since! Fritzi, the Russians are heading now for Kiev.'

'*Der Endsieg wird kommen*. Final victory will be ours, never fear.'

'Fritzi – ' Tarnera sighed ' – those airy sunlit homes they promised us; they're all over the Reich now – thanks to the

RAF. And do you remember the days when we were going to sweep up the British Isles with a vacuum cleaner? What happened to that? If a referendum were held now to end the war, there'd be a hundred and twenty per cent vote, the odd twenty per cent voting twice. You're beginning to regard the war as an end in itself, irrespective of whether it can be won. *Alles klappt*. Everything's ticking over. We haven't lost, so everything's fine. Anybody with half an eye can see the way things are going. That nonsense about one folk, one Reich one Führer only papers over the cracks. There's no direction any more. The Party stalwarts have boozed away what grey matter they had.'

'The Führer will make things come right.'

Klein-Wuttig spoke doggedly and Tarnera threw up his hands. 'Oh, God, Fritzi, all this Hitler worship's just Catholicism without Christ!'

Klein-Wuttig stared stonily at him then he gathered up his belt and cap and strode to the door. As he opened it, he turned and jerked out his arm defiantly. 'Heil Hitler,' he shouted.

'Oh, go to the devil!'

As Klein-Wuttig disappeared, Klemens arrived.

'What was all that about?' he demanded.

'Only Fritzi insisting that we can't lose the war.'

Klemens frowned. 'Of course we can't,' he said. 'We started it and now we're stuck with it and we might as well enjoy it because the peace will be terrible.' As he tossed down his hat and whip, he stood for a moment, staring at a picture near the door. It showed a village street and seemed to have been painted entirely in the left-over browns and greens of a one-armed house decorator.

He frowned and gestured at it. 'Those paintings we're after,' he said. 'They couldn't have painted over them, could they? I mean, could *that* be one? I've heard of that sort of thing being done by shady dealers. They scrape it off afterwards or something.'

Tarnera smiled. 'I've checked, Herr Oberst. That paint's years old. You'd never scrape it off.'

Klemens scowled. He also had begun to notice the new

spirit in the village and it worried him because sabotage was rife all over France. Despite everything, the French were still managing to urinate into the petrol tanks of lorries, and concrete bastions along the coast were said to be rotten because French labourers had discovered that sugar dropped into a concrete mixer formed calcium saccharate which robbed the concrete of its strength.

None of this, of course, applied to the district of Néry–St Seigneur–Rolandpoint, which had been stiff with Germans since 1940, but it didn't mean that the villagers weren't scheming. He was no fool and was as conscious as Tarnera that time was running out. Apolitical himself, he was none the less aware that when Armageddon came, it would be well worth his while to have stacked away against the future everything he could find, and it bothered him that he was sitting on a set of art treasures that no one had yet thought to remove.

'That inventory I asked for,' he said. 'Is it ready?'

Tarnera fished in his briefcase and produced a thick folio of papers, which he passed over together with a signal flimsy. 'I've also tracked down Colonel Marx,' he said. 'That's his reply.'

Klemens snatched at the signal and stared at it. 'So much for that damned old woman!' he said. 'Well, *I*'ve got something too! Let's have the old witch in.'

Because of the warmer weather, the Baronne had discarded her husband's sheepskin jacket but she still looked cold. Klemens gestured to a chair and she sat in it as straight-backed as if it were a bed of nails. Klemens started off gently. 'We're not receiving the co-operation we're entitled to, madame,' he said.

'You can hardly expect it,' the Baronne snapped. 'Unless, of course, you were to decide to leave, and then we'd willingly help you pack.'

Klemens smacked the table with his hand. 'You realize that as maire you could be held hostage for the good behaviour of the village,' he said. 'How would you like that?'

The Baronne was quite unmoved. 'At my age, it wouldn't bother me at all. My only regret would be that I wouldn't be here to see you all trailing back to Germany in defeat.'

Klemens scowled. She was so old his threats were meaningless. He changed the subject. 'The pictures,' he said.

The old woman looked at him blankly. 'Which pictures?'

Klemens reddened. 'You know damned well which pictures, madame!' He waved the telegraph flimsy. 'It's taken a little while to check your statement that they'd been stolen because, as you know, we expect the British and the Americans to try to land in France and, due to the allied bombing and the disruption of communications, Colonel Marx has taken some tracking down. However, we *have* tracked him down, and he states in his message that the paintings were here when he left.'

The old woman pulled a face. 'Perhaps he took them himself and doesn't want anyone to know.'

Klemens scowled, knowing she despised him. 'That's not all, madame!' His voice rose as he began to lose his temper. 'What you don't perhaps realize is that paintings have to have something called provenance. Do you know what provenance is?'

The Baronne shrugged and Klemens smiled. 'Provenance, my dear lady,' he said, 'means pedigree. I've been in touch with General Dannhüber, who's an expert, and he was kind enough to provide a catalogue of the paintings and artifacts in this house. It's an old one, of course, produced before the war, but it lists nineteen pictures as well as a number of etchings and several sketches. With this list I've contacted art dealers in Munich, and General von Stülpnagel in Paris put me in touch with one or two of your compatriots who are more friendly to us than you are. I now have descriptions of every one of these paintings. In some cases, even photographs. I now know all there is to know about them and when I find them – '

'*When*,' the Baronne reminded him.

Klemens ignored the comment, '– when I find them, I shall know if they're the ones I'm looking for. They're all listed here, madame: Five Greuzes – five, madame! – a Nattier, a Watteau, a Lancret, a Fragonard, a Vigée Lebrun, a Corot, a Troyon, a Daubigny, a Monet, a Kucharski, a

Prud'hon, a Desvosges, a Quantin and a Truat. There's also a small pencil drawing by Rembrandt, engravings by Legros, a red chalk sketch on green paper attributed to Leonardo da Vinci, a folio of pencil drawings of rocks by Dali, a charcoal drawing of washerwomen by Degas, and water colours by Dufy and Orissa. To say nothing of framed chromos of one of your family at Abd el Kader and the defence of the legation at Peking by another of them; drawings by Détaille and de Neuville, three Nîmes vases, a set of Rouen plates, a Chippendale mirror, four Louis XIII chairs, a surveyor's compass used in America during some war against the British, an 18-carat gold fob watch, English, French and American antique toys and automata, and various items of jewellery on red velvet in flat glass cases.' He turned to Tarnera. 'Have you seen any jewellery in flat glass cases, Tarnera?'

'None, Herr Oberst.'

Klemens laid a folder on the table and leaned forward, his hands on the desk, to stare with narrowed eyes at the Baronne.

'This catalogue, madame, was issued by your husband. It bears out what I've been told.' He opened a page. 'For instance: the Lebrun. Two metres by one and a half.' He flipped the page. 'The Monet. Two and a half by two. These are big paintings. Where are they hidden?'

The old woman's face remained blank. 'I've told you. They were stolen.'

'They're in this house!' Klemens' bottled-up frustration came out in a shout.

The Baronne didn't even blink. 'Not to my knowledge.'

'We'll search the place!'

The thin shoulders lifted in a shrug and the Baronne stood up. 'Then, monsieur, I suggest you get on with it.'

Klemens stared after her as she closed the door. 'Tarnera,' he said, his voice bitter. 'She knows those damned paintings are here! But she also knows they're sufficiently safe for her to challenge us to find them. Very well, we'll show her what we're made of. Turn the place inside out. And, to make sure that while you're in one room they're not passing something through the ceiling to the next, we'll have the whole damn lot of them out on the gravel in front.'

Half an hour later, they were all out on the drive – the Baronne, Euphrasie, Joseph, and the cook. It took another half-hour to find Psichari, the gardener. He was in the lavatory at the back of the house, enjoying a smoke, and being half crazy, refused to leave until he'd finished. With them all finally standing in an indignant group by the great front door, Unteroffizier Schäffer prepared to send his men through the house.

'What are we searching for, Herr Oberst?' he asked.

'Canvases. Paintings. They may be flat. They may be rolled.'

'Not the ones on the walls, Herr Oberst?'

'No, you idiot! Search every room. Every cupboard. Every carpet. Every mattress.'

An hour later it began to rain and the indignant Baronne demanded to be allowed inside. Unwillingly, Klemens moved them into the hall. They were there until late afternoon by which time Schäffer's men had to admit defeat.

'The damn things must be somewhere,' Klemens scowled. 'They wouldn't destroy them out of spite.'

'They just might, Herr Oberst,' Tarnera pointed out.

'Have they searched the place properly?'

'From top to bottom.'

'Attics?'

'Every one. I checked.'

Klemens stamped up and down, his hands clamped behind his back. 'They were here when Colonel Marx was here,' he insisted doggedly. 'He even says that if he'd been on his way home, he might have helped himself to one or two.'

'Perhaps they're in the village,' Klein-Wuttig said.

'Very well,' Klemens slapped his hand down on the table. 'Tomorrow we search the place with a fine-toothed comb.'

The following morning, Klein-Wuttig and his men surrounded the village. At first there was a certain amount of panic, but when one of the soldiers actually handled papers with a list of the members of Reinach's réseau and did no more than glance at it, it dawned on them that the Germans weren't looking for weapons and they began to enjoy themselves.

In Reinach's house, there was great excitement when Schäffer gave a shout and Klein-Wuttig was inside the house in a moment, yelling for Klemens.

Klemens was waiting near the church, alongside a rusting iron crucifix that clawed at the sky next to the notice board announcing the times of the masses. Behind him was the cemetery, at the end of a small dusty path which had been stirred by the feet of countless mourners and the hooves of generations of scrawny horses. It was desolate and full of frugal crosses of cast-iron, beadwork wreaths and marble slabs supporting yellowing photographs under glass. Among the stonework, the edgings of granite chips, weeds and lachrymose angels, there was a large family vault inscribed 'Famille St Angéac-Brieuc de Frager'. It was giving Klemens the creeps, and he was glad to go into action as Klein-Wuttig called.

Schäffer had discovered an ancient frame, its gilt blackened with age, from which the canvas had been cut. A further search had produced from under a bedroom rug a canvas of a man and a woman.

Klemens stared at it joyously. 'Now we're getting somewhere.' He glanced at his list and Tarnera saw him frown. 'I've no mention here of a painting of a man and a woman,' he said. 'You're sure that's a man and a woman.'

'One of them has a bust and the other a beard, Herr Oberst,' Tarnera pointed out.

Klemens scowled and looked again at the painting. It was a deep brown in colour. 'What's its pedigree, do you think?' he asked.

'By amateur out of dud, I imagine,' Tarnera said. 'If that's an old master, Herr Oberst, I'm the Führer's dog.'

'Fetch Reinach in.'

As the carpenter was brought in, his face blank and stupid, Klemens jerked a hand at the canvas. 'Where did you get that?' he snapped.

'From my father, monsieur.'

Klemens turned to Tarnera. 'Get him!'

Reinach's eyebrows lifted. 'You'll have a job, monsieur. He's in Heaven. He died in 1936.'

'Then what the devil was he doing with the Baronne's painting?'

Reinach's eyebrows shot up again. '*That* doesn't belong to the Baronne, monsieur! It was painted in 1934 by my brother who was taken prisoner in 1940. It's supposed to be my parents, only he was never very good at painting and his colours were always muddy.'

Klemens glared. 'If it's of no value,' he yelled, 'what was it doing under the carpet? And why did you cut if from the frame?'

'Because we heard, monsieur, that you were collecting things to take back to Germany. It hasn't any value, but it means a lot to my family.'

Klemens shoved him aside and stamped out.

Two houses further along, Dréo's one-legged son appeared holding a small picture of a battle. It showed French troops in red trousers and képis driving off a group of Prussian soldiers in spiked helmets with a great deal of slaughter. It was a very bad painting. 'It shows our people defeating your people north of Tours in 1871,' he said to Schäffer, his face serious. 'You can have it for fifty francs.'

In the street Klemens conferred with Klein-Wuttig and Tarnera. 'They're shifting the stuff along,' he said, 'from one house to the other. Split your men up. One lot to start at the east, the other at the west. Where they meet, that's where the pictures will be.'

But they weren't, though they searched the decaying environs of the church, the bell tower, the barns and sheds, and even broke open the de Frager vault because one of Schäffer's men said he thought he detected the marks of a crowbar on the stone. All they got for their trouble was a vituperative complaint from the Baronne, spat into their faces with all the venom she could muster.

'Didn't you find anything at all?' Klemens asked wearily.

'A few hidden bottles of wine,' Tarnera said. 'An odd bottle of brandy. No guns. No paintings. No jewellery.'

12

The Germans hadn't even found Balmaceda's copies that he'd painted during his long love affair with the Baronne. He'd sent them to Dijon ages before to raise the wind and, since no Frenchman had enough money to spend on paintings and he refused to allow them to be sold to Germans or collaborators, they were still there and his studio was empty.

Néry enjoyed the joke immensely and began to think they were winning, because this was the second time they'd put something across the Germans. They were in such good spirits Reinach even made himself a rubber stamp with the words 'Read but not approved – Charles de Gaulle' with which he crept round the village after dark and stamped all the Occupation notices the Germans had put up. There was a new feeling of defiance abroad. Glued every night to their radios, trying to hear in spite of the fading batteries and the static, they were far more worried that they'd miss the message about their parachute drop than they were about the Germans catching them listening to the BBC.

In the meantime, the forest behind the village had suddenly become of great interest to everyone. There were always mushrooms to look for – chantrelles d'automne or the shy little trompettes de mort, black shapes under the leaf mould. Others went with ferrets after rabbits or, if the evening was warm and they were young, with girl friends. What Klemens didn't know was that, deep in the undergrowth, Urquhart had started giving instructions on the weapons they'd rescued from Rolandpoint.

It wasn't easy because the villagers liked to preserve their individuality and since there were forty million Frenchmen there were also forty million different political parties and forty million different ways of absorbing knowledge.

'The Bren's an ideal gun,' Urquhart intoned, in his North of England dourness looking and behaving almost like the high-country Burgundians themselves. 'Strong, portable and accurate, while the Sten's just the thing for street fighting, wood clearing or anywhere the enemy might appear suddenly at close quarters.'

'I wish I were at close quarters with those filth,' Sergeant Dréo growled.

'Or better still with the Widow Bona in Rolandpoint,' Guardian Moch grinned.

Urquhart drew a deep breath. 'It's easily handled,' he struggled on, 'and can be fired in single rounds or in bursts from the shoulder or waist. It's easy to hold and fits snugly into the hand.'

'There are other things that fit snugly in the hand, too,' Moch said and Ernouf rounded on him.

'There's a Frenchman for you!' he snorted. 'It's weapons he's talking about!'

Moch grinned. 'It's weapons *I*'m talking about!'

At the end of May, de Frager and Lionel Dring returned. 'The area round Besançon's stuffed with armed men,' they reported. 'They could stop a whole German division. On the Vercors massif they're receiving weapons all the time.'

'Then where are the ones *we* asked for?' Reinach demanded indignantly. 'We've heard nothing and there's a full moon due.'

Sergeant Dréo rubbed his bottle nose and twanged his moustaches. 'I thought they were going to give us the message last night,' he said wistfully. 'There was something in his voice, I thought. As though he were looking directly at me.'

It was decided that Urquhart should cycle to St Seigneur to demand action and, to Neville's surprise, Marie-Claude insisted on accompanying him to make it look like a shopping expedition. It was a long ride and they took a satchel containing bread and cheese and wine and stopped at midday to eat it.

The summer was on them now and there was a breathless stillness about the air and a heat haze over the valley. The trees were in full bloom, thick and heavy, and the roadside where they sat was dotted with flowers. Marie-Claude was quiet, as she had been with Urquhart ever since they'd snatched the Rolandpoint weapons from under the noses of the Germans. He knew what was troubling her, but he made no effort to help her and after a while it came out – cautiously at first, then in a rush. 'When you were in Rolandpoint those nights,' she said, 'I prayed for your safety. That you returned unharmed was due to my constant prayers to the Virgin.'

Urquhart grinned. 'How about giving Ernestine some of the credit?' he said. 'She worked hard at it, too.'

Her lips tightened and she tried a different tack, aware of a strange new loneliness, and a sense of uncertainty and insecurity such as she'd never known before. She looked at Urquhart but, as usual, his face was secret and enigmatic. He always puzzled her because, while he could smile – and when he did his whole face lit up – he was nevertheless a reserved man not given to showing his feelings much.

'While you were there I had a long talk with Neville,' she said. 'He's a very rich man.'

'Very.' Urquhart was still not being helpful.

'He talked a great deal about luxury and wealth.'

He looked at her. She was wearing a faded blue dress that was spread about her strong thighs as she sat in the grass beside the bicycles. The breeze had blown wisps of dark hair loose and her face was pink with exertion. As his gaze travelled over her, a blush coloured her cheeks further.

'Of course,' he said. 'Trying to impress you. Who wouldn't? You're splendid.'

The words brought a still deeper colour to her cheeks and her body glowed. But then Urquhart's face was empty again and she found she was suffering from a restlessness that harried her to distraction. After a while he spoke again, his mouth twisted in a smile.

'Was he offering them to you?' he asked.

She brushed an insect off her leg. 'It seemed so.'

'Marriage?'

'That's what I thought.'

Urquhart said nothing and she went on in an off-hand manner. 'We have many strange marriage customs in Burgundy,' she said. 'In the middle of the wedding feast the people bring in pieces of silver or things for the house; and with the dessert someone fires three shots under the table, like when they knock three times on the stage at the theatre before the performance.'

Urquhart listened politely – a strong, nerveless man who could never be pushed into anything he didn't want – and she went on doggedly. 'If *you* were going to marry a girl, Urk't, what would *you* offer her?'

Urquhart grinned. 'Same as *I*'ve always had,' he said. 'Hard work.'

She sniffed. 'I already have plenty of that.' Her face set in a frown. 'Why *aren't* you married, Urk't? You're strong and capable. Do English girls not attract men?'

'Oh, yes.' He sat, still as a rock, watching her. 'They attract men.'

'I think perhaps English girls are not aware of what they have to offer.'

'The ones I've met seemed to be.'

She frowned but persisted. 'Why, then, did you *not* marry?'

Urquhart seemed untouched by her worry. 'Because I haven't met the right girl,' he said.

'It's wrong not to marry!' She was beginning to grow irritated by his calm. 'God created Eve out of Adam's rib so that when she's not at his side he feels the loss! I was married at seventeen!'

Urquhart still showed no reaction and, torn by her emotions, she struggled on, throwing out hints like confetti and trying to pretend it was all just a joke. 'Love's a violent emotion,' she went on. 'Men sometimes fight over a girl. Sometimes with fists and sometimes with knives. If it were you and Neville, unfortunately, the police would have to take away the winner to languish in the Tower of London.'

'Yes,' Urquhart said.

She stared at him furiously, aware that in that strange quiet manner of his, he was well aware of her tactics. 'Would you marry *me*?' she demanded bluntly.

The question was without artifice and Urquhart answered it in the same manner. 'No,' he said.

'I'm not poor!' She sounded indignant that he should refuse her. 'The farm's mine. I would bring a good dowry.'

Urquhart was still unmoved. 'Englishmen don't expect their wives to bring a dowry. But that's not the point. When I get married, *I'll* do the asking.'

Her expression sagged and the fierceness went out of her. For a moment she stared at her feet, bewildered and ready to cry. Urquhart didn't move and slowly she gathered her courage again. She was determined to have it out. 'Neville's perhaps not very good with his hands,' she said, 'but he's very handsome and he makes me laugh. Perhaps *he'll* marry me.'

'Why not ask him? He might even say yes.'

'I *must* have a husband.'

'For the farm?'

'Yes.' She stared at him unblinkingly. 'And for me, too.'

When they reached St Seigneur, the ride proved to have been for nothing. The agent had vanished towards the south where things were said to be stirring and the radio operator had gone with him; the only help and advice they could get came on the way back from Brisson, of the bereft Rolandpoint réseau.

'If he said it'll come,' he insisted, 'then it'll come. Our drop came exactly when they said it would.'

'We don't even know how to welcome the damn thing,' Urquhart said.

Brisson drew three dots on the oily surface of his bench. 'Three of you have to stand in a triangle,' he said. 'Like that. With the summit pointing upwind. All with white torches. There must also be a red at the apex. When you hear the aircraft you change it to three white lights, a hundred yards apart.'

He agreed to ride back with them to the field where they were expecting the drop, and they took nets and ferrets so that it would look as if they were rabbiting. In the middle of the field, they stared about them and Brisson pointed to where they should stand.

'I'll be here when it happens,' he promised. 'I can get up from Rolandpoint in an hour. Just have your transport ready, that's all. They'll be flying as slow as they can, and everybody must count the parachutes as they come down. Everybody.'

'Why?'

'Because if you miss one and it's seen by the Germans, they'll know there's been a drop and then – ' Brisson drew his finger across his throat and made a slitting noise ' – that's it for the lot of you.'

Marie-Claude remained so nervous the walls seemed to tremble and bulge with her efforts to keep silent. Again and again she went over what they needed. 'Hercule and the platform with enough hay on it to cover everything,' she kept saying. 'Butter, cheese, bread, and a bottle or two of wine – '

'And hard-boiled eggs,' her mother added. 'They're very good for the muscles.'

'Torches,' Marie-Claude went on. 'Rope. Spare batteries . . .'

Urquhart grabbed her by the arms and forced her to stand still. 'Stop it,' he said. 'Stop it, Marie-Claude! There's no need to make a meal of it. It'll be all right on the night.'

She felt choked and dizzy and despairing with the sense of obligation that swept over her. Except for one or two like Reinach, she knew she was surrounded by a lot of elderly men and young boys given to too much patriotism, and she felt responsible for them. She tried to explain, moving in Urquhart's grip, but he refused to let her go, holding her until she calmed down.

'Stop tearing round like a cyclone in a barrel,' he said quietly. 'That way you forget things.'

'You would perhaps like me to do as the English do – sit down and make some tea?'

He smiled. 'Just calm down, that's all. You'll do what you have to do much better that way.'

She looked desperate. 'They're such old fools, so many of them.'

'I'm not.'

She stopped trying to escape and stared up at him with a perplexed face. 'What are you expecting out of it all, Urk't?' she asked.

'I owe the Germans as much as you do,' he said. 'I was also in that defeat you like to recall so much, you know. We got away at Dunkirk but we were beaten just as you were.'

'Is it important to you, too, that they suffer?'

'For God's sake, yes,' Urquhart exploded. 'I want to see the whole lot of them marching past me into captivity, like we did and you did in 1940, with their heads down and their eyes on the ground because they *know* they've been beaten. I don't believe in turning the other cheek. I believe in the Old Testament and an eye for an eye and a tooth for a tooth. I want to see them going through what they've put everybody else through. And they will, Marie-Claude, with you or without you. There are so many men and guns and aeroplanes in England now, just waiting for the word "go", there's no room for any more.'

Her eyes widened. 'There are?'

He nodded. 'And when they come, the Germans won't know what's hit them. Already we've damaged their cities more than French and British cities have been damaged. I've seen them. Soon they'll have the pleasure of seeing us march through their streets, too, and this time they'll not be able to say that the politicians stabbed them in the back, because they'll be defeated and they'll *know* they've been defeated.'

She stood silently for a moment, staring at his face. Then she nodded and he allowed his hands to drop from her arms.

'You're right, of course, Urk't,' she admitted. 'Thank you.'

Without embarrassment, she kissed him on the cheek. 'Thank you, Urk't,' she said again. 'I think it will be all right now.'

Nevertheless, it was as well for her nerves that the message arrived the next night. Almost as if Brisson had contacted London, it came in the high plummy voice the BBC seemed to favour even in French. 'D'Auguste à César!'

Marie-Claude, who had been listlessly eating her meal, sat bolt upright at once. 'That's this area!'

Immediately, there was a suggestion of electricity in the air. As Neville laid down his knife, it clattered against his plate and Marie-Claude irritatedly shushed him to silence.

'Here he comes again,' she said, her eyes glowing with fervour. She'd heard of allied intervention in other parts of France but this was where it became personal, because this was for her alone.

'*Maître Corbeau, sur un arbre perché –* '

That was all and it seemed almost an anti-climax but they knew at once that they were in the war again. Marie-Claude rose, her eyes alight. Turning to Neville and Urquhart, she kissed them both with great ceremony as the representatives of the country across the Channel that had brought her hope.

'Those lines were chosen by us,' she said solemnly. 'No one but us. I was there.' She hurriedly cut more bread. 'You must finish your food and you must have plenty. You'll be hungry.'

As soon as he'd finished, Neville dragged out one of the ancient bicycles to set off to warn Brisson. He hadn't even reached the road when he met Reinach hurrying up the dusty drive.

'It's tonight,' he said. 'Did you hear it? I've told everybody. There's Théyras and Ernouf and Father Pol. We've also got three boys and the Dring family and Yvon Guélis and the Péroutins.'

They exchanged cigarettes in a way that to Neville seemed to scream out loud of conspiracy. 'It's not enough,' he whispered. 'Urquhart said we'd need at least twenty. The more the better.'

'I can get de Frager. And Dréo and his son. They're not much good at walking with their stiff legs but they can lift. I'll get young Hénault as well, and Rapin and the Gaudins from the other end of the village. And Vic Letac, Mère Ledoux's barman, and Roland Razzo, who works for Théyras. Is that enough?'

At Rolandpoint there was no sign of Brisson, and the garage was closed. 'He's at his mother's,' Ernestine Bona told Neville. 'Are you going to stop the night? It'll soon be time for the curfew.'

'No. It's the parachute drop.'

'Then bonne chance, mon brave.' She nodded at the bicycle. 'Can you ride it?'

'Yes.'

'Fast?'

'I'm almost as good as a Frenchman on a bike now.'

Her lips curved in a smile. 'Just be careful. With that between your legs you could end up no good to anybody. Certainly not to Marie-Claude Defourney. I'll bet she's after you, isn't she?'

Neville grinned and she disappeared, to return wheeling a petrolette. 'Borrow this,' she said. 'And just be careful the Germans don't catch you or they'll "friction" you. I'll find Brisson.'

Marie-Claude and Urquhart were waiting with the horse and cart when Neville returned. The brigadier of police had stopped him on the outskirts of Rolandpoint to demand what he was doing there; in a sudden inspiration he'd said he was going to see a woman whose husband was on night work, and the French love of 'l'amour' – especially illicit 'amour' – had worked and he had been waved on.

As he clattered into the farmyard he saw Marie-Claude was wearing her men's boots and hat and was bundled into one of the heavy coats the French called 'canadiennes'. As the sun sank, the woods became russet. Then the eastern horizon took on a shade of misty blue and a strong scent of hay filled the air.

They set off as soon as it was dark, leading the old horse along the track that ran round the farm, the wheels crunching on the flints. After a while, they met Théyras who was waiting with a bicycle, hump-backed and still.

'They'll never come,' he said sceptically.

'Of course they will,' Marie-Claude replied fiercely. 'You heard the message. It came through on the nine-fifteen broadcast also. *Maître Corbeau sur un arbre perché . . . Maître Corbeau . . .*' she repeated it excitedly.

Soon afterwards, they met Ernouf, then two more men with spades and sacks, and they followed the cart in single file through the trees. Ernouf was trying to imitate the announcer's voice and sounded as if someone was clutching him by the throat. '*Maître Corbeau . . .*' he said. 'Exactly as we suggested.'

'He had a catch in his throat, I thought,' Ernouf commented.

'Of course he didn't, you old fool! Do you think he's just concerned with you?'

Ernouf scowled. 'Well, he read it better than any of the other messages, and it's the first we've had for ages.'

The argument stopped as Reinach appeared, jolting down the lane in his lorry with Father Pol. The exhaust was broken and it was making a tremendous noise.

'They'll hear us all over the Côte-d'Or,' Marie-Claude wailed.

Reinach seemed unperturbed. 'I gave the garde-champêtre a lift,' he said. 'He won't bother us. Father Pol made him promise to look the other way.'

'Priests shouldn't be involved in this work,' Marie-Claude persisted anxiously.

'Neither should young girls,' Father Pol said. 'And since the man and the priest are inseparable, the priest couldn't live with his conscience if the man didn't do his duty.'

It was pitch dark now and their shoes were already saturated with dew. The cows on the dropping zone had rushed away in alarm as they'd arrived but now they were edging close again, full of curiosity, black and white patches in the darkness, filling the silence with the sound of chewing and belching. Reinach went among them with a stick and they heard the thump of heavy feet as the cows moved away. Ten minutes later they were back once more, standing in an inquisitive ring round the little group of humans, breathing heavily and occasionally mooing a soft welcome.

After a while the moon came up, flooding the countryside with orange light, and as they chewed cold rabbits' legs they saw a wild boar racing across the field to the woods, its tail up like a pennant against the sky.

'A big one,' Dring said to Urquhart. 'If you go into the woods, look out for their runs. They're like tunnels in the undergrowth. And that's the sort that'll charge.'

Father Pol sighed at the thought of the fats and greases they'd let go, and looked at his watch. 'It's time,' he observed.

'I don't think they're coming,' Marie-Claude said.

'The English are never on time,' Sergeant Dréo grumbled. 'They weren't at the Marne.'

There was no sign of Brisson and Marie-Claude went into a riot of nerves.

'He won't come,' she muttered.

'If he doesn't we'll manage on our own,' Urquhart said.

Dring was frankly sceptical. 'I served in the air force in 1920,' he said. 'No aeroplane could navigate to a single small field.'

Reinach shouldered his way among them, shoving at them with his big hands. 'Stop arguing,' he growled. 'There's a trench to be dug for the containers. Get on with it.'

Marie-Claude was standing with her hands clenched, and Neville drew her on one side.

'They'll come,' he reassured her.

Her head turned quickly. Her face was set, as though she were willing the venture to succeed, trying to project her determination to the aircraft they were expecting, to its crew, even to the people in England who had despatched it. 'It *must* work,' she said. 'It *will* work.'

He put his hands on her shoulders and turned her so he could see her face in the moonlight. 'It'll work all right,' he said. 'It will, Marie-Claude. 'You've made it so it'll work.'

He was trying to say more than merely that he believed she was brave, and he hoped she'd understand. He believed, in fact, that she did understand and was grateful for her comprehension as she reached up to give him a chilly little peck on the cheek.

'Yes,' she said. 'It will.'

Reinach tried to cheer her up. 'You can have one of the parachutes,' he offered. 'They make good underwear, so long as you don't let the Germans see it.'

Her eyes flashed. 'What makes you think I'd let a German see *my* underwear,' she snapped, and Reinach grinned.

The men digging the trench had started work by the light of hurricane lamps, grumbling at the effort it entailed. But Reinach didn't let them rest. He'd been a good choice as leader because he had the gift to make them do as they were told just by the strength of his personality.

'The ground's like concrete,' Dring complained.

'So's your head. Dig.'

Brisson arrived at last in a lather of sweat. He was still fighting off Marie-Claude's indignant accusations when she stopped dead. 'Hush!'

As they listened, they made out a low drone somewhere in the sky, though it was impossible to tell from which direction it came.

'That's it!'

After a while the drone died and they were all silent.

'They've missed us,' Dring said. 'I knew they couldn't do it.'

The moon was high now and the landscape was silver blue. There wasn't a cloud in the sky and the stars were bright lamps in the heavens. Faintly they could hear the sound of crickets and the shuffle of night birds.

'It was a false alarm,' Théyras said.

'No! It's coming back. Listen.'

Then they heard the beat of unsynchronized engines and Reinach yelled. 'That's it! Get to your positions!'

'Let me hold the lamp,' Théyras said, grabbing at Ernouf's arm.

'No! I want to hold it first!'

'Shut up,' Reinach snapped. 'You're like a lot of kids!'

The torches were switched on and, as the droning sound grew louder, they strained their eyes.

'There!' It was Neville who spoke, and they all saw a black patch drifting across the sky.

'Four engines. Twin rudders,' Urquhart said. 'Halifax. Lucky bastards. They'll be home tonight.'

The black patch vanished and the sound died. They all became jumpy, and were peering skywards when they saw the moon making a star of reflection on a perspex nose. There was a brief glimpse of a light inside an open hatch and the sound of the propellers drumming against the earth. Then the sky exploded in a spray of round black mushrooms.

Marie-Claude flung her arms round Neville and hugged him. 'They've come!' she crowed. 'They've come!'

Father Pol crossed himself and raised his hand in a

blessing to the crew of the aeroplane. 'Bless you, my sons,' he said quietly. 'God's love be with you in your travels.'

Ernouf was not half so circumspect and was yelling at the top of his voice. 'Vive la France!' he screamed. 'Vive de Gaulle!'

Reinach cuffed him at the side of his head and sent him staggering. 'Shut up, you old fool! Do you want every German in Néry up here? Start counting.'

There was a series of tinny clonks as the containers hit the ground and the parachutes deflated, then a stampede of excited men across the stubbly grass. It was a good drop and all the containers were together. They were the length of a five-hundred-pound bomb and heavy enough for the edges to dig into the hand. Théyras gaped at them, startled. 'Mother of God, do they expect us to carry these?'

Brisson showed them how they hinged down one side like a pea-pod. Inside were three shorter containers, all heavy but all supplied with handles. There was a lot of puffing and panting as they were carried into the trees, and curses as someone cut his hand on a bent lid. A wheelbarrow was lifted off the platform to help; then Reinach's lorry started up and they all stopped dead, aghast at the noise the defective exhaust was making.

'They'll hear us in Dijon,' Marie-Claude panted.

'Not them,' Reinach said. 'Throw the stuff on the lorry! By the time they wake up we'll have finished.'

His confidence paid off and the containers were in the woods within a few minutes.

'Make sure they don't leave anything behind,' Reinach whispered to Neville. 'And make sure you've got all the parachutes. They're daft enough to forget something.'

The parachutes and cords were stuffed into the metal shells and buried in the trench they'd dug. The excitement was intense.

'A Bren,' Ernouf said. 'Automatic pistols. Grenades. And oh, *mon dieu*, look at this!'

There were mortars, a bazooka, a radio no one knew how to use packed in sponge rubber, incendiary pots, time pencils, detonators and silver coils of cordtex. They were all chattering noisily, indifferent to the racket they were making and asking when they could do it again. When Marie-Claude begged them to be quiet, they became motionless. petrified in whatever they were doing before continuing in whispers. But two or three minutes later, they were all chattering noisily again.

Then Théyras gave a yelp of delight. 'Coffee,' he shouted. 'And sugar! *And* butter! I must have one of those to take to my wife so she'll believe me when I tell her where I've been and won't think I've been with the Widow Bona.' He grinned. 'And cigarettes! French cigarettes made in England! We don't have to smoke that filth made out of cow dung and bat shit the Germans provide.'

He handed the packet round and they all lit up, standing still and drawing in the smoke with delighted smiles, pulling it down to the depths of their lungs. For a moment it seemed as if it would appear from their ears, their trouser bottoms, from inside their hats, even through the lace-holes of their shoes.

'My friends,' Reinach was saying proudly, gesturing at the weapons, 'weve become men again. Chics types once more. We have weapons. All we need now is something to do with them.'

They all stood round him, grinning and pleased with themselves. All except Marie-Claude, waiting alone with the horse a short distance away, staring with a puzzled expression at Neville and Urquhart. She had provided the cart and all the food and wine. To a certain extent she'd provided a lot of the driving force. But now, with the weapons in their hands and cigarettes in their mouths, they seemed to have forgotten her, to have moved into a different sphere where women didn't belong.

Staring at them, she was suddenly aware that they had reached the beginning of a new, urgent and probably dangerous phase, and she was conscious of a terrible loneliness.

Part 2
FIRST LIGHT

'Périsse l'univers pourvu que je me venge.'
Savinien de Cyrano de Bergerac

1

There was something in the air.

The invasion was on its way.

They all knew it was on its way. The whole of Europe knew it was on its way – even the Germans. The only thing they didn't know was where and when.

It stuck out a mile that it was coming from the increase in messages from the BBC. It was obvious from the amount of training going on across the Channel, the collection of invasion craft and warships, the number of men gathered in Southern England; it was clear from the urgency that showed in everything the Germans did, the way they moved their men, increased their security and watched the French like hawks in case they knew something the Germans didn't. Everything suddenly seemed to be on the move, aircraft, guns, lorries, men, all turning to face the north where they knew the threat existed.

Though Radio Paris had stepped up its appeals to the French not to be deluded by British and American promises, and the Germans had stepped up their threats about what would happen if they were, the messages from London continued to grow in intensity. Despite the fact that Gestapo agents seemed to be everywhere – fortunately easy to recognize because of the German love for green that manifested itself in the colour of their hats or jackets – the whole of France was on the alert. The next messages from London would surely indicate invasion in a matter of hours and the beginning of guerrilla warfare against railways, roads and telephones. In Néry, Reinach, Urquhart and Neville stayed up all night preparing explosive charges, grenades and incendiary pots until the almond-paste smell gave them all a headache. The feeling that the end of their ordeal was in sight had grown so strong it was almost possible to reach out and touch it, and it no longer occurred to either Neville or Urquhart to question their stay in the district or complain that they were not being sent on their way. Almost without being aware of it, they had become involved in Néry's determination to be free.

Few of them had realized that Cassino was the key to Rome or that Rome was the key to the invasion, but on 4 June they heard that the Italian capital had fallen and that Roosevelt had announced that Berlin would be next.

Marie-Claude was short-tempered with worry. With Hössenfelder's help no longer welcomed, the farm had begun to go down again. Neville had no time to soften the blow by paying her the small attentions she'd grown used to, and this only served to increase the tension. Like everyone else, Neville was absorbed in the endless discussions that went on nightly about what they could do with their weapons now they had them, the endless counting and re-counting of ammunition – as if they thought that it might have evaporated or been eaten by mice – the constant admiring of the shining inner workings of their machine-guns. It was a man's world in which she no longer had any influence, and it left her desolate.

Only Urquhart stood aloof. He continued his training sessions in the woods. He even entered into the endless discussions of what they should do. But always he was slightly cynical, slightly sceptical, as though he felt they were only playing at soldiers. Yet he too paid no attention to Marie-Claude, and she was starved of affection. Desperately wanting to be in love with someone, she wasn't sure whom; and, filled with angry frustration, she could only take her problem to Father Pol. Her eyes filled with infinite distress, she sat opposite him, bolt upright in her chair and hostile in her misery, expecting – demanding – help. The old man had long since guessed what was troubling her and he poured her a measure from his dwindling store of marc and placed it carefully beside her, saying nothing, waiting for her to speak. She didn't even seem to notice as he sat down opposite her.

Adjusting his thick glasses, he stared at her warily. She was an attractive girl, with a flair for dress when she wasn't wearing the men's clothes she used about the farm. Everything in the cluttered and ugly little room, smelling of the old man's body odour, looked shabby and colourless beside her.

'Is it possible to love twice, Father?' she asked bluntly.

Father Pol sighed and scratched at the emery of blue bristle on his chin. As he'd watched her grow up through the war, seeing her grief as she'd lost her husband and then the man she was going to marry in his place, he'd often wanted to take her head in his hands and comfort her. But he'd been anointed to console only with words, and sometimes – to a young girl – words were as dry as old bones and just as uninteresting.

'Are you in love again, child?' he asked.

Marie-Claude lifted her head, her face full of solemn beauty. There were tears on her eyelashes and she wasn't sure whether they were caused by sadness or just plain frustration.

'I think so, Father,' she said.

'Who?'

'I'm not sure. I don't know.'

Father Pol was puzzled and she went on. 'I loved my husband when he was alive, Father.'

'He was a fine, virile man.'

'But he's been dead now for four years. Is it wrong to forget him?'

'It would be a miracle, child, if you didn't.'

Marie-Claude sighed. 'I have a farm, Father,' she said. 'I need a man for the farm and I need a man for me.'

'I'm sure you won't find it hard, my child,' the priest said. 'I'm sorry sometimes that I'm old and married to the church.'

'There's so much to do.'

'The Lord never intended that the Via Crucis should be travelled with ease. Duty is bitter, child, but the rewards are splendid, and Almighty God in His wisdom knows best.'

Marie-Claude drew a deep breath. '*My* worries probably seem unimportant to God. Ernestine Bona – '

Father Pol held up his hand. 'There's a statue of the Sacred Heart in the bedrooms of many wanton women,' he said. 'It doesn't seem to make young men wish to possess their vessels in honour, or their vessels want to be so possessed. Even so, though I sometimes find the conduct of Christians deplorable, I still think the arm of the Lord is round us.'

'Do you think the English are hypocrites, Father?'

Father Pol's face was expressionless. This was something he'd been half-expecting. 'Our two friends at the farm?' he asked.

Marie-Claude frowned. 'I hear that after ten o'clock at night the English are the same as Frenchmen. Yet they don't seem to notice *me*.'

'Perhaps they feel their duty lies elsewhere.'

Marie-Claude's head jerked up at once, her eyes ablaze with indignation. 'Who?' she demanded.

Father Pol smiled. 'Not "who", child – "what". Their country, for instance. Perhaps to them love's a luxury they can't afford at the moment. Perhaps, like you, they're waiting for the right time.'

Marie-Claude sniffed. 'When it comes, they'll probably go away.'

'That's a possibility. God teaches us not to count our chickens before they're hatched.'

'And anyway, what can *we* do? Just because we've got some weapons, it doesn't mean we know anything about fighting.'

Father Pol gestured. 'We do what we can,' he said. 'You've heard the story about the juggler who wanted to make an offering but, as he was poverty-stricken, all he could do was toss up his knives and plates in front of the statue of the Virgin until the sweat ran down his face. But since this was all he had to offer, the Madonna herself stepped down from the pedestal and wiped the sweat from his brow. It's only a legend but it's beautiful, and in the same way we shall know how to behave when the time comes.'

'In the meantime, Father, I live like a nun.'

Father Pol drew a deep breath. 'Are you troubled by impure thoughts?'

Marie-Claude moved restlessly, her mouth mutinous. Sometimes, she felt, she derived her only pleasure from them. It was the absence of action that bothered her. 'If they looked at me, Father, it would help. Underneath my clothes I'm a woman.'

'I'm aware of that; like most of the men in Néry. God made the human body. Even the bits the religious perfectionists don't always like. But these are troublous times, child, and you must possess your soul in patience. What bothers us all is nerves and the fact that we're growing a little on edge. I try to be consoled by the fact that the Germans are too.'

By this time half Néry knew about the parachute drop and, listening to them, it appeared that they had all taken part in it.

'I've just been talking to another one who was there,' Urquhart said as they ate their evening meal. 'This one swore he carried two of the big containers away under his arms.'

Neville laughed, but Marie-Claude kept her eyes down on her plate.

Reinach couldn't sit still. 'If they don't invade soon,' he complained, 'it'll be too late! It's June now. For God's sake, it'll be autumn again before long.'

That evening the weather was bad, with the rain heavy on the roof and the wind roaring through the trees to rattle the windows and shake the shutters. The atmospherics on the old radio made it impossible to hear and, after thundering on it for a good half-hour with her fist, Madame Lamy switched off in disgust.

'They'll not come tomorrow,' she said. 'That's certain. They'd all drown.'

But within half an hour, Reinach was tapping at the back door, wearing a rubber coat dripping with water. His eyes were bulging with excitement. 'It's on!' he announced, his wide empty mouth splitting his face from ear to ear. 'Didn't you hear the messages?'

Marie-Claude dived for the radio but Reinach grabbed her arm. 'It's finished! They've stopped now! But I heard him! It might have been de Gaulle himself for all I know. He said we had to gather and transmit information and that it would be of the most vital importance to the progress of the operation.'

Marie-Claude ran to where Urquhart was repairing a broken stall in the cow-byre with Neville. 'It's on!' she yelled. 'Come quickly!'

Reinach was still dragging off his rubber coat when Father Pol appeared, coming through the back of the stackyard. Almost immediately behind him was young de Frager. 'The message came,' he announced. 'We must start at once!'

Urquhart's expression showed his usual disbelief. 'To do what?' he asked.

De Frager gestured wildly. 'This is a great date in history,' he said. 'We must be part of it.'

'Well, go on, how?'

De Frager glared and Father Pol leaned forward. 'You spend too much time asking how, my son,' he said.

Marie-Claude was also staring angrily at Urquhart. He puzzled her. Sometimes he seemed sympathetic towards what they were hoping to do. At others he was merely cynical.

'And *where*,' she said. 'And *when*.'

Urquhart looked up at her and smiled, refusing to be drawn into the acrimony of an argument, and Neville pushed forward.

'Surely we can do something,' he insisted.

'What?' Urquhart asked.

'For Christ's sake, stop saying "how" and "what".'

Urquhart's eyes narrowed. 'When you can prove you have some idea what the hell you're wanting to do, I will,' he said.

'All you do is sneer at everybody else's suggestions.'

'And all *you* do is hypnotize yourself with your own

bloody visions of glory – like *they* do. We're nothing. Remember that. Nothing. A group of bloody amateurs who won't even give their full attention to learning to use what weapons they've got. We couldn't even put on the simplest field exercise.'

De Frager pushed between them. 'They're probably on their way already,' he said. 'Any day now we'll be free! God's surely on our side!'

Father Pol shrugged. 'God's been on so many sides already,' he said gently. 'Sometimes on both sides at once.'

De Frager gestured. '*Someone's* got to have the courage to stand up to them! The Lord didn't come down from Heaven just to prevent men getting into bed with the wrong women or to tell old ladies it's time they went to church again! There are Germans on the sacred soil of France! We should drive them back to their own filthy country!'

'When they're beaten they'll go on their own,' Urquhart pointed out.

'Merely letting them go isn't enough,' Reinach growled, for once grudgingly siding with de Frager. 'When it's all over, other men will say "We helped to free France." *We* need to say it too.'

Tarnera had also heard the broadcast but when he passed on its contents to Klemens, the colonel looked at the rain pouring down the windows and the wildly tossing trees outside. He couldn't believe that the allies would risk all their elaborate plans, their fleet of ships and thousands of men's lives, by launching them into such diabolical weather.

The possibility worried him, nevertheless, and he telephoned General Dannhüber for instructions. Dannhüber sounded as much on edge as everyone else.

'How can I give you instructions,' he demanded, 'when I don't know what to instruct against?'

'Is it the invasion, General?'

'Rommel says it isn't imminent. My advice to you, Klemens, is sit on it. They haven't come yet, that's for certain. I've just been in touch with Paris.'

Mollified, Klemens telephoned Major Doench at Rolandpoint and Major Rieckhoff at St Seigneur, and discussed possible action with them before coming to the conclusion that, lacking information, the only thing they could do was wait. As he finally put the telephone down, Klemens called in Klein-Wuttig and Tarnera.

'Are we ready?' he asked.

'We have an alert out throughout the command,' Klein-Wuttig said. 'Guards have been doubled, all vehicles have been immobilized and every man's been told to sleep fully dressed, with his weapons alongside him.'

'Good. Good. Security?'

'Checked,' Tarnera said. 'Patrols in the village and sentries doubled on the château.' He smiled. 'I should hate anyone to burst in and slit *my* throat.'

Klein-Wuttig scowled at him and Klemens waved them away before they started arguing. 'You'd better get some sleep,' he said. 'But make sure the telephone orderly knows there's to be no dozing. And one of you had better be on call all night. Arrange it how you like.'

After they'd gone, Klemens went to bed himself. When the allied parachutists arrived, they'd not drop near Dijon, he knew, and certainly not at Néry. Then he remembered that the roads from the south and from Paris back to the Reich cut the command north of St Seigneur and, realizing the allies might well try to stop supplies from Germany, he started to worry again.

He tried to make himself sleep, but he remained uneasy and twice he sat up, once to make a note of something he felt he'd need to check the following day, once to make sure the telephone orderly had had no messages. He finally managed to drop off just before dawn but it was a restless sleep and he was still tossing when the telephone alongside his bed rang. It was Tarnera.

'I thought you'd like to know, Herr Oberst,' he said. 'They *are* coming.'

'Who're coming?' Klemens was still befuddled.

'The allies, Herr Oberst. I've just received a report that glider troops and paratroops have been flying over the Normandy coast in millions.'

'Nonsense!' Klemens could still hear the rain against the window.

'I'm afraid not, Herr Oberst,' Tarnera said. 'It's just been confirmed.'

Then Klemens realized it was daylight and sat up sharply. 'What's the time?' he asked.

'Five fifty-five, Herr Oberst.'

'It must be just another raid, like the Dieppe thing. Surely.'

'Not this time, Herr Oberst. It seems the sea's black with ships and they're firing on the coastal defences.'

'The Führer said it would come in the Pas de Calais area.'

Tarnera sounded sceptical. 'I'm afraid that's a figment of the Führer's imagination, like the Reich that would last for a thousand years. Quite a lot of it's already crumbled in Russia and Italy.'

'Shut up, Tarnera!' Klemens was wide awake now and bad-tempered with lack of sleep. 'You ask for trouble. How did you find out? From Dijon?'

'No, Herr Oberst. It came through headquarters at La Roche-Guyon and via Le Mans.'

'I find it hard to believe.'

'Perhaps we've *all* been kidding ourselves,' Tarnera said dryly. 'I gather Paris didn't believe it either.'

They didn't even believe it in Néry.

Marie-Claude was picking up the twigs and small branches that had been snapped off by the wind, and her mother was sweeping up the petals of the blown roses that scattered the front of the house, when Reinach fell into the yard over the wall at the back.

'Haven't you heard?' he yelled. 'They've landed in Normandy!'

'What!'

'Four o'clock this morning! Near Caen! Put the radio on!'

As they switched on, the BBC was already playing 'La Marseillaise', and Reinach, Madame Lamy and Marie-

Claude stood still and solemn and straight. As it finished, they were all reaching to embrace each other when it changed to 'God Save The King', and they all looked hurriedly at Urquhart and Neville and stiffened again. As the last notes died away, Marie-Claude's face split in one of her wide electric grins. It died immediately as a new tune started.

'What's this?' she demanded.

' "Star-Spangled Banner",' Neville said. 'It's the American one.'

Marie-Claude's eyes blazed. 'For God's sake, do we have to listen to "The Red Flag", and the Dutch and the Belgian and the Australian and Scottish national anthems before we can move?' She dived for the kitchen and came back with a bottle of marc and began to splash it into tumblers in vast helpings that burned their throats.

'Eisenhower made a broadcast in French,' Reinach said. 'His accent wasn't too bad. I almost understood him. De Gaulle's going to speak at lunch-time. The allies have kept their promises. It's up to us now to keep ours.'

The yell was already going round the fields – 'They've landed!' – and Lionel Dring appeared at Father Pol's presbytery, his eyes blazing with excitement. 'They've come, Father! We should ring the bells.'

'There aren't any bells,' Father Pol pointed out. 'The Germans stole them to make guns.'

'Then, for God's sake, let's bang a drum or something! The allies have come back to France!'

Caught by the tempest, Father Pol sent word that there would be a special mass, and by mid-morning black-clad figures in their best clothes were heading towards the church. Everyone in the village turned up – even Neville who wasn't a Catholic. The shabby old building with its carved stations of the cross and its agonized Christ, its worn seats and peeling pink-washed walls, was full of optimism and joy and hope. The Baronne arrived on the arm of her great-grandson and followed by old Balmaceda – looking like an ancient doll with her bright artificial hair set against the dramatic black of the Baron.

Father Pol had decided that it was time to follow the example of Father Xavier in Rolandpoint and was already thundering away. 'Nazism and Vichy fascist institutions are anti-Christian!' he was shouting. 'It is our duty to contribute to their defeat!'

When they'd finished shouting 'Vive la France', they sang 'La Marseillaise', the tune surging to the roof, then they all streamed out into the sunshine purged and sanctified.

Klein-Wuttig watched them, puzzled. There was no sign of war in Néry and his orders were not to provoke trouble. Yet it filled his brain with worms as he saw tricolours being waved at him by children too small to argue with, because he was fully aware that older brothers and sisters had passed them out and were carefully watching his reactions.

The radios remained on all day, heavy with German announcements and threats, and instructions from Radio Paris and Radio Vichy. Later, de Gaulle spoke.

'It is he!' Madame Lamy breathed, almost as if she were hearing a god give tongue.

'He's only a man,' Marie-Claude said, looking at Neville and Urquhart.

'He's France! He means France to us!'

'He means nothing at all unless we hear him.'

There was a lot of static and a few precautionary thumps from Madame Lamy; nobody in the whole village was making any pretence of doing anything else but listen. 'The Battle of France has begun,' the sombre voice intoned. 'In the nation, in the empire, and in the armed forces there is now one purpose, one desire. Look upward. There, where the burden of our blood and years lies like a lowering cloud upon us, there the light of our greatness is shining through.' It struck exactly the right note and left them all elated and entranced.

'He said we had to destroy the enemy,' Sergeant Dréo yelled.

'And the Germans,' Father Pol pointed out dryly, 'have said that their troops have been given orders to shoot anyone co-operating with the invasion.'

'That's right,' Guardia Moch agreed. 'In fact, Pétain says we're going to be plunged into civil war, and Goebbels says the allies have done exactly what the Germans wanted and walked into a trap.'

'You'll have us believe soon that Hitler *planned* the invasion to make a German victory,' Marie-Claude snorted. 'The Germans will collapse.'

'No,' Sergeant Dréo said. 'They're good fighters. I know. It'll be a long struggle. We must make preparations. Is everyone in the réseau ready?'

Reinach looked sheepish. 'Some of them.'

'Why not all?'

'Because some of them have gone off north to see what they can do. Gaudin's brother. Yves Rapin. And young Guélis. The barman from the Frontière came over from Rolandpoint for them. Even young Hénault. He rolled up his father's 1914 kit and set off after them. They said they were sick of waiting here for something to happen.'

They stared accusingly at Urquhart, as though it were his fault, and Dréo pounded the table.

'*We must do something!*' he shouted, and his words seemed like a special plea to the Almighty for guidance.

But what?

With few young men left – even, for that matter, few middle-aged men who'd been brave in the other war – the knowledge that they were old and rusty made the following days bitter. There was an enormous sense of anti-climax, and they sat far into the night waiting for things to crystallize.

More youths vanished, to appear in the hills behind the village, wearing scarves round their necks and clutching rifles and Sten guns, magazines sticking out of every pocket. De Frager was prominent among them and there was a great deal of show, but not much action except that a few telephone lines were cut. There were also rumours of Milice and collaborationists further to the east being caught and beaten up or even shot. Then they heard that the narrow-gauge railway down to St Seigneur had been torn up five kilometres from Rolandpoint, and the feeling that something was happening at last lifted their hearts and filled them full of elation – until they learned that the job had been so badly botched it had been repaired almost immediately. Brisson's brother, who was a garde-voie and responsible for that stretch of track, had been taken out and shot although he'd had nothing to do with the sabotage. His son was said to be walking round with a gun in his pocket swearing to kill the Communist who'd done it. It made them all hesitate a little.

Finally they learned that at Noidan-sur-Clamery, over to the west of Dijon, the villagers, made bold by a parachute drop, had openly attacked a German column. Two lorries had been set on fire and three men killed, but the following day German-controlled Cossacks had swept up from Dijon; fifteen men and boys had been shot and several women raped. The guns that had appeared in the woods round Néry vanished immediately and the young men were back in their homes that night, worried sick in case they'd been seen.

'We must *do* something,' Reinach nagged. 'London have said we must.'

'You're not strong enough,' Urquhart pointed out. '*Your* strength lies in simply existing.'

Neville sighed. He was profoundly touched by the need of the people of Néry to salvage their pride, but he'd also read enough history to know in his heart that Urquhart was right and they were wrong. Night after night he had defended their need to do something and every time Urquhart had demolished his arguments with his experience. Yet, despite his emotional involvement, his common sense told him that the time hadn't yet come for them to act.

'In case you haven't noticed it,' he said, 'you live in what will probably be the last bit of France to be liberated. You're a long way from British airfields, close to Germany and in an area that's strongly held.' He saw their eyes on his face and drew a deep breath. 'Wait,' he urged. 'The Germans are avoiding trouble because they think you're stronger than you are, and one of the first historical principles of war is to make your enemy think just that. If you attack them, they'll know you're not.'

Father Pol frowned. 'I notice you talk a great deal about this history, my son,' he observed thoughtfully.

'History's a part of warfare,' Neville said. 'English soldiers learn it at Sandhurst, the French at St Cyr, the Americans at West Point, the Germans at Potsdam. It helps them to avoid trouble the next time the same situation arises. British cavalry have always been careful to avoid getting themselves into the mess they found themselves in at Balaclava.'

Father Pol's eyebrows rose. 'There were *British* cavalry at Balaclava?' he said, surprised. 'I thought it was the Chasseurs d'Afrique who won that battle.'

'It wasn't won,' Neville said more harshly. 'And it wasn't the Chasseurs d'Afrique who lost it.'

For a moment, Father Pol seemed about to take up the challenge but then he changed his mind. 'This history,' he probed. 'You have studied it?'

Neville nodded.

'And it is this same history which makes you suggest that we should not yet attack the Germans?'

Neville leaned forward. 'Time's on your side,' he pointed out. 'Any military planner would tell you the same.'

'Even this Wellington you speak about?' Dréo asked.

'Even Napoleon. And if anyone knew his history, he did.'

Father Pol nodded, satisfied. 'Very well,' he said. 'I am convinced. We will wait.'

The others seemed to agree with him. All except Reinach who got to his feet and stared at them with angry eyes. He seemed as taut and tense as a tightly wound spring.

'I just wish *I* were in Normandy!' he growled.

2

'If something doesn't happen soon,' Urquhart said, 'this bloody place will explode.'

For a whole month there had been no sign of the liberation they'd expected, no sign of any backward movement from the Germans. And when the weather at the end of June deteriorated into gale force winds which wrecked shipping off the Normandy coast, broke up floating piers and swept away helpless vessels, it even began to look as though it would be 1948 before Burgundy was freed.

'For the love of God,' Reinach raged, 'when *shall* we be able to do something?'

Though in Dijon and Besançon railway engines were being disabled, and points, roundhouses and bridges blown up, seen against the vast panorama of the invasion, they were mere pinpricks which the Germans always savagely avenged. In Gascony, twelve hundred of them had wiped out eighty men of the Maquis, shooting the wounded or smashing their skulls with rifle butts before forbidding their families to collect their bodies so that they were left in the sun to rot. Only on the Vercors massif, near Grenoble, was there any organized resistance.

'They've been free there since the eleventh,' Reinach said. 'They simply hung out flags and sang "La Marseillaise", and got away with it.'

The news stirred the men of Rolandpoint to demand their weapons back. If resistance were possible in the south, they argued, then it should be possible in the Côte d'Or. For many in Néry the invasion had been set up to liberate not France but Néry, and more young men dug out their fathers' equipment from the other war and disappeared towards the fighting.

'If we don't do something soon,' Reinach said, 'we shall have no young men left.'

'Wait,' Neville insisted. 'For God's sake, wait! When you move it's got to be when they can't call in the tanks or the Luftwaffe. Guerrilla warfare must never condense into a solid body. Clausewitz said that. He was a German, and German generals have all read him. Your time will come; every German scheme in history's contained the seed of its own destruction.'

'This doesn't sound like the fair-play English,' Ernouf growled.

'It's a good way to fight a war,' Urquhart growled back.

In the atmosphere of frustration and fearful hope, the news of Oradour-sur-Glane in the Haute Vienne dropped like a bombshell. The Germans had mistaken the place for Oradour-sur-Vayres, where fighting had taken place, and the SS had swept down to shoot all the men and lock all the women and children in the church which they had then destroyed with explosives. As the people died, the village itself had been drenched with petrol and set ablaze. Six hundred and forty-three people had died and when a mass was held by the Bishop of Limoges, time bombs, planted by the Milice, had been discovered in the crypt of the cathedral.

Nobody else argued with Neville.

Unknown to the villagers, the Germans were as edgy as they were.

To Colonel Klemens things seemed to be getting out of hand. Intelligence reports stated that fifty thousand Frenchmen had been secretly armed and were only waiting their chance.

'It's exaggerated, Herr Oberst,' Klein-Wuttig insisted. 'It's not possible. They haven't enough ammunition. Unskilled soldiers waste it. They'd need millions of rounds.'

'There are three thousand people on the Vercors massif,' Tarnera pointed out, 'simply defying us.'

Klein-Wuttig's mouth twisted. 'If *that's* all they're doing,' he said, 'they don't bother me.'

With the tension building up, the news came that the allies were at last on the move again in Italy and had reached the Arno, Ancona and Leghorn, and on 20 July General Dannhüber arrived at Néry for a hasty conference. Klemens drank a little more than usual, so that as soon as Dannhüber had gone he found himself dozing at his desk. The telephone jerked him back to wakefulness. It was Tarnera.

'What is it?' he demanded. 'Not another invasion, surely?'

'Perhaps even more, Herr Oberst. I've just had Paris on the telephone. They've got a report that the Führer's been assassinated.'

'*What?*' Klemens was wide awake and bolt upright at once. 'It's not possible!'

'It's not even sense with all those drugs he takes these days, it's like killing a corpse.'

'Shut up, Tarnera,' Klemens shouted. 'If you can't keep quiet, I'll have you posted away from here – if only for your own safety. Sturmbannführer Frobinius was up here the other day and he was asking about you. If *he* gets it into his head to dislike you, there's nothing I can do. Go on with your report.'

There was a long silence on the telephone and when Tarnera's voice came again it was quiet and controlled and devoid of sarcasm. 'It was heard on the Swiss radio, Herr Oberst. They picked up a Berlin announcement. There's a state of emergency in Germany and the Wehrmacht's taken over the protection of the Reich. It seems the conspirators are also in control in Munich, Vienna and Paris.'

Klemens drew a deep breath. He was an uncomplicated man. For a long time he'd seen victory slipping through German fingers, and this new situation was one he'd been envisaging with a sort of transfixed horror for some time.

'Have you heard how they regard it in Dijon?' he asked.

'With what I would call doubt and confusion, Herr Oberst,' Tarnera said. 'They're waiting for confirmation.'

'What do you think we ought to do?'

'The same as Dijon, Herr Oberst. Nothing.'

By evening, they were all sweating on the radio news. There had been warnings of an announcement and at six o'clock it came.

'An attempt has been made on the Führer's life,' it stated. 'But he has received only slight burns and bruises and no other injuries.'

Tarnera frowned. 'He's got a charmed life,' he said.

Klein-Wuttig turned. 'Were you expecting he might die?'

'I think we'd better make our number with Dijon,' Klemens said. 'Please call them for me, Tarnera.'

As Tarnera handed over the telephone, Klemens seated himself at the Baronne's table. 'I've just heard the announcement, General,' he said smoothly. 'Let me be the first to state my loyalty to the Führer.'

'I should hold your water,' Dannhüber barked back bluntly. '*I*'ve just had a signal by teleprinter signed by Field Marshal von Witzleben who, as you'll doubtless remember, was dismissed in 1942. It states quite categorically that the Führer's dead and that non-combatant Party leaders have seized power. It declares a military state of emergency with Witzleben in command of the armed forces.'

Klemens' jaw sagged. 'Where does that put *us*?'

General Dannhüber was in no doubt about where it put *him*. 'It puts me,' he said, 'exactly where I was before. And, if you've any sense, that's exactly where it should put you.'

As Klemens put the telephone down uncertainly, Klein-Wuttig reached for his hat. 'I'll make a tour of the command,' he said. 'These French bastards are bound to try to make something of it.'

He wasn't far wrong. In St Seigneur a man ran from a bar shouting, 'This is it! The swine will collapse without him to shove a ramrod up their backsides!'

Yelling hysterically, he tried to snatch a rifle from a German sentry and for his trouble was immediately seized and shot. From tearful relatives it appeared he was a habitual drunkard, known as the Fleabag because of his indifferent personal habits, and only his dying had redeemed a wasted life. Since the news of the Berlin conspiracy had not yet been broadcast on the French radio, the owner of the bar was also shot – for listening to the BBC.

It was an uncertain day, broken only by the news that the Vercors cell had at last been attacked by elements of three Wehrmacht divisions with air support. It was an even more uneasy night, and Klemens slept badly, dreaming that French Communists and German Gestapo were coming through the window. There was no mention of any assassination in the next morning's papers and until noon the Germans and the French in Néry, all of them well aware of what had happened, were eyeing each other cautiously for a sign of weakness.

Late in the afternoon, Klemens was holding a signal

from Dijon on which several words stood out '. . . it is recommended that nothing should be done until the situation can be assessed . . .' when the radio came to life.

The harsh voice made him jump. 'If I speak to you today,' it said, 'it is first in order that you should hear my voice and know that I am unhurt and well, and secondly, that you should know of a crime unparalleled in German history . . .'

'He doesn't sound very dead,' Tarnera said flatly.

'. . . The bomb,' the harsh voice went on, 'was placed by Colonel Count von Stauffenberg. It exploded two metres to my right. One of those with me has died. A number of colleagues very dear to me were very severely injured. I myself sustained only very minor scratches, bruises and burns. I regard this as a confirmation of the task imposed upon me by Providence . . .'

They heard him out in silence and the angry voice went on to order that no one, from private to field marshal, should obey any orders passed out in the name of the conspirators.

'. . . It is everyone's duty to arrest, or if they resist, to kill at sight anyone issuing or handling any such orders.'

Klemens dropped the signal he was holding as if it were red-hot, his heart shrivelling as details were given of the round-up and execution of the conspirators.

As the radio stopped, Klein-Wuttig appeared and tossed his hat on to the table. 'They've brought gliders in,' he said.

Klemens' head jerked up. 'What the devil for? I thought they'd caught them all.'

'All who?'

'The conspirators.'

'Oh, that!' Klein-Wuttig shrugged. 'That's finished, Herr Oberst. I heard it down at the command post. No, this is Vercors. It'll be all over before long.'

After Oradour, no one had any doubts about the outcome of the fight going on to the south. The gaiety that had existed after the rescue of the Rolandpoint weapons, their own parachute drop, and the defeat of the Germans in the search for the Baronne's paintings drained away again. Those events belonged to a different epoch, a period when they had almost begun to believe that the Germans were just fools who could be toyed with. What was happening to the south was the reality, and it was as though the whole village was holding its breath in an aching tension as the fighting continued.

Moch brought back little snippets of information which had come from Grenoble, and they all waited, praying the Germans would be repulsed. The Germans were equally on edge and went everywhere preceded by motor cyclists who continually dismounted and deployed to make reconnaissances. They were stony-faced, giving nothing away, and when Elsie, out with Jean-Frédéric Dréo, barked at Klein-Wuttig's car, the driver stopped and gave her a boot up the backside that sent her yelling to the farm. Two weeks later, an SS man appeared from Dijon and stuck up a large notice outside the mairie informing them that the Vercors resistance had been wiped out and reprisals were now taking place.

Urquhart showed no emotion. 'If you want to play at generals,' he said, 'join the liberation army.'

Marie-Claude turned on him at once. Her expression was angry but there were tears in her eyes as well. 'They tried,' she snapped. 'They just didn't have your experience.'

Urquhart's shoulders moved. 'It'll not be the experience of a couple of shot-down airmen that'll do the job when the time comes,' he said flatly. 'It'll be common sense and plain French guts. I shan't be here, anyway.'

Marie-Claude's eyes widened. 'You're leaving?'

'We're doing no good here.'

She caught her breath, shocked and bewildered, and it was a moment or two before she spoke. 'You *can't* go,' she said.

Urquhart's expression was blank. 'I think I can.'

She stared at him, her scrutiny close and accusing. 'What will become of us?'

'The allies will come soon. All you have to do is lay low and keep quiet. Néry will be all right.'

'I didn't mean Néry.' Her eyes showed the depth of her distress, and they gazed at each other in silence, her face entreating pity. 'I meant me.' She paused and gave a helpless gesture. 'My mother. The farm. There'll be no one here. Will Neville also be going?'

'If I can persuade him.'

Marie-Claude's eyes grew angry. 'We've already lost the German,' she said.

Urquhart's eyes glowed with anger. 'We're supposed to be airmen,' he said, 'Not day-labourers.'

She made no further comment but, that night, Urquhart discovered that his papers had disappeared. For a while he stared at the wallet with its few French notes, then slipped down the winding stairs from the attic under the roof. Marie-Claude's bedroom showed a light under the door and she was sitting up in bed with a shawl over her shoulders, staring at a Michelin map of the district. She glanced up as he entered but made no comment at his appearance in her room. She even seemed to be expecting him.

'Where are my papers?' Urquhart demanded.

'I don't know.' Her eyes were still on the map. 'If you've lost them, they'll be hard to replace, with travel restricted by the invasion.'

Urquhart's face was grim. 'You've got them, haven't you?' he said. 'You never intended us to leave! You wanted us here – to put fences up and mend the barn and feed the pigs. You just wanted a couple of free farmhands.'

'Is there anything wrong with that?' She lowered the map and stared at him defiantly, aware of her guilt but sickened at the thought that she would be on her own again, bearing all the responsibility, doing all the work.

She lifted the map again as if she regarded the matter closed, trying to assert her will by bluff, but Urquhart smashed it from her hands and grabbed for her. His fingers in her hair, he pulled her head round to face him, so that her neck was curved back, a vein at the side of it throbbing. Then he saw that there were tears in her eyes and abruptly he released her and pushed her away. For a moment she stared at him; then, standing stiffly upright by the bed, her head up, her hands at her sides, she quietly began to cry.

Urquhart frowned. 'Does our being here mean so damned much to you?' he asked.

She stared at him, her mind full of fearful uncertainties, and for the first time he noticed the faint lavender circles under her eyes that indicated how tired she was. 'The farm's all I have,' she choked, dizzy and despairing as she saw it being snatched away. 'It's all I've ever had. I've fought to keep it ever since my husband died.'

Then her eyes became fierce again. 'Go, if you want to!' she said. 'Those who are dead are dead! There's no going back! I've accepted that! But no one's ever going to beat me! This is my country and this is my land and it's a part of me that never changes! There's no land in the world like this!'

She was making no appeals to him, stating no case and asking no mercy, but, because he was of farming stock himself, he knew exactly what she meant. She reached into a drawer beside the bed and, taking out the documents he was seeking, she flung them at him. 'There you are!' she said. 'You can go now, if you wish!'

Urquhart didn't move and she looked up at him, her eyes still bright with tears. Then a huge sob racked her body and, as she turned her head away so that he shouldn't see her misery, he pulled her to him and let her weep out her unhappiness against him. Her whole frame was shaking, the first sign of weakness he'd ever seen in her, the first crack in her armour.

'Oh, Urk't!' she wailed.

He held her for a while, letting her exhaust herself with her weeping. Then he swung her into his arms and lifted her on to the bed. She stared up at him, her eyes wide, her lips parted, a vague disquietude in her heart, wondering what he intended. But he simply pulled the sheet up to her chin and tucked it about her neck.

'Very well,' he said. 'Not yet. We'll stay a little longer.'

She was quiet the following morning, not looking at him, and for the first time she seemed uninterested when Father Pol arrived with Reinach and Ernouf with news of what the Germans had done on the Vercors massif. Men had been shot and tortured. One woman had been raped seventeen times with a doctor holding her pulse. Another, a Maquis officer, had been disembowelled and left to die with her intestines wound round her neck. It had stopped all demands for action in Néry.

Father Pol sighed. 'Perhaps,' he said, 'the time's coming when it'll be *worth* dying despite the odds.'

'There's nothing to fear in death,' Reinach muttered. 'What we really fear's the prelude, the process of dying. We should take the risk and face the Germans.'

'Who?' Marie-Claude asked quietly. 'Sergeant Dréo with his wooden leg and Father Pol with his belly? There are no young men left.'

'I think there are,' Father Pol said quietly.

'Who?'

Father Pol shifted himself in his chair for comfort. 'One is an ex-soldier with a great knowledge of fighting. He has fought the Germans on three fronts and knows how they behave. The other is an expert at battle plans and military history.' He stared at Neville. 'You've lived long enough here to become part of this village,' he went on. He glanced at Marie-Claude. 'You've even entered into the lives of some of us. But we can't ride into Heaven on a lot of historical quotations, my son. We have finally to take a chance on dying to destroy this monstrous cruelty called Nazism.'

Neville looked uncomfortable. 'You can count on me,' he said. 'I'll help.'

Father Pol was not satisfied. 'Helping isn't enough,' he pointed out. 'Tell us what to do! Tell us how to destroy the Germans! From the depths of history and for the love of Heaven, produce us a plan!'

3

The fighting in the north continued, but nothing had changed in Néry.

Depressed by the charge he'd been given, Neville wrapped a billhook in a piece of sacking. Tying it to the handlebars of Madame Lamy's bicycle as if he were going hedging, he set off out of the village and up the slopes. His face wore a dogged look of determination because he knew Father Pol was in earnest and was waiting now with the others for something brilliant to emerge. He returned in the evening to sit at the kitchen table with a map of the district and a piece of paper on which he wrote down scratchy notes – deliberately illegible so that no one could guess at the blankness of his mind.

Because the Germans were still in control in Burgundy, the breaking of the iron ring round the Normandy bridgehead at the end of July and the beginning of August came as a total surprise. Fourteen days later, as they heard that the Americans had landed in the south, hope leapt up once more.

'On the Feast of the Assumption,' Father Pol crowed.

'Obviously divine intervention,' Reinach said dryly.

Neville said nothing. Conscious of the eyes of Father Pol on him, he was aware only of the dreadful dearth of ideas.

The following week, with the allies already well into Brittany and as far south as Nantes, news arrived that Pétain, the father-figure of Vichy France, had disappeared towards the German frontier with his jackal, Laval; and, as the Americans began to pound up the valley of the Rhône, it seemed that liberation was actually coming at last. Suddenly the Germans were retreating everywhere and German air activity, which had stopped with the invasion, started again, searching for the Maquis and stirring up the thoughts of revenge and the salvaging of honour all the more.

'We are still waiting,' Dréo hissed at Neville as he cycled past the forge.

Putting his head down, Neville drove doggedly at the pedals. When he returned to the farm, he refused to satisfy Marie-Claude's curiosity about what he'd been doing – chiefly because he'd been doing nothing but stare helplessly at the curves and angles of the countryside from the ridge of land that ran round the village, his mind empty except for the despair of ever filling it with anything worth while. Producing a military plan was a very different thing from admiring one that had already been formulated.

The following day he tucked his trousers firmly into his socks once more and rode off yet again. Marie-Claude stared after him, bewildered.

'What is he doing?' she asked Urquhart.

Urquhart grinned. 'He's playing at Peter Pan. You've heard of Peter Pan?'

She sniffed. 'I have been educated too. But to a Frenchman, Peter Pan is unthinkable.'

When Neville returned he was still not forthcoming and there was even a look of anguish on his face as he disappeared to his room with a map and nothing else but a piece of cheese. Marie-Claude's warm heart, longing to give love and sympathy, went out to him and, seeing Urquhart smiling at her, she whirled on him.

'Why don't *you* go and help him?' she snapped.

The tension in the village was obvious. To Tarnera it was just like a spring wound up too tight.

'I think they're measuring our throats for the nooses,' he observed.

Klein-Wuttig took out a small pocket book and made a note in it. 'I suppose you realize this is defeatist talk, Tarnera?' he said.

'What's odd about defeatism when we're being defeated?' Tarnera asked. And he was right because, with a whole German army destroyed in the killing ground at Falaise, the allies were now into open country and driving on Paris where the Resistance was already out in the streets and the German garrison preparing to throw in its hand.

The village hotheads began to talk loudly of action once

more and Communists from St Seigneur, their hair en brosse in best Resistance style, began to appear. They were neither countrymen nor even honest workmen but demagogic windbags who saw everything only in terms of their own politics.

'Our party's proved its right to rule France,' they said. 'We're already sending miniature coffins to collaborators as a warning.'

'I'll wager a few are also being sent to old ladies with weak hearts by relatives hoping to inherit their money,' Father Pol snorted. 'If the music of the holy trumpets has to be paid for with twisted guts, then let us twist the guts about the right things!'

Despite his indignant disapproval, he was nevertheless driven to climbing on his bicycle and riding at full speed to the farm to demand when Neville was going to produce his plan.

'All the world knows,' he said, 'that we not only invented democracy but also patented it and own the world copyright. But it won't live long in the hands of people like those. It's time *we* did something, if only to thwart the yahoos who wish to turn France into a political prison.

'They've blown up a roundhouse in Dijon,' he shouted accusingly from the door as he left. 'And smashed a crane – the only one in the area they had for lifting wrecked engines back on the tracks. What are *we* doing?'

'For God's sake,' Neville said as the door slammed. 'I'm not an expert! I'm only a student of history.'

Urquhart grinned. 'You and your bloody history!'

Neville whirled, 'And you and your bloody Dunkirk,' he snarled. 'You needn't think that *you* won't be part of the blasted plan when it comes off! It's not the field marshals who fight the battles! It's the brigadiers! Well, since you've fought the Germans hand to hand, teeth to teeth, eyeball to eyeball, when I finally come up with something, *you* can be the bloody brigadier!'

That night electrifying news arrived. The allies were on the outskirts of Paris and the whole of the capital was surging into the boulevards to meet them. By next morning the

Americans were in front of Notre-Dame, and Free French armour was driving down the Champs Elysées. The following day de Gaulle himself marched across the Place du Parvis Notre-Dame to attend a Te Deum in the cathedral. Paris had purged her soul and was breathing free air again after four years of humiliation.

As though at a signal, the German troops in Bourg-la-Chattel just to the north disappeared into thin air, and trucks with tricolours or red Communist banners were reported rushing through the streets containing bearded and ferocious-looking Frenchmen in uniform.

'There are flags everywhere.' Dr Mouillet had just returned from a visit to his lady friend. 'Especially outside the homes of ex-Vichyites. And they're shaving the heads of the girls who've been sleeping with Germans.'

'They should shave their pussies, too,' Lionel Dring said. 'And tattoo a swastika on each of their tits.'

Marie-Claude whirled on him. 'What do *you* know about it?' she demanded. 'How do *you* know what drove them to it?'

Dring looked surprised. He had long since ceased bothering to call on her, and he glanced angrily at Neville. 'Well, since you have the taste for a foreign lover yourself, perhaps you would too – '

Marie-Claude silenced him with a round-arm slap across the face that startled them with the noise it made. 'Get out,' she spat. 'Get out!'

When he'd gone, Neville saw she was crying and put an arm round her.

'I lost my husband in 1940,' she sobbed. 'I knew what happened between a man and a woman. I'm not just a virgin waiting for her lover. I had grown used to a man and sometimes I cried myself to sleep for want of one. And sometimes, when one of the Germans noticed me, God help me, I wondered what it would be like with him.'

As she pushed him away, her eyes full of tears, and vanished into the kitchen, Neville stared after her helplessly.

Urquhart's face was expressionless. 'It's no good, lad,' he

said quietly. '*You*'ll not get her any more than Dring will. He's too impulsive; you're not impulsive enough.'

Neville glared at him and for a moment it was on the tip of his tongue to blurt out what had happened between himself and Marie-Claude on the night when they'd saved the Rolandpoint weapons. But Urquhart was watching him with his usual cynical expression, and for a moment he even had the horrified feeling that he knew anyway.

The excitement went on into the next day. Young Dréo went over to Bourg on his Spitfire and brought back the information that the partisans of both Right and Left were opening headquarters there. There had been a parade with tricolours and red flags and a band of bugles and drums, and the place had gone mad at the sight of disciplined Frenchmen.

He could hardly speak for excitement. 'Communist execution squads are shooting Miliciens,' he said, 'and beating up shopkeepers, and the policemen who harried them in 1940. They've got the Vicomtesse de la Chattel and her boy friend in the jail, as well as all the black marketeers and members of the Croix de Feu.'

That night, to everyone's surprise, the Germans in Néry also disappeared. It was an incredible, unexpected thing, but it happened. Neville was the first to be aware of the growl of engines down the street, and together he and Urquhart and Marie-Claude pressed their faces to the gap in the shutters on the landing. Down the dusty drive to the farm and between the empty gateposts, they could see lights flashing beyond the trees and hear the grind of lorries.

The next morning, Reinach came hurtling into the kitchen. 'They've gone!' he yelled. 'North-east towards Mary-les-Rivières and Germany!'

Immediately, tricolours appeared from windows; and a few unexpected bottles appeared from the cellars. People who'd been careful to keep out of the way during the hard days conveniently forgot that they'd always previously referred to the Maquis hiding in the forest as 'terrorists' and 'woodlice', and begged to be allowed to join them so they could say they weren't collaborationists. Even old Balmaceda arrived in Mère Ledoux's bar, very drunk, with his wig over one ear and clutching an ancient dusty flask.

'Glasses, patronne,' he yelled in a cracked boozy voice. 'It's absinthe! The real stuff! It only needs a drop of pump water to make it perfect!'

A few boys, already wearing berets, scarves and illicit armbands proclaiming them members of the Gaullist Forces Françaises de l'Intérieur, were carrying carbines and had festooned their chests with belts of ammunition. Sergeant Dréo caught Neville in the stackyard and began to bellow indignantly at him. 'They've gone!' he yelled. 'Without a scratch! All we have to show for our war is four years of humiliation!'

As they argued, Elsie began to bark, and the old man's grandson came tearing down the hill on his Spitfire, his head down over the handlebars, his hair wild, his eyes bulging with horror.

'They're coming back!' he was shrieking. 'The Germans are coming back!'

As if by magic, flags, weapons, berets and armbands vanished back to their hiding places, and bottles were hurriedly stuffed out of sight. At the château, Patrice de Frager, who'd insisted on all the rooms the Germans had occupied being disinfected, hastily changed his mind. The discarded items of German equipment which had been tossed indignantly on to the lawn were quickly collected and returned to where they'd been found.

The first two Germans to appear were motor-cyclists, wearing helmets and sweating in the heat. They were grey with dust and looked tired.

'Back again!' Reinach said with strained cheerfulness from the door of Mère Ledoux's bar.

The soldiers eyed each other and one of them grinned.

'Yes,' he said. 'We're the vanguard of an SS division, and we've arrived complete with Gestapo hangmen and torture chamber.'

He was only joking, but nobody else asked questions.

Within an hour, the whole lot of them were back, and this time the village could see the SS among them. By evening, they'd learned what had happened. The Germans had circled to the north and arrived in Bourg-la-Chattel to find the place celebrating. The Vicomtesse had been released along with her collaborator lover and the members of the Croix de Feu; and the town was now short of thirty of its senior citizens, shot by Milicien survivors, together with one or two drunks and defiant youths who'd dared to shout 'Vive la France!'

It seemed that Néry wasn't intended to take part in great events, and the best they could do was fall back on working out what humiliation they could wreak on the Germans *when* they got the chance.

'How much bloody humiliation do they want?' Neville asked bitterly, conscious that Reinach, Dréo and the others had taken to watching him carefully, as though expecting his ideas would suddenly light up in little balloons above his head as they did in comic papers.

Urquhart was pitiless. '*Complete* humiliation,' he said. 'As complete as theirs has been.'

The prospect of being responsible for the deaths of men – friends as well as enemies – was too much for Neville. Organizing a battle and overseeing it at close quarters was very different from the impersonal business of dropping bombs from an aeroplane. 'Wouldn't it be sufficient if the Germans surrendered?' he asked.

Urquhart shook his head. 'They want an eye for an eye and a tooth for a tooth, and, anyway, the Germans would never surrender to the Maquis in case they were shot out of hand.'

Neville shifted uneasily in his clothes. He was an easy-going young man and his whole life had been one of avoiding decisions. Money had smoothed the way for him. You didn't make decisions when you had enough money to pay other people to make them for you. Even his service in the RAF had been short because he'd been allowed to finish his university course before being pulled into uniform.

'I don't like it,' he said uncomfortably.

Urquhart grinned. 'I was always told,' he said, 'that it was from your class that leaders came. Born to leadership, they always told us in the Regulars. In the habit of giving orders.

Ingrained ability for command. Didn't they ever tell you that you were all budding Montgomerys? Or perhaps they've begun to realize at last that an army's run by its sergeants and its colonels, and everybody in between doesn't count.'

'For Christ's sake, stop needling me,' Neville snapped. 'I'm doing what I can.'

'But not fast enough, old son.' Urquhart was infuriatingly calm. 'For a bloke who knows all about the war, you're singularly slow in showing much appreciation of it.'

'What the hell do they expect of me?' The words burst out despairingly and Urquhart laughed.

'The plan for a battle, old son,' he said. 'Drawn up like the wiring chart for a wireless set. A moves to the left in threes. B marks time while C advances at the double. Lots of little red arrows. That sort of thing.'

'You don't fight battles that way.'

Urquhart's grin died abruptly. 'I know bloody well you don't,' he snapped. 'I've been in one or two. But you've either got to prove that you don't or back out of it.'

'I wouldn't be able to look 'em in the eye if I did back out.'

'Who? Marie-Claude?'

'What do you mean?'

'Come off it. You paw her like a farm boy.'

Neville glared. Urquhart had eyes in the back of his head. 'I don't think she even looks at me,' he said.

'Just goes to show, doesn't it?' Urquhart said mildly. 'People are sometimes as bloody as they seem to be.' His smile returned. 'Still, love's a bit like war, isn't it? You might pull it off yet, if you can only produce a plan.' He gestured. '*The* plan, the masterpiece that's going to win the war, clear the Germans out of Néry, and leave her breathless with admiration.'

Neville writhed. 'I'm not arranging a bloody massacre,' he growled.

Urquhart shrugged. 'You're a fool if you think they'll settle for less,' he said.

As Neville tied the billhook to the handlebars of Madame Lamy's cycle again next morning, Marie-Claude appeared, her eyes entreating, longing to be of assistance. 'Perhaps I could help you,' she said. 'I know this land as I know my own flesh.'

Neville looked at her, his face expressionless. Then he nodded. 'All right,' he said.

This time, he took the Fond St Amarin, the third of the three roads leading from Néry to the east. As it left the village, it dipped for a while, then rose steeply between the trees where Guardian Moch's house stood in a field at the top of a steep lane, surrounded by the crates and boxes and barrels which had once held his black market discoveries. He halted to examine one of the tunnels made through the undergrowth by wild boar, then pedalled away again to stop near the ridge and stare round him once more.

Marie-Claude caught up with him, panting. He was sitting in the saddle, his feet on the ground, looking back at the valley. Without speaking, he took out his cigarettes and lit one. Then he seemed to remember her and, offering the packet, went on staring fixedly at the road.

She watched him without speaking, not wishing to break his train of thought. He made no attempt to enlighten her, but rode higher up the slope to stop again just below the cutting where the road crossed the ridge. At this point the land to the left rose abruptly to a sheer chalk cliff called the Escarpment St Amarin, which was topped by undergrowth and trees. Beneath it, there was a narrow strip of land, then the river rattling in shallow pools over its stones in a four-foot gully that had been cut by the passage of the water. Alongside the river the road ran along a stony ridge higher than the land on either side. Beyond the road the fields fell away into a shallow hollow, made muddy by the seepage of the river under the road and full of lush green grass, then rose to a green meadow that lifted in folds as if it had been ridged by deep dykes – up and up to where the Crête St Amarin swept round in a semi-circle above the escarpment. Just below the crest at the top of the meadow there was another ditch, covered by a deep belt of undergrowth, cutting off the ridge from wandering cattle as effectively as barbed wire.

'The dam,' Neville said unexpectedly. 'The dam above the village I've heard about. Where is it?'

Marie-Claude pointed to the trees. 'Up there. Dring's supposed to look after it.'

'What about the pump in the square? Does the water come from there?'

There was a new urgency in his manner. He seemed to have thrown off his gloom at last and was peering intently at the slopes.

'Is it the plan?' she said, drawn to him again by her warm heart and the wish to see him succeed. 'You have thought of something?'

His eyes were still following the curves of the land. 'Come on – ' he sounded impatient and her heart leapt at his enthusiasm ' – the pump in the village. Does the water come from the dam?'

'No, it's fed by a spring on the other side of the hill. It's a good spring. It never fails. The dam was built by the army in 1917 when they thought the front line might be pushed down as far as here.'

'How much does it hold?'

'Not enough to drown the Germans. It sprang a leak once but all it did was turn the ground in the dip there into deep mud. Some of it came on to the road.'

'What if the spring dried up?'

She stared at him, puzzled. 'It won't. It never has.'

He shrugged. 'It might this year. What about the Baronne? Could she tell a lie? Some people can't.'

Marie-Claude gestured. 'Her whole life's been a lie. On his death-bed her husband told Father Pol she'd been the best wife in the world.' She looked puzzled. 'This is also to do with the plan?'

Neville ignored the question and, propping the bicycle against a tree, sat down and lit another cigarette. He suddenly seemed depressed and uncertain again, overwhelmed by the responsibility that had been handed to him. 'I wonder if Urquhart isn't right,' he said after a while, 'and you wouldn't be a lot wiser just to let them go.'

'No!' She was indignant. 'Surely you of all people understand! You've lived in France before the war.'

'Nice. Promenade des Anglais. That's not France.'

She paused. She knew what she wanted out of life as much as Reinach and Father Pol and the others. For months now she'd been working for it. Soon France would be free – with true Gallic arrogance, she couldn't believe that the German occupation of a nation as cultured, noble and intelligent as the French could go on for ever – and, though she was far from being a peasant, she still had a peasant's straight-thinking contempt for vacillation.

'Would you live in France again, Neville?' she asked.

Neville looked round, startled by the question. 'Yes,' he said. 'Any time.'

'Although you are English?'

'France's every man's country,' Neville said, and he could see she was pleased.

She paused and she seemed unexpectedly shy. 'Would you do it for someone else?' she asked. 'Not because of France? Not for yourself alone?' She lifted her head, her eyes shining. 'For a girl, for instance?'

'If she were the right girl.'

'Permanently?'

'No.' Marie-Claude's face fell and Neville went on easily. 'My family's wealthy, Marie-Claude. We don't stay anywhere permanently. We go to the south of France for the season. To Salzburg for the festival. To Switzerland for the skiing.'

'Would you take your wife with you on these trips? When you had a wife, of course.'

'Certainly.'

She hesitated. 'What if she were lacking in culture?' she asked quietly. 'Lacking in poise?'

Neville glanced at her out of the corner of his eye, then he leaned across and kissed her. 'There's no better teacher than money,' he said.

Two evenings later, Marie-Claude invited Reinach to the farm for coffee.

Neville's idea had grown so suddenly he was almost afraid of it, and he had first tried it out on Urquhart. Urquhart had listened carefully, for once without a trace of cynicism in his expression, asking a lot of searching questions and even supplying a few answers to things that had worried Neville. And when Neville had finished, he'd sat back and looked at him with an odd, awed look on his face.

'You're all right, lad,' he said.

Neville frowned, uncertain what he meant and suspecting sarcasm. 'Thanks,' he said sourly.

Urquhart was unperturbed. 'Don't look a gift horse in the mouth,' he said. 'I'm not in the habit of telling many people – especially officers – that they're all right.'

Then Neville realized he'd meant what he'd said, and Urquhart grinned.

'It's a good plan,' he said. 'If we can only get these buggers to hold their water until the right moment, I think it'll work.'

For the first time in months, Neville felt a real warmth for Urquhart. The distance between them had closed, and he now saw some meaning in what they'd been through together, some understanding of the comradeship Urquhart had felt in the regular army.

'Thanks,' he said again, and this time he was smiling too.

When Reinach arrived, Dréo and de Frager were already in the kitchen with Father Pol who was sucking down coffee with his vacuum cleaner noise. Neville was staring at a map, and Reinach was immediately aware that he seemed cheerful.

'You have a plan?' he asked.

'It depends,' Neville said warily, 'on what you wish to inflict on them.'

Reinach looked quickly at Marie-Claude. 'As much as possible, of course,' he admitted.

Neville gestured. 'Suppose they surrendered? Several hundred Germans throwing down their arms to a few Frenchmen ought to be enough humiliation even for you.'

Reinach's gaze switched to Dréo who frowned. 'We wish

to destroy them as Napoleon destroyed the Austrians at Austerlitz,' the old man said.

'I'm not arranging a massacre.'

Dréo plucked at his moustaches. 'Not even a small one?' he asked.

'At Bourg they shot the Miliciens when they were wounded,' Neville said. 'I'm not having any part of that. I'm aiming at surrender.'

'*We* want dead.' Reinach glanced again at Dréo, then at Father Pol, then back at Neville. 'You aren't losing your nerve, are you?' he asked.

Neville said nothing because Reinach had put his finger on the very thing that was worrying him. He had begun to see that a general, whose responsibility was immeasurably greater than that of a factory manager because he was operating with human lives, had to take this hardest of all courses unflinchingly. He wasn't sure he could. 'I'm not a general,' he said.

Reinach paused. 'Very well. I'll hold everyone in check.'

'Can you?'

'I can punch them in the jaw.'

'What about the Rolandpoint men and the St Seigneur men.'

'We shall need *them*?'

'Yes.'

Reinach's eyes narrowed as he accepted his responsibility as leader in a way that Neville knew *he* never could. 'I'm not having our people set against the Rolandpoint and St Seigneur lot,' he said bluntly. 'Our enemies are the Germans. Tell us the plan. There are only three roads out of Néry. Which one do we use?'

Neville refused to be rushed. 'However we do it,' he said, 'wherever we do it, we need men. How many have you got?'

Reinach looked round. 'Me and Ernouf and Sergeant Dréo.'

'Me,' de Frager added.

'And me.' Father Pol put down his coffee cup. 'I can pray to God for the gift of courage.'

'That's five.' Urquhart spoke for the first time. 'You've produced five.'

'I'll help,' Marie-Claude said.

She'd half hoped he'd say No, she mustn't, or that it would be too dangerous; but all he said was, 'Six,' and she frowned at his matter-of-factness.

'Théyras,' Dréo said. 'Dring and Lionel Dring. Perhaps Gaston Dring too. He's fifteen.'

'Ten,' Urquhart said. 'Six of them getting on in years.'

'Duclos. Guardian Moch. The Hénault boy and Jacques Jacquelot. Yves Rapin's back too. Then there's Gaudin and his sons, and Vic Letac and Dr Mouillet.' Reinach sat for a while, thinking. Then he fished out a stub of pencil and began to write on the edge of a newspaper. 'Thirty-seven,' he said. 'Including boys.'

'Against what Klemens has got, it makes poor odds,' Neville pointed out. 'And to the two hundred Germans in Néry, you have to add five hundred from St Seigneur and two hundred from Rolandpoint. When they leave they'll pass through here and move on as a unit. That makes it even poorer odds. What about the other places? Rolandpoint? St Seigneur?'

'Rolandpoint have said they have thirty-nine,' Urquhart said. 'That makes seventy-six. It's still not enough.'

'How many do you want?' Reinach demanded angrily.

Urquhart leaned forward. 'The man who wins the battle is always the man who can bring most soldiers into action at the same time and at the same place,' he said. 'We need a lot, or it won't be humiliation. It'll be a disaster – for *you*!'

Reinach glanced at Father Pol. Then he shrugged. 'We can contact Courbigny and Araigny and Tarey, I suppose. And I can telephone Drumont at Roches-les-Drapeaux and Armandeau at Dijoine.'

'Go on,' Neville said. 'You're doing better.'

'Do you want the whole damned district?'

'Why not?'

Reinach looked at Father Pol again and didn't answer. Why not indeed? Every village that wanted one seemed to be getting a parachutage these days and there were thousands of Frenchmen just waiting for their opportunity to rise up and bash some German's head in. 'All right,' he said.

'We want men from Luchy and Lingeau,' Neville went on. 'And St Verrier and St Bringt and Beauzois and Violet. Even the hill villages round Metz-la-Montagne. All of them.'

Reinach's eyes were wide. 'That'll be hundreds.'

'We *need* hundreds.'

Reinach frowned, suspicious. 'This is a good plan, Neville?' he asked.

'Urquhart thinks it'll work.'

'And that's important?'

'He's got to put it into effect. He knows where to site the weapons and what the Germans will do.'

Reinach shrugged. 'Okay,' he said. 'I'll get the Bourg-la-Chattel, Diepape and Pailly men. They have a few scores to pay off. And probably a few more.' He leaned forward. 'When do we put this plan into effect, Neville? Soon?'

'When the Americans are closer. So that the Germans don't have time to turn round and lash out.'

'What do you think they are? Of course they'll lash out. You've heard of Vercors. You've heard of Oradour.'

De Frager shifted uneasily. 'And I hope you haven't failed to notice that an SS major's joined the staff at the château. What about the old people and the children?'

'I've not forgotten the SS major,' Neville seemed almost smug. '*Or* the old people and children. And I've heard of Vercors and Oradour. This time, though, the Germans will be *helping* us.'

'I can imagine it!' Reinach snorted.

'They will,' Neville insisted. 'We'll get them to.'

Reinach's eyes flashed. 'Then, for the love of God, tell us where and when! Are we going to fight like your famous Milord Wellington at Waterloo.'

'No.' Neville looked young and excited. 'The battle's Sedan, 1870.'

There was a sudden chill in the room and an immediate freezing of expressions. *Sedan!* There might have been glory in defeat at Salamanca and Waterloo but there was none at Sedan. The war of 1870 against the Prussians had been only blunder, stupidity and corruption, and the hated name of its climactic defeat made them look at each other quickly.

'Sedan!' Reinach said.

'Sedan!' Dréo echoed.

Neville's enthusiasm washed over their indignation. 'The Prussians got your army into a valley,' he said, 'and surrounded them with guns. Moltke said he'd got them in a mousetrap.'

Sergeant Dréo stared at him, wooden-faced. 'The French fought well,' he rumbled. 'I had a great-uncle there.'

'They were beaten before they started,' Neville said. 'Ducrot knew it. "We're in a chamberpot," he said. "And we'll be in the shit right up to our necks." ' He leaned forward, his eyes alight. '*We* can get the Nazis into a chamberpot.'

Dréo scowled. 'Does it have to be a *German* plan?' he growled.

There was a sudden deadlock and it looked as if they'd reject what Neville had to offer. Tears came to Marie-Claude's eyes, then her face lit up and she rushed to his help.

'What irony if the Germans *were* defeated by a German plan!' she said.

Her enthusiasm turned the trick and there was an immediate lightening of glowering expressions.

'I can just imagine their faces,' Sergeant Dréo crowed. 'Tell us what we must do, Neville, and let us get on with it before it's too late.'

Part 3
DAY OF GLORY

Le jour de gloire est arrivé.

Rouget de Lisle

1

'Tarnera,' Klemens said thoughtfully. 'Have you noticed a new attitude in this village?'

Tarnera nodded. 'I have, Herr Oberst. 'They're suddenly more approachable.'

'Why is that, do you imagine?'

'Perhaps *they*'re also beginning to think we're losing the war.'

Klemens stared at the map on the wall. The front line ran now from south of Le Havre through Paris to Château-Thierry and Troyes, then back on its tracks north of Auxerre to the Atlantic coast. In the south it probed upwards from Italy, east of Switzerland towards the Balkans, west deeper and deeper into France.

'There'll be a stand on the German border, of course,' he observed.

'By that time,' Tarnera said, 'we shall have lost everything we ever gained and that in itself will be defeat. I doubt if the régime could stand it.'

Klemens frowned and Tarnera went on earnestly. 'People like you and me, sir, will then need to know where our loyalties lie, because the allies will never accept Nazism.'

Klemens turned. 'Have you talked to Klein-Wuttig about this?' he asked.

'We shall get no help from him, Herr Oberst. But *I*'m a born survivor.'

Klemens frowned. 'I hope you are, Tarnera, because Wuttig and this damned SS man are as thick as thieves. I think Fritzi's keeping a diary.'

'Of his boy friends' affairs?'

'No, Tarnera. Of yours. The things you say. Take my advice, if Sturmbannführer Frobinius talks to you, be careful not to make comments. I know you enjoy your wit. Sometimes, even I do. But Fritzi doesn't. And Frobinius won't. Keep a tight hold on your tongue.'

Tarnera smiled, and Klemens went on more sharply.

'I know you regard it all as rather a joke,' he growled. 'But if you're a born survivor, then make sure you *do* survive. It might be worth it because there's something in the wind.' He laid a letter on the table. 'That arrived this morning.'

The door clicked and Klein-Wuttig appeared. Klemens looked round. 'We're discussing the new friendliness in the village, Fritzi,' he said. He indicated the letter Tarnera was holding. 'That arrived in my post this morning, marked "personal". What do you make of it?'

The letter consisted of a single line of typing – 'Look in the cellars' – and Klein-Wuttig stared at it for a moment before studying the envelope carefully. 'Postmarked St Seigneur,' he said. 'But it could, of course, have been posted there by someone from Néry or Rolandpoint.'

Tarnera's expression was amused. 'Think it's a bomb, Herr Oberst, designed to blow you and me and Fritzi to Kingdom Come?'

Klein-Wuttig frowned. 'It's a possibility, Herr Oberst.'

'Then why warn us?'

'Perhaps it's from the Baronne's maid,' Tarnera suggested. 'She and Corporal Goehr have been making eyes at each other a lot. Perhaps she's afraid that Goehr's going to Kingdom Come too.'

'Can we question her?'

'It wouldn't do much good. She'd obviously deny everything.'

Klein-Wuttig's face set. 'We could ask Sturmbannführer Frobinius – '

'No!' Klemens' hand chopped down in a quick gesture. 'I'm not having Frobinius and his black-collared gentry in this. We'll handle it ourselves.'

'Very well, Herr Oberst.' Klein-Wuttig's expression registered disapproval. 'In that case, it would seem sense to search the cellars.'

'*Which* cellars?' Tarnera was frowning. 'I've never seen any cellars. And that, come to think of it, is odd – don't you think? – a house as big as this without cellars. Didn't the Baronne tell us that they once had vineyards? With wine you need somewhere to keep it.'

Klemens smiled. 'Tarnera, I believe you're on to something.'

'There *is* a little wine, of course – kept in the pantry off the kitchen, but that's hardly big enough to swing a cat round and it has a stone floor, stone walls and a stone ceiling. You couldn't hide anything in there.'

'You know what I think?' Klemens' small eyes narrowed and he slapped the table. 'I don't think he's talking about a bomb at all. I think he's talking about the paintings!'

That thought had also occurred to Tarnera but with his sympathy entirely on the side of the Baronne, he'd hesitated to state it.

Klemens had got the bit between his teeth now, and was looking excited. 'Let's have the old woman in,' he said.

The Baronne looked tired but defiant, and for once Klemens didn't bother to offer her a chair.

'Madame – ' he sat back, flicking at his boots as usual with his riding crop – 'the Corot, the Daubigny, the Madame Lebrun.' The Baronne said nothing and Klemens looked up at her, smiling. 'They're still here, aren't they?'

The Baronne's eyes flickered. 'They were stolen,' she said.

Klein-Wuttig leaned forward. 'We don't believe you, old woman,' he snapped. 'And you know what we do to liars and cheats and thieves and people who defy the Reich.'

The old eyes fastened contemptuously on him. 'I take it

you mean roughly what people who belong to the Reich also have done to them when *they* cheat and lie and steal.'

Klemens waved Klein-Wuttig aside with a weary gesture and, reaching out to the letter, he tossed it across the table towards her.

'That's just arrived, madame. There's no need to read it. I'll tell you what's in it. "Look in the cellars," it says.' He leaned further forward. 'Where *are* the cellars, madame? *We*'ve seen no cellars.'

For a long time the Baronne was silent then she shrugged. 'Are there cellars?'

'Of course there are cellars! You don't imagine a family as old and powerful as this bought their wine by the bottle from Mère Ledoux, do you?'

Klemens sat back, smiling. 'And the cellars?'

'They're still there. If they'd been taken away the house would have fallen down.'

'Then where, old woman!' Klein-Wuttig shouted. 'Where?'

'Where cellars are usually situated,' the Baronne snapped back. 'Below the house!'

Klein-Wuttig leaned forward. 'The paintings are hidden there, aren't they?'

The old eyes, still bright and black as jet, settled on his face. 'Why do you wish to know? So you can steal them when you are defeated?'

Klein-Wuttig's face went pink. 'Germany will *not* be defeated.'

The Baronne gave a bark of laughter. 'Then why is the Wehrmacht running like rabbits? When Hitler is hanging from a lamp-post in the Unter den Linden, will you call *that* defeat?'

Klemens began to move the papers on his desk thoughtfully. 'These cellars,' he prompted. 'Where is the entrance, Madame?'

'There was one through the kitchen but that was bricked up years ago. The only one there is now is in the rear courtyard. There's a pile of hay in front. We hid it because occasionally we kept a pig or two down there that no one knew about.'

'You could be shot for that,' Klein-Wuttig said triumphantly.

The Baronne smiled. 'But I don't think I shall be,' she observed dryly. 'Not with the allies beginning to cry out about war crimes.'

As she disappeared, Klemens sat for a moment staring at his feet. Then he looked up, smiling, and heaved himself from his chair. 'Get a torch,' he said.

Followed by Tarnera, Klein-Wuttig, Unteroffizier Schäffer and three men, they left the house by the front door and walked in a self-important little procession along the crackling gravel path to the stables. Halting in the courtyard, Klemens stared at the outbuildings and coach-houses. Then he turned and gazed at the hay packed in the arches under the château.

'Get rid of that rubbish,' he snapped.

The three men behind Schäffer began to pull away the hay. Within minutes one of them shouted. 'There's something here, Herr Oberst!'

Klemens moved forward through the fodder piled about his boots. He could see the weathered boards of an old door.

'Open it,' he said.

More hay was dragged away and Schäffer pushed at the door, so that they found themselves standing in a short passage.

Klemens smiled. 'I think we've found our cellars, Tarnera,' he said. 'Very well, Schäffer. You can go.'

When the soldiers had disappeared, Tarnera moved into the dark passage. Ten yards in front of him there was another door, even more dilapidated, set between crumbling stone pillars. As he heaved on it, it swung back with a groan of rusty hinges. The white beam of his torch probed the darkness and they saw picture frames, dusty and chipped, stacked against the wall. Klemens smiled.

'Let's have a look at them, Fritzi,' he said.

Klein-Wuttig pulled out one of the heavy frames and turned it. Tarnera shone the torch on it while Klemens glanced at the list in his hand. 'One metre by one and a half,' he said. 'That's a millpond, isn't it?'

'It looks like one, Herr Oberst.'

'It's the Corot. I have it here. Try the next one.'

Klein-Wuttig turned the next frame round. 'Two girls listening to a minstrel playing a mandolin.' He sounded as if he were reading the charge at a court martial.

Klemens slapped the list in his hand. ' "The Lesson" by Lancret! These are the paintings we're looking for, Tarnera. I'm certain of it. Next.'

'Man in a red coat with horse and servant. The servant looks a bit like that smith, Dréo.'

' "Baron de Frager, with horse and groom". It's a Greuze. It was painted in this village.' Klemens grinned. 'Fritzi,' he said, 'in case you don't know it, you're handling a fortune. Get that artist chap down here.'

When Balmaceda arrived, Klemens was sitting on an upturned wooden bucket staring at the painting of Baron de Frager.

He looked round. 'Seen that before?' he demanded.

Balmaceda frowned. 'I have indeed, monsieur.'

'These are the paintings we're looking for, aren't they? How did they get down here?'

Balmaceda shrugged. 'Monsieur, I don't know. When they disappeared, we assumed the villagers had hidden them. They're very parochial and regard them as their own, and we knew they'd turn up sooner or later.' He glanced about him at the dusty walls of the cellar. 'They picked a good place,' he ended.

'They did?'

'Oh, yes, monsieur. I was once an art dealer. I know about paintings. It's dry down here. Of course, they should be properly wrapped and crated.'

Klemens considered. 'If this place is all that good,' he observed, 'they might as well stay here. If I take them upstairs your damned Baronne might well organize a raid to have them removed, mightn't she?'

'She's a woman of spirit, monsieur.'

'Then we'd better have them under lock and key and place a sentry outside. Could this place be made secure?' Klemens reached for one of the barred windows and yanked at the bars. One of them came away in his hand. 'For instance,' he said. 'That! We'd better have it bricked up, hadn't we? We'll also have a new door here and have the outer one repaired. Could that be done?'

'Of course, monsieur.'

Klemens thought for a moment. 'Fix it,' he said.

There was a long silence, then Balmaceda coughed.

'Monsieur,' he said. 'There's no stone. The quarry's not been worked for eight months.'

'Very well, work it.'

'We should need your permission, monsieur. Colonel Marx forbade anyone to go near it after the trouble with the Resistance last year. He decided it had been used for hiding explosive.'

Klemens waved his hand. 'We can keep an eye on it. What else do you need? Have you a stone-mason?'

'Théyras, monsieur. You'd also need a carpenter for the door. We have a good one: Reinach. He's from Alsace. They're well known there for their ability to work in wood. Their carving – '

'I don't want carving,' Klemens said. 'I want a door. And I want crates. Tell Reinach and anybody else who's involved to come and see me.'

That evening while Colonel Klemens was dining, Reinach, Théyras, Sergeant Dréo, Ernouf, Dring and Balmaceda were ushered in by Tarnera.

Klemens wiped his mouth with his napkin and looked down the length of the Baronne's table. 'Are you skilled men?' he asked.

Every head nodded earnestly.

'Sound at your jobs?'

More nods.

'Very well, I have work for you.'

Reinach looked at the others and smiled at Klemens. 'It's

a long time since we did a decent job of work, monsieur,' he said.

'You know what you have to do?'

'Make crates, monsieur.'

'Do you know what for?'

'Unfortunately, monsieur.'

Klemens smiled. 'Does it bother you?'

Reinach shrugged. 'They aren't *my* paintings, monsieur. I'm more interested in wages.'

'How about the others?'

'They aren't their paintings either, though Dréo's great-great-grandfather or something is on one of them. We pull his leg about whether he's the horse or the groom.'

Klemens grinned. 'You will make covers. Unteroffizier Schäffer will find old army blankets for you to tear up. You will make crates. Good crates. Nothing shoddy. To fit the pictures. You can do that? I want them well protecting.'

'Will you be taking them away, monsieur?' Reinach's expression was innocent and Klemens frowned.

'Why do you ask?'

Reinach shrugged. 'In the days when the Baron was alive, if I made a crate for simple storage, it was light. If it was to be sent to a dealer, it was heavy. If it was to go by rail, it was heavier still. They throw things round a bit at the station.'

'Make them very heavy,' Klemens said. 'I shall also want the cellar door replacing. Can you do that?'

'I shall need one or two assistants, monsieur. I can't do it all myself. And there'll need to be men in the forest cutting and stripping. There's nothing in the village we could use. It's all been burnt as firewood.'

'Enlist anyone you need.'

Reinach gestured and pulled a face. 'Well, that raises another point, monsieur. Colonel Marx forbade anyone to go into the woods. It was after that fuss with the Resistance last year. People do go, of course. After rabbits and game. A few of the boys with their girl friends. But that's unofficial. They won't go if the soldiers are watching.'

Klemens frowned. 'I've already given permission for wood

to be cut for transportation to St Seigneur and on to the Reich for winter relief.

'Cut, monsieur,' Reinach said.

'Then cut some more. As of now, you have permission to cut as much as you require and to employ as many men in the forest as you need. What else will you want?'

Reinach considered, his clown's face twisted with the effort of thinking. 'Not much, monsieur. Soft wood for the crates. Harder wood for the door. While we're at it, we might as well make a good job of it. The Baronne won't object, I suppose, and it'll be all right for after.'

'After what?'

'After the war's over, monsieur.'

Klemens leaned forward. 'You talk too much, Reinach,' he growled. 'Just do your carpentering and keep your mouth shut. What else do you want?'

'Petrol for my lorry and the tractor, and for the saw in Dring's woodyard. You can't cut trees into planks by hand, monsieur. We shall also need charcoal for Sergeant Dréo's forge. That means a bit of extra wood, but we've plenty of old iron we can use for the hinges. Théyras'll seal up the windows and rebuild the pillars for the door.'

Klemens nodded. 'Can it be kept quiet?'

'Like the grave, monsieur.'

'Very well, get on with it.'

Reinach nodded and turned, then he stopped and swung back to face Klemens. 'Just one thing, monsieur,' he said. 'Who told you?'

Klemens was full of food and wine and he was feeling cheerful. He pretended he knew the identity of the informer. 'So you can go and burn his house down?' he asked. 'Oh no! I'm not telling you that.' He wagged a finger at Reinach. 'And if I hear of anyone being beaten up, I'll be holding an enquiry. Understood?'

Reinach grinned, clicked his great feet together and even had a shot at a salute. 'Understood, monsieur! Absolutely, completely understood.'

2

The grumbling had stopped.

The invading armies were now heading towards Sens, and in his bones Captain Tarnera knew it wouldn't be long before the German retreat – already increasing in speed – became a rush and every Frenchman started grabbing for a gun. Allied aircraft were known to be dropping them now in enormous quantities and, despite Vercors and Oradour, there was a mounting resistance in the Dordogne, the Auvergne, the Jura, Savoie and Corrèze. The tactics had also changed from sabotage to straightforward attack, and the reports that came north now indicated that down there no road was safe.

In Néry there was still no sign of open hostility, but suddenly the village seemed to be on tiptoe. There was no difference and yet there *was* a difference. The villagers were now watching the Germans as closely as the Germans had watched them in the past. It was as if they were studying every move and timing everything they did. Tarnera guessed they were up to something, but could only suspect it had something to do with the fortuitous discovery of Klemens' paintings, which they were surely far too hard-headed to enjoy losing. As for the anonymous letter Klemens had received he put that down to some private quarrel – perhaps some father who objected to young de Frager seducing his daughter.

The village was bright with sunshine that made the old stonework glow. As the German lorries moved past, they threw up dust in a fine cloud that coated the sweating faces of their crews and settled on windows and flowers, dulling their colour. Tarnera sighed. He had an uneasy feeling that somehow, somewhere, Klemens had made a mistake. Yet, going over it all again and again, he couldn't imagine what it was.

Reinach appeared from his workshop. He was carrying two large four-handed saws which he tossed into the rear of the ancient lorry he drove. With him were Théyras the mason and Ernouf the quarryman, clutching a bag of hammers and chisels, and several youths who'd been taken on as assistants.

Reinach waved. 'Good morning, Monsieur Tarnera,' he called gaily. 'How's everything?'

Tarnera waved back and Reinach continued, lifting the bonnet of the lorry to prime the carburettor. 'I've heard the allies are planning to land half a million men at Bordeaux. Have you heard that, monsieur?'

Tarnera smiled. He knew Reinach well by now. 'No, I've not,' he said. 'Any more than I've hear that the Führer's about to invade Scotland from Norway and attack them from behind.'

Reinach grinned, his head half inside the engine. 'It'd go hard for you if they did land half a million men, though, wouldn't it, monsieur?'

'Not half as hard as it would for you if Major Klein-Wuttig heard you dispensing such gems of sedition as that one.'

The lorry was taking some starting and Reinach, who was hitting something with a hammer, lifted his head and gave his wide clown's grin that Tarnera reckoned wasn't half as stupid as it looked. 'Ah,' he said, 'but I wouldn't dispense gems like that to the major, would I? Not likely. I prefer to stay alive. With you, monsieur, it's different.'

He got the lorry's engine going at last, and the old vehicle rattled and chugged out of the village. Tarnera stared after it, frowning, well aware that Reinach's cheerfulness didn't come just from the look of the day. Perhaps, he thought, it was due to the promise of work and wages. Then he frowned again because he suspected Klemens had no intention of paying.

The gates to the yard behind the château were now kept closed and there was a sentry on duty. Unteroffizier Schäffer had instructions that only his most reliable men were to be given the job and he'd set up a special little guard-house in one of the harness rooms, where a corporal spent most of his time sitting outside in the sunshine, watching everything that went on.

That afternoon Tarnera took the car and two men with machine pistols, in case of an attempt at ambush, and drove out to the forest above the village. He could see nothing unusual. The quarry overhung the Rue des Roches, one of the three roads east from the village, but there was nothing there to worry him. Ernouf and Théyras were busy under the eyes of a sentry measuring up boulders and taking an occasional swipe at them with a hammer. They'd already collected a pile of square stones near the road.

'Everything all right, corporal?' Tarnera asked the sentry.

'All correct, Herr Hauptmann. Nothing wrong.'

Tarnera wasn't so sure. Just over the ridge, Reinach was busy at the saw-mill. They'd already felled one of the big spruces and used the ancient tractor to drag it to the saw. Three men were now manoeuvring it on to the bench with the aid of a purchase fastened to a derrick. As he watched, Tarnera saw Reinach swing at the handle of the saw's motor and heard the clatter as it started. Two of the men put their weight against the end of the log so that it moved on the rollers towards the whirling blade. A cloud of sawdust flew up, golden against the sunshine, and the high scream of the steel teeth biting into the wood filled the forest with sound.

Klemens was staring at his maps when Tarnera returned. He looked up with a smile. 'How did it go, Tarnera?' he asked.

'I don't trust them,' Tarnera said.

Klemens sat back. 'You worry too much, Tarnera. What can they do to harm us? Did you see the Resistance up there?'

'No.'

Klemens shrugged. 'Well, they can't kill German soldiers with hammers and chisels. Tomorrow I'll take a look myself.' He bent over the table. 'At the moment, I've got other things to handle. We've to prepare an appreciation of the situation round here. When our people finally pull back to the border they'll be passing east of us to Langres on the N74, or north from Auxerre along the N65 to Chaumont and Nancy. We found those pictures just in time. Which one would you like?'

'I've never been much interested in art, Herr Oberst.'

Klemens' head jerked round. 'Who said *I* was? *I*'m interested in keeping body and soul together after the débâcle. Fritzi's accepted one.'

'Managing, no doubt, to reconcile his incorruptible German conscience.'

Klemens laughed. 'If he uses what little brains he possesses, he ought to be able to keep his head above water until Germany's sorted out her problems. How about the Fragonard?'

Tarnera nodded non-committedly. He had no intention of accepting anything; not simply because he regarded it as dishonest but because he felt it downright dangerous. He tried Klein-Wuttig on the subject, but he was quite uncompromising in his attitude.

'The French have no understanding of art,' he said. 'I've chosen the portrait of Countess Matejko by Kucharski.'

'A good choice, Fritzi. A good Aryan painter.'

Klein-Wuttig glared. 'And why not? And my name is Friedrich-Johannes Klein-Wuttig. Not Fritzi. *Nor* Wuttig as the Colonel sometimes calls me. I have to accept insults from him, but nothing from a mere captain.'

'Not even such good advice as "Get rid of it"?' Tarnera said. 'It'll be as dangerous as high-explosive when the war's over.'

Klein-Wuttig didn't answer but he didn't forget either, and that evening Klemens drew Tarnera aside. 'What have you been saying this time,' he demanded. 'Frobinius wants to see you.'

Tarnera smiled. 'I've been pulling Fritzi's leg, that's all.'

'I notice he never laughs,' Klemens said bluntly. 'Now go and see Frobinius. And, for God's sake, don't be provoked into losing your temper.'

Frobinius was sitting in Klemens' chair, his black uniform sombre in the grey light. His cap with its death's head badge lay on the desk before him. He was only in his twenties with the round face of an eager schoolboy, his uniform well padded to compensate for narrow shoulders and the thin neck that protruded from his collar as if he were an adolescent outgrowing his clothes. His pale face was intent as he stared down at a file in his hands.

'Captain Tarnera,' he said cheerfully. 'Our German traitor!'

'I beg your pardon, Herr Sturmbannführer?'

Frobinius gestured. 'A figure of speech,' he said. 'Fritzi Wuttig's view. Haven't you noticed that he has his knife into you?'

Tarnera answered warily. 'A matter of temperament,' he said. 'We just don't see eye to eye about most things.'

'Especially, it seems, about Germany's chances of winning the war.'

Frobinius' face was cherubic but Tarnera was aware of danger.

'I've never refused any duty,' he said, 'no matter what it was. But I was a newspaperman and newspapermen see things clearly.'

'Newspapermen have been shot for seeing things too clearly, Tarnera. Sometimes it doesn't pay.'

'Frederick the Great's generals didn't always agree with him,' Tarnera said, 'but they continued to do their duty.'

Frobinius looked up sharply. 'The Führer's decisions aren't expected to leave room for the sort of disagreement Frederick the Great's generals indulged in. And as for generals, I'm a historian of sorts too, and I know that Napoleon's generals didn't always agree with *him* and continued to do *their* duty – *until they forced him to abdicate*. There's a later example: Witzleben, Stauffenberg and Beck and the July 20 plot. Fortunately, we were too quick for them.'

There was a long pause then Frobinius leaned forward. 'Do you consider us ruthless, Captain?' he asked gently.

Tarnera swallowed and searched for words. 'I sometimes think there might be more room for mercy,' he said.

'No one ever became strong by dispensing mercy.' Frobinius' smiling face had changed. 'We aren't seeking popularity. You know what Reichsführer-SS Himmler said. "We don't expect to be loved. We're the black band of brothers." If Germany's position's in any doubt at the moment, it's because people have chosen to be merciful. I promise you I shan't.'

The realization that he'd not impressed Frobinius was confirmed for Tarnera when Klemens called him into his office before the evening meal.

'For God's sake, Tarnera,' he said. 'What did you say?'

Tarnera shrugged. 'I was careful, Herr Oberst, to say as little as possible.'

'You still said enough for him to think you a bad security risk.'

Tarnera's shoulders moved. 'Herr Oberst, at this stage of the war, I think I've grown tired of trying to impress murderers – '

'Shut up!' Klemens roared. 'I won't have it! I've allowed you far too much rope as it is: If I continue, *I* shall be involved. And *I* want to get back to Germany in one piece. I've not gone in for murder. I've not indulged in loot – ' he stopped ' – except for the pictures, Tarnera. Except for the pictures. And those I mean to have. If we lose this war – '

'I think, Herr Oberst, it's now a case of "*when* we lose".'

Klemens' shoulders sagged. 'Have it your own way. When it comes, I shall offer my surrender as a soldier. I'm not a member of the Party. I'm not even a regular officer, merely a reservist. If they insist, I'll walk into the prisoner of war camp and close the door with my own hands. They can't keep me there for ever.'

He took a turn up and down the room; then, recovering his spirits, he swung round to face Tarnera once more. 'They'll have to get Germany going again when it's all settled down,' he said. 'And for that they'll need men who've been in positions of authority. By that time there'll have been a change of climate and I don't intend to starve, believe me. That's when we shall be glad we've got the pictures away.'

Tarnera said nothing because he had a strong suspicion that the people of Néry had no intention of allowing the pictures to leave the village at all.

They hadn't, but their chief concern at that moment was that Brisson had arrived from Rolandpoint smiling all over his face and demanding a share in their ideas.

'I've heard of a plan,' he said.

Marie-Claude's face was blank. 'You must be cleverer in that fly-blown village of yours than we are,' she said. 'Do you think we're stupid enough to try anything with an SS major at the château?'

'Ernestine heard something was in the wind.'

'In bed, I suppose,' Marie-Claude snapped.

Brisson went away chastened and Urquhart went with him, to see Ernestine Bona.

Marie-Claude frowned but she didn't argue. When he returned he was as silent as usual about what he'd been doing and Marie-Claude served his meal with a sullen expression on her face. When he'd finished, he looked up. 'Someone else's trying to get in on the act,' he said.

No one spoke or moved and he went on after a pause. 'The radio operator at St Seigneur says they want to send us an agent to organize us.'

Marie-Claude turned at last. 'We *are* organized,' she exploded. 'Tell them to send him elsewhere!'

Urquhart smiled. 'I did,' he said. 'But that's not all. It seems they have more weapons in London these days than they know what to do with. They're giving them away without being asked. We're to have another drop.'

3

When Colonel Klemens visited the forest to see for himself what progress was being made, Ernouf and three assistants with crowbars and ropes were hauling rocks about the quarry. Ernouf beamed as Klemens appeared.

'Only using the best stone, Colonel,' he announced.

'I don't give a damn whether it's the best or the worst,' Klemens growled, 'so long as it stops thieving fingers.'

Escorted by Tarnera, Klein-Wuttig, Unteroffizier Schäffer and a dozen men, all with their weapons at the ready,

Klemens marched over the ridge to the saw-mill. The number of Reinach's assistants had swollen considerably, and with him also were Sergeant Dréo and several youths selecting pieces of wood and burning them on a fire packed with sods.

'Charcoal, monsieur,' Dréo said with a wide smile. 'For the forge.'

Reinach came forward. Behind him, two men were loading planks on his lorry. Further down the hill near the road, four more men with a large saw were staring up at a tree gauging its straightness. 'Pine for the crates,' he said. 'But not so resinous it weeps and spoils the pictures.' He pointed down the valley. 'Oak for the doors, of course, so it won't warp.'

'I don't need a diatribe,' Klemens snapped. 'Just get on with it.'

'Of course, monsieur.' Reinach paused and coughed. 'There's just one thing.'

'And that is?'

'The crucifix, monsieur.'

'Which crucifix?'

'The statue of Christ in the church, monsieur. Monsieur will understand because no doubt he's a good Catholic.'

'I'm a Lutheran. For God's sake get on with it.'

'It's said to be made from the wood of the true cross, monsieur, and we'd like to store it somewhere safe. Two years ago it was damaged – by the soldiers. They were drunk. They had no discipline. Not like monsieur's soldiers. Perhaps monsieur would permit us, since we're already up here, to cut wood for a new one.'

'Go ahead.'

'And for the float?' Reinach's face was full of innocence. 'It's carried through the village in procession on Good Friday. The men get underneath it. You'd think it was on wheels the way it glides along.'

'Cut the wood.'

'And also for the plinth where the cross stands in the church? Since it's a big cross, it'll need to be a big stand.'

'Were you also thinking of re-flooring the church?' Klemens spoke sarcastically.

Reinach's eyes widened. 'Well, it's certainly old, monsieur. One day someone will break his ankle.'

Klemen's bent down, his nose within inches of Reinach's 'No,' he snapped. 'I've given you permission for your cross, and your float and your stand. Let that be enough.'

As the Germans turned away, the Frenchmen watched them go, straightening their backs for a moment.

'We should have laid on an ambush,' Sergeant Dréo growled, his smile gone at once, his eyes narrow and glittering. 'My old chassepot could have done for the lot of them.'

When Klemens returned to the château he found a deputation waiting to see him, led by Gaudin the farmer from the west side of the village. Marie-Claude was among them.

'We represent the agricultural interests of the valley, monsieur,' Gaudin said. 'Since wood's being cut again in the forest, we've come to seek permission to use some of the branches for stakes. Our barbed wire fences haven't been repaired for two years.'

Klemens considered. 'I see no reason why not,' he said.

Gaudin coughed. 'That, of course, monsieur, leads to another point.'

'Out with it.'

Marie-Claude stepped forward. 'Some of us haven't got any wire. Mine's rusted completely away.'

Klemens looked at her. He saw a pretty young woman with an appealing smile, and he'd always had a soft heart for appealing young women. He turned to Tarnera.

'I think we can help, don't you, Tarnera?' he said. 'I think we might spare a roll or two of ours.' He smiled at Marie-Claude. 'Bring a cart down, madame. My men will load it for you.'

That night the platform arrived, driven by Marie-Claude and pulled by the Spanish war veteran Hercule – the same cart and the same same horse that only two nights before had been hauling arms from a huge new parachute drop. Four rolls of barbed wire, a little rusty but otherwise undamaged, were thrown aboard by two of Schäffer's men. A bottle of marc produced two more rolls, and a joint of pork a third. Marie-Claude drove off with a tarpaulin over them, watched by the grinning soldiers.

The following evening, the platform was down again; this time with a load of logs. Reinach was driving it. It had been raining all day and he had a sack over his head and shoulders like a cape, and Hercule's hide was streaked with water.

'With our compliments, Colonel,' Reinach said cheerfully. 'The nights will soon be growing cold. I'm afraid there's some acacia among it, and no self-respecting forester would normally include acacia in the firewood, but they're the ends of trees we selected. It's not bad for crates, you see.'

Klemens watched them unload the logs. Three men were already busy in the stable finishing the crates, and Reinach was working on the heavy new door. At his forge in the village, Dréo was hammering happily at the hinges and, as Klemens well knew, more than one horse had appeared surreptitiously for shoeing on the understanding that the Germans were paying. He leaned forward, smiling. He was enjoying the game he knew Reinach was playing with him.

'You're making sure you're looking after yourselves too, aren't you?' he said. 'A new crucifix, a float, a stand. And how about firewood? Have you made sure there's some for yourself?'

Reinach grinned back, his wide foolish mouth empty, his expression indicating that he realized Klemens was a shrewd man. 'A little, monsieur,' he admitted. 'Here and there.'

Klemens eyed him cheerfully. The season of cold nights with ground mists creeping from the river had started. And with the rain, the old château, without proper heating of any kind for two years, had a chill about it that got into the bones. That night, full of food and drink and enjoying the huge fire the mess orderly had built, he turned to Tarnera. 'Let that fellow Reinach know that we wouldn't be averse to more logs like these,' he said.

The following evening, Reinach arrived with another cartload. As Klemens appeared he bobbed his head, reached under a sack on the platform, and produced a brace of pheasants.

'For the colonel,' he said. 'In token of our appreciation. We got them with nets and, between you and me, monsieur, they belong to the Baronne.' He gestured at the logs. 'We had to cut a few small trees down especially, but I thought the colonel wouldn't mind.'

Klemens was sufficiently impressed to hand over a bottle of good German wine. 'Cut all you want,' he said.

He'd had a fire in his bedroom the night before and was enjoying the permanent hot water for baths.

Unfortunately, the next morning, the well dried up. And not only the well but also the stream that had once turned the mill, which might have supplied an alternative source of water.

Klemens noticed it first when he went into the village. There were always a few women round the pump, gossiping and drawing water, and always soapy puddles from the public wash-house across the road. But this morning there were more men than women and, as Klemens' car slowed down for the crowd, Father Pol stepped forward. He'd been working at the pump and the odour he gave off was at its fruitiest.

'Monsieur le Colonel,' he said. 'There's no water.'

'Why not?'

'The well's gone dry.'

'Well, use the stream.'

'That's dried up, too. I expect it comes from the same source.'

Klemens climbed from the car and solemnly inspected the bed of the stream that ran under the disused mill. The water had vanished, exposing the old cigarette packets and tin cans which rested among the stones and drying mud.

'Why not get water from the river?' he asked.

Father Pol looked indignant. 'Do you realize, monsieur, how far the river is outside the village?'

Klemens shrugged. 'Well, what do you want me to do about it?' he asked. 'It's your affair, not mine.'

But when he returned to the château at lunch-time he discovered it *was* his affair after all, because Corporal Goehr was complaining that there was no water to cook with.

'Why not?' Klemens snapped.

'Well, you, Herr Oberst, had a bath this morning, and so did the Sturmbannführer and the Herr Major and the Herr Hauptmann. And so did the Baron and the Baronne and Herr Balmaceda. When we came to organize the lunch, there was no water left in the tank.'

'Where's Unteroffizier Schäffer?'

Schäffer appeared, looking worried. 'There's no water in the tank, Herr Oberst,' he announced.

'I know there's no water in the tank,' Klemens snapped. 'What are you going to do about it?'

'I'm already doing what I can, Herr Oberst. I've been up to look at it. It's empty. All that's left are the jellified bodies of bats and a few dead beetles, and nothing else.'

Klemens scowled. 'Where does the water come from?'

'It's pumped up from the village, Herr Oberst. The pump's switched on every day. We've got it attached to one of our generators. Unfortunately, it doesn't take more than about three or four baths to empty the tank. It's far too small for a place this size.'

Klemens waved him aside and glared at Goehr. 'What about the meal?' he demanded.

'Cold collation, Herr Oberst.'

'I was expecting pheasant.'

'There's no water, Herr Oberst. We can't prepare them.'

Klemens stared at him, his face reddening. Then he threw back his head and shouted.

'Tarnera!'

Tarnera appeared almost immediately. 'There's no water,' Klemens snapped.

'No, Herr Oberst!' Tarnera said. 'I understand the tank's empty. It's pumped from the village – '

'I know it's pumped from the village and the well's run dry! Find out why!'

They didn't have to bother. Reinach appeared with a deputation, headed as usual by Balmaceda and the Baronne. Since it was an official visit, the Baronne wore her maire's sash of red, white and blue.

'The well's dried up,' she announced. 'The notice, "Trinkwasser", that you and your men had the gall to put on what is a French pump is therefore pointless.'

'It's the spring, monsieur,' Reinach explained. 'It comes from the hills. The source is up there somewhere and it's stopped.'

'Why?'

'It does sometimes.' Reinach shrugged. 'Last time was five years ago, just before the war. We had a water engineer come from Dijon to look at it. He brought a geologist, and they said the hills are honeycombed with underground streams and sometimes the land settles and they change course. It might be months before it comes back.'

'It's typical of you French dimwits,' Klemens snapped, 'not to have done anything about it before. What happens now?'

'Last time, we rigged up a temporary pipeline from the dam to the stone gully from the hills. It was built centuries ago but it'll still carry water.'

'Rig it up again.'

Reinach's shoulders lifted to his ears in another vast shrug. 'The rubber piping's perished, monsieur. But, if monsieur will help us a little – '

'Don't worry,' Klemens growled. 'I'll get the Wehrmacht engineers up from Dijon.'

As they left, he snatched up the telephone and rang headquarters. 'General Dannhüber,' he said, 'we're having a little trouble here. Water supplies have dried up. Something to do with the spring. I'm wondering if the engineers – '

'No!' General Dannhüber didn't hesitate for a second. 'They can't! Arrange something yourself, Klemens. Every engineer we've got is south of Dijon. The damned Maquis have started blowing bridges down there and General von Weizsache borrowed them. I've also got a group near Beaune repairing a railway line that was sabotaged, and two groups at Auxonne shoving a derailed engine back on the rails. And I've got to keep some by me in case we have trouble ourselves. Use watercarts.'

There was a crash as the telephone was replaced. Two minutes later the deputation was back.

'It seems the engineers are – ah – engaged elsewhere,' Klemens said. 'You'd better get on with it yourselves. Can you produce enough for drinking?'

Reinach shrugged. 'We don't *drink* water, monsieur,' he explained. 'We use it for sprinkling on the ground outside the bar to lay the dust. Of course, perhaps the children will need a little now and again and perhaps the women, but it'll have to be boiled first because the only hose we've got has been used for pumping out cesspits.'

'Let Captain Tarnera know what you need,' Klemens said hurriedly. 'I'll send lorries to Dijon to collect it.'

By the following afternoon, men were working up in the woods by the dam, laying reinforced rubber pipes to the ancient stone gully that ran down the hillside. From the bottom, more pipes were laid to the village square where a big canvas tank was being erected.

'We need a flat stone base for it,' Reinach decided. 'There's plenty of slate in the quarry.'

'Then get it,' Klemens said.

When Klemens went up to the dam, Reinach and Dring had already rigged up a heavy pump and were pumping water out in a steady stream. By evening at the château it was just possible to cook and wash. Despite the problems, Klemens considered he'd done a good job. Every water cart in the district – and most of the farms had one – was going to and from the dam in a regular stream, and Klemens noticed that they all brought back bundles of the sharpened stakes for the new fences. There was already a large swathe cut into the forest where thick fir branches lay in heaps, heavy with the smell of resin.

There was a marked difference in the air traffic over the valley now. The aeroplanes were all moving north, and many of them were Junkers 52s.

'Carrying wounded,' Neville said.

'Or German generals abandoning their troops,' Urquhart suggested.

According to the rumours, parachute drops were coming all the time to the south now. British, American and French officers, openly wearing uniforms and carrying arms, were arriving with them. The countryside down there was said to be stuffed with every kind of illegal weaponry imaginable, from rifles to field guns. There were stories of German cars being destroyed by phosphorous bombs, and of prisoners taken.

'All claiming to be Poles, Cossacks, Austrians, Czechs and Pomeranians forced to fight for the Nazis,' Guardian Moch reported. 'It makes you wonder where the Germans have got to.'

The reports from the battle front grew wilder. The American 7th Army was approaching Dijon and Besançon and units of the 3rd Army from the north were now approaching Auxerre and Chaumont, en route for the Vosges and the Belfort gap.

Then Moch brought news that German civilian workers and clerks were leaving the area and trains were moving north through Dijon, Besançon and Vesoul towards Belfort and Mulhouse and the German border.

'All packed with women clerks and loot,' he said. 'They say the guard's vans are full of pictures.'

'But not yours,' Neville pointed out. 'Not yet. Where are the Americans?'

'South of the Doubs. They're shelling Valentin.'

The next afternoon, Urquhart cycled to St Seigneur to find the radio operators. He returned with the news that the Americans had reached Troyes.

By this time an impromptu system of communication had sprung up so that they always knew exactly what was happening elsewhere. Messages were carried by travelling salesmen like Moch in their 'valises diplomatiques', by priests moving from village to village to celebrate mass, by anglers heading for the rivers, by train drivers and guards, by farmers in town looking for seed. They were also sent by the railway telegraph and the post office in a crude code that everyone but the Germans understood. Villages were referred to by their nicknames and figures were indicated by the number of windows there were in a church, or the height of a tower. To people brought up in the area, it was simple and highly effective.

The day after Urquhart had been to St Seigneur they learned that Vangouillain was full of German soldiers, and then they knew that the Wehrmacht was in full retreat. Vangouillain was jammed with them because a continuous stream was passing along the Dijon–Langres–Nancy road. Most of them were going straight through the village, stopping all other traffic, forcing the people indoors, their heavy vehicles frequently battering the houses as they turned the sharp corners. A few were stopping to get water from the pump, or to try to buy milk or fruit.

'They look exhausted,' Moch reported. 'I saw them. I was down there on the petrolette.'

'Were they well behaved?'

'They were quiet. But they seemed worried. It was a good sight, Neville. Their clothes and transport looked as though they were only held together by dirt.'

That night they heard a dull thump over the hills and guessed that someone was at work somewhere with explosives. They soon learned where.

'Someone blew the bridge at Assômes,' de Frager informed them. 'I heard it at the château. They retaliated by taking twelve men, including the maire, and shooting them in the square. They've got engineers on the bridge now. It'll be working by tomorrow.'

That night, German cavalry passed through Néry, tough-looking men on tall horses. American Thunderbolts caught them the next morning at Cheuny and when Neville cycled over with Reinach, all they found were half a dozen dead horses by the roadside, a little scattered equipment, and a man spread-eagled in the bushes staring up into the trees, the flies on his dead eyeballs.

'The war's coming closer,' Neville said bleakly. 'Let's hope they don't decide to make a stand here or you'll get all the fighting you've been wanting.'

There was an air of apprehension in the village when they returned. Gaudin's wife had been accused by a passing group of Germans of sheltering Maquisards and punished by the removal of all the food in the house.

'It was an excuse, that's all,' Marie-Claude said, 'Someone was hungry.'

The following day they saw Germans moving north of the village to the Langres–Belfort road, passing close to the Crête St Amarin, and two days later Jean-Frédéric Dréo and Gaston Dring found six of them lying dead in the swampy grass at the other side of the ridge. No one knew who'd shot them. They seemed to be only boys and someone had removed their weapons and boots.

German traffic was now building up on the side roads to the south of the plateau as the drivers tried to avoid the crush on the Dijon–Langres road.

They watched them from the tall grass on the hillside and could see that the men in the lorries were beginning to look tired, their uniforms dirt-encrusted and creased, and there was a strained look of defeat on their faces. Many of the vehicles were old or filched from French civilians and they were battered, worn-out and rickety.

'They're from south of Dijon,' Guardian Moch said, searching with a pair of black market field glasses for divisional and regimental signs with the shrewdness of an army intelligence officer. 'I saw them down there last week. They're beginning to evacuate.'

'They're blowing the bridges after them, too,' Reinach said bitterly. 'Couldn't we do something?'

Moch shook his head. 'It's not the same as shooting two engineers on their own. These days they're working in the middle of their own army.'

The cellar was finished the next morning, and Reinach asked Klemens to inspect it. He'd carefully repaired the outer door and replaced the broken one inside, while Théyras had rebuilt the pillars that held it in place and filled in the barred windows.

'A mouse couldn't get through there now, monsieur,' he beamed. 'Not even a flea.'

'And look at the door,' Reinach said. 'It fits like a glove and moves like a dream.'

He put his weight behind the heavy woodwork and it swung to with the precision of a railway carriage door.

'Though I say it myself,' he crowed, his face wearing an expression of pride, 'I know my job, and Dréo's hinges are perfect. It's twelve centimetres thick and made of oak but, with a little grease supplied by Monsieur Schäffer, it moves without a sound.'

Klemens nodded his approval. 'What about the paintings?'

'All done, monsieur.'

The crates stood together at the back of the cellar, all labelled.

'I had two men here every bit of the time, Herr Oberst,' Schäffer said. 'If the crate says "Baron de Frager with horse and groom", then that's what's inside it.'

He handed over the key, and they all stood back while Klemens inserted it. As he turned it in the ancient iron lock, removed from the stables and oiled and refurbished by Sergeant Dréo, there was hardly a click.

Klemens smiled. 'You've done a good job of work,' he said. 'It's more like a prison than a store-room.'

Reinach grinned. 'Yes, monsieur,' he agreed. 'It is, isn't it?'

4

The Wehrmacht started arriving in the Néry–St Seigneur–Rolandpoint valley the next day.

Mère Ledoux's youngest son, who entertained ambitions to play football for one of the big French teams after the war, was kicking a ball against the wall of the bar and kept careful count of them as they passed. Everyone knew that the Gestapo was beginning to crack and were collecting civilian clothes – in Dijon there wasn't a suitcase left in the shops –

while the French police were actually beginning to round up the gangs who'd lived off the possessions of the Maquisards hiding in the woods.

Then a German lorry carrying pigs for troop rations was shot up on the Vangouillain–Mary-les-Rivières road near Salutre. In the atmosphere of mounting dread, the German soldiers left their dead behind, climbed into the escorting kübelswagen and bolted. Since the réseau who'd done the job had also had casualties and bolted, the pigs were left unattended until discovered by young Dréo and his friends on their bicycles. By evening they'd all been slaughtered, cut up and hidden by the overjoyed Néry men.

It was as they were turning their backs on the bullet-riddled lorry that they saw the column of Germans pouring up the road from Dijon; a long stream of armoured cars, motor cyclists, staff cars, lorries, even occasional tanks. Lacking any kind of formation, they moved very slowly and there were frequent halts to investigate possible traps – a sure proof that the Maquis were beginning to be feared.

'I think,' Reinach observed grimly as they watched from the trees, 'that our friends are finally heading for le dernier round-up.'

There was already a great deal of hither and thither between Rolandpoint and St Seigneur that seemed to indicate Klemens' men were preparing to leave. But nothing had yet happened in Néry. To the south, they heard, Villebasse was drowning in Germans who in their rage and fear had set fire to the village and partly destroyed it. Assômes was also sunk deep in the German tide and the young men had tried to avenge the earlier atrocity by sniping at the retreating columns as they passed, while the girls kept watch for the next lot. But, though they were harassed, the Germans were by no means throwing their hands in. While the troops remained in the lorries, tanks were called in and machine guns set up, and the whole column finally went into action with mortars and light artillery plastering the woods behind the running Frenchmen. The village was left devastated, a terrible sight with burning houses, mutilated men, and weeping women and children.

All transport began to disappear – lorries, petrolettes, cars, even bicycles. The Germans had been harried for miles and were willing to shoot to obtain something on wheels.

'There's a rumour at the château that the Americans are being held up north of Chaumont,' de Frager announced. 'The Germans are blowing the bridges across the Marne, and the Maquis are having to fight to hang on to the crossing at Vignogny.'

'That's all we need,' Neville said bitterly. 'We can't do a thing if we can't rely on the Americans coming up on time.'

'We can do a bloody lot even *without* the Americans,' Urquhart growled. 'What's the matter, lad, losing your nerve?'

Neville's head jerked up but for once there was no sign of a smile on Urquhart's face.

'You don't think everything went dead right with Montgomery's plan at Alamein, do you?' he said. 'I bet he bit his nails a bit here and there, in spite of what they say. It's a good plan you've thought up. *Boy's Own Paper* couldn't have done better. And it'll work. All we have to do is keep an eye on Klemens so that we know the minute the bastards look like leaving.'

The praise surprised Neville because Urquhart had never been one to offer much encouragement, and he began to take heart again.

That afternoon, Reinach found a reason to take his lorry to Haute Falin in the hills. It was noticeable as he left that several mothers with young children were taking the opportunity to visit relations and were packed on boxes in the back. Other women were stuffing perambulators with babies and treasured possessions and setting off in well-spaced groups on foot, ostensibly with the same purpose in view. Half of them carried messages demanding help while their husbands busied themselves digging holes in their gardens, packing valuables into boxes and old suitcases, and burying them under footpaths and dung-heaps and vegetable plots.

After dark the horizon to the south flickered with flashes and they could now hear the sound of gunfire. As they talked,

Commandant Verdy de Clary arrived, his cold indifferent eyes hard. 'I am a French officer,' he told Reinach. 'I request the right to join you.'

Reinach glared. 'You've waited long enough,' he snapped.

Verdy's eyes flickered. 'There was no point in aggression when the Germans were powerful,' he said stiffly.

'No,' Reinach snorted. '*C'est comme au bal des pompiers. Ce sont toujours les mêmes qui dansent*. It was always the same people who took the risks. Did you expect them to lay down and let you walk on them? There were some who didn't. Most of them are dead.'

The old man's eyes flickered. 'I'm a French officer,' he repeated. 'I demand a command.'

'I don't fight under some parvenu who sat back and enjoyed the war,' de Frager retorted. 'We don't want people who've rejected us.'

'*I* want them,' Urquhart said quietly. 'He's a trained soldier, and I want every man I can get who knows his job.'

'No one would work with him!'

'They will if I say so,' Urquhart snapped. 'I want someone who'll do as he's told, not just some farm-boy who'll let off his gun when he thinks the time's right.'

The following morning, Euphrasie, the Baronne's maid, brought the information that she'd been told to complete the German officers' laundry before midday.

'They're moving!' Reinach said, and half an hour later Jean-Frédéric Dréo came hurtling into the village on the Spitfire.

Neville and Urquhart had been sitting at the table, Neville frowning at his map, Urquhart sharpening a billhook with a stone as if the normal work of the farm had to go on and there was nothing else in the world to think about.

'They're burning papers in St Seigneur and Rolandpoint,' Dréo panted.

Urquhart looked at Neville, then at Marie-Claude who was helping her mother to dry the breakfast dishes. 'It's time we went,' he said quietly.

He put down the billhook and the stone and rose unhurriedly. As he followed him, Neville's heart was pounding.

At the door he turned and saw Marie-Claude's eyes on them, troubled and concerned.

'Better start things moving, Marie-Claude,' he said. She nodded silently, drying her hands on a towel, her eyes never leaving their faces.

By lunch-time they were on the slopes above the village where a surprising number of men had discovered there was work to do. As the village emptied, several of the older children slipped surreptitiously out of school and set off on their bicycles to play truant. One or two went fishing, passing on their way to the river through the hamlets of Araigny, Tarey and Violet. One boy went to visit his grandmother in Metz-le-Bois, and another cycled through the villages of Cheuny, Amizy and Beauzois before disappearing with his girl friend into the woods at Bois Seul. 'What you do afterwards is your business,' his father told him. 'What you do before belongs to Néry.'

Their arrival halted all activity in the hills. Harvesting stopped. Men and youths disappeared into barns and started digging under dung-heaps and piles of hay, lifting boards or burrowing into the roofs of their cottages, even into the walls at the backs of pigsties. Old rook guns appeared, with twelve-bores and long hunting rifles, even ancient muzzle-loaders that had been in their families for generations and hadn't seen the light of day for years. The action was largely symbolic because the hill villages had also had parachute drops and there were anti-tank weapons, Stens, Brens, mortars and rifles. Bicycles, petrolettes and horses appeared in the streets and it was surprising how many of their owners found they had business in the direction of Néry. At four in the afternoon, a message reached Reinach from the St Seigneur post office.

'Those parcels you asked me about – they're on their way. They've just left. They should arrive tomorrow.'

Reinach dug out the old lorry, tossed his tools into the back for the look of the thing, and set off for the woods. Men were already waiting near the saw-mill with their bicycles and petrolettes, watching a German light plane circling just above.

'Reconnoitring the route up the valley,' someone said. 'They don't trust anyone these days.'

'When Major Rieckhoff's people from St Seigneur reach Rolandpoint tomorrow,' Colonel Klemens was saying, 'they'll pick up Doench's men and von Hoelcke's tanks and press on here. When we leave we'll be in strength.'

'Route, Herr Oberst?' Klein-Wuttig asked.

'Rue des Roches to the Langres road.' Klemens looked at a sheet of paper in his hand. 'All food to be removed. All surplus stores to be destroyed. The first vehicles, consisting of two of Captain von Hoelcke's tanks, will leave here at 10 a.m. the following day. I don't want to be caught in the Forest of Frênes after dark.'

He paused, glancing again at the paper, aware of Frobinius watching him carefully from near the fire. 'The second part of the column under Fritzi,' he went on, 'will leave as soon as the tanks and the following lorries are clear of the village. All men will carry weapons, ammunition and rations for three days. Lorry-mounted machine-guns will be manned at all times. Look-outs will watch not only the sky but the trees as well. I shall be in the centre of the column with Tarnera. The rear will be made up in the same way as the van, with von Hoelcke's remaining two tanks coming last. That way, we shall have armour and guns handy at any point. If trouble comes, it'll come where the road starts to rise to the St Amarin ridge. Questions?'

'Women?' Tarnera said. 'There are still women clerks in St Seigneur.'

'They leave this afternoon. Their buses go straight through. I don't want to be hampered with them.'

'Sniping?' Klein-Wuttig said. 'Suppose it starts as we leave the village?'

'No mercy,' Frobinius snapped.

'I want no women and children harmed,' Klemens said.

Frobinius smiled. 'We don't differentiate. We take the whole family.'

'I would remind you that this is my command.'

'And I would remind *you*, Herr Oberst, that since July

20th, on the Führer's instructions, all commands are subordinate to the SS and the Gestapo. *I* will handle the security. The first family that's shot, the first house that's burned, will serve as a warning for everybody else along the route.' Frobinius rose. 'And now, if you'll excuse me, I have things to attend to.'

As he left the room, arrogant in his shining boots and black uniform, Klemens glared after him.

Klein-Wuttig coughed. 'One other question, Herr Oberst.' He'd been worrying for some time over whether he should inform Frobinius about what was hidden in the cellar. In the end he'd decided not to, and now his eyes glanced downwards meaningly.

Klemens' frown disappeared. 'The lorry containing the – ah – secret equipment – will be immediately behind *my* car. Fritzi,' he said. 'I'd be obliged if you'd get Transport to provide their best driver. I also want a lorry with a machine-gun in front of my car and another behind the lorry.'

'What about loading the lorry, Herr Oberst?'

'I shall attend to that myself,' Klemens said. 'At the last moment. There'll be a commanding officers' conference this evening to finalize details. Let's make it as late as possible – say nine o'clock – so that there can be no leaks. We don't want the orderlies guessing what's happening. We'll also keep the Baronne and her staff confined to their quarters. I don't want *them* to know when we're leaving.'

'Ten o'clock tomorrow.'

Euphrasie brought the information the following morning as she arrived at the farm to buy eggs for the Baronne's midday omelette. 'Corporal Goehr told me. There's an officers' conference tonight and they're putting a sentry on our corridor so no one sneaks out to listen. Goehr usually comes down with a pot of coffee about then and he had to tell me why he couldn't tonight. He fancies me.'

Reinach scowled. 'Very soon,' he growled, 'with God's help, you'll be able to use those eyes of yours on French boys.'

Euphrasie sniffed. 'You think I *chose* to use them on the Germans? That Schäffer tried to put his hand up my skirt.'

As she left, Urquhart rose. 'I'm off to Rolandpoint to see Brisson.'

'Tell him to get that radio operator of theirs to contact the Americans,' Neville said. 'Tell them they've got to hurry. 'We need them.'

'Tell Ernestine to get to work on him,' Marie-Claude advised. 'You ought to be able to persuade her. Half an hour in bed – '

Neville turned on her. He was tense and nervy and his good humour had gone, but this time he was at one with Urquhart. 'It doesn't matter if he goes to bed with the radio operator himself so long as he gets the Americans,' he snapped.

Marie-Claude looked hurt, and Urquhart winked at her and slapped her behind as he went outside.

From the château that afternoon, they heard the gunfire in the south more plainly.

Worried, Tarnera walked through the village, expecting to see signs of hostility and preparations for their departure. But the place looked normal enough, though somehow to Tarnera things still didn't feel right. He could see an old man leading a horse into a farmyard. Two or three more, holding billhooks and sickles wrapped in sacking, were standing and talking outside the bar. He noticed they were all smoking, something that was unusual at a time of tobacco shortage and he assumed that some 'tabac' owner in Dijon or St Seigneur had been cleared of his stock by the Maquis.

Reinach stopped his lorry alongside him. Lionel Dring was in the cab with him, and several other men and youths with axes and billhooks were in the back.

'More logs for the colonel,' Reinach called. He jerked his head to the back of the lorry. 'They're all getting in on the act now. The woods are full of wood chips just waiting for the collecting.'

Tarnera offered him a cigarette. 'What about the dam? Are they still working on that?'

'Oh, yes, Herr Hauptman. It's almost dry, but Ernouf's

digging above the Fond St Amarin. He thinks he might be able to get the spring coming down to Néry again by next week.'

By next week, Tarnera thought, they'd all be in Germany with a little luck.

As the lorry drove off, Reinach was grinning. ' "How's the dam?" ' he said, mimicking Tarnera. ' "Nearly dry, Herr Hauptmann." "And how's the dip?" "Sopping wet, Herr Hauptmann." '

Dring gave a laugh and Reinach's great empty mouth opened in a guffaw. '*C'est le sang-froid*,' he said. 'A crétin's face and *le sang-froid*.'

High up the hill, he stopped the lorry and looked back. The smoke from the German fires round the village was lifting slowly to form smudges in the sky. The road in front of him was growing narrower and steeper, cutting into the slope more deeply as it rose to the crest. Over the still air, he could hear the drum of engines and knew they belonged to German vehicles approaching from St Seigneur and Rolandpoint. They were going to swamp Néry when they arrived because only a token number of older men and women now remained in the village, stoking fires with whatever rubbish they could find to make smoke so that empty houses looked occupied, turning radios up so they could be heard outside, and letting themselves be seen a dozen times or more so that there would seem to be more of them than there were. Only a few places like the shops, the bar, the presbytery, the office of the mairie, which would be noticed if they were empty, remained occupied.

Having offered up prayers for the success of what they were going to do, Father Pol dusted the little figurines above the altar in the church, gave a quick flick to the Henri IV window and cleaned the halo of St Peter with brass polish. Putting away his cloths, he genuflected and knelt before the statue of the Madonna. 'Remember, oh, most gracious Virgin Mary . . .' he began.

He had got only as far as '. . . despise not my petitions . . .' when Father Xavier from Rolandpoint arrived.

'Praying for success?' he asked.

'Clergymen managed to equate Napoleon's victories with evangelical counsels,' Father Pol said stiffly. 'And no doubt Lutheran pastors manage to do the same with Hitler's, so there's no reason why *I* shouldn't. Are your people on the way?'

'At this very moment,' Father Xavier said. 'Shall we join them?'

The first men to arrive on the slopes above the village came from Rolandpoint. Led by Brisson, they came through the trees and over the hill in a bunch, having left Rolandpoint in ones and twos. Like the Néry men, most of them were magnificent shots.

Ernestine Bona was with them. 'You said there wasn't a plan,' she accused.

'It just shows you can't rely on anybody,' Reinach grinned.

'The St Seigñeur group'll be here after dark,' Brisson said. 'They're bringing a few from Bourg-la-Chattel.'

Soon afterwards, Verdy de Clary appeared. He was dressed in his uniform complete with képi, harness, revolver and map case.

'I will fight in my uniform,' he said.

Urquhart nodded. He was also wearing his uniform, the grey-blue freshly pressed, the stripes bright and the gold crown above them polished. It was important to him too.

Then the men from Tarey, Araigny, Violet and Courbigny began to trickle in with other little groups from Roches-les-Drapeaux, St Verrier, and the hill villages. Neville and Reinach watched them, counting them as they appeared. Urquhart was near the road, siting weapons, arranging caches of grenades and marking the ranges with white stones. Above him on the slopes, Lionel Dring and Patrice de Frager were dragging up their new playthings. The last parachute drop had proved an embarrassment of riches, with money, tobacco and food – even chocolate – to say nothing of a vast mass of weapons which had even included two 28mm airborne anti-tank guns. Since they'd learned how to use them in the Doubs, Dring and de Frager had claimed them at once and contemptuously handed over their bazookas to younger members of their teams.

These men were now scraping shallow positions near the Bren gunners, which they were protecting with logs and boulders. The youngest of them, a boy of sixteen, held his tube-like rocket launcher lovingly. Among the trees, doctors from Rolandpoint and St Seigneur, led by Dr Mouillet, checked bandages and humped first aid boxes. Men and boys stacked tins of food, along with cans and bottles of water. Gaudin's elder son had thrown a sheep on its back across a log and cut its jugular vein. As it was skinned, fires were started to cook the strips of flesh for rations.

Deep in the undergrowth overlooking the road, Sergeant Dréo, his medals in a bright row across his chest, was planting his old machine-gun, limping backwards and forwards with his son, their artificial legs thumping and creaking as they secured the folds of undergrowth with string. 'One snip,' Sergeant Dréo said, 'and we have a clear field of fire.'

Underneath the trees, boys made up explosive charges and primed grenades, their beardless faces intent. Among them Sergeant Dréo's grandson worked quickly and efficiently, watched by Elsie, his bicycle close by. There was a low murmur among them and occasionally, as an aeroplane passed overhead, their heads lifted even while they continued to work.

'Everything ready?' Urquhart asked.

Reinach nodded. 'By the time we've finished, the Boches'll be so confused they won't know which way they're going.'

In the early evening they slipped back into the village and gathered at Mère Ledoux's bar. The barman was stuffing bottles into an old suitcase.

'Everybody must be out of the village before dawn,' Neville insisted.

As they waited in the doorway, the German troops from Rolandpoint appeared. It was a long and heavily armed convoy and there were a lot of uncovered vehicles with machine-guns mounted on them. The occupants all wore steel helmets but many of them were officers.

'St Seigneur headquarters,' Brisson said.

Shortly afterwards it started to drizzle, and through the rain six big buses arrived, camouflaged in the jaundiced colours of the Afrika Korps. Infantrymen in full battle-kit climbed out of them and waited as they drove into one of Gaudin's fields. There were gunners with them, and three 88mm guns, and they began taking up positions round the village.

Guardian Moch appeared, coming down the hill from the west. 'Germans up there, too,' he said. 'I think they're from Pailly. Some of them are cavalrymen.'

'Probably Ukrainians,' Reinach said. 'There were some at Diepape.'

Moch grinned. 'For Cossacks, they don't have much knowledge of horses. They've got horrible saddle galls.'

When the cavalrymen appeared they turned out to be U-boat sailors from Bordeaux, who'd been mounted and uniformed in grey to fight their way back to Germany, and everyone breathed a sigh of relief because the White Russians were notorious for their cruelty.

By dusk the village had filled with Germans, the Panzer men sitting on their tanks to watch the others straggle in. Their commander was a good-looking man with blond hair and blue eyes of the sort so much admired by Hitler. He was wearing a white peaked cap.

'He'll stand out like a bull's-eye in the woods,' Reinach observed thoughtfully.

Then they noticed that the backwash from other roads was also finding its way into Néry, and Moch pulled his 'Anthony Eden' over his ears and went round the village on a bicycle to count them.

'One thousand two hundred,' he said. 'Give or take a few.'

'It's more than we expected.'

'There's a general, too. He just drove into the château.'

The curfew was carefully observed. The bar emptied before it grew dark and they all faded away through the thin drizzle, warning the maire's secretary, the postmistress and all the others to be ready to slip out over the walls early next morning. By dusk the village was still as the grave.

Except for four boys and a dog.

Jean-Frédéric Dréo, Gaudin's younger son, Euphrasie Doumic's brother, Louis, and Gaston Dring had been working all afternoon preparing grenades and plastic explosives. They had slipped away through the woods, accompanied by the inevitable Elsie, for a view of the assembling Germans. They were tense and excited, and quivering almost as much as Elsie herself, aware that the following day something tremendous was going to happen.

'It's going to be the biggest defeat the Germans have ever suffered,' Jean-Frédéric said.

They had just clambered to their feet and left the shelter of the trees when Gaston discovered his shoe lace was broken. Bending to repair it, he heard the sound of an approaching car. So did Elsie who immediately bolted towards the road, barking wildly.

'Oh, Jesus,' Jean-Frédéric said, putting two fingers to his mouth to whistle her back. 'She'll be shot!'

Dréo's whistle was heard clearly over the noise of the car bringing Sturmbannführer Frobinius back to the château for Klemens' evening conference. He had spent the afternoon in Rolandpoint checking on rear-guard security, and, alert to danger, he turned in his seat as the car slowed to a halt. Silhouetted against the lighter blue of the night sky, he could see three figures running along the ridge. 'Stop!' he yelled.

The boys hesitated, then swung away in a panic. Frobinius didn't hesitate. 'Get them,' he said quietly.

The SS men jumped out at once and began to run along the edge of the field. As the boys saw them they turned again to head back for the trees, but they'd already been cut off and they swerved desperately in the direction of Rolandpoint.

'Shoot, you fools!' Frobinius shouted, standing in the car to direct the beam of a powerful signalling lamp up the field.

The three figures looked like leaping spiders in the white light, and the first shots brought down Louis Doumic with a shattered knee. The other two stopped dead. Frobinius climbed through the hedge and began to walk slowly towards them, watched from the shadows in the trees by the horrified Gaston Dring.

'Where were you going?' he demanded.

The two unwounded boys glanced at each other. 'Home,' Jean-Frédéric said.

'Why didn't you stop, then, when you were told to?'

They were almost speechless with fear. Jean-Frédéric managed to speak. 'We thought our parents would be after us, monsieur. We've been in the woods.'

'Why?'

Godefroy Gaudin had a brainwave. 'With a couple of girls,' he said.

'Show me your hands,' Frobinius demanded.

Gaudin put out his hands and Frobinius lifted them to his nose and sniffed.

'Plastic explosive,' he said. 'I know the smell.' He turned to the sergeant who was bent over the moaning Louis Doumic. 'These men are terrorists,' he said. 'Shoot them.'

The sergeant straightened up. 'They're only boys, Herr Sturmbannführer.'

'A boy can kill as easily as a man can. Shoot them.'

They stood the two boys against a tree and dragged the moaning Louis to join them.

'Sturmbannführer – ' As the sergeant tried again to protest, Frobinius snatched his gun away.

'You're like all the others,' he snapped. 'This is what I ordered! This is what I want done!'

The rattle startled animals in the wood and they heard the flap of wings as a bird crashed through the undergrowth.

'Leave them there,' Frobinius said, and, turning on his heel, he strode back to the car while the scared Elsie, who had been watching from a distance, her tail between her legs, crept closer in the dark to sniff at the blood on the bodies.

5

The crash of the shots echoed all over the village. It had a special quality and those who heard it instinctively knew what had happened even before young Dring arrived, shocked and sobbing, with the news.

Slipping over the hedges with blankets, they found the bodies against the tree, their faces wet with rain. Elsie approached, nervously wagging her tail, then returned to the bodies and nudged at Jean-Frédéric with her nose, bewildered by his stillness. Lifting them over the wall, they buried them deep in the wood. Father Pol bent over the graves. '. . . *Endormis dans la paix du Seigneur. Ouvrez pour eux les portes du Paradis . . .*'

'Think we ought to let their mothers know?' Dring asked.

'Their mothers are in Mont Algérie,' Reinach said.

'*They* ought to have been in Mont Algérie too,' Neville muttered.

'But they weren't, Officer Neville,' Reinach said harshly. 'Because war isn't tidy, and because they were French and wished to take part.'

Sergeant Dréo was as stiff and erect as a statue when they told him. Behind him there was activity among the trees and small moving lights as an extraordinary number of men moved about in the undergrowth. Groups had arrived from the villages to the south. They'd heard there was to be a great victory and, wishing to be part of it, had arrived by the back lanes on foot, on bicycles, on horses and on petrolettes, and in cars resurrected from haystacks, caves and woods. There was a sound of digging and saws and muted swearing among the undergrowth that drowned the muffled sobbing of Dréo's son, the dead boy's father.

'I shall kill that man,' Sergeant Dréo said. 'They were just boys with a little pride.'

Neville's expression was sick and wretched and Dréo looked hard at him. 'There'll be no surrendering to *me*,' he went on. 'And I shall kill anyone who tries to stop me.'

Leaving the old man to comfort his son, they moved into the undergrowth where a headquarters had been set up. Dr Mouillet was bent over his bandages and dressings with a few frightened girls who'd heard of the shootings. One of them, Jean-Frédéric's girl friend, was sobbing bitterly. A telephone engineer from St Seigneur, who'd been a signaller in the army, was working over a radio set.

'We're in contact with Verdy de Clary,' he said. 'I'm trying to get de Frager now.'

Ernestine Bona pushed through the grass into the area of light round the lantern. 'We've picked up a message from the Americans in the south,' she said. 'They're heading for Dijon. The Spahis of the Free French First Division are with them. They were heading up the valley of the Saône but they've been told by Chaumont to get through to us instead. They say that if we can stop the Germans here for a while, they'll have to retreat via Roches-les-Drapeaux, and the American tanks are heading down there. It'll be like Falaise in Normandy all over again.'

'How long do we have to hold them?'

'Until the evening.' The radio operator had a curiously dry voice that sounded like the rustle of old leaves.

'That's a whole day!' Neville said. 'We can't hold them that long! We hadn't planned to!'

'Then for the love of God,' Reinach said. 'Let's think about it.' He turned to the radio operator. 'Tell them we'll do it.'

'How?'

'Let's burst into the château tonight and shoot the bastards down,' Lionel Dring said. 'They'll be no good without officers.'

'Shut up!' Reinach's authority sat on his shoulders as if he'd been leading military formations all his life. 'We can do better than that. What do you think I had in mind when I built that cellar?'

It was dark when the staff conference started, and the air seemed to be full of the distant thuds of explosions.

Klemens had been taken aback by the arrival of General Dannhüber who had had to leave Dijon in a hurry. When the

Gestapo had started firing on police stations there had been an unexpected retaliation, and before they'd known what was happening the whole town was in the streets. The Germans had withdrawn hastily, and in the rush Dannhüber's car and two others had been cut off. Petrol bombs had finished off one of them at Vangouillain and a burst of firing at Assômes the second. Knowing that Klemens was still in control to the north, with tanks under his command, Dannhüber's car had headed as fast as possible for Violet and up to Néry.

Klemens had been none too pleased to see the general. When Frobinius had arrived and made his report, his plans for leaving the village without trouble had begun to collapse about his ears.

'For God's sake,' he snapped. 'All the SS do is to make the job harder for the army! For every Frenchman you frighten into submission, another dozen are driven into opposition!'

'I must inform Reichsführer-SS Himmler of your view,' Frobinius said.

Klein-Wuttig watched the clash of temperaments warily. There was something electric in the air and he was beginning to worry about his accusation of Tarnera. Frobinius had no such doubts.

'Have no fear,' he told him quietly. 'He'll be arrested as soon as he sets foot in Belfort. Probably Klemens as well.'

The conference opened in a cool atmosphere, with Klemens icy with fury at the sight of General Dannhüber sitting opposite him in the most comfortable chair in the room. Von Hoelcke, the panzer captain, sat next to the general, his uniform as smart as if he were about to go on parade for the Führer's birthday. Rieckhoff and Doench, the majors from St Seigneur and Rolandpoint, both looked tired and rumpled and they were clearly uneasy. The Afrika Korps commander, Captain Witkus, wore an air of indifference because he was secure in the knowledge that if he didn't think much of Klemens' orders, he'd do as he'd learned to do in Africa and follow his own instincts. The naval man, Fregattenkapitän von Hassbach, still startled to find himself not a sailor but a cavalryman, was entirely bewildered.

Tarnera was the last to arrive. As he'd driven through the

village he'd heard radios playing and seen chinks of light between shutters and curtains, and smoke rising into the damp still air. The bar had been closed, he'd noticed, and the only people he'd seen were German soldiers. He felt vaguely troubled and realized that he'd seen remarkably few people about the village all day.

Outside the door, Unteroffizier Schäffer had whispered to him about the arrival of General Dannhüber and acquainted him with Frobinius' shooting of the three boys. Tarnera had said nothing but he was white-lipped with anger and the tension in the Baronne's dining-room was clear.

Klemens outlined his plans sullenly. 'I'll take the centre rear of the column,' he said. 'Perhaps the general would like to take the centre van.'

'What do you mean by that?' Dannhüber asked.

What Klemens meant was that he wished to be as close to his lorry-load of pictures as possible and well away from General Dannhüber who, he hoped, would be able to restrain Frobinius with his rank. He explained that the column would be led by tanks and lorries, followed by the Afrika Korps buses.

'Experienced fighters, every man, General,' he said. 'Then I think perhaps your own car. There'll be an 88 just ahead, then more lorries, and finally my own car followed by the marine cavalry and von Hoelcke's last two tanks. How does that seem to you?'

Dannhüber considered. He was an intellectual general, thin-faced to the point of gauntness and deeply lined. The position Klemens had given him seemed sound as far as he could see. He was in one of the strongest parts of the column, near the tanks and 88s; and close enough to the experienced Afrika Korps men who at least wouldn't make a shambles of anything they did, as the mounted sailors inevitably would. It seemed as safe as Klemens' place, which he assumed would be as safe as anywhere. He glanced at his chief of staff, Colonel Kaspar, who sat alongside him, looking less like a soldier than the curator of a museum that he'd been until the war had snatched him up. He stared at the route Klemens had marked on his map.

'Why this route?' he asked.

'Room to manoeuvre, sir,' Klemens said. 'The Fond St Amarin's too narrow and the Chemin de Ste Reine has trees. The Rue des Roches is open all the way to the ridge and, since we have horse-mounted cavalry, we might even use them if we have to.'

'God help us if we do have to,' Dannhüber said, in which sentiment he was silently echoed by Fregattenkapitän von Hassbach. 'What about the other roads?'

'There'll be strong patrols at the bottom of the Rue des Roches to make sure there's no activity there. I'd rather keep my people out of the Chemin de Ste Reine altogether, with those trees.'

Dannhüber nodded his approval and Klemens turned to von Hoelcke. 'Any questions?'

'Can my tanks get off the road?'

'The road's wide enough for two columns of traffic and you can move alongside it to any point of danger.'

'I don't want to be caught in any woods.' The gunner major had fought his guns all the way up from the south and he wanted to keep them.

'There are no woods in the Rue des Roches,' Klemens pointed out, and the gunner nodded his assent.

'That's it then, gentlemen,' Klemens said. 'Perhaps we'll take a drink before we go to our posts.'

As he rose, Goehr came forward with a tray of glasses of champagne. Since it might be their last chance to drink graciously for some time, Klemens had decided to put on a little show of ceremony. To Tarnera there was a strange air of unreality about the room. In the candlelight, with the rumbling of gunfire outside, they seemed like a lot of aristocrats in a revolution waiting for the tumbrils, and he wondered if this was what it had been like when Germany had been defeated at the end of the other war.

6

Tarnera was the last to appear for breakfast the next morning. He'd been to the village with final instructions for Captain Witkus of the Afrika Korps. General Dannhüber had felt that four buses in front of his car would prevent him from seeing enough, and had decided it might be wiser to have only two – one in front and one behind – with the others further back near Colonel Klemens.

Witkus grinned. 'The old bastard's frightened that if anything happens they'll prevent him nipping to safety,' he said.

Returning between the crowding lorries, Tarnera remembered the shootings of the night before and was surprised that there were no weeping women or shaken fists and hysteria. The French were an emotional people, and he'd seen too many deaths in the course of the last four years not to know how they acted. But the houses were silent and, feeling that every shuttered window hid a pair of eyes, he drove through the village conscious of a collective German guilt.

The shops hadn't opened, he noticed, and the shutters were still up outside the bar. He decided it was a sign of mourning, but then he realized he'd seen no children about either and could only assume that their mothers were keeping them safely out of the way of heavy wheels. Yet there was a strange stillness about the place, an absence of humanity that filled him with a sense of foreboding. Something was wrong, he was certain, but he couldn't say what it was.

The rain had stopped and the sky was clear. Under a blazing sun, the centre of the village was jammed with vehicles and horses. It stank of petrol, diesel fumes, ammonia, and the sweat of hot human beings. A cart had mounted the pavement near the bar and the driver was wrestling with his animals, which were nervous at the throbbing vehicles and the streams of men laden with ammunition and weapons who threaded between them. One or two of them wheeled stolen bicycles loaded with loot, and there were a few civilian cars among the army vehicles – ancient Citroëns, Renaults and

Matfords, even the big black traction-avants the Gestapo liked to use – all piled high with kitbags and suitcases.

As he turned into the grounds of the château, he heard a cow bellow in a field opposite. It sounded as though it were in agony with the need to be milked. There was a whole group of them standing where they normally gathered in the evenings and he realized he'd heard them on and off all night. It puzzled him a little that the French weren't doing anything about it, but he decided that they were keeping out of the way until the Wehrmacht had shaken the dust of Néry from their feet. With liberation so close, they probably preferred to avoid trouble.

When he reached the dining-room, Klemens was giving last-minute instructions to Unteroffizier Schäffer. Frobinius was just rising to his feet and, jerking his jacket straight, he buckled on his pistol and reached for his cap.

'Hello, Tarnera,' he said. 'Been out creating discord?'

Tarnera couldn't manage to answer him and Frobinius swept past him with a grin. Klein-Wuttig was waiting down the corridor, and Frobinius grinned again. 'Have no fear, Fritzi,' he said. 'I shall be waiting for Herr Tarnera when he arrives in Belfort.'

By this time, having sorted out the problem of the general's position in the column, neither Klemens nor Dannhüber was in the best of tempers. It had been Dannhüber's intention, thinking in terms of a long and dusty journey in the heat, to have a bath to start the day. But there was no water, not even for washing, and only a minimum amount of coffee for breakfast; something which had also irritated Colonel Klemens.

'I want all orderlies, their kit and equipment away by 9 a.m.,' he was saying quietly to Schäffer. 'Immediately behind the general. But not you, Schäffer. I want you in the yard behind the house with a lorry, a driver, one orderly, and one sentry. I want your equipment and their equipment to go in that lorry. You understand why, of course?'

Schäffer stiffened. 'Of course, Herr Oberst.' His eyes went down to indicate that he knew what was below their feet.

Klemens nodded. 'Exactly,' he said. 'Loaded properly,

what there is in the cellar shouldn't occupy more than half the lorry. The rear end will be stacked as high as possible with your equipment and yourselves. Understood, Schäffer?'

'Jawohl, Herr Oberst.'

'There'll be something in it for you, Schäffer, of course. Promotion and the additional pension it'll bring when you leave the army. Perhaps even a little – '

Klemens gestured with finger and thumb, and Schäffer stiffened. 'Very good, Herr Oberst.'

As he saw Tarnera eating, Klemens sat down alongside him. 'I shall need you later, of course, Tarnera.' He tapped the table, nodding pointedly downwards. 'We shall wait until the general and Colonel Kaspar have left. Then I want the rear gates closed and the cellar doors unlocked and the paintings stowed in the lorry waiting in the yard. Quickly, you understand. At that time, there'll be only you, me, Klein-Wuttig, Schäffer and three men. Understood?'

'Understood, Herr Oberst.'

'Good. Get plenty to eat. A good meal carries a man a long way.'

Sitting round the table in the Baronne's kitchen, Reinach, Dring and Ernouf were tucking into rolls, butter, coffee and slices of excellent German sausage which had found their way there from the Germans' pantry.

'A good meal carries a man a long way,' Ernouf pointed out.

Reinach was staring with brooding eyes at a vase standing on the table in front of them. The Baronne sat opposite him, her face a mask.

'How valuable is it, madame?' he asked.

'Probably priceless,' the Baronne said.

'It's a lot to ask.'

The Baronne eyed the vase. 'It's in a good cause, Hyacinthe. Joseph got it out of the roof last night.'

'I can't guarantee they won't break it.'

'We have to accept that. I'll happily give it up to see the back of those filth. What are you going to tell them?'

'That there's more where that one came from – '

'I hope you're not.'

' – but that they're hidden in the cellar in one of the wine casks.'

'Will it work, Hyacinthe?'

'There are eight more of us hidden in the stables, madame. They came through the park last night. The same way we brought the crates.' Reinach paused. 'Madame, you should leave.'

The old head went up. 'No, Hyacinthe. I've waited for this day for years. I want to enjoy it.'

Euphrasie appeared. 'They're at the cigarette stage,' she said. 'There are seven of them left, including the general.'

Reinach rose. 'Right. Lead us to the orderly.'

As the German officers began to collect their papers, weapons, map cases and binoculars, Klemens' orderly appeared with a tray.

'There's that chap Reinach outside, Herr Oberst,' he said.

Klemens was preoccupied with explaining to General Dannhüber the schedule of his movements to the frontier. 'For God's sake,' he said in a low voice, 'I don't want his damned logs just now!'

The orderly didn't move. 'It isn't about logs, Herr Oberst,' he said. 'He has a large package.'

Klemens frowned, and from behind Dannhüber's back he signed to Tarnera to attend to the matter.

Reinach was waiting in the corridor with Ernouf and Dring, their caps in their hands. Unteroffizier Schäffer was with them.

'They insist they have something for the colonel,' he explained. 'They say it's to do with – ' he looked at the floor ' – you know, sir.'

Reinach, his face split in his empty smile, was clutching a large object wrapped in cloth. 'I found it, monsieur,' he said. 'It's for the colonel.' He opened the cloth and Tarnera saw a wide-topped case with white classical figures on a blue background. 'It was in one of the old stables at the other side of the estate.'

Tarnera frowned. Somehow, he'd believed that no one in Néry would be guilty of collaboration. For a warm fire and

H

to fool the Wehrmacht a little, yes, but not with such as this.

Reinach's smile had a shifty look about it and Tarnera sighed, disappointed and obsessed with the depression brought on by the shootings and his own foreboding. 'The colonel won't be interested,' he said.

Reinach stared back at him. There was a hard look in his eye that Tarnera hadn't seen before, a cold calculating look that made him decide he'd misjudged his fellow men. 'I think he will, monsieur,' he said.

Klemens was just lighting General Dannhüber's cigar when Tarnera opened the door. Before he could stop them, Reinach, Ernouf and Dring had slipped in behind him.

Dannhüber's head jerked up. 'What the devil's this?' he snapped.

Reinach gestured. 'We just wanted to see the colonel, monsieur. That's all. We have a gift for him.' He opened the top of the cloth-wrapped parcel. 'He's been good to us and we thought he'd like this.'

As Klemens moved forward, so did Dannhüber. 'What's that?' he demanded.

The cloth fell at Reinach's feet. As he put the vase on the floor, Dannhüber stared at it. Kaspar joined them. 'Good God,' he said. 'Where did you find that?'

Reinach chuckled. 'Plenty more where that came from, monsieur,' he said. 'We found it in the loft of the old stables at the other side of the estate.'

Colonel Kaspar had picked up the vase with an expert's gentle hand and was examining it. 'Hard paste biscuit porcelain with white classical figures applied on a blue ground.' He turned it upside down. 'Mark: A.B. for Alexandre Brachard, jeune.'

Dannhüber's eyebrows rose. 'Genuine?'

'Without a doubt, sir. His blue and white jaspar-ware Wedgwood vases, in the neo-classical styles of the late eighteenth century, were copied by several contemporary potters in similar material. This is a surprisingly late reproduction.' Kaspar turned to Reinach. 'Did you say there were other things?'

Reinach scratched his head. 'At least four, monsieur. One of a dancer playing some pipes.'

Kaspar turned to Dannhüber. 'Probably a Siot-Decauville made for the Paris exhibition in 1900. Go on.'

'A white inkstand thing with a chap on it.'

'Mennecy porcelain probably.'

'And a thing like a bucket with birds on it. It's got a mark on it like a fort with crossed swords underneath.'

'Peterinck.' Kaspar's eyebrows rose. 'Probably around 1750. Tournai porcelain.'

Watched by Klemens who was now beginning to grow distinctly uneasy, Dannhüber turned to Reinach. 'Did you find the others in the stable, also?' he asked.

Reinach grinned his gaping smile. 'Yes, monsieur. Ernouf's cousin – this is Ernouf – let the cat out of the bag. Before he went to Marseille to look for work.' Reinach leaned closer. 'He and some others hid them months ago. There are more in the wine vats, monsieur. Near the paintings.'

Dannhüber leaned forward. 'What paintings?'

Klemens' complexion was rapidly changing colour. Reinach picked up the vase and wrapped the cloth round it again.

'The colonel found some old daubs belonging to the Baronne,' he said. 'They were pretty filthy. Somebody said one of them was a Corot or something. I wouldn't know. About nineteen of them, I think there were. Somebody said they were valuable.'

Dannhüber frowned. 'Where are these paintings now?' he asked.

'In the cellar, monsieur. All crated up.'

'We had them prepared for transport to Germany, General,' Klemens said hurriedly.

Dannhüber eyed him. 'I'll bet you did. I'd like to look at these paintings, Klemens.'

Klemens' heart sank and he glanced at Tarnera. 'Ask Schäffer to come here, Tarnera,' he said.

Tarnera was feeling better as he went to fetch Schäffer. 'All is discovered, Schäffer,' he said cheerfully.

'All what, Herr Hauptmann?'

'The colonel's little scheme for the paintings. The general's discovered it.'

'What's going to happen?'

'I'm afraid the Baronne will still lose her pictures but I doubt if the colonel will get them.'

When they entered the room Dannhüber was still questioning Klemens.

'What did you intend to do with these paintings, Klemens?' he was saying.

Klemens' mouth opened and shut for a moment and Tarnera stepped forward. 'We intended to deliver them to the curator of the first museum we came to, Herr General,' he said. 'The first one of any size would be Breisgau, I think. I had it in hand.'

Klemens flashed him a grateful glance as Dannhüber studied the scheme.

'Good idea,' the general said. 'On the other hand, of course, we have to accept – and we must face this – that within a few weeks the Americans and the British will be at the borders of Germany and – who knows? – perhaps soon afterwards in Breisgau.'

Tarnera was recovering his spirits rapidly. 'Of course, Herr General. Unless the Wehrmacht stops them at the frontier as the Führer instructs.'

Dannhüber gave Tarnera a look that seemed to indicate that he thought the Führer hadn't a cat in hell's chance of stopping even a boy on a bike.

'Under the circumstances,' he resumed, 'I think it might be wiser if the collection were not simply dumped in Breisgau, as you suggest, because as soon as they cross the border the French will be looking for it. I know these paintings and I think perhaps they should be split up. Shall we say, some to your home, Klemens? You have somewhere to keep them, I presume?'

'Of course, sir.'

'So have I. So I think some to my home also and some to Colonel Kaspar's. We can keep things quiet there until the uproar dies down and we can convey them deeper into the Reich.'

'Of course, Herr General.'

Tarnera coughed, enjoying himself. 'The colonel, Herr General, indicated that *I* might be able to hide one of the pictures too, and Major Klein-Wuttig another.'

Dannhüber's look suggested that Klemens was a fool to let so many people into the secret. 'If he said so,' he conceded. 'You'd better take them from the group Colonel Klemens will be caring for.' He glanced at Reinach and the others waiting patiently in the background, Reinach still clutching the vase, and turned back to Klemens. 'I think we just have time to take a look round the cellar. Sèvres vases shouldn't be allowed to rot in old wine casks, should they?'

It was noticeable as Schäffer led off – followed by Tarnera, then Dannhüber, Klemens, Kaspar and Klein-Wuttig – that Major Doench from Rolandpoint, Major Rieckhoff from St Seigneur, and Fregattenkapitän von Hassbach joined them. Not only were they highly intrigued by what was happening, but it had also occurred to them that there might well be a piece of Sèvres porcelain lying about loose which was small enough to be stuffed in the pocket.

Schäffer led the way out of the front door and round to the back of the house, his boots crunching on the gravel. Reinach, Dring and Ernouf brought up the rear. As they reached the yard, Klemens glanced round. His orderly was standing with the driver by the waiting lorry and there was a sentry on the open gate. Beyond was the tumult of the village street where the column was trying to get under way.

'Close the gates, Schäffer,' Klemens said.

The big wooden gates were slammed to. They could still smell petrol and diesel fumes and hear engines revving up.

'Shift the hay, Schäffer,' Klemens said, his mind seething with frustrated rage.

Schäffer clicked his heels and signed to the sentry. There was a long-handled fork leaning against a cart, and the sentry and Schäffer got to work.

'You had them well hidden, Klemens,' Dannhüber observed cheerfully.

'It seemed wise, General.' Klemens gave a sick grin.

'Tarnera, Wuttig and I worked on this with Unteroffizier Schäffer.'

Schäffer, Klein-Wuttig and Tarnera exchanged glances. The old bastard was shopping them all.

'Open the door, Schäffer,' Klemens said as the worn boards appeared. Schäffer fished out his key and unlocked the heavy padlock.

'Light, Wuttig!'

There was a hurricane lamp standing in the corridor behind the door. Klein-Wuttig lit it and replaced the glass. Dannhüber stared at Reinach's new door with interest.

'Nice piece of work, Klemens,' he said.

'*We* built it,' Reinach said loudly from the rear of the party. 'We're proud of that door. It moves like a dream. Not a sound.'

Dannhüber wasn't listening. He was examining the woodwork with interest.

'Well, if nothing else,' he said, 'you've given the Baronne de Frager an excellent new door at the expense of the Reich, Klemens. Nobody will ever rifle *her* wine cellar.'

'It isn't at the expense of the Reich, monsieur,' Reinach said politely. 'It's at Colonel Klemens' expense. It's still to be paid for.'

'Has it now?' Dannhüber smiled. 'How much is it to cost?'

'Around seven thousand francs, monsieur. And cheap at the price.'

Dannhüber grinned suddenly and looked maliciously at Klemens. 'Under the circumstances, Klemens, you'd better pay up. It might be your last chance.'

'Of course, General,' Klemens fished in his wallet and sourly handed over the notes to the delighted Reinach. Then, moving a pick handle leaning against the door, he fished for the key. At the back of the group, Tarnera was smiling broadly.

'Open it,' Dannhüber said.

Klemens inserted the key. The great lock slid back silently, and Klemens lifted the latch.

'Light, Major.'

Klein-Wuttig stepped forward with the hurricane lamp.

In its light they could see the nineteen crates stacked against the wall.

'Made a nice job of those too, Klemens,' Dannhüber observed. He peered into the darkness. 'And the wine casks?'

'Beyond, monsieur,' Reinach shouted from the back of the group. 'Further in the cellar.'

'Let's have a look, shall we?'

The general advanced deeper into the cellar with Klein-Wuttig followed closely by Kaspar; by Klemens who was determined to hang on to everything he could; and by Schäffer who was determined to get what he'd been promised. Behind them, Major Doench and Major Rieckhoff grinned at each other and followed with Fregattenkapitän von Hassbach. Tarnera stood in the entrance, holding the vase. He was just about to follow when something screamed out in his mind.

The cows that needed milking! The empty shops! The locked-up bar! The absence of women and children! This!

He knew at once what was happening and he was just whirling round when he heard the sentry behind him give a yelp of pain. Then the pick haft, wielded by Reinach, clanged on the back of his helmet, throwing him forward into the cellar.

With his last second of consciousness, he heard the heavy oak door thud to behind him.

7

As Reinach turned the key, they heard a muffled shot and something thump against the other side of the heavy door. Reinach grinned.

' "Moves like a dream, monsieur," ' he said. ' "You can't even hear it shut." They can shout till the cows come home. Dréo's locks would stop a cannon ball.'

As he moved to the outer door, he saw Klemens' orderly and the lorry driver in the yard go down beneath a pile of men in blue smocks and berets. Immediately, several more Frenchmen appeared and Reinach gestured.

'The sentry's in there! Out like a light!'

As the Germans were stripped of their weapons and locked in the stables, the lorry was driven to the front of the house where the staff cars were waiting. Reinach went back to the cellar. There was only the faint sound of voices beyond the door.

'They couldn't shift that with a Tiger tank,' he said.

In the street, Captain Witkus of the Afrika Korps was growing worried. The gap which had been left for the staff cars between his men and the front half of the column was widening and he knew better than anyone that it was dangerous.

'Where the hell are they?' he snapped.

Glancing at his watch, he climbed from his car just as von Hoelcke appeared. He was as angry as Witkus.

'It's ten-thirty,' he said. 'Where are those fat bastards?'

When another quarter of an hour passed and still no one had appeared, von Hoelcke walked across to the wooden gates of the château and hammered on them. There was no sound from the other side and he was suddenly suspicious.

'Up to the house!' he snapped, and, scrambling into Witkus' scout car, they roared up the street and turned into the drive leading to the front of the château. The Baronne, Euphrasie, the cook, Joseph and Reinach were standing on the steps staring across the park.

'Out of the way,' von Hoelcke said.

Stamping into the house, he stormed through the downstairs rooms with Witkus. There was nothing but scattered papers and dirty plates left from breakfast.

Euphrasie watched him from the doorway. 'If you're looking for the others,' she said, 'they've gone. Half an hour ago.'

'Where?'

'Across the park.'

The two Germans clattered to the steps. Quite clearly they

could see tyre tracks across the soft turf disappearing from sight among the distant trees.

'Where do they lead to?' Witkus demanded.

'There's a gate over there,' Reinach said. 'It opens on to the Cheuny road. From there, you can get to Langres and up to Belfort. They loaded up the lorry ages ago. There were a lot of crates.'

'*Flat* crates,' Euphrasie said. 'There were also some packages wrapped in blankets.' She glanced at the Baronne, her face suddenly shocked. 'Oh, *mon dieu*, madame! The paintings!'

The Baronne stared at her. Then she screamed and began to hobble into the house. The Germans stared after her, then Witkus shoved his Luger into Reinach's face and slammed him back against the door jamb. 'What's this about paintings?' he snarled.

'The Baronne had some paintings hidden upstairs!' Reinach stammered. 'Everybody knew about them.'

Witkus flung him aside and dashed into the house followed by von Hoelcke. At the bottom of the stairs, the Baronne was weeping in Euphrasie's arms. Up on the third floor Joseph was standing in an open doorway, gaping.

'They've gone,' he was saying.

'What have gone, you old fool?' Witkus demanded.

'The paintings! They were in here.'

Reinach had followed them up the stairs. 'That's what they wanted me to make those crates for, madame,' he called down the stairs in a hollow voice. He turned to von Hoelcke. 'Nineteen there were. We even cut trees down.'

'The porcelain's gone too,' Joseph said.

'What porcelain?' Witkus demanded.

'Sèvres porcelain.' Reinach turned to shout down the stairs again. 'That's what they were stuffing in the cars, madame.'

The two Germans hurtled down the stairs again and stood on the steps staring into the distance.

'The bastards have ditched us,' von Hoelcke said. 'For loot!'

'They wouldn't do that!' Witkus said.

'Wouldn't they?' von Hoelcke snarled. 'You must have heard what they caught them with at Falaise. Fur coats. Paintings. Jewellery. The British radio was full of it.'

'Do *you* listen to the British radio?'

'Of course I do! It's a damned sight more reliable than that he-goat Goebbels' effusions in the *Völkischer Beobachter*. They were getting away with half Normandy. It wasn't in the tanks or on the guns, though. It was all in the damned staff cars!' Von Hoelcke's arm shot out as he pointed. 'Look at the tracks, man! They speak for themselves! Come on, if we hang on here any more, the Amis'll be on our tails. Let's get that column moving.'

'Stop firing that damned gun,' Dannhüber shouted. 'It isn't doing a scrap of good.'

'I'm trying to smash the lock, Herr General.' Klein-Wuttig fired again and the bullet whanged against the metal of the lock, and whined round the cellar.

'Stop it, you idiot! You'll kill us all.'

Klein-Wuttig stood back and Kaspar inspected the lock. 'Quarter-inch iron,' he observed. 'It looks as though it was made in the eighteenth century, and it's heavy enough to stop any small-calibre bullet.'

His head still spinning, Tarnera sat on one of the wine gantries and listened to them with a strange feeling of satisfaction. The French had planned the whole thing, he realized, and he was aware of a joyous sense of relief that he'd not misjudged them.

Dannhüber turned on Klemens. 'A damned nice mess you've got us into,' he snarled.

Klemens stiffened. 'I seem to remember, General, that it was *your* idea to come down here.'

Dannhüber glared. 'You could be court-martialled for this. In fact, I'm damned sure you will be.'

'If we get out, Herr General.' Tarnera said quietly. 'It strikes me, in fact, that the only trial *we* shall face will be a war crimes trial set up by the Americans. They're great on war crimes.'

It stopped the argument dead. Dannhüber jerked at his

jacket and turned to Klemens. 'You might as well have built a prison,' he snapped. 'In fact, you *have* built a prison. And, in the meantime, your column's heading for Germany without half its officers. God knows what'll happen to it.'

Urquhart and Neville waited. The noise of the grasshoppers in the dry grass seemed deafening. Behind them, not speaking, Sergeant Dréo crouched behind his mitrailleuse.

The trees were full of men, because more had arrived during the night, even from places on the other side of the Vangouillain–Mary-les-Rivières road. Alerted by the women from Néry, they'd pushed across the road with the weapons that everybody seemed to have in quantity these days, eager to kill a few Germans.

I know these men, Urquhart thought with surprise. I know them like the back of my own hand. They're no different from the men of the fells in Cumberland where I come from, from the moors of North Yorkshire and the lowlands of Scotland. They were like his own father and his four stubborn brothers, slow to take offence but quick to defend their land, their own soil, willing to quarrel to the death with a neighbour or even their own family where the rights to a strip of meadow were concerned.

He glanced at Neville alongside him. Neville had worked hard but he was no more part of these surroundings than a university professor would be. He belonged in the hothouse atmosphere of wealth, museums and great houses, not part of the countryside like himself and the men taking their places around him in a rumble of unexcited conversation.

Reinach came stumbling through the grass. He was grinning broadly. '*Toujours le sang-froid*,' he panted. 'We got them! We got every one of them!' He snatched at a Sten gun that was handed to him. 'Every single one!' he crowed. 'All we have to do now is destroy their columns.

Neville stared at him unhappily. 'You've got everybody who matters,' he said. 'Isn't that enough?'

Reinach's head turned. 'If we had Hitler himself, it wouldn't be enough,' he growled. 'Not after what happened to those boys last night. I want a life for a life – and more!'

He stared down the valley, his eyes glinting. Then the old silly grin came back. 'I should think that about now there's the most unholy tangle brewing up in the Rue des Roches.'

There was.

The German column, commanded now in the absence of Colonel Klemens by Sturmbannführer Frobinius, had come to a stop on a corner half-way up the hill. Two miles from the village a motor-cyclist outrider had run up against a vast rock slide that had blocked the road with a tangle of soil, stone and young trees from the steep side of the hill, and within a minute he was back with his report. The column waited, its tail still in the village, while a scout car went up to investigate. Then von Hoelcke edged a tank up the slope, too, and when Frobinius arrived, it was waiting hull-down behind the curve of the hill, the ugly snout of its gun pointing at the fallen rocks.

Frobinius stared at the barrier. 'What do you make of it?' he asked.

'Brought down by explosives,' von Hoelcke growled.

Witkus's little scout car arrived in a rush.

'What's the hold-up?'

Von Hoelcke jerked his head and Witkus stood up in his seat and stared.

'Can we get infantrymen up there?' Frobinius asked. 'The Afrika Korps, for instance.'

Witkus looked down his nose. 'We don't know how tough that barrier is,' he said. 'And we can't spare half an hour to find out. We'd have every damned Frenchman from here to the frontier joining in if we did.'

Von Hoelcke nodded agreement. 'My orders are to report to 14th Armoured at Belfort,' he said. 'Not fight a battle. We'd lose half our vehicles and a hell of a lot of men.' He waved an arm at the column behind him. 'Most of these people are headquarters staff and cypher clerks. They're inexperienced. They're unfit. They're old. They're useless. We need the Afrika Korps to support my tanks, and there are two other routes out of Néry.' He eyed the barrier. 'We'll try just one shell,' he said. 'And see what happens.'

The crack of the gun set the echoes clattering in the valley. The missile struck the base of the pile of young trees. There was a huge cloud of smoke and dust, and clods of earth and splinters of stone and wood flew into the air. When it settled down, the tangle of trees, soil and rock was still there, a few flames licking at branches where the shell had exploded.

Over the drum of engines behind them they could hear the grasshoppers and the hum of bees and a skylark high in the heavens. A man coughed somewhere and it sounded like a small explosion.

'Nobody there,' von Hoelcke said.

But as he spoke, over the aching stillness there was the distinct click of a gun being cocked. As they ducked, a light machine-gun in the trees beyond the rocks started playing on the head of the column. The bullets struck the tank and whined away into the fields. The turret lid clanged as von Hoelcke disappeared, while Frobinius cowered with Witkus alongside and all the heads in the column on the corner behind them vanished from sight.

'The bastards are just waiting for us to try to get past,' Witkus said.

Frobinius' eyes narrowed. 'Very well,' he said. 'We turn back. I wish to God those sewer rats of the staff could see what's happening.'

The 'sewer rats of the staff' were far too occupied with their own problems to be concerned with Frobinius. They were still struggling with Reinach's heavy door and rapidly coming to the conclusion that there was no way through it, round it, over it or under it.

They stood back and stared at it furiously. Tarnera still sat on the gantry. His head was feeling better now and he was almost enjoying himself.

'How valuable are these paintings. Klemens?' Dannhüber asked suddenly. 'I don't suppose you checked?'

Klemens stiffened. 'I imagined they were priceless, Herr General.'

Dannhüber scowled. 'They were indeed! Well, by God,

Klemens, if *we* can't have them, the French shan't! Open those crates!'

They got the lid off the first crate and pulled the painting out. It took a lot of doing because there was only one small jemmy. Reinach had made sure there would be.

Klemens fished into his pocket and brought out the list. ' "Greuze, Jean-Bapiste," ' he read. ' "Woman combing her hair". One metre by one and a half. Circa 1780. Signed." You see the woman there, of course, Herr General.'

Dannhüber approached the painting and bent closer to it. Then he took out a pair of glasses from his breast pocket and stuck them on his nose. 'Hold the light up, Kaspar,' he said.

Kaspar did so and Dannhüber pointed at the canvas and said something to him that no one else heard.

'Let's have a look at the others,' Kaspar said.

Schäffer set about the second crate. The nails came out after a struggle and they lifted out the picture and stood it alongside the first one.

'Vigée Lebrun,' Klemens said. '1830. The date's in the corner. Two metres by one and a half. "Graf von Hodossy." The description says, "This painting testifies to Madame Lebrun's triumphal progress through the courts of Europe. She had visited Vienna, Prague – " '

'I know what she did,' Dannhüber snapped. 'Let's see the next.'

By this time Schäffer was beginning to wonder what was going on and even Klemens was becoming uneasy.

'That's the Daubigny,' he was saying. 'Charles-François. "Cross-roads near Barbizon". Painted 1864–5. Signed. Oils. Ninety-one by sixty-nine centimetres. The painter's best period".'

Dannhüber studied the painting carefully, whispered to Kaspar, who also studied it, then he jerked his hand. 'Get the lot out,' he said.

It took them a long time to get the rest of the paintings out. Reinach had done a very thorough job.

'Go on!' Dannhüber sounded bored. 'Tell me.'

Klemens didn't like the sound of his voice. 'Jean-Bapiste Greuze,' he said. 'Those four. The next one's the Kucharski.

Then there's the Fragonard, the Lancret, and the Nattier – '

Kaspar interrupted him. 'Let me see your catalogue,' he said.

Klemens handed over the folder. 'Printed in 1938,' he pointed out. 'Written by Professor Phillippe Gautier of the Faculty of Arts, Dijon University. He ought to know his business.'

'He did,' Dannhüber said. 'A pity you didn't.'

Klemens stiffened. 'What do you mean, Herr General?'

Dannhüber gestured. 'I mean – and Colonel Kaspar agrees with me – that not only have you built yourself – and me and these other gentlemen – a prison no one can get out of, but you did it for no good reason. These are copies.'

Then Tarnera remembered the Baronne and her lover who had spent half his life copying the Baron's paintings as an excuse to climb into bed with his wife. Balmaceda's attic, he had heard, had once been full of the work of years, effective and creditable, but worthless because they were only copies – Balmaceda's payment for all his years of illicit love – and Tarnera began to laugh softly to himself.

Klemens was staring at the paintings. 'Copies, Herr General?' he gasped.

'Copies, Klemens,' Dannhüber said. 'Every last one of them.'

8

It took a long time to turn the column round.

Standing in the shelter of von Hoelcke's leading tank, Frobinius sent his instructions back along the line of vehicles and the shouts went echoing down the valley.

'Turn round! Turn round! Back to Néry!'

There were yells of disgust and anger as sweating men jumped from the lorries, while the drivers wrenched at the steering wheels and cranked their gear levers. There was a gap half-way down the hill where a scout car managed to pull out, and behind it a lorry also turned, swinging with difficulty in the road and backing and filling to reverse direction.

Frobinius appeared, his face furious, and pointed at the wide slope of the field at the side of the road.

'What in God's name are you doing?' he roared. 'Use the field! Pull the fence down!'

A group of soldiers began to work on the fence and dragged it flat. Then lorries swung off the road and turned in the field, before returning to the road further down, facing the other way. Despite the speed of the operation, it wasn't designed to avoid confusion: seeing what had happened, other groups of men began to break down more of the fence and the lorry crews, many of them from non-combatant units and nervous as the uneasiness spread through the column, swung out without waiting for orders.

There was only one thought in everybody's mind: they must not abandon their vehicles. Without their vehicles, without the means of towing their guns or carrying their ammunition and light weapons, they would become virtually defenceless against the Frenchmen they all knew were now crowding into every wood and hiding behind every hill all the way back to the frontier. By leaving their tanks, their scout cars and lorries, they could have fought their way through and over and round the barrier but, after the experiences of Normandy and Falaise, they all knew that on the other side they would be entirely vulnerable to attack. Without transport they could never hope to reach Germany.

Down the hill, the scout car waited. The lorries which had turned after it began to form up behind. More heavy vehicles joined them, their drivers helped by sweating, dusty men shoving at the front wheels. A gun crew, trying to swing their heavy weapon, ran over a straining man's leg and the crack as his thigh bone snapped could be heard for yards. He started to scream and, without a great deal of tenderness, they lifted him into the back of a lorry where a medical orderly bent over him.

But there was no more firing and nothing stopped the

vehicles turning. Even the big Afrika Korps buses managed to jolt in a wide circle in the field, swaying behind the guns until they were back on the road and facing downhill. All Klemens' carefully made plans for the column had already fallen apart. Frobinius hadn't thought to organize the turning and it was now impossible to change places, so that the tanks which should have been at the front of the column were all now at the rear, and the soft-skinned vulnerable vehicles, because they had found it easier to change direction, were more often than not at the front.

Frobinius' black Mercedes went hurtling down the road, its horn screaming, Frobinius standing up and yelling to the panting soldiers to get themselves and their vehicles out of his way, so that he could reach the new head of the column. With him in the car was von Hoelcke, transferring from the leading tank to the one which had been bringing up the rear. Reaching the back of the column, he found his second-in-command sitting with his head out of his turret, sweating in the dusty sunshine and wondering what the hell had gone wrong.

'Out!' Von Hoelcke yelled at him. 'Get up the hill! Take over my tank! I'll take over this one!'

A motor-cyclist was stopped and, swinging his machine round, he roared back up the slope to where von Hoelcke's first two tanks still waited, half-hidden by the corner and occasionally engaging the hidden snipers with bursts of machine-gun fire to make them keep their heads down.

As the lieutenant climbed into the turret, the two panzers on the hill began to disengage, edging backwards to the bend where they hauled off the road and turned into the field, their tracks scattering clods of earth, before following the column streaming back to Néry. Ahead of them, Frobinius' Mercedes pushed into the village. It wasn't easy because more lorries, trying to escape from the Americans in the north, were now beginning to crowd into the valley from the direction of Châtillon and Troyes, while his own vehicles returning to Néry found themselves facing those still trying to get out. There was already a ghastly traffic jam near the château where military policemen, their metal gorgets dulled with dust, struggled to bring some order to the confusion. As they finally managed to make a gap, von Hoelcke's rear two tanks pushed their way through and out on to the Chemin de Ste Reine. As soon as they were free of the village, they halted again to wait for the column to form up in some sort of order behind them.

Waiting among the villagers on the slopes above Néry Urquhart turned as a man came scrambling over the brow of the hill.

'They turned back!' he was yelling excitedly. 'There were shots! It was terrific but we beat them!'

'It hasn't even started yet,' Urquhart growled.

He had arranged his men like an arrowhead with the long straight road up the hill as the shaft, his forces increasing in density as they reached the point, and another concentration of weapons in the trees at the lower end where the feathers would have been. Between them they could bring a tremendous fire to bear at the tip and tail of any German column. There was also a large group under Neville – with rifles, Stens, Brens and grenades – acting as a reserve half-way down. Heavier weapons were on the hillsides.

Urquhart frowned as he watched. He knew what he was doing but he wasn't so sure anyone else did. Under him, he had over three hundred men and the problem was chiefly one of discipline. Neville's plan was complicated, ambitious, even wildly optimistic, and one wrong shot could destroy it. Gathering the group commanders round him, he told Reinach once more what he wanted.

Reinach started to harangue the half-circle of men like a born leader. He wore a beret with fluttering ribbons that some former conscript had given him, and stood with his hands on his hips, his body leaning forward, in a manner that was typically French. 'Nobody,' he said ' – repeat nobody – fires until the Very light's seen and the first shot comes from here. If anybody does I'll break his jaw. Understood?'

Heads dipped in acknowledgement.

'If anybody gets excited and fires too soon the whole thing falls apart. Got that?'

More nods.

'And if we have to, we break off and scatter. We want no repetition of Vercors here. They won't chase us far. They haven't time. So we don't want anyone killed unnecessarily. Understood?'

The heads nodded again.

'Then don't be brave. There's no one to admire you except your friends who're doing the same. So don't stand up or leave cover. Only shoot if the Germans are within range, because we have to watch the ammunition. If we're going to do what we've planned, let's do it properly.'

As the men scattered, Urquhart moved back to the headquarters they'd set up, where the women were waiting with the wireless operator and the signallers. Ernestine and Marie-Claude seemed to be having an argument. Ernestine was pointing at him, and at the same time gesticulating wildly with her other arm. As he approached, she stopped and they faced him, looking guilty, Ernestine still flushed with the argument, Marie-Claude pale and angry.

Neville was watching him.

'What's wrong now?' Urquhart demanded.

Neville gave him a twisted smile. 'The usual. Just seeing it from the other chap's point of view.'

'Bugger the other chap's point of view,' Urquhart grinned. 'You've done your job, Field-Marshal. And bloody well, too. Now it's the turn of the brigadier.'

Determined not to be forced into the humiliating confusion of the Rue des Roches, Frobinius, von Hoelcke and Witkus decided to be more careful this time. It irritated Frobinius to have to act in concert with the other two. But, despite his seniority of rank, his rôle had always been that of a policeman, while they had both fought their way through the débâcles in North Africa and Normandy and were tough, experienced in war, and as anxious as he was to stay alive.

While the vehicles heading into Néry were halted by men of the Militärpolizei, a short column consisting of an armoured car with infantrymen, backed up by one of von

Hoelcke's rear two tanks, was sent out of the village to reconnoitre the Chemin de Ste Reine. As they moved away, the first lorries, some of whose drivers had been caught a month before in the valley at Falaise and could see another killing ground looming up, began nervously to edge after them. Others began to follow. After a while, Frobinius caught on to what was happening and sent men to halt them, but it was already too late and a large number had already followed von Hoelcke's leading tank as it clattered after the armoured car. Once more they were committed.

As the armoured car and the leading infantrymen reached the corner where the road began to wind up to the Crête St Amarin, von Hoelcke halted and Frobinius joined him.

'Edge up to the corner, driver,' von Hoelcke said. 'But keep her hull-down.'

As they moved forward, von Hoelcke nervously eyeing the slopes on either side, one of the infantrymen from the armoured car came running back, waving his arms.

'The road's blocked, Herr Major,' he said.

'Gottverdammt!' Von Hoelcke scowled. 'What with? More rocks?'

'No, Herr Major. This time it's trees.'

As the tank edged forward, Frobinius raised his binoculars. It was quite clear that the trees that formed the barrier ahead had all been chosen because they had leaned over the road and would fall across it under their own weight at the last saw stroke. He could see traces of mud round the tops of the lopped trunks.

'Those bastards couldn't all have been cut last night,' he said. 'They must have been sawing through them all the time they were cutting their logs and planks. They stuffed up the cuts with mud and came out this morning to finish them off.'

'See anyone?' von Hoelcke asked.

'No. Nothing.'

But again a machine-gun opened up and everybody dived for cover.

Frobinius lifted his head. 'Surely we could break through,' he suggested.

Von Hoelcke was staring up the slope at the fallen trees. 'My tanks can't,' he snapped.

Frobinius looked back down the valley. The sky was brassy with heat and the column of vehicles behind them was covered with a shimmering haze from the engines. Over it hung a pall of yellow dust through which the sun flung the shadows of the overhanging foliage. 'What are the chances of dragging those trees clear?' he demanded.

Von Hoelcke stared at him. 'Have you seen the size of them? They've obviously picked the biggest they could find. And those bloody Frenchmen are sitting right on top waiting to pick us off. There's still another route.'

'The Fond St Amarin's dangerous and they've probably blocked that, too. There's a chalk cliff close to the road. They could have weapons there.'

Von Hoelcke looked coldly at Frobinius. 'Do you have any other alternatives?' he asked.

Frobinius scowled. 'No,' he said. 'We'll take it.'

By this time, however, Néry was packed with vehicles and it was difficult even to approach it. Only by turning out the Afrika Korps men with their guns at the ready could Frobinius force a passage.

'What the hell's happened?' he screamed above the shouts, the din of engines, the revving motor-cycles and the rumble of exhausts. 'Where have all these damned people come from?'

A military policeman appeared. 'The Americans are south of Troyes now, Herr Sturmbannführer,' he yelled. 'They're only forty-odd kilometres away and heading for St Seigneur. All the traffic from the Sens–Nancy road that wasn't cut off is trying to get out this way, too!'

They got the armour through at last, with von Hoelcke back in his own tank again as they reversed direction yet again. In a fury, he drove his vehicle at a cart drawn by four horses that happened to be in his way. Forcing it from the road, dragging the screaming animals backwards until they fell, he backed off and pushed a lorry after it until there was a gap.

'Shoot those animals.' he roared. 'Right, Witkus, are your people ready? This time, it's all or nothing!'

With a struggle, they got the column moving again. The crumpled lorry that von Hoelcke had pushed off the road had started to burn. The flames were licking the side of a wooden barn while the blazing petrol had reached the spot where the four horses lay, so that the stink of scorched hair and flesh filled the nostrils with sickening intensity. Then the cart caught fire and the flames increased, filling the road with smoke. One heroic man with a lorry tried to drag the wreckage aside, but it didn't help much. The following vehicles had to feel their way through the smoke, while the men on foot held handkerchieves in front of their mouths and eyes and stumbled past, their sweating faces fixed under their helmets. The column was moving again but by now there was no order, no cohesion. Units had twice been broken up and scattered, and their officers were sometimes half a mile from their commands. All too often the clerks, the unfit and the elderly were at the front simply because fear and inexperience had made them the fastest off the mark.

As the column halted on its way out of the village to the Fond St Amarin, Frobinius stopped his car alongside von Hoelcke's tanks. Just ahead and on their left, Guardian Moch's house stood alone at the end of its narrow lane, surrounded by the scattered debris of its owner's black market activities. The road in front swung in curves through the trees. Then it dipped into a hollow before turning and rising alongside a chalk escarpment, topped with more trees and undergrowth, and finally climbing steeply to the ridge. The chalk cliff was thirty feet above the road while on the right, the land dipped into a hollow full of lush grass, brambles and nettles, before sweeping up to another thick belt of undergrowth below the final steeper slope to the tree-lined ridge.

The valley was silent beyond the throbbing of the engines and the mutter of tired voices as Witkus' scout car pulled up.

'What now?' he demanded.

They were worried about the silence and had almost decided to send an armoured car ahead with infantry to feel their way through the hollow, when a bright red petrolette ridden by a girl in a yellow dress hurtled down the lane from Guardian Moch's house and swung into the road half a mile ahead of them. It was going at full throttle, which was how the villagers always tackled the steep slope of the Fond St Amarin. Anything less failed to carry them to the brow of the ridge, and that meant pushing their machines for the last quarter of a mile.

'She's going fast,' von Hoelcke said.

Witkus grinned through the paste of dust and sweat on his face. 'Perhaps she was scared,' he said, 'when she saw what was following her. Perhaps she thought it a very big operation for a very small rape.'

'It isn't a joke!' von Hoelcke snapped.

'Hasn't the whole damn war become a joke?'

Frobinius was gesturing excitedly. 'There's only one place this road leads to,' he said. 'On to the Chatillon–Langres road! If *she* can get through, we can! Follow her up, Hoelcke!'

Stephanie Moch had a good start, however. After her wild ride to Rolandpoint, she had volunteered willingly for the job. She knew exactly what to do and, as she hurtled down the slope into the dip, her skirts fluttered up to her waist. By the time Frobinius and von Hoelcke came to life, she was almost a mile ahead of them in the dip, going as fast as she could.

9

Up on the hill, squatting behind the Bren, Urquhart's eyes were everywhere. The countryside below him looked warm and rich with the hot colours of late summer. It was friendly and real and he remembered how alien and foreign he'd felt when he'd first arrived in the spring. He frowned, uncertain of his emotions but sure that in the months he'd been there he'd become part of this little corner of Burgundy. He'd heard it said that France was the land all men loved, even the Germans, because here all men walked free and the sun shone down softly, as it did on no other place on earth. Now he knew what it meant.

He turned on his side and stared down the valley. As though they sensed the tension in the air, the grasshoppers had stopped their croaking and the silence was immense. No one moved except for the occasional messenger, standing on the pedals of his bicycle to drive the machine over the lumpy ground.

'There's a gun barrel glinting down there!' Urquhart pointed out. 'Tell them to rub dirt on it and push up the foliage a bit.'

Reinach's head lifted. Over the silence they could hear nothing but the hum of bees. The stillness seemed to be a living thing, breathing alongside them in a curious kind of menace.

'Tanks!'

They all heard the drum of engines and the clink and clatter of tank tracks. Reinach pointed and they saw the rising cloud of grey-white dust appear in the valley. Then they saw the flash of the sun on windscreens, and Reinach's arm shot out again.

'Here they come!'

A scout car appeared first, then a group of infantrymen, followed by two tanks moving like grey-green slugs up the winding road beneath the trees. Behind them was a group of lorries, then two more tanks, followed by buses and big troop-carrying lorries.

Neville caught his breath at the strength they implied and glanced uneasily at Urquhart. Urquhart was watching calmly, his eyes glinting, a tough self-reliant man in no doubt about what he was going to do.

'Got the bastards,' he said.

'They're not here yet.' Neville looked along the ridge of the chalk cliff. 'Some clot's bound to fire too soon.'

Urquhart didn't seem to hear him. 'Grenades?' he asked.

'A dump every twenty-five yards. Ammunition caches in

the trees.' Neville scowled. 'I don't like this business. And neither will you by the time you've finished.'

Urquhart turned slowly. 'Who said I ever did?' he asked.

The head of the column had now reached the corner where the road turned and began its last straight climb up to the crest of the ridge. Two changes of direction and the confusion in the village had brought a weird mixture of old cars and lorries, men on stolen bicycles and motor bikes, even weary infantrymen on foot, up among the leading military vehicles. The column was moving with the speed of a tortoise because there were even horse-drawn vehicles interspersed among the lorries and, with no room to pass, they were all reduced to the pace of the starved and tired animals.

Urquhart's teeth showed in a grin. 'For the first time,' he said, 'the buggers are beginning to *look* defeated.'

As von Hoelcke's tank turned the corner and ground to a halt, the road ahead looked deserted and Stephanie Moch on her petrolette was nowhere to be seen. Frobinius climbed out of his Mercedes and walked up to join the panzer captain, a puzzled frown on his face.

'Where did she go to?' he demanded.

'She certainly didn't carry on up here.' Von Hoelcke's eyes were sweeping the silent, empty landscape. 'That machine just couldn't go fast enough to be out of sight yet.'

'Well, she couldn't turn off.'

Von Hoelcke shook his head and pointed grimly at a narrow gully, its entrance half-hidden in the undergrowth. It was less than half a metre wide and disappeared like a tunnel into the trees. 'Wild boar,' he said. 'I come from East Prussia and I've seen those things before. She pushed the bike down it, hid it, and kept on going.'

'Why, for God's sake?'

Von Hoelcke lifted his eyes. 'We'll know before long,' he said.

High above the Germans, Urquhart continued to watch. Apart from one spot where the road beneath him was obscured by a curve of the land, he could see the whole valley. Several times, Reinach eyed him, waiting for a signal, but Urquhart didn't move, sitting behind a Bren, his back against a stump of tree, relaxed, almost as if he were resting after a morning's work. Behind him, among a group of girls who had refused to be sent away, Ernestine Bona and Marie-Claude waited with Doctor Mouillet, sitting under a little shelter they'd made out of branches to keep the sun off the wounded. As he glanced round at them, Ernestine waved but she didn't give her usual smile. Marie-Claude's expression remained frozen. Then he saw Gaston Dring running through the trees. 'Stephanie's arrived,' he said.

Urquhart nodded and turned to Reinach who was muttering alongside him to the radio operator. 'Where are the Americans?'

'Other side of St Seigneur. They're bringing up artillery. They'll make a hell of a mess.'

Urquhart stared down the slope towards Néry. There'd be other places in a mess before the day was out, he thought.

'What about the Free French?'

'Coming as fast as they can. They're at Champagnole. That's still three and a half hours away.'

Urquhart crossed himself. 'God help us,' he muttered.

Von Hoelcke's tank stopped and the big gun barrel had begun to swing. The machine looked formidable with the bundles of camouflage netting for night bivouac strapped to its hull. Then changing gear with high-pitched whine, it lurched and moved on another few yards before stopping again.

'The bloody plan was too complicated,' Neville said uneasily. 'The buggers are suspicious.'

An armoured car, followed by a truckload of troops, moved forward and stopped alongside the tank. The tank's hatch opened and a figure stuck its head out.

There was a mile-long drop back to Néry. It was hot in the tank and von Hoelcke was gulping at the warm afternoon air. They had already wasted far too much time getting away from this god-forsaken place, but at least the road ahead didn't appear to be blocked, and he could see all the way to the crest and across open fields on the right where his tanks and guns could manoeuvre. 'They must have decided this road couldn't be held,' he said.

As the tankman turned to speak to the man in the black uniform standing in the road, Urquhart's eyes narrowed. The sun was hot on his back and he was sweating. Neville was staring through his binoculars.

'That's the SS man,' he said. 'The bastard who shot young Dréo.'

'So what?' Urquhart's voice was harsh. 'Are you thinking of challenging him to a duel?' His hand sliced down. 'Forget him! You know your bloody history. We don't have man-to-man fights any longer. You made a good plan. Don't spoil it by going at it half-cocked.'

Neville became silent. Not far away, crouching in the bushes at the edge of the chalk cliff, Théyras was gnawing at a piece of bread and sausage. Sergeant Dréo and his son were sitting on rocks beside the old mitrailleuse, their stiff legs stuck straight out in front of them, the old man's face like wood beneath the steel helmet he'd brought back in 1918. Near them Lionel Dring crouched behind his anti-tank gun, his eyes narrow. Balmaceda sat beside him, clutching fresh ammunition to his chest. He looked ancient, and, with his toupee slipping again, even a little drunk.

The smell from the engines below wafted up to them, and Neville could hear the putter of diesels reverberating against the flat white face of the cliff. The leading tank had the number 375 painted on its turret in white, and it seemed to have been newly camouflaged in brown and green splodges. From where he sat, he could almost see into the hatch.

It was an ideal position for snipers and there were plenty of people lining the cliff who could shoot. But no one succumbed to the temptation.

Urquhart turned to him. 'Right,' he said. 'Get down there! The first two vehicles are to be allowed through.'

Neville began to move away, running in a crouch.

'And, Neville!'

Neville stopped and turned. Urquhart's face was hard.

'No backing away! None of your bloody compassion! Every German dead today means one less of our people dead tomorrow!'

Neville nodded, but was still shocked by Urquhart's cold-blooded attitude.

Then Urquart grinned and waved him away. 'Here's to a short war,' he said.

By this time, the two tanks in the lead had moved a little higher up the slope. The road was steep, the surface worn smooth, and the tracks slipped. As the engines screamed, the first tank slid sideways on the camber of the road and tucked its nose into the bank. The officer climbed out. He'd abandoned his jacket and they could see the sweat on his face and darkening the back of his shirt and under his arms. He was peering towards the rear of the tank as though he was having trouble with the engine.

The driver also opened his hatch and climbed out. Then the officer began to shout something to the commander of the second tank who emerged on to his turret. He was in shorts and looked like a boy with his ash-blond hair. His head disappeared, but as his tank moved it too slid to the side of the road and ended up alongside the first tank.

Reinach was grinning. 'We've got them,' he said. '*Dans le pot de chambre*.' He looked expectantly at Urquhart, who shook his head.

'Wait!'

'But we have them!'

Urquhart ignored the urgings, watching carefully as an armoured car began to edge past the tanks.

'Wait,' he said, his eyes glinting. 'They're going to try the soft-skinned vehicles. That makes it easier. And if the tanks want to move now, they'll have to wait for the jam to clear and come at it with a rush. Tell the radio operator to let de Frager know.'

Reinach was puzzled by Urquhart's intentions, and it was Marie-Claude who scrambled to her feet.

'I'll go!'

As she hurried off through the trees, a big troop carrier

followed the armoured car in low gear past the stalled tanks, an exasperated officer standing in the road waving it on. Helmeted men clung to the tarpaulin frames shouting insults at the tankmen. They were festooned with ammunition belts, some of them with grenades round their necks. Every one of them held a machine-gun or a sub-machine-gun.

The carrier negotiated the jam with difficulty and slipped out of sight beneath the escarpment. Urquhart held his breath. Just in front below him he could see a lizard on a rock basking in the sun. Father Pol crouched among the bushes behind it, clutching a rifle, his spectacles down his nose, his shovel hat tilted forward; he was sweating in the sun.

'Blessed be God,' he was muttering. 'Blessed be His holy name. Blessed be Jesus Christ, true God and true man.' He looked up and saw Urquhart watching him. 'Agony isn't mitigated because others share it,' he pointed out.

Urquhart nodded and crossed himself and Father Pol lifted his hand, two fingers raised in blessing. 'Blessed be our venture today, my son. God grant that France will soon be free.'

Urquhart turned. Théyras caught his eye and, brushing his moustache with the back of his hand, made a gesture as though he were drinking from a bottle. Urquhart licked his lips. His heart was thumping but he was quite calm. He turned again and looked down the valley.

Negotiating the corner, the young lieutenant commanding the armoured car stared ahead. The road rose in a straight line in front of him to where it traversed the crest by way of a cutting. Beyond, it appeared to be unoccupied. There were more trees up there, but they were set well back from the road and there seemed a chance. There were probably men with guns sitting among the rocks by the cutting, however, and he jerked his helmet down and tapped the driver.

'Straight ahead,' he said. 'And fast. Ready?'

'Ready, sir.'

The lieutenant stood up and waved to the driver of the

lorry-load of troops behind. 'If we can get to that cutting and hold it, we're all safe!' he yelled. 'Let's go!'

The driver let in his clutch and the armoured car jerked. The engine of the lorry behind roared, then the two of them headed up the hill. The cutting came closer and, expecting a blast of fire, the lieutenant drew his head down into his shoulders. Just in front there were patches of dirt and stones on the macadam and he suspected immediately that they concealed mines. But, by a miracle, they were past and nothing had happened. The road beyond was clear!

'Radio,' he snapped, and as he was handed the microphone, he shouted into it. 'Eifel calling Schnee Elbert! Eifel calling Schnee Elbert!'

Von Hoelcke's voice came back. 'Schnee Elbert to Eifel. Go ahead.'

The lieutenant's voice broke with his excitement. 'We're through!' he yelled. 'There's nothing up here! Nothing at all!'

Rising from the turret, von Hoelcke shouted down to Frobinius waiting alongside.

'The road's clear,' he said.

'Typical of the French,' Frobinius grinned. 'They've only half done the job.'

He ran to his car as von Hoelcke waved his arms to the vehicles behind. He wanted them out of the way so that he and his tanks could reverse and take the hill at speed. The column edged backwards, the gaps between the vehicles closing until they were bumper to bumper, and the lurch rearwards travelled all the way down to Néry in another vast concertina movement like a caterpillar in reverse until it came to a stop on the outskirts of the village, where the jam in the street brought it to a halt.

As a little space was cleared, von Hoelcke's tanks edged backwards, too, reversing from the bank and down the hill until the road flattened out a little. As they stopped again, von Hoelcke touched his driver's shoulder with his foot.

'Right, driver,' he said. 'Full speed ahead! And this time stop for nothing!'

The tank's treads slipped and for a second it slithered sideways on the camber of the road; then it began to pick up speed. As the corner drew near, von Hoelcke held his breath, but the tank negotiated the turn flat out, clattering round and filling the valley with the noise of its engine as it began to climb. Beyond the cutting they could see the armoured car waiting with the troop carrier, the soldiers lining the side of the road, alert for any signs of trouble.

They were within a hundred yards of the ridge, approaching the dirt-patched stretch of road, the first of the lorries behind them level with the face of the escarpment and going at full speed, when von Hoelcke saw the tarmacadam patches in front of him erupt in a sheet of flame and the whole road lifted in a shower of dirt, stones and chunks of soil.

10

The young lieutenant in command of the armoured car was watching the cutting as instructed when he saw the surface of the road climbing out of the valley beyond it suddenly explode. The earth shook and, at the same moment, a great flare of flame gouted from the rocks on either side of the cutting, and boulders leapt into the air to crash down and form a solid barrier that effectively jammed the narrow opening in the ridge. More explosions followed and tons of earth slid after them. Between the lieutenant and the rest of the column there was now a high barricade of stones and soil, and beyond it a deep trench had been blown in the road, across which he knew neither he nor anyone else would ever get anything less manoeuvrable than a tank. He was in trouble.

'For God's sake,' he screamed. 'Open fire!'

'What at?' the machine-gunner alongside him yelled. At that moment they saw a streak of smoke heading towards them, and in their last second of life they heard a thump on the bonnet of the armoured car. The explosion flung it to the side of the road as a heap of twisted metal and molten glass, its crew hurled from it like rag dolls. Only one man survived and he lay trapped and screaming as the flames edged closer.

As the rest of the advance group ducked their heads to avoid the falling debris, a blast of fire from what seemed hundreds of weapons started from the trees and shrubs along the ridge, the bullets striking sparks from the road and the rocks where they crouched and whining off into the distance. Another bazooka rocket finished off the troop carrier and a corporal, trying heroically to drag a Spandau into position, was lashed by the fire before he could set it up. A second man running to his assistance was lifted off his feet by another burst, and when a third man was killed the sergeant sensibly called a halt and they lay with their heads down, scrabbling with fingers in the earth behind every scrap of cover they could find.

'Leave it,' the sergeant yelled. 'Leave it!'

Then, as the fire from the ridge suddenly lessened, he realized it had changed direction and that the weapons were firing into the valley beyond the blocked cutting. As he became aware of the volume of sound from the other side of the ridge, his jaw dropped and he realized that, despite what had happened, he and what was left of his men were probably luckier than they knew.

The first shot into the valley was a shell from de Frager's anti-tank gun positioned above the blocked cutting, and a puff of dust erupted in the meadow just beyond the first tank as it began to draw back from the shattered strip of road. Behind the tank, the following vehicles, also brought to a sudden stop, had crashed into each other all the way down the column, and up on the ridge the Frenchmen could hear the shouts and yells of fury and fear.

Then the anti-tank gun fired again and there was more dust.

'For God's sake,' Urquhart snapped, as if he could be heard at the top of the hill, 'Raise the bloody sights!'

As the tank began to back away, the Germans were already jumping in dozens from the lorries and scrambling behind them for shelter. Their automatic weapons started to chatter, but they had no idea where the shells had come from and their firing was wild and largely directed across the open fields on their right towards the line of trees lining the crest. There was a thump as de Frager got the tank at last, and a column of oily smoke lifted into the sky to drift away in the breeze. The explosion had torn off the port track and the tank had slewed round and started to burn. The driver, his clothes on fire, fell out on to the road and was dragged to shelter by a group of soldiers who were frantically covering him with coats to put out the flames. The second tank, also trying desperately to back away, crashed into a civilian car just behind that was full of infantrymen, crushing it so that the screams of the injured men were added to the din.

'Get that gun firing!' Von Hoelcke was standing by the side of his blazing tank, trying to direct the fire of the second tank. 'They're up by the cutting! For God's sake, bring that damned gun to bear!'

Urquhart was still watching with narrowed eyes. Apart from de Frager's shells and the shooting of the Germans, still no one had fired. Reinach looked at him eagerly.

'Wait!' Urquhart was gesturing with the flat of his hand. 'Wait!'

De Frager's gun fired again and was answered immediately by the whiplash of high velocity shells, but even now the Germans had not managed to pinpoint de Frager's gun. The rattle of Spandaus was answered by the ripple of Brens from the ridge, the sound pouring down the valley in waves. Spent bullets sent leaves drifting down, and from near the tank they could hear someone screaming orders. Then Urquhart nodded at last and pointed, and Lionel Dring's gun banged. A lorry went up in flames as it tried to pull out and turn, so that its blazing shape blocked the road. As he fired again, a second lorry followed, and square-helmeted men ran for shelter, heads down, their equipment bobbing at their hips. A wounded soldier was dragged away, his bare head lolling back, his arm round another man's neck.

Ducking down the road to the second tank, whose commander was still uncertain of the direction of the firing and was busy demolishing the rocks near the cutting, von Hoelcke started pointing wildly to the escarpment on their left. As the Spandaus started to shred the trees, Urquhart heard someone yelp. Glancing round, he saw Yvon Guélis being dragged away, blood across his face and chest. Dr Mouillet bent over him and, in a fragment of time, Urquhart saw Ernestine's jaw drop and Marie-Claude's face bleak and white with shock.

Turning back towards the fight below him, he squatted behind his Bren, his back still against the stump of tree. A German, his arm limp at his side, began to stumble back instinctively towards the shelter of Néry. Other men, trying to get away from the flying splinters of metal and stone, began to follow. Among them were the crew of von Hoelcke's tank, shouting and gesticulating angrily. A few more men, less shaken by the shock of the attack, were underneath their vehicles, pointing towards de Frager's position and the hill at the top of the meadow on the other side of the road, where it might be possible to circle round among the trees along the ridge to the cutting.

Frobinius was yelling to the commander of the second tank. 'Off the road,' he shouted. 'Get up there! Get those bastards with the gun!'

The tank driver reversed his starboard track and the blunt nose swung. The gun was still pointing to the cutting, still firing as the tank lurched into the fence and edged off the road. In front of it, the land fell away into the shallow dip filled with undergrowth, brambles, nettles and bright green grass, and as the tank's nose dropped, the gun seemed to whip as it dipped with it. Then, as the tank moved into the hollow, dragging the fence with it, its tracks began to throw up watery mud and, before its crew knew what had happened, its bogeys were hub deep in thick black slime. The commander's head appeared.

As it jerked into reverse, Urquhart sat up. 'Now,' he said and, lifting a Very pistol, fired a signal cartridge across the valley. As the red light burst, he swung the Bren in front of him, lined up on the tank and pulled the trigger. The tank commander, his head up, instinctively watching the flare, slid out of sight inside the turret. Then, as Urquhart's gun fired again, the whole escarpment above the road burst into flame.

From his position further down the hill, Neville saw everything with shocked eyes as if it were magnified, its colours multiplied and doubly gaudy. Just below him, a lorry slewed sideways to a halt and a man jumped out and started to run. Three more men followed, and he recognized the last one as Hössenfelder, the dumpy Westphalian who had appeared at the farm to help, the little man whose love of the soil had driven him to work even for the French.

Gaudin's elder son, taut and bitter since the murder of his brother, lifted his rifle. As Neville turned to stop him, Urquhart's warning came back to him and he choked on the words in his throat. As the rifle cracked, Hössenfelder's running feet grew slower and his body leaned further and further forward before he finally went down, his body sliding along the surface of the road. As he came to a stop, he rolled over, and Neville could see tar, melted in the hot sun, smearing his face.

Caught in the flank behind their vehicles where they'd been sheltering from the firing from the cutting, men went over like shot rabbits. The tank in the dip was swinging wildly now, its tracks having difficulty gripping the sticky mud formed by the diverted spring and the leaking dam on the slopes above. Then Dring's gun fired again and the tank caught fire. The hatches opened and the crew began to scramble clear. The first man out reached down to where another man was pushing up the body of the commander, but a Bren burst caught him across the waist and he fell headfirst into the turret. As the flames took hold, an incandescent flare shot upwards from the hatch, and someone inside started screaming.

At the back of the column, down in the valley, a command car driven by a cypher clerk from St Seigneur was trying desperately to turn on the narrow road to head back to the safety of Néry. As the driver fought with the wheel, a lorry-mounted machine-gun behind him began to fire at figures running among the trees on the higher ground alongside. One of them fell but was snatched up and dragged out of sight; then an explosion behind them sent the high bank of the road toppling down across the road and on to the bonnet of the car.

'Get rid of it,' the lieutenant in command of the group screamed, but as his men jumped from their lorries with shovels and began to tear at the loose earth, a series of cracks made them look up. Greyish smoke was drifting away between the trees and half a dozen tall firs were teetering across the blue skyline above them. As they ran for safety, the trees crashed down across the road in a cloud of dust and flying twigs, the last one falling across the trapped car to pin the driver in his seat with a broken spine. As men ran towards him, machine-guns started firing from the trees and a phosphorous grenade landed among them. Car, driver, rescuers and all disappeared in a cloud of white smoke and stabbing flame.

On the Néry side of the fallen trees, the drivers of the vehicles crowding up from the village were also trying to turn to escape from the firing higher up the valley. One or two broke clear and were already pushing their way back to the village alongside the jammed column. But as they reached the first of the houses, they found themselves facing the last of the vehicles leaving the Chemin de Ste Reine. Two of them collided and blocked the road and the whole lot became hopelessly jammed near the burning barn where the smoke drifted thick and golden across the glaring sunshine.

'They've closed the road!' The yell was taken up on all sides. 'Turn round!'

In the narrow streets, however, it was impossible to change direction. A man, frightened and drunk on brandy looted in Rolandpoint, kicked in the door of the nearest house and, snatching up a burning plank from the blazing barn, tossed it inside. One of Frobinius' men, cut off from his group after the retreat from the Chemin de Ste Reine, caught the spirit of the thing at once. This was the sort of occasion when he knew exactly what to do.

'Burn them out,' he roared. 'Burn out the French filth!'

Bursting open the next house, he flung in an opened jerry-can of petrol and hurled a grenade after it. The crash of the explosion and the whoof of the petrol going up blew out the windows and flapped the shutters, and smoke poured out in a thick cloud. Another drunken man ran into the church and sprinkled petrol among the pews. Yet another let fly with his Schmeisser at the altar, and the intricate carved and painted figurines leapt and toppled, wooden heads and arms flying through the air. The great metal pipe from the stove, running across the church like the bowels of a submarine, collapsed in a cloud of rust and soot. Then the Henri IV window fell out and flames began to rise as still more German soldiers dragged benches forward to feed the blaze.

The door of Mère Ledoux's bar was smashed down and when they found no drink, the Germans fired at the shelves, and glasses and bottles leapt into the air. A moment later, flames started there, too. Reinach's home followed, then Balmaceda's studio, the Gaudin farmhouse, and Dréo's smithy where the work of destruction was made easier by the embers still glowing in the forge.

It was only when half the village was alight that it dawned on the infuriated Germans that they were endangering their own escape. The smoke and flames had been caught by the breeze and were roaring across the street. With the Americans pushing into St Seigneur and the routes from the south jammed by troops fighting to get north, there was now only one way out of Néry and that was to the north-east.

Already groups of men, abandoning their vehicles, were drifting on foot up the Rue des Roches and the Chemin de Ste Reine. Indifferent to the shambles which had started in the Fond St Amarin, their only concern was to get through to the Mary-les-Rivières road beyond and on to Belfort. Not many of them did.

By this time, the third tank had been stopped by Yves Rapin's bazooka and the column was becoming a tangle of burning vehicles. Since the attackers were thirty feet above their heads and overlooking them, it was almost impossible to bring the 88s to bear. An attempt was made, only to be defeated by the mortar fire coming over the trees. The bombs dropped among the lorries, killing men, tearing away limbs, and smashing more vehicles.

The commander of the fourth tank tried to bring his gun round but a fresh shower of grenades came down from the cliff. Several of them burst against the turret and one went straight into the open hatch. The thump of the explosion was followed by silence. The crew of the third tank had already abandoned their disabled vehicle and run for shelter.

Lorries were still trying to turn off the road, and one or two of the smaller ones had swung into the dip alongside in the hope of reversing direction there. But the dip had become a bog and not one of them managed it. Only one small tracked vehicle managed to reach a ridge of stones built as a cattle crossing, but it was promptly hit by a burst of heavy machine-gun fire and stopped, burning furiously, to block up the only escape route.

Alongside Urquhart, Sergeant Dréo was hammering with the old mitrailleuse, his bullets punching holes in the sides of vehicles and dropping men. Guardian Moch, still wearing his 'Anthony Eden' hat, was shooting as if he'd lived all his life as a huntsman. Dring and Ernouf, in shirt sleeves, were handling their long rifles expertly as they talked and smoked, while Stens and Brens rattled from the shattered cutting where a wildly excited Patrice de Frager was hopping about between the rocks and trees, shouting orders. A group of hated Miliciens in their distinctive uniforms became a sitting target, and automatic weapons opened up on the struggling mass as they tumbled from their trucks. The frenzy was infectious; cheering started and a few heads popped up.

'Get down,' Urquhart yelled furiously. 'Get down, you stupid bastards!'

No one could hear him above the din, and a boy in a group of excited youngsters running wildly along the lip of the escarpment was seen and caught by a machine-gun burst from the road. He was lifted off his feet and flung down in front of his girl friend, his head almost torn from his shoulders. Another boy, his eyes glassy with the shock of battle, stared at the body then stood up, a grenade in his fist.

'For Christ's sake, Reinach!' Urquhart stormed, infuriated by the blind courage the French boys were showing. 'Tell them to cut out the heroics!'

But he was too late and the boy was hit in the legs. Spinning round, he fell across a bush, which slowly sagged and deposited him in the grass, watched by the girl who was still frozen into immobility with horror.

One of his friends began to crawl towards him but suddenly he stopped yelling and, rolling with difficulty on to his face, his trousers shining with the blood pouring from his thighs, reached for the grenade. His hand scrabbled weakly about in the grass before he managed to clutch it. Then he began to crawl forward again, his face torn by the bush and ghastly with his agony. At the edge of the escarpment he forced himself to his knees and wrenched at the pin of the grenade. It landed under the petrol tank of a lorry which went up like a bomb.

'Got the bastard,' he sobbed, and fell back in the grass writhing with pain. '*Merde*,' he moaned as he was carried away to safety. 'My legs! Oh, God, how they hurt!'

Close by the burning lorry, a troop of horses pulling a gun and terrified by the flames and the explosion, began to rear and plunge in a confusion of twisted leathers and shouting men. The gun swung across the road, its wheels caught in the rusty barbed wire that edged the tarmacadam. Urquhart jabbed at Sergeant Dréo and yelled in his ear. The flash of eyes in response showed all the bottled-up hatred of four years. The old machine-gun swung and one after the other the horses dropped, their heavy legs threshing in the roadway, their bodies effectively forming a barrier against either advance or escape. Dréo went on firing until the last of them was still.

Below them, Frobinius was screaming at the naval lieutenant who, now that Fregattenkapitän von Hasbach was incarcerated in the cellar of the Château de Frager with

Klemens and General Dannhüber, had taken over command of what he had cheerfully called the Marine Cavalry. He was not so cheerful now because Frobinius was pointing at the silent trees at the top of the sloping meadow at the right-hand side of the road beyond the dip.

'Get up there,' he was yelling. 'Horses can cross that mud. Get up the field and among those trees. Get on to the ridge and come round behind the bastards!'

The lieutenant didn't think much of the idea but he was willing enough. Having been a sailor until a few weeks before, he hadn't the foggiest notion of what he should do and his men were equally in the dark. Cavalry charges, he knew, were usually delivered with a sword or a lance and the sheer momentum of the swiftly-moving weight of a hundred or more horses. He had no idea how to deliver a charge with rifles, but he drew his pistol and tried. He got his men into some sort of order in the smoke, his unskilful sailors wrenching at their nervous mounts. Then, as he waved his arm, they began to form into a ragged line and plough through the brambles and undergrowth in the bog, avoiding the disabled tank and the burning scout car.

As they moved clear of the undergrowth, the firing from the cliff caught them. A horse screamed and went down, shot through the spine, its rider leaping clear as the agonized animal tried to drag itself away, trailing its hindquarters. More horses fell and riders toppled from the saddle. Then mortar bombs began to land among them, and they opened out, leaving three animals struggling on the grass and a man climbing to his feet and limping away. They kept going, however, and from the top of the escarpment Reinach stared across the valley. 'It's up to Verdy de Clary now,' he said. 'Let's hope he can wait.'

Urquhart's eyes narrowed. 'He'll wait,' he said with the confidence of a soldier in the durability of army training.

The horsemen were half-way up the slope when the whole line of the trees where Verdy de Clary waited burst into flame. More horses went down and the whole line lost cohesion. In a moment there were a couple of dozen dead and dying animals scattered across the grass, their riders running back to the road, and more horses galloping away with empty saddles.

The sailors struggled back. One of them had been kicked in the chest by a wounded animal. As he was helped to shelter he was breathing agonizedly in terrible snoring whispers, choking on his own blood under his shattered ribs. Several of the riderless horses trotted back with them, mingling with the lorries and scattering men in their panic until the machine-guns brought them down.

Furious and sickened by the butchery, the lieutenant limped to the shelter of a wrecked tank. 'Whose damned silly idea was that?' he snarled.

11

Crouching behind von Hoelcke's tank, Frobinius stared horrified at the ruins of the charge he had ordered. As far as the Germans were concerned, the Frenchmen thirty feet above them might well have been three hundred feet up. He was baffled what to do next and it was von Hoelcke who decided that the only alternative was a proper attack by the few experienced infantrymen they had up the slopes of the field where the horsemen had failed.

Like Urquhart he had faith in training. The meadow on their right rose with occasional dips like shallow trenches behind which attackers could hide and at the top there was a belt of thick undergrowth which could shelter them for a last rush into the trees. It didn't seem impossible that they could fight their way along the ridge to the groups of men firing from the cutting and round to the lip of the escarpment.

He managed with a struggle and the aid of Captain Witkus to get the assault organized. By manhandling them, they got two of the 88s pointing towards the trees. It was difficult because the slopes were steep and there was no time to dig the guns in tail-down. Somehow they also directed one or two heavy machine-guns up the slope, then von Hoelcke turned to Witkus.

'Right,' he said. 'Off you go! I'll support you with everything I can bring to bear.'

The machine-guns began to hammer and the 88s got off one or two shells, but then a bazooka rocket hit one of them, throwing it on its side and killing its crew. The second gun was already being showered by grenades.

The infantrymen had set off, stumbling and cursing, into the bog at the side of the road. Fighting their way through, their clothes snatched at by brambles, they flung themselves down behind the sloping bank, only to find they were still exposed to the fire from the escarpment. With no alternative but to go forward – and as fast as possible – Witkus waved his arm and set off running, bent double, up the slope.

By this time, the second 88 had been silenced and one by one the heavy machine-guns had had to retreat across the river to the trees on the narrow strip of stony soil under the escarpment. But it was almost as dangerous there because grenades could be tossed down on to them and, though they couldn't be seen so easily from above, the smoke from the burning lorries obscured their view of the opposite slope.

Witkus' infantrymen had now reached the belt of undergrowth near the crest and, feeling that at least it hid them from view, they plunged into it. Almost immediately, they found themselves caught up on a criss-cross of barbed wire – their own wire, German wire – the wire Klemens had handed over for fencing French pastures. There wasn't enough to be completely effective but it delayed them.

Cursing and sweating, Witkus urged them on. 'Keep going,' he yelled. 'Keep going!'

At the other side of the belt of wire, deep in the tangle of bushes and brambles, the land dropped into a small ditch. The first man leapt thankfully for its shelter, only to scream as a pointed stake ran deep into his groin, and Witkus saw that the ditch was filled with dozens of interlocked sharpened poles like an ancient cheval de frise.

'You can get through that,' he yelled. 'Keep your heads!'

As the soldiers struggled on, Witkus noticed an ominous silence from the weapons at the top of the hill. Perhaps his men couldn't be seen, he thought, because he could still hear the guns from the escarpment hammering away and the occasional thump of a grenade. They were no longer firing at him, however, and biting his lip, knowing that the Wehrmacht had been fooled by a set of French farmers, he gathered his men together for the final rush forward.

Néry was a shambles by this time, with furious German soldiers shooting the cattle in a lunatic welter of slaughter. Two old men and a sick woman who had refused to leave the village were dragged out and shot. So was a boy who had sneaked back against orders with his girl friend to find her cat. His body was stripped and flung on to the steps of the war memorial, then the girl was dragged into a house and raped.

More lorries had managed to force their way into the village from the west. The Americans near St Seigneur were close behind them, creating havoc with their artillery among the tail-end of the stream of vehicles heading east, and those in the lead simply ignored the shouts of the military police in Néry until, in the confusion of vehicles facing in every imaginable direction in the village street, it became impossible to move out in any direction at all. Through the confusion lines of men threaded, desperately seeking safety, fires roaring on both sides of them. Officers were ransacking their baggage for food and weapons they could carry on foot and there was no longer any talk about beloved Führers or thousand-year reichs. They were all just hoping to get home in one piece and that somebody would stop the slaughter before it caught up with them.

To the east, up the Fond St Amarin, they could hear the rattle of machine-guns and rifle fire and the thump of mortars, and they knew without doubt that their only hope was to get out via the Rue des Roches or the Chemin de Ste Reine. The village was like a scene from hell. Dead cattle and horses lay in the fields and farmyards, and men who were too old or too young or too sick to be in the front line

– clerks and cooks and waiters and orderlies – watched, their minds numb, as wounded stumbled back, covered with blood and dust. Those who had come through the pocket at Falaise knew they were going through the same thing all over again.

Men fought their way between the jammed vehicles, grim-faced and filthy. Occasionally a doctor bent over an injured man or tried to set up a dressing station in a cottage garden. The village was already littered with abandoned rifles, knapsacks and scraps of uniform, and the crowd of angry soldiers milled round, aware of a failure in command, seeking food, drink, a way to safety. With the pressure growing from the west, the stream of men from that direction was turning now into a flood and the flood into a stampede. A horse-drawn gun locked its wheels with a waggon, and the carriages and lorries piled up around it in inextricable chaos until the road became quite impassable. Carts and screaming horses with crushed limbs tried to fight their way free, and desperate men climbed over the bonnets and wings of cars to make any progress at all. And, all the time, soldiers, exhausted by the long retreat and indifferent to what was happening in their weariness, were falling asleep in doorways and front gardens.

On the slope of Mont St Amarin, Captain Witkus was crouching with his men for the last dash forward to the crest. He grasped his pistol and waved.

'Off we go!' he yelled.

But as they started to scramble up the bank, they found they were in a minefield and the explosions cracked in their ears, deafening them, flinging them down again, blowing off feet and hands, and tossing them back into the ditch on to the sharpened stakes. Among the first men out was Captain Witkus himself. In front of him, beyond the ditch, lay a line of fir branches brought down from the top of the slope where Reinach had been cutting trees. It was sufficient to stop his men once more and stank ominously of paraffin and petrol.

He turned. Down in the valley he could see the whole length of the German column, paralysed under a hanging pall of dust and smoke. Shouts and the neighing of horses drifted thinly up to him through the firing.

His men began to appear in ones and twos. Some of them had fought with him all the way back through the desert from El Alamein into Libya, across Sicily, and finally up the length of Italy. Although he was only twenty-three, Witkus loved every tough one of them. They had never failed him as long as they were on their feet.

Heads were bobbing in the trees not forty yards away and he fired desperately at them. But his attack had lost its impetus because it was quite impossible to move forward against the weight of the weapons ahead. Then he smelt smoke and heard the crackle of flames and realized that the paraffin-soaked fir branches and the undergrowth at the end of the ditch were now burning, and the breeze was sweeping the fire swiftly towards him. A man scrambled out of the ditch and plunged back into the belt of undergrowth, struggling through the criss-crossed barbed wire, his uniform torn, and began to head down the slope to the doubtful safety of the column on the road. As he ran, he was caught by a burst of fire from the trees and rolled over like a shot rabbit. Then a sergeant, a man who'd been with Witkus since long before Alamein – a quiet, intelligent, hard-working man who'd taught Witkus his job in the days when he was a mere novice, covering his mistakes and quietly giving advice – broke from the ditch in front of him and set off for the trees with two men. They'd not gone ten yards before a bullet hit the sergeant in the face and he spun round, spraying blood, half his neck and jaw shot away. The two men immediately turned and bolted back to the ditch.

Witkus looked back again. The road had become a deathtrap not only for the horse-drawn artillery but also for the mechanical transport. Dead horses, limbers and guns with human bodies scattered among them lay across the road and in the muddy dip. One of his buses, sideways across the road where a bazooka rocket had flung it, was burning furiously and he could see quite clearly that the German fire was slackening. Any moment now, a rush back into Néry would start.

He felt hot tears stinging his eyes and, knowing perfectly well that he'd come to the end of the line, he waved to what was left of his men and began to walk slowly back down the hill, indifferent to the bullets that were flying past him.

Urquhart watched the attack die away into scattered groups of running men. Among them he could see the officer quite clearly, walking slowly, his pistol hanging from his neck by its lanyard, his hands empty. Young Gaston Dring stood up and, resting his rifle on the bough of a tree, put his eye to the sights.

'No!' Urquhart yelled, but he was too late and, as the rifle cracked, he saw the officer stop, sway, then fall flat on his face. Urquhart's arm scythed round and Dring was flung on to his back, startled and bewildered. Urquhart stared at the officer. He'd known exactly what was going through his mind, what shattering of the spirit he was suffering, because he'd suffered it himself – all the way back to Dunkirk, in Greece, in North Africa.

As he turned to apologize to Dring, he saw old Balmaceda, a thin stick of a figure, dancing a wild dance. His monocle had disappeared and his toupee had slipped over one ear. Beyond him Marie-Claude and Ernestine Bona were bent over Théyras.

They were far from finished yet, he knew, and he turned to the radio operator who'd pushed forward to the edge of the escarpment.

'Where are those damned Free French?' he demanded. 'For God's sake, tell them to hurry!'

'I am doing! They're coming as fast as they can. They've asked the air force to help.'

'Tell them to seal up the Rue des Roches and the Chemin de Ste Reine. And Reinach – '

The carpenter's head turned.

'Can we spare one or two boys on bicycles to act as guides?'

'They won't leave here! Not now!'

Urquhart's face twisted. 'What the hell do they want? To be in blood up to their elbows? Send them, Reinach! They're supposed to be soldiers of the Resistance! Make them go! Make them obey your orders!'

Reinach's jaw dropped. Then he nodded and vanished.

The firing had slackened now, and when Reinach returned it was coming from below them only in short bursts.

'They've gone,' he said. 'Hénault wants to enter the Tour de France after the war so he should make it.'

There was little control among the Germans in the valley now. Von Hoelcke had been wounded in the head and Frobinius was crouching behind his wrecked tank, shocked and bewildered at the disaster. A few men were still resisting the impulse to break back to Néry and were exchanging shots, and every now and then one of them went over backwards as one of the Frenchmen pulled a trigger.

For the most part, those Frenchmen who'd served between 1914 and 1918 or had been conscripts between the wars were calm. Father Pol, a black bulk among the undergrowth, was working the bolt of his rifle without looking up, while Dring and Ernouf chattered away quite calmly and swopped cigarettes as they fired. Then the Germans' spirit began to break, and a few of the younger Frenchmen, growing excited, stood up to get a better shot.

Near Urquhart a boy from Haute Falin, who had been firing steadily and effectively with his brother, rose to throw a hand grenade. A heavy calibre bullet flung him down at once and his brother grabbed the grenade instead. As he turned, he too was hit in the back and flung on to his face. On wobbly legs, he rose and staggered forward, but a machine-gun burst laid his leg bare to the bone and the grenade lifted into the air to fall harmlessly into the river and burst in a shower of spray.

'For the love of God,' Reinach yelled. 'Keep your heads down!'

A few of the Germans who had waded the river to the narrow strip of ground beyond were clinging to the shelter of the cliff. One of them, an officer, found the steep pathway that led to the top. Gathering a few men, he led a rush up the slope. Neville's group had worked their way instinctively higher up the hill to where the main fight was and, leaning over the edge where the escarpment bulged, they picked the Germans off one after the other. As the survivors dived back to the bottom for shelter, youngsters appeared from the trees and began to roll boulders down on to them and Neville could see the Germans cowering against the slope, firing off snapshots as heads appeared. His revulsion at the butchery churning in his guts and mounting to his throat, he signalled to one of the Rolandpoint men nearby. He had three phosphorous bombs in an old French steel helmet but was motionless, staring down in shocked fascination.

'For Christ's sake!' Neville yelled. 'Throw them!'

Coming to life, the Rolandpoint man snatched at the grenades and the men by the cliff were enveloped in a cloud of smoke and flame.

There were still experienced Afrika Korps men clinging to the shelter of the vehicles and one group had got a heavy machine-gun working. Shells began to flash along the edge of the cliff near Neville. Then, as the gun lifted, twigs and small branches began to fall on them. One of the shells hit a Néry boy in the chest, and for one frantic second Neville saw the startled look in his eyes before he died.

He had hardly flung a blanket over the body when Yves Rapin appeared with his bazooka, running in a crouch through the trees, and began to set it up among the bushes. Under cover of the machine-gun, the few Germans left across the river under the cliff began to wade back, and as one of the Rolandpoint boys leaned over to fire at them he began to slip. His face showed his horror, as he went crashing through the foliage along the edge of the escarpment to roll the whole thirty feet to the bottom. One of the Germans, a tough-looking sergeant, ran forward to kill him but he was shot as he ran, and went down, still shouting in triumph, as the boy bolted for safety. Then the bazooka fired. The machine-gun and all its crew vanished in stabbing flame and flying splinters, and the Afrika Korps men decided they were wasting their energy and their lives where they were.

Many of them were wounded and every man's hair was grey with the chalky dust, as though youth had departed, leaving only prematurely aged and grimy men. The gunner major had been shot as he tried to organize a fresh resistance and by now there was no hope at all for the lorries. They couldn't go on and they couldn't turn or reverse. The 88s had all been knocked out from close range and as the gunner officer fell it became a case of every man for himself. In sixes and sevens, followed by panting, terrified ex-clerks and orderlies, the Afrika Korps men tried to cut their way out. The bewilderment of the scrambling men was obvious to the Frenchmen on the escarpment as the first groups began to coagulate and join together in a mob, with no thought in their minds but shelter from the holocaust and relief from the slaughter.

Then the heavens filled with an iron howling and, looking up, they saw nine rocket-firing Typhoons turning in a steep bank beyond the crest of the hill. Reinach jumped to his feet and everybody started cheering hysterically.

'We have them,' Reinach howled. 'We have them in Ducrot's chamberpot!'

Urquhart grabbed him and slammed him to the ground, then, running back to where Dr Mouillet's team was working, he grabbed Marie-Claude in his arms and pulled her down with him.

His toupee almost falling off and looking not only old and drunk but mad as a hatter as well, Balmaceda was doing a crazy dance of excitement as the aeroplanes howled down the valley. Their first salvo of rockets crashed into the head of the column to stop it dead, but this time there was no need for the formality because the column was already a rabble and, as the missiles slammed into the chaos of men, cycles and animals, it was as if the end of the world had come.

Rockets exploded among packed vehicles, hurling guns, wheels, wings, bonnet covers, tarpaulins, frames and human beings into the air. The fields and floor of the valley were suddenly alive with desperately running men and galloping horses. As the rockets flung vehicles one on top of another, they burst into flames and huge pyres began to blaze, filling the blue sky with mounting columns of black smoke from burning rubber. Then the running men themselves were caught in the sweeps of cannon shells as the Typhoons swung again over the burning column to complete the work the villagers had begun, all the way back to Néry and beyond. Cars lay nose-down in the river, while all the way up the hill, jammed nose-to-tail, they burned in inextricably mangled heaps, choking the road even to men on foot. Even the undergrowth in the hollow where the Germans had been dragging their wounded had caught fire now, crackling and roaring in the breeze to drown the screams of injured men unable to move and being slowly roasted to death.

The last three aeroplanes were a long way behind the others. As the men and women on the escarpment lifted their heads in awe at the destruction below them, they came howling down the valley. The first salvo landed like the others in the middle of the German column and they saw more men and animals and machines hurled from the road in a bloody mixture of flesh, steel, soil and stone. The second salvo thumped down round von Hoelcke's wrecked tank and the heavy turret lifted as if it were a cardboard box and slid over the side, the big gun thumping to the ground in the welter of flame and smoke. The third salvo was less well aimed and. as it caught the edge of the escarpment, Balmaceda's toupee shot high into the air in the blast as he was lifted in a whirl of arms and legs over the edge. Rocks, stone and pulverized earth flew skywards and there was a landslide down to the river which carried three men with it. A huge tree fell, crashing through the undergrowth on to the last of the group of Germans who had crossed the river and were sheltering against the cliff face below.

As the stones and dirt and pieces of splintered wood showered down on them, Urquhart held Marie-Claude tightly against him, so that he could feel her breath on his cheek and the warmth of her trembling body against his. Then the aeroplanes were gone and, as he released her and ran to the edge of the cliff, she rose to her feet, brushing the dirt and twigs from her skirt, her expression bewildered and unhappy.

As Urquhart began to shout orders, Witkus' last few men, still in good order despite the butchery, tried once more to retreat, only to be caught by a new hail of fire from the escarpment which drove them into the burning brambles at the side of the road. By this time, the weapons were so hot from the sun and the continued firing, the metal burned the skin. Ignoring the pain, Urquhart emptied his Sten at them then, running along the edge of the cliff, he seized a cache of grenades and began to pull out the pins and hurl them into the valley below. There was a gush of white smoke and a German helmet flew high into the air, spinning like a humming top, end over end. Aware of a terrible power and conscious what a tremendous weapon the grenade was – as if it had been thought out specially for this particular job – he ran backwards and forwards, flinging them into the road as if he were fielding at cricket.

All the lessons he'd ever learned about throwing them were forgotten as he swung his arm backwards and forwards in a whirling motion. He couldn't miss and there was no need even to duck because the face of the cliff took care of the splinters. Caught by the excitement of victory other men began to do the same. The road below was filled with smoke and under its cover six of Frobinius' SS men made a despairing scramble for safety. Reinach saw them and, snatching up a rifle, jammed in a clip of cartridges and picked them off one by one.

By now, despite the orders, the excited Frenchmen were advancing steadily from the trees opposite and down the slope of the meadow to the road, and both they and the men on the escarpment were in danger of being shot by their own side. The Germans in the middle were spraying the air indiscriminately, frantic under the shower of bullets and grenades. Then, unexpectedly, a white sheet appeared on the end of a ramrod and started waving, and a tremendous shout went up.

'They're surrendering! They're surrendering!'

More sheets, towels, even handkerchiefs, appeared. Cut off, leaderless and defeated as the hard core of battle-hardened men were shot down, the Germans began to step out from between the lorries, throwing down their weapons and raising their hands. An officer in the uniform of the SS began to shout at them and, when they ignored him, he lifted his pistol to threaten them. Ernouf picked him off as if he were shooting crows, and as he fell, more men stepped out, their hands in the air.

Leaving the old mitrailleuse, the two Dréos began to make their way to the road with rifles, struggling with their stiff ungainly legs through the undergrowth and down the rocky path, their faces grim and unsmiling. Ernouf was still chatting cheerfully with Dring as if they were working together on the harvest. Above them the sky was no longer blue but a dirty brown with the smoke of burning vehicles, branches, undergrowth, cordite, melting rubber and lifting dust. The place seemed to reek of the sour odour of Germans, the acrid smell of sweaty tunics, stale cigars and fear.

The Frenchmen were all on their feet now, cheering and chattering wildly. Hytier, the bar-owner from Rolandpoint, wearing his old steel helmet, was handling his Sten with impressive efficiency, letting off short bursts at a group of SS men still trying to hold out among the lorries. Some of the Frenchmen had reached the river now and were wading across. Among them was Brisson, the Rolandpoint garage proprietor, followed by the two Dréos. Just ahead of him was Father Pol, who had abandoned his rifle only too willingly and was holding in front of him the cross he carried on the chain round his neck, ready to give absolution to the dying. 'Blessed be those who hear the will of God,' he was shouting. 'Blessed be God in His angels and His saints – '

'Father!' Urquhart yelled.

But Father Pol couldn't hear him for the racket and, as he reached the road, one of the SS men lifted his machine pistol and fired. Father Pol's hat flew off as his head came up with a jerk. For a second, he stood stock still in the road, a vast black bulk, his face blank and startled; then he went over backwards like a log. Urquhart saw the dust puff out as he hit the ground, and he swung round to Neville who was climbing towards him. 'What a bloody fine plan we made!' he shouted in fury.

The advancing Frenchmen had dropped to the ground, and Brisson began to creep forward holding a Mills bomb.

Unseen, he reached the other side of the lorry where the SS men were crouching and, pulling out the pin, gently rolled the bomb between the wheels and dived for the shelter of the river bank. As the grenade went off and the black-uniformed figures were flung aside, flames started from the petrol tank of the lorry and Brisson stepped forward to spray the writhing men with his gun.

They found Frobinius leaning against a wrecked car near the single strand of barbed wire that bordered the road. He'd been wounded by a splinter from Brisson's bomb but, as the Dréos approached, he lifted his pistol. The bullet hit the younger Dréo in the mouth and he reeled away, spitting blood and teeth until he collapsed. His father lifted his rifle and shot the German in the chest.

Frobinius staggered back, putting out one hand to the wire to retain his balance, indifferent to the barbs that tore at his flesh. The pistol dropped from his fingers and he stared wildly at the old man who stopped in front of him, not speaking, his face expressionless. Then Dréo lifted the rifle again and shot him once more in the chest. As Frobinius fell backwards, the wire caught him behind the legs, so that he toppled over to land on his back with his head in the mud, his black-booted feet held up by the sagging wire in an attitude of gross indignity.

He wasn't dead but was gasping with agony, the blood bubbling from his mouth, his eyes wild with the desperation of a cornered animal. Sergeant Dréo stood staring down at him, his eyes hard under the old steel helmet. It was almost as though the old man were allowing him time to absorb what was about to happen. Then he put the rifle muzzle to the writhing German's face so that he could look straight down the barrel for the last second or two of life, and shot him between the eyes. The bullet punched in his nose and blew out the back of his head. As his blood and brains oozed into the muddy grass of the slope, the jackbooted feet gave a last convulsive kick and were still.

12

By 4.30 p.m. it was all over.

More of the Frenchmen began to scramble down to the road as the resistance died, Dring and Ernouf still talking incessantly and handling their long rifles like experts. A young German, stumbling as he tried to drag out an ammunition box, stopped as a bullet shattered his arm. Another just behind him promptly dropped his weapon and waved a white handkerchief, his face terrified. Young Gaston Dring, his face like a choirboy's, walked forward and with only a slight tensing of the muscles of his features, lifted a Sten he'd acquired and fired two copybook bursts. The bullets struck the wounded German in the chest and flung him aside. The other man staggered back, still clutching his handkerchief, fell over the ammunition box, and collapsed with his legs across it, moaning. A man in a blue smock from Bourg-la-Chattel, walked forward and, holding his rifle with one hand, leaned over to shoot him in the head, then turned to another man in a beret who appeared behind him and held out a cigarette for a light, as though he had merely paused in cutting a hedge.

Neville, his face grimy with battle, was suddenly sickened. 'Stop it,' he yelled at Reinach. 'It's over! It's finished! How many more lives do you want?'

Reinach stared at him and began to shout so that the shooting died away. The road was littered with smashed vehicles, the bodies of men, immobilized guns, and four burning tanks whose ammunition was still exploding. Even the river bed had proved a death-trap, the swiftly-flowing water washing over the remains of horses, limbers, guns and human beings which had tried to find shelter there or had crashed from the road in the panic.

Every staff car seemed to be filled with loot. There were glasses, typewriters, pistols and small arms by the hundred scattered among the wreckage along with cases of wine, tinned food and medical stores, leather goods, clothing and –

oddly enough – corsets. Across the seat of one car, clutching five looted fur coats to her, was the body of a woman. Further down, surrounded by dead men, whose unweathered faces, uncalloused hands and spectacles proclaimed that they were clerks and orderlies, were two dead girls dressed in grey uniforms, women office workers who'd somehow been left behind and been caught up in the horror in the Fond St Amarin. They had once been pretty, and as they sprawled in the road they looked small and childish and somehow twice as pathetic. Neville stared at them with empty eyes, his stomach churning with nausea.

Here and there stray shots still rang out as Miliciens or SS men were dragged out. For them there was no mercy. A last pocket of resistance in the bushes where they'd hidden was destroyed by the simple expedient of scattering petrol on the undergrowth on the windward side and setting fire to it; as the SS men appeared coughing and spluttering, they were mown down with Stens.

One man, wearing the jacket of a grenadier, was standing with his hands in the air being questioned by Reinach in Polish and insisting in German that he was a Pole.

'Then why are you wearing SS trousers?' Reinach demanded.

'I am a Pole. I was born in Warsaw.'

'When did you join the German army?'

'I am a Pole. I was born in Warsaw.'

'It's a lovely day.'

'I am a Pole born in Warsaw.'

Reinach shook his head. 'He's an SS man,' he said, and Hytier lifted his gun and pulled the trigger.

Prowling among the dead, Gaston Dring brought a packet of papers and an army pay book to Urquhart. He seemed a little afraid of him.

Urquhart scanned them. 'Justus Witkus,' he said. 'Captain Afrika Korps. Holder of the East Medal for the Winter War. France, Greece, Africa, Italy and back to France. Poor bastard, I've probably exchanged shots with him before.'

He opened the wallet. There was a picture of a young woman and a small child, both of them good-looking and smiling and a letter congratulating Witkus on winning the Knight's Cross.

Urquhart looked up. Dring was holding out a wrist watch and the enamelled medallion.

'Keep it,' Urquhart said. 'It's worth keeping. He must have been quite a soldier.'

When the relieving troops arrived, coming over the ridge in a long khaki line, they said they were Spahis of the Free French First Division. They were good troops and well equipped and, though they looked tired after their headlong dash from the coast, they showed no sign of wear and tear apart from their dusty uniforms.

'Thanks to you,' their colonel told Reinach, 'we've got around nine thousand Germans bottled up between Néry and St Seigneur because the Americans have just arrived at the other end of the valley. How many did you kill?'

'Around a hundred and eighty,' Reinach said bleakly. 'That's a fair exchange for the lives they took. There are a hell of a lot of wounded as well.'

The colonel stared down the valley at the wreckage. Flies from all over the province seemed to have scented the spilled blood already and were swarming over the chaos, great fat creatures that pestered even the living. Now the shooting had stopped, in the sudden stillness they could hear the singing of birds.

'You've done a good job,' the colonel said. '*La Patrie est reconnaissante.*'

Walking up the hill, gathering the various groups together, Urquhart was aware of an enormous lassitude. The whole valley stank of burning oil, scorched flesh and melting rubber and the men searching for wounded among the wreckage coughed and spluttered in the smoke. Those Germans who could walk were disarmed and sent stumbling down the slope towards Néry.

At the roadside, Ernestine Bona and Marie-Claude were weeping together over a dying boy. Dr Mouillet had laid out the French dead in the meadow and had now moved down to the road to examine the bodies of others as they were brought down. There were thirty-nine altogether, including several youngsters who, excited by the battle, had rushed forward to be able to claim they'd shot a German and been caught themselves. There were also old Balmaceda, Sergeant Dréo's son, Yvon Guélis, Théyras, and the black bulk of Father Pol, their bodies watched over by a group of men with stiff, saddened faces.

'Dear God, what a mess,' Neville said, staring at the dead priest.

'He always said that there'd be a time when it would be worth dying,' Urquhart said flatly. 'I suppose he'd have considered this was it.'

Someone produced a tricolour and tied it to a tree. It caught the breeze and fluttered in the smoke that drifted up from the road. Urquhart saw there were tears in Reinach's eyes and, when a small group of boys and girls started to sing 'La Marseillaise', none of the older men joined in so that it sounded thin and reedy in the afternoon air and finally died away.

Bottles of wine began to change hands and there was a lot of excited chatter, but not among the older men. They were family men who'd learned the value of life and, for all their hatred of the Germans, they didn't enjoy seeing the slaughter they'd wrought. It had been too easy. Neville's plan had been too clever, and the springing of the trap so perfect there was not much satisfaction from their success.

Reinach stood watching his men dragging dead Germans to the side of the road and laying them in rows. 'This is how they left *our* young men,' he said. 'In neat rows by the roadside.' He drew a deep breath. 'Why do I feel so little satisfaction, Urk't,'

Urquhart lifted his head. 'Because these weren't the ones who did it,' he said.

'There were SS men among them.'

'Most of these were headquarters clerks.'

'They didn't fight like clerks.'

Urquhart gestured. 'And poor stupid bloody Klemens, locked in the cellar down there.' He jerked a hand at the smoke filling the valley. 'They've killed the cattle and burned your homes. Was that what you wanted?'

Someone handed him a bottle and he drank from it, aware of the rough wine grating against his throat. Neville still looked pale and shaken under the dirt as he passed it on to him.

Almost everyone was down from the slopes now, moving between the abandoned vehicles, filthy and exhausted by the fury and passion of the fight. Looted bottles of brandy had been found and there was some laughter, high-pitched and edgy, compounded of shock, excitement and relief that it was all over.

In Néry, it seemed as if half the German army was crammed among the burning houses. The French colonel, who was looking for war criminals and seemed eager to find some, insisted on Neville, Urquhart, Reinach and a few others accompanying him. They rode in a German lorry behind a French tank. Other villagers began to follow them to find out what had happened to their homes.

There were already Americans on the western slopes and apart from a few determined men still firing sporadically from hiding places, the Germans had thrown down their arms. American tanks were driving them into one of Gaudin's fields, where they were being searched, and out at the other side in a long dusty column heading west to imprisonment. The French troops started doing the same thing on the the eastern slopes, using the yard of the château for the interrogation. Colonel Klemens and General Dannhüber were among the first to appear.

'Do we hold them as war criminals?' the French colonel asked.

Reinach shook his head. 'Not for us.'

As Tarnera passed, Reinach stopped him. 'I'm sorry I had to hit you so hard,' he said. 'I have no personal feelings towards you.'

His head bandaged, Tarnera lifted his eyes and managed a smile as he vanished.

Moving through the village, their ears caught by the occasional bursts of firing as the last pockets of resistance were winkled out of barns and cottages, they stared at the burned and wrecked houses. The Free French had got a bucket chain working from Reinach's big water tank. They had stopped the blaze inside the church, but the Gaudin farmhouse was in ruins. Only the fact that the Defourney house had been used as a dressing station had saved it.

'They couldn't burn Néry,' Reinach said in a dry, proud voice. 'It was too old and too well built.'

De Frager appeared. He seemed suddenly to have grown up. There were no wild declamations and no histrionics. 'My great-grandmother would have liked to have seen them in defeat,' he said. 'But they set fire to the house and she and Euphrasie and Joseph tried to fight it. She had a heart attack.'

Looking for Marie-Claude, Neville found himself staring up the dusty drive of the farm that they'd used now for nearly five months. The bicycles lay in the yard, twisted and ruined as if a lorry had been driven over them. Beyond the stack-yard, he could see the cattle dead in the field. Though the house seemed untouched, the wooden porch had been set on fire and had burned completely away so that there was a scorch mark across the whitewashed wall. The haystack lay in a heap of glowing ashes and the air was full of floating black flecks. Here and there piles of hay had been scattered by running feet.

Madame Lamy had returned to the village ahead of them through the fields at the back of the house and was standing among the wreckage, weeping quietly. 'There are wounded Germans on the beds,' she said slowly. 'And two of them dead in the vegetable patch waiting to be buried.'

Abandoned weapons lay about the drive with scattered clothing and German equipment. Neville's eyes were agonized. 'Poor Marie-Claude,' he said.

Urquhart surveyed the wreckage not as a city dweller but as a countryman whose family had faced such disasters before.

'We can get it going again,' he said quietly. 'Work's all that's needed.' He sounded surprisingly like Reinach.

More villagers were beginning to appear from the slopes

in lorries and German cars and on foot. Lionel Dring arrived with his father, Brisson and Ernestine Bona. They were standing in the yard staring at the cows sprawled in the field beyond the stackyard gate, the pigs dead in the sties, the dead chickens with spread wings and scattered feathers, when a fusillade of shots sent them all diving for shelter.

Crouching behind the thick wheels of the platform, Neville realized that Urquhart was not with him and, lifting his head, he saw him lying among the scattered hay, moving feebly, blood shining on his face in the sun in a vivid red splash. Then a dozen Free French soldiers, attracted by the shots, crashed into the yard, firing at the barn with everything they possessed. A German fell from the loft and thudded to the ground, his helmet clonking tinnily on the roof of the pigsties.

In the silence, as they rose slowly to their feet, the French sergeant bent over Urquhart. A bullet had sliced across his cheek near the bone, cutting it open. Despite the blood it was only a slight wound and he was already sitting up.

'Is he all right?' Neville asked as he knelt down with Reinach and Ernestine.

Ernestine nodded. 'He'll be with us a long time yet,' she said.

'I'll bandage it,' Reinach offered.

Ernestine gave him a shove. 'Never mind the bandage,' she said. 'Go and get *her*.'

Reinach stared. 'Who?'

'Use your wits, you oaf! Who do you think?'

As Reinach dashed off, Ernestine looked at Urquhart who was drawing his feet under him to rise. He looked dazed but not much hurt, and she pushed him back quickly. 'Stay where you are,' she said. 'Have you no sense of drama?'

Then a scout car stopped outside the gate with a squeal of brakes and Marie-Claude, her face twisted with apprehension, hurried down the drive, followed by Reinach. As she saw Urquhart, she ran towards him, crying his name. As she passed, Neville made to stop her, but she brushed him aside as if she didn't even see him and, falling on her knees beside Urquhart, she pulled him to her, his head cradled against her breast. 'Urk't,' she begged in a broken voice. 'Oh, Urk't! For the love of God, say you're all right!'

As Ernestine began to push the others away, Urquhart struggled free. 'It's not much,' he said, shaking the blood from his eyes and trying to gather his senses.

Marie-Claude seemed surprised but she was determined to have her moment, and, ignoring his protests, she wrenched dramatically at the skirt of the cotton dress she wore. He was still protesting as she brushed at the blood on his face with a torn-off piece of the material. 'I thought you were dead, Urk't,' she was whispering. 'I thought you were dead!'

Urquhart sat up abruptly, taking her shoulders in his broad strong hands. 'Stop it, Marie-Claude,' he commanded. 'Stop it! I'm not going to die, you little idiot!'

She stared at him, her eyes agonized and still uncertain, and he grinned. 'I'll be here for years yet,' he said. 'And by the look of things, I'll need to be, too, to get this place on its feet again.' And Neville knew then that, in his sturdy, self-reliant way, he had made up his mind long since about her.

Marie-Claude was sitting back on her heels, staring at him, an expression of bewilderment on her face as though she couldn't believe him. 'You *want* to stay here?' she whispered.

'That's what *you* wanted, isn't it? A man about the place.'

She gazed at him a moment longer and Neville could see tears streaming down her cheeks, her expression a mixture of joy, wonder and guilt all mixed up together. 'It isn't a farm labourer I want, Urk't,' she said, her words coming in slow miserable steps. 'I don't care about that! I don't care about the farm!'

Urquhart grinned and, in the first real show of affection he'd made towards her since he'd arrived in Néry, he pulled her to him and kissed her properly on the lips. 'I'm a farmer,' he said. '*I* do!'

As she flung her arms round him, hugging him, her face deep in the angle of the neck, making little sobbing noises of happiness, Neville turned away. He suddenly knew what

Urquhart had meant when he'd told him that he was too gentle for Marie-Claude. She needed strength, not to lean on, but to match her own strength, and he didn't have to ask himself twice how Urquhart had managed to seize hold of her heart. He'd done no begging or pleading but had remained aloof, making Marie-Claude do the asking, sensing all along that she was suffering from an insecurity of which she was totally unaware that needed the example not of love but of determination. Remembering ruefully his concern when they'd first arrived that Urquhart might not find it easy to fit in, he realized Urquhart had fitted far better than he had himself, for the simple reason that he had sprung from a community identical with Néry, from a people with the same roots, even to the needs and the hopes and the ambitions.

He drew a deep breath and began to walk towards the street. As he did so, he almost bumped into Madame Lamy. She managed a smile. 'A new start,' she said. 'A new start for us all. *C'est bon pour le courage*.'

Neville tried to smile in return, and, to his surprise, found it worked. Then, as he stopped, staring at the damage and appalled by what he'd done with his plan, Reinach, bundled out of the farmyard by Ernestine, came up behind him and put a hand on his shoulder.

'Cheer up, Officer Neville,' he said. 'It can all be put together again. And history *does* work. Without any doubt. It was the finest plan I ever heard of.' He slapped Neville's shoulder and gestured at the Germans sullenly filing away and the Free French tank by the war memorial, the snout of its gun pointing towards them. 'It's obvious,' he said. 'You've only to look.'

Neville nodded and the smile came again, more easily this time and a little stronger as the sense of defeat slipped away from him. Suddenly he felt better and knew he'd manage to survive. As Reinach shoved an arm through his in a curiously French manner, they walked together down the drive.

'Yes,' he agreed. 'You've only to look.'

Then, as life flowed back into him and the chill round his heart began to disperse, he suddenly realized that, having survived, having endured it all, he would not have had things

other than as they had been. For the first time he knew that in the years to come, when the shock and the hatred had died away, he would think the better of himself for what he'd done. His senses would reject all the destruction about him and, above all, he'd be glad he'd achieved more than he thought he could when the challenge came. They would all of them – every one of them – look back on what they'd done with satisfaction and pride. Despite everything, when they were old, they'd remember this day of glory as the finest of their lives.

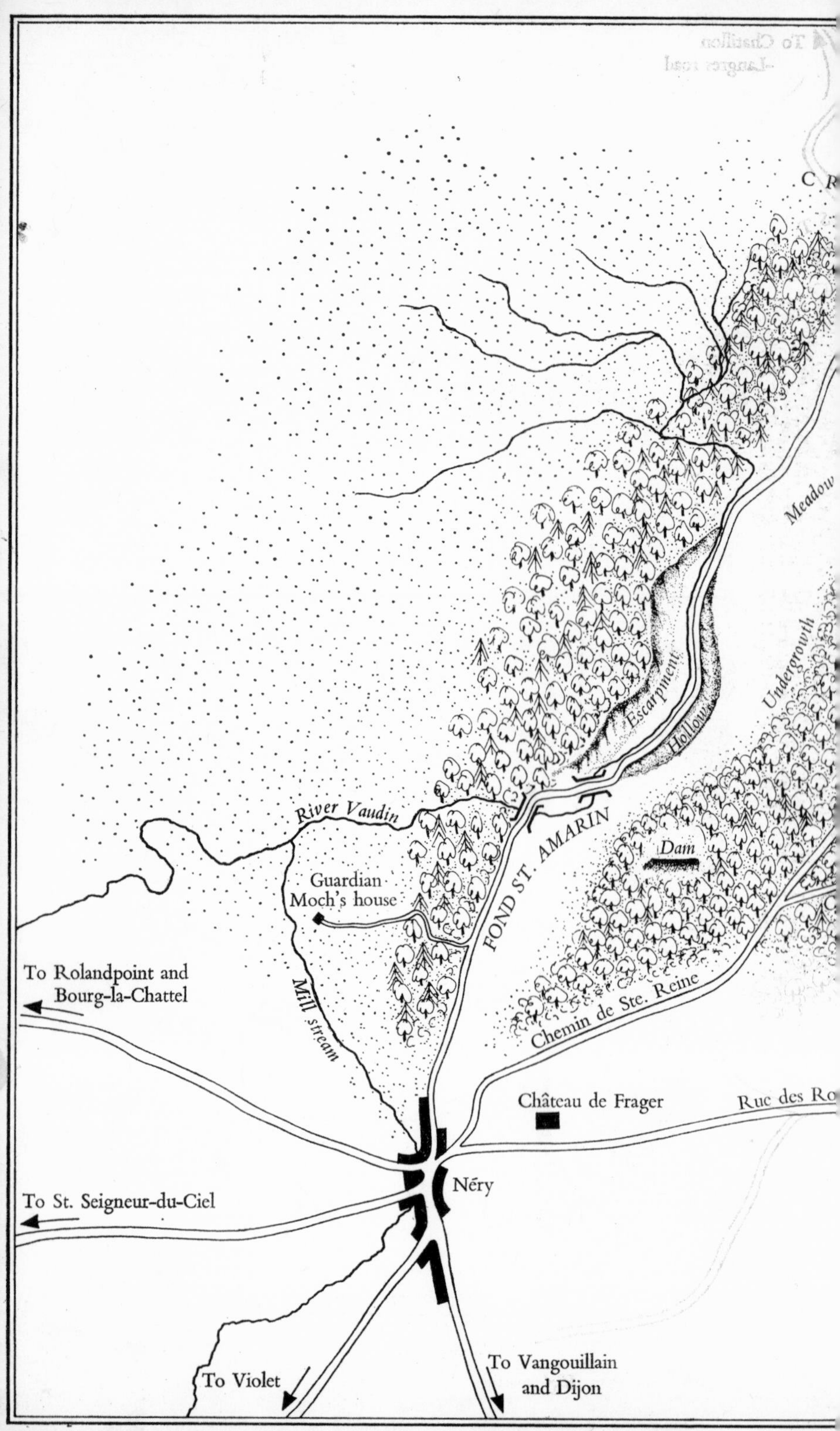

River Vaudin
Meadow
Escarpment
Hollow
Undergrowth
Dam
FOND ST. AMARIN
Guardian Moch's house
Mill stream
Chemin de Ste. Reine
To Rolandpoint and Bourg-la-Chattel
Château de Frager
Néry
To St. Seigneur-du-Ciel
To Violet
To Vangouillain and Dijon